NOT
WHO WE
EXPECTED

Books by Lisa Black

NOT
WHO WE
EXPECTED

LISA BLACK

KENSINGTON
PUBLISHING CORP.

kensingtonbooks.com

KENSINGTON BOOKS are published by

Kensington Publishing Corp.
900 Third Avenue
New York, NY 10022

Copyright © 2025 by Lisa Black

All rights reserved. No part of this book may be reproduced in any form or by any means without the prior written consent of the Publisher, excepting brief quotes used in reviews.

All Kensington titles, imprints, and distributed lines are available at special quantity discounts for bulk purchases for sales promotion, premiums, fund-raising, educational, or institutional use. Special book excerpts or customized printings can also be created to fit specific needs. For details, write or phone the office of the Kensington Special Sales Manager: Attn. Special Sales Department, Kensington Publishing Corp., 900 Third Avenue, New York, NY 10022. Phone: 1-800-221-2647.

Library of Congress Card Catalogue Number: 2024946453

KENSINGTON and the K with book logo Reg. U.S. Pat. & TM Off.

ISBN: 978-1-4967-4968-0
First Kensington Hardcover Edition: March 2025

ISBN: 978-1-4967-4970-3 (ebook)

10 9 8 7 6 5 4 3 2 1

Printed in the United States of America

For Pam

Chapter 1

It might not be the largest private home Rachael Davies had ever visited, but it definitely made the top ten. She stepped out of her car, leaving it on the wide circular drive, behind two haphazardly parked SUVs. Slightly biting air refused to pretend it was still fall; winter approached, without subtlety.

The building's rectangular footprint spanned half an acre, according to her quick estimation. A balcony ran the length of the upper floor, held up by graceful white columns. Dead leaves rustled along the brick porch under white-shuttered windows. More cars were scattered around a detached garage. The former pathologist wondered as she approached if the house had originally belonged to one of the Founding Fathers or some other wealthy colonialist. They were less than fifty miles outside DC. It might have been a plantation. . . . Either way, it was a place where someone like her would once have had to go around back to the servants' or the delivery entrance.

She marched up the brick steps to the front door and knocked.

No one objected. No one answered at all.

The door consisted of clear glass panes arranged in a looping, almost floral pattern, allowing her a broken-up view of a cavernous entryway. She found a doorbell set in brass, rang it, heard the peal inside. Waited. Still no response.

She checked her watch to see if she had arrived on time, neither too early nor too late. Not an easy task when she had to drive nearly two hours from the Locard forensic center on the Chesapeake Bay, through DC traffic—always a nightmare—simply because rock legend Billy Diamond had asked her to.

Billy Diamond had shredded his guitar onstage with the band Chimera from the time he was fifteen. He tended to be coy as to exactly how many decades had passed since then. The band's total record sales had waxed and waned over the years but generally had fallen somewhere between Billy Joel's and Taylor Swift's. At least they had until their very public and acrimonious split several years ago.

Rachael tried the knob, which turned easily. Sound escaped through the open crack—voices, music, clattering, as if someone in the kitchen had dropped an armful of metal pots. She pushed the door and stepped inside. The commute had been too many miles to simply turn around and leave.

Besides, Rachael was as much a rocker as the next girl. Meeting Billy Diamond was not an opportunity to be passed up lightly.

Sounds came from everywhere, voices and shouts and laughter, the occasional snap of a snare drum. These echoed off the marble floor, the high ceiling, and the stone steps leading up a curving staircase. An ornate round table had been centered under the chandelier. It held a vase of wilting roses and a Starbucks cup with lipstick on the rim.

Hallways ran off to the right, left, and center. She began *eeny-meeny-miny-moeing* her options, but then a wiry older man with a small snare drum tucked under one arm tripped down the steps, his sneakers squeaking with each riser. He noticed Rachael only when he nearly ran into her.

"Oh, hey, Mama," he said.

"Hello. I'm—"

He continued past her without slowing. Lacking a better idea, she trotted to keep up, an Alice in business attire following the White Rabbit.

They passed through a sitting room of sorts with white chiffon curtains and overstuffed settees. A woman of indeterminate age vaped on an ottoman while running her fingers through wild auburn hair. She didn't seem to notice either Rachael or the snare drum, directing her conversation to a gorgeous young man on a couch who appeared to be asleep.

The wiry man and the drum came to a stop in a hexagon-shaped sunroom with band instruments set up in its center—guitars, drum set, a saxophone lying across a chair, music stands. It looked convincingly haphazard, but Rachael wondered if it was some kind of photo shoot rather than a practice or concert spot. No amplifiers, and temporary-appearing heavy black curtains covered some of the windows.

"Excuse me," she said to the man, who nearly dropped the drum while attaching it to a stand. "I'm here to see Billy."

"Aren't we all," he muttered, then seemed to remember his manners. "He's upstairs."

"Could you be more specific? I'm guessing 'upstairs' covers a lot of ground."

He got the drum attached, straightened, and surveyed his handiwork. After moving a music stand four inches to the left, he continued. "Yes, sorry. I'll help you find him. Who are you? All media requests need to go through me, but I can see you're not a reporter." His eyes swept her from top to toe and back again. "Besides, if you were, you'd have a photographer with you."

Why her looks told him that, she couldn't guess, and she didn't bother trying. "I'm Rachael Davies, from the Locard Insti—"

"Ohhh, *yes*. You're Isis's sister."

She was, but she was still startled to hear it mentioned for the second time in as many days. Isis had been dead for what, almost two years now? "I am, but—"

"Come with me."

And he was off again.

She followed him through a kitchen, littered, but not badly, with used plates and the detritus of take-out food, and up to a normal-sized elevator which rested in a corner. The rear of the house looked out over a short expanse of lawn that ended in a waist-high field that might be some kind of crop or a very large English garden.

"I hope you can help him," the man said as the electric doors closed and the cage began its ascent. "He's driving me nuts. I'm Newton Garcia, by the way. Don't call me Newt. I'm the manager for Billy Diamond. I used to be the manager for Chimera, but when they split, I stuck with Billy. Wasn't *that* a brilliant idea!" he finished, adding this last as if to himself.

"Okay." She realized she had no idea how many people had made up Chimera or what their names were. Rachael might obsess over a favorite song here and there, but she was no groupie. "I'm not quite sure yet why he's asked to see me."

The aging rocker had called her personally at the Locard Institute, a center for forensic research, training, and investigation. He had told her he needed her help to find his missing daughter, and asked if she would come and talk to him about it, because he had been a good friend of Isis, and Isis had always said that her sister Rachael was the smartest person she knew and could solve anything. Rachael had very much doubted that Isis ever said anything of the sort, but the combination of famous rock star and missing child had made her willing to sacrifice an afternoon in the lab.

"It's about Devon," Newton said, and the elevator came to a stop.

So the missing child wasn't a secret, but still, Rachael needed to talk to the client—potential client—before anyone else. "How is he driving you nuts?"

The elevator opened onto a long hallway with doors on either side of the marble floor, the perfect place to use the child's Big Wheel beside a half-moon table. The table held a small lamp and a red lace bra. Voices and at least one television sounded along the way.

Newton held the elevator door as she stepped out. "How *isn't* he driving me nuts? The venue is too big, it's too small, the sound is off, a solo tour is a terrible idea, a solo tour will sell millions, and Samson is the worst drummer ever, so let's get Mitchell. Mitchell is a . . . . It's just nerves, that's all."

Rachael glanced in some of the rooms as they passed. Nothing outrageous: beds, pieces of classic furniture, the occasional pair of jeans on the floor. A canary in an ornate cage, carefully monitored by a pensive tabby cat on the window seat. No beer can pyramids or smashed guitars.

"If this touring as a solo act is a flop, it will be a financial and emotional disaster for all concerned, including me. Very definitely including me. But it will be a body blow to the guy's ego. Of course it will be. How could it not? All that's at stake is his entire musical legacy. Did he make Chimera, or did Chimera make him? I didn't know Billy when he was younger, but I'll bet he's never handled stress very well." He waved her ahead of him, into a room near the end of the hall.

"That's not true," Billy Diamond said as they entered. "I handle stress excellently well."

Chapter 2

Rachael had met a number of famous, semi-famous, and not at all famous people through her work at the Locard—but never a rock star, a genuine rock star, with thirty albums totaling well over three hundred million in sales, a star on the Hollywood Walk of Fame, inclusion in the Rock & Roll Hall of Fame. Her nerves hummed, something that hadn't happened in a while.

That he knew Isis did not surprise her. As DC's premier party planner, Isis had handled events for all sorts of people. That Isis had ever mentioned her, *that* surprised Rachael. The two sisters had never been enemies, but Rachael didn't think they'd ever truly been friends either.

And now here was Billy Diamond.

An amp cord caught his toe as he hastened to shake her hand. Even more wiry than his manager and dressed in a pair of plaid pajama pants and a T-shirt so faded she couldn't read the lettering, Billy Diamond first pumped her hand with a firm grasp and then held it in both of his. Thin black hair liberally spiked with gray had been gathered into a ponytail; he had tattoos on both arms, a collection of bracelets, and bare feet, which he now shook free of the amp wire.

Given that most of the walls were covered in acoustic tiles and that a soundboard with enough electronics to run the International Space Station was on display, this had to be the actual practice space. A man in sweats and sporting a braided beard tuned a guitar; he gave Rachael a quick but friendly smile. A woman with seriously toned arms and a shock of pink hair didn't even glance up from the pile of electrical cords she seemed determined to untangle.

Meanwhile, Billy was saying, "Thank you so much for coming out. I'm desperate, I'm telling you, really desperate, and Isis was such a friend to me. She said you were so sweet and softhearted, you'd never leave anyone in pain."

Again, *Isis* said that? As if.

"And I am in pain, believe me, and I know you understand, because you're raising her baby now, aren't you? Danny?"

"Danton," she corrected. "He's two and a—"

"I saw that in a magazine or the paper. Does anyone read the paper anymore? Do I? I'm not even sure. But I need your help, please." He raised her knuckles to his lips. "Please."

Who could resist such an awkwardly cheesy appeal? Even spoken with breath smelling of orange juice and rum. "Why don't you tell me what the situation is, and we'll see if the Locard can help."

"Yes, yes, of course." His head snapped in one direction, then the other. "Let's sit . . . Oh, there's nowhere to sit. This is where we—Well, let's go to the parlor. It's actually called a parlor, do you believe that? The people who had this place before me, they called it that."

"It's beautiful," Rachael said. A little small talk often helped to put clients at ease, and this one needed to come down a notch or two. "I had no idea you lived so close to the capital."

"Yeah, well . . . I had to get away from the craziness, you know, the . . . just . . . LA and Nashville and New York. I'd had enough—"

"He thought he might go into politics," Newton translated.

Rachael felt her eyebrows rise and tried to stop them midflight.

"I didn't . . . it's not . . . It was a good deal. The house was a good deal," Billy finished after a sharp look at his manager. "Let's go."

"The photographer will be here at two," Newton called after them.

"Yeah, yeah, yeah."

Rachael caught the manager's eye roll just before Billy led her away, looping one arm through hers, as if they were going to stroll across the green bank of *La Grand Jatte*. Or as if she might try to escape.

"The parlor" now had a pool table and a poker table, heavy red curtains layered with dust, and a bar in the corner, which didn't seem too dusty at all. "Drink?" Billy offered. "We've got everything. Wine, liquor—even sweet iced tea if you want it."

She said that water would be great and found a grouping of armchairs, then pulled one closer to another. This interview needed to stay under control and on topic, she could see, or they'd be there all afternoon. Not that that would be a bad thing.

He handed her an ice-cold bottle. "Water. *Ugh*. You know what fish do in that?" He slumped into the adjacent armchair without waiting for her reaction to the punch line. Ice tinkled in his own glass—probably not full of water, to judge from the darting gaze and the frenetic speech. But she could be wrong. He might just be stressed and chronically hyperactive.

"So . . ." she began.

"Do you like music?"

"Uh, yes. Yes, very much. I'm a huge fan of Chimera, a huge fan of yours, always have been," she added, assuming his question had truly been, "Do you like *my* music?"

She'd guessed right. His face dissolved into a smile of pure happiness. "Really? Which one is your favorite? Wait, don't tell me. It's 'When You Wake,' right? You look like a hope-less romantic. *Hopeful* romantic."

Not the way she'd describe herself, but she didn't tell him so or that she'd never heard that particular song. "I'm not sure I could pick a favorite. I considered 'New Road' my theme song when I got my first car."

He laughed merrily, then launched into a longish story about how the lyrics had popped into his head while he was driving through gorgeous Canadian mountains on his way to join the band in Alaska. She could have listened for hours but wanted to get home in time to make Danton's dinner. Her mother had book club tonight, and Loretta took book club very seriously.

It took some gentle prodding to get him back on track.

The singer clasped his hands together. "Okay. Oh gosh, where do I begin? It's my kid, Devon. I have only one kid. Like you now, right? She's nineteen, amazing, she's so smart, and I know you must think, she's my kid, grew up with . . . this."

He gestured around the room, maybe at the high ceilings and crown moldings, the beautifully maintained antique windows, or maybe at the wastebasket next to the bar, with the fruit flies hovering over the discarded bottles, an ashtray overflowing with cigarette butts and glass pipes. Rachael couldn't tell.

"You'd think because she's Billy Diamond's that she'd be stealing cars by the time she's ten. But she's not like that! Devon is . . . She's the most hardworking person I know, and I know a lot. The music business is *not* all drugs and jamming. It takes a massive amount of—Anyway, Devon has always been straight As, soccer team, takes a homemade cake to her nana on her birthday, just the sweetest kid ever. *Smart.* I don't know where she gets it. Certainly not from me."

He stopped, and Rachael wondered if he was waiting for her to disagree. For all she knew, Billy Diamond might make pancakes every Sunday morning before church and tutor disadvantaged math students. What she wanted to do was ask about Devon's mother, but he went on before she could finish the thought.

"She's not part of this . . . life, I mean. She doesn't trade on my fame like other celebrity kids, and I've tried to help her not be part of it. Like . . . no social media. She doesn't party. Paparazzi don't follow her around, because she's convinced them that she never does anything interesting. Most of my fans don't even know I *have* a daughter, and most of her friends at Yale don't know I'm her dad. And that's the way we both like it."

"She's a student at—"

"Yeah. Supposed to be in her sophomore year now. You know she qualified for three scholarships but turned them down? 'Cause they need to go to the kids who need the money, not people like us."

Rachael nodded her approval.

"I see what you're thinking. If Devon's such a perfect kid, why am I here?"

"Take your time. Background is vital."

"Well, here's the foreground. Now she's disappeared."

A kid who didn't look old enough to drive walked into the room, carrying an electric guitar in each hand. The paint jobs were impressive. One had a waving flag motif over a field of grayscale zombies. The other had a collection of wild cats—tigers, lions, cheetahs, jaguars—of varying colors, all peering with menace through bright green reeds.

"Which one?" the kid asked.

After the briefest consideration, Billy pointed at the one with the cats, and the young man exited without another word. The rock star flopped one hand at his wake in a dismissive gesture. "We donate those. I don't play them. They're just painted up to look cool for a charity auction. *Real* fans know I don't play anything but Geneva. She's been with me since . . . Let's see now . . ."

"Devon has disappeared?" Rachael prompted. "Have you reported—"

"From my life, I mean, not disappeared like you're thinking. I know where she *is*, but she won't answer my calls, won't text. She's gone . . . What is it? Incommunicado. And I'm worried."

He rubbed his eyebrows with both hands before summarizing. Devon wanted to take a gap year, have a break, do some traveling. Billy wasn't crazy about it—he knew all about losing your momentum, which was how he had screwed up the fourth album. But if anyone deserved a little time off, it was Devon. Then summer began, and instead of backpacking through Malaysia, she went to a sort of life coach retreat spa in Nevada. That was Devon, through and through. Even her downtime must be productive. It sounded to Billy as if she was rethinking her major—economics, with the aim of going into nonprofit guidance—so perhaps taking some time to reassess would be the smart thing to do. She sounded enthusiastic about this retreat place at first, but then he heard from her less and less, until "less" became "not at all." Cell phone service was spotty, and soon he couldn't get ahold of her *or* Carlos.

Rachael jotted down notes on a small spiral-bound notebook. "Carlos?"

"Her boyfriend. That's another reason I didn't give a thought to her going, because it *wasn't* Malaysia and because she wouldn't be alone."

"And the boyfriend is—"

"Sweet kid. They were two peas in a pod, really. He needed somewhere to go over last Christmas break, so Devvie brought him home, and that was that."

"What does Carlos's family think about this spa?"

This stumped him. "I . . . I don't know anything about his family. I don't even have their number. I'll get back to Carlos in a minute, though I'm sure it was Carlos's idea . . . the counseling aspect of it. And it's not actually a spa, more like a ranch. It's called Today's Enlightenment, or something ridiculous like that."

"And you've tried calling this ranch?"

For the first time an expression of true annoyance crossed his face. "Of course I did. I'm not *stupid*."

"No, of course not," Rachael soothed. "I'm sorry if my questions sound a bit ridiculous at times, but I have to establish what has and has not been done."

"Oh. Yeah, okay. Some chirpy girl in their office says, 'Yes, Devon and Carlos are there. They're fine.' But every time I called, they're out picking beans or in motivation class or doing finger paintings or whatever and can't come to the phone. I'd leave a message, and no callback. Finally, I told the chirpy girl that either she put Devon on the phone or I was going to show up at her door that night. She got a lot less chirpy after that, but I talked to Devon. That was three weeks ago. September twenty-third." The flow of words stopped without warning.

"And?"

"She said she was fine."

"But you had your doubts?" Rachael asked, guessing that was the case.

"Yes and no," he said. "She said that I shouldn't call her

anymore, that I was interrupting her 'progress.' She talked about that a lot, *progress*. She said she was tired of defining herself by my standards and counting on unreliable people. She said my life revolved around myself and that was fine, but hers needed to revolve around herself, and a bunch of other gobbledygook like that. Basically, she was ticked off because Carlos had bailed on her and I was a shit father. She put it more gently than that, because she's Devvie, but that's what she meant."

"Okay." *I wasted a trip*, Rachael thought. The Locard Institute could wow the world in many ways—training scientists, researching innovative new ways to solve crimes, explaining the inexplicable to private clients—but talking a daughter out of a delayed teenage rebellion fell outside those areas of expertise. What Billy needed was some family counseling. "I appreciate your concern, Billy, but—"

Newton materialized next to the coffee table. "Photographer will be here in five. We have to get you into makeup."

"In a sec."

"Now."

"Talkin' about my *kid* here," Billy snapped.

"You can talk and get your face prettified at the same time." Newton said this lightly, jollying the great man along, but Billy wasn't having any.

"In. A. Minute."

"They charge by the minute," Newton warned.

"They charge by the photo, and only the ones we purchase. Now, get out of my face, Newton."

His tone sufficed to make the manager turn and leave, though he muttered, "No one says that anymore," as a last act of defiance.

The man's shadow hadn't left the doorway before Billy said, "No matter how this tour goes, when it's over, I'm firing that guy. I know what you're going to say after 'but.' But why don't I go myself if I'm that worried?"

"Or send . . ." She didn't know how to phrase it. A flunky? One of his minions?

"I can't. For one thing, you see what it's like here. I don't get time to pee without interruption. But most importantly, I don't want Devvie to think I'm checking up on her." He leaned forward, staring into Rachael's eyes. "Devvie's a celebrity kid. It's . . . it's hard on them. You don't know."

"No," Rachael admitted.

"They're expected to be a normal person after growing up in abnormal circumstances. There's no going to school with the same kids year after year, riding bikes in the driveway. It's all Dad's work, Dad's entourage, moving around and trying to do homework with a tutor on the road. They can't trust anyone. Either people try to be her friend because she's my kid or they want to tell her why her dad is a bum who can't sing. Kids like her are in therapy by the time they're ten, in rehab by the time they're fourteen, and that doesn't come as a surprise to anybody, does it?"

He paused for a response here, so Rachael nodded.

"Devon's *different* than that. She's been so strong all these years—and this is the first time she's ever jumped out of her box to do something on her own. I *can't* let her think I don't have confidence in her. My dad did that to me. I won't do that to her. After she *finally* took a step on her own path, I can't go charging in, putting the whole place in an uproar, and it becomes all about me and autographing some chick's boob. See?"

Rachael tried to picture her son as a timid college sophomore. *Timid* didn't describe him, but things might change when he left the security of their home. The thought made her heart flutter.

"And I can't send anyone else. First, Devon knows everyone who works for me, probably better than I do. She was handling my schedule before she could drive. Second"—he glanced at the open doorway, leaned closer, and lowered his voice a decibel or two—"I can't trust anyone here. My new band is grumbling about their placement, the roadies don't want to be called roadies anymore, both groups want a lot more money, and Newton is trying to kill me. I need someone neutral. I need the Locard."

As sympathetic as Rachael felt toward a parent in distress, and though Billy had already promised to pay the kind of fee that could launch a new research study, she had to make something clear. "This is not the type of thing in which the Locard has a lot of expertise, Mr. Diamond."

"Call me Billy."

"It sounds as if you want us not only to check on your daughter's welfare but also to convince her to reconcile with you, without mentioning you or letting her know that you are involved or even aware."

He considered that. "Yes, exactly."

"I don't see how that would be possible."

He brushed this away with a wave of one hand. "Isis said you could figure out anything."

Speaking of that . . . "How did you know Isis?"

What she meant was, "How *well* did you know Isis?" Her sister had a long and varied history, the kind that had given their father prematurely gray hair and driven a wedge between the two siblings. But she had made a success, at last, of a party-planning business, catering to the wealthy and high-profile clients of DC. And Billy looked like he threw a lot of parties.

It tugged at Rachael, this opportunity to find out a little more about her sister's life during the past eight or ten years, the years in which they hadn't spoken much other than in quick, bitter arguments. The birth of Danton had repaired some ties, but only a fraction.

The abrupt change in topics had silenced Billy, so she prompted, "Through her business? Elite Events?"

"Yes! Yes. Uh yeah, Isis and I did a lot of business together. She put together great stuff, and you know, I trusted her, and I don't trust many. She said you were the smartest person who ever existed."

No she didn't.

"Just, please, go to Nevada or have someone else go there. You look too much like your sister."

No I don't, Rachael almost said aloud.

"Make sure she's okay. Beautiful blond girl, you can't miss her. And maybe find out why she stopped talking to dear old Dad. If she needs some space, fine. If Carlos or someone else has gotten her into something . . . not good. Then I'll charge in, chaos or not."

It sounded like easy money for the research department, Rachael found herself thinking. A plane ticket, spa fees, or whatever, put this hyper dad's mind at rest. But she couldn't let her desire to learn about Isis bias her. "I understand. But if you think she's simply taking some space—"

He shook his head so sharply that the ponytail flopped between his shoulders. "That *is* what I thought until yesterday. Until I found out Carlos was dead."

Chapter 3

Ellie Carr paused with a coffee cup halfway to her lips. "I'm going to do what, now?"

Rachael had made it back to the Chesapeake Bay area in time to stop in at the Locard before everyone started heading home. She'd caught Dr. Ellie Carr in her office. The ex–FBI agent and crime scene expert had worked undercover before and, at thirty, might have a slightly easier time talking to Billy's daughter.

"Here's the time line," Rachael told her. "Three weeks ago Devon tells Billy that Carlos left the ranch, bailed on her. Yesterday Billy finds out that Carlos is dead. He apparently drowned in the Truckee River. His body was found last week at a dam east of Reno. The structure of this particular dam—it caused considerable damage to the body. The local medical examiner puts time of death at three to six weeks ago, which coincides with when Devon said he left the ranch."

Ellie sat behind her desk. Her office didn't have much space but did have a large window overlooking the center courtyard, already deep into the shadows of dusk. The Locard started life as a boys' school, nestled in heavy woods, and had three floors in a U shape. It had laboratories of every kind, offices, a gymnasium, even a cafeteria, but somehow the radiators and heavy wood framing never let its occupants forget its humble origins. "Ah. Carlos was dead before Billy last spoke with Devon, so no need to panic that she went into the same river with him."

"Yep."

"Does Devon know Carlos's dead?"

"There's no way to know. He did try to call, but she wouldn't come to the phone, and he didn't want to tell her that in a message. Billy's worried that she'll be depressed or grieving if or when she finds out, even if she sounded more annoyed than upset about Carlos. He thinks she'd been cooling on the romance for a while now, but it's hard to tell with young emotions."

"What do her friends think? Usually when a girl is dumped, she runs to her BFFs."

"It didn't sound like the poor kid had many. She grew up on the road, with adults, roadies, groupies, and managers."

"What about her mother?"

"Billy doesn't think much of her, to put it mildly, though I always take an ex's opinion with a few handfuls of salt. He said she blew a few months after the girl was born and he doesn't know if she's even still alive. Gave me her last known address, though."

"And Carlos's family hasn't contacted him? Do they know who Devon is?"

"I asked that too. He couldn't remember either of the kids ever mentioning his family, which, he claimed to realize only as we were speaking, was weird."

"Maybe, maybe not."

Rachael wondered if Ellie was thinking of her own childhood, of being orphaned at four, growing up with various loving relatives. But at least Ellie had always had somewhere to go on a school break. "He *had* a family, though. The medical examiner notified them, and they called Yale to let them know Carlos wouldn't be returning this fall and to cancel the automatic billing. Yale called back about a refund and got Billy instead because Carlos had put the Diamonds as his next of kin. From there Billy turned to Google, which told him the rest."

Without another word, Ellie woke up her computer and found a map of Nevada. Rachael stood to peer over her shoulder. They found the long Truckee River, which flowed from Lake Tahoe northeast through Reno, then continued into the desert, through Derby Dam, and up to Pyramid Lake.

"How did they identify him after all that time in the water? He have ID?"

"Not on him, but again, considerable damage. If he wore a shirt, it had been completely ripped off, along with most of his chest. Nothing left but tattered khaki pants and one purple Air Jordan. But someone managed to get a fingerprint."

Ellie raised an eyebrow. "He had a record?"

"Nope. In high school he was printed during the application process to be a camp counselor."

"Cause of death is drowning?"

"I'll see about a copy of the autopsy report, but according to the *Reno Gazette-Journal*, the ME chalked it up to an accident, means unknown. He's hardly the only person who has drowned in that river this year. The city has a large homeless population, and the river is prone to flooding in some months."

"Where is this ranch?"

Rachael read off the address, which pinpointed a spot southwest of Reno, between it and Lake Tahoe. "Looks pretty close to that same river."

Ellie sat back, crossing her arms. "So . . . possible scenarios . . . accident, suicide, murder. Accident . . . Carlos falls into the river at the ranch, can't swim, the stream carries him through Reno without anyone noticing and up to the dam, and Devon assumes he bailed on her. Suicide . . . Devon breaks up with him, and Carlos heads for Reno, where he contemplates his broken heart, ponders how he gave up a Yale education to pursue a girl who doesn't want him, knows he's not going to get much sympathy from his disinterested family, then throws himself into the water."

"Seems extreme," Rachael had retaken her seat but now checked her watch. She should still make it home in time.

"Last, murder . . . Carlos broke up with Daddy's girl Devon, and she didn't care for it and brought a river rock down on his head, leaving him to float through Reno and so on. Maybe all the above . . . Carlos sours on the whole self-help thing and/or Devon, heads to the nearest city with an airport—Reno. He gets good and drunk or runs up some gambling debts with the wrong casino owners and winds up in the water either accidentally or on purpose."

"That's a lot of extrapolating," Rachael pointed out. Ellie thrived on forming scenarios, but Rachael had to admit that all the same ideas had run through her mind while stopping for red lights through DC.

"I said *possible*." Ellie fell silent, then added, "I don't blame Billy for his concern. His daughter goes out there with this guy, and now the guy is dead."

"Yeah . . . I don't love that either."

Ellie finished the last of her coffee. "But if it were my kid—"

"You'd be on a plane right now, instead of interviewing private investigators for the job. Me too."

"But not our client," Ellie said, her statement a question.

"My take? Billy wants to be a good father. But he wants

to be a fabulous rock star more, and he can't be in two places at one time. Delegation is necessary."

"And priorities must be established." Ellie made a face, something between a deep frown and a pucker of distaste, as if she'd bitten into a rotten lemon. "All right, I'm all in. *Someone's* got to look out for this girl."

"That's what I think too." Rachael stood up, ready to go home to her own child, who, she thought with no little gratitude, was still too small to leave the house without her. Part of her wished he always would be.

"So I have to go to Nevada and establish that Devon Diamond is physically and psychologically healthy and maybe talk her into giving her dad a call, without letting her know that Dad is the one who sent us. You know that might be difficult. Maybe even impossible."

Rachael said, "I have every confidence in you."

Ellie made that face again.

PART I

THE WELCOME

People started around us. "Welcome. Welcome [a]ll of [y]ou. [G]lad you are with us." This was Jonestown. I was here at last, here with the people that love me without condition. It felt wonderful.

Leslie Wagner-Wilson, *Slavery of Faith*

Chapter 4

Ellie hired a car to drive her to the ranch. It was exorbitantly expensive but would make it harder for the group to send her away if she dumped herself on their doorstep like the thirty-year-old foundling she was. She and Rachael had thought that through. They had tried to think everything through.

Google Maps had told them the ranch sat at the foot of an unnamed mountain—the nearest town, on the other side of said mountain, was a tiny burg with the pretty name of Topaz. As near as Ellie had been able to determine from the local topography, it appeared to be a relatively level five-mile hike from the ranch to Topaz if she went around the mountain or two miles of much steeper terrain if she went over the top of it. Closer than Reno, at ten miles away. One of the tenets of undercover work: always be aware of your escape routes. Old habits died hard.

Agnes, the Locard's amazing and slightly frightening digital forensics whiz, had helped her research Today's Enlightenment and its director, Galen. No last name, just Galen. The Today's Enlightenment web page provided his résumé—

one of the youngest to graduate from MIT, went on to Harvard, IQ measured at 166, studied meditation in Tibet and New Zealand before designing his own program. To Agnes's frustration, the man didn't seem to exist outside his own website. Galen *wasn't* the name his mother had given him.

Of course, Devon Diamond didn't exist online either. Billy had given Rachael only one snapshot to pass along, and it wasn't a great one, Devon at a high school dance, her face partially turned, a slender white girl with blond hair to her waist. In an age when nearly every young person plastered the internet with selfies, Devon didn't even have an Instagram account. Of course, it was also an age acutely aware of the dangers of releasing your personal information across the internet—for celebs most of all. But Agnes would keep looking.

The ranch itself had pages across all major sites, with photos of beaming people arm in arm, an expanse of desert plus a mountain in the background. Tripadvisor reviews were resolutely positive, with comments along the lines of "Best thing I ever did," "Really helped me out of a dark place," and "I left with new meaning and direction in my life." The harshest criticism came from a Minnesotan, who complained that living conditions were "sort of roughing it" and that the dinner entrées could have used more flavor.

No news articles to be found, but then finding inner peace didn't grab media attention like prostitutes and the Comstock Lode. Nevada had been founded in gold and silver mining rushes, with many legal but still not super-profitable brothels as well as legal and quite profitable gambling. In fact, the world-famous Mustang Ranch brothel also sat along the Truckee River, between Reno and the dam where Carlos's body had turned up. Perhaps he'd gone there for some comfort after the break with Devon, found that physical pleasure could not soothe his troubled soul, and plunged into the Truckee's depths. Or was tossed in by some angry working girls after he welched on his bill. Neither theory seemed particularly likely.

She did find it interesting that the Nevada legislature met only every other year. Ellie couldn't decide if she found that enormously sensible or simply lazy, but either way, it seemed to work for them.

And too soon, she arrived, not *actually* in the middle of nowhere, though it certainly appeared as such. The car ground to a halt at the graveled ribbon, the only visible drive branching from the road in either direction, and the guy at the wheel got out without a word. He opened the trunk to hand Ellie her backpack. Then he gazed toward the group of nondescript buildings scattered along the flat earth, the nearest about a hundred feet away. No people in sight, the only movement that of a lone chicken pecking at a clump of weeds.

"Are you sure this is where you want to be?" the driver asked her.

Nope. Not sure at all, popped into her mind. But Ellie was a grown-up and a former FBI agent, with more than a passing acquaintance with deception and violence, and should have a better than average ability to handle whatever Today's Enlightenment could throw at her. If Devon figured out why she was there, she might feel a little embarrassed. Billy might withhold part of their fee. That would be the worst that could happen.

At least that was what she told herself.

"Yes," she told the driver. "I'm sure."

Chapter 5

The sun warmed Ellie's shoulders, welcome after the air-conditioned vehicle, but with a firmness that told her she'd be seeking an escape from it before too long. The plains stretched in all directions until interrupted by mountains, with visibility for several miles. No fence, nothing like a guard shack or even a reception booth. If anyone there wanted to leave, like Carlos, they had only to walk away. Of course, it would be a long, hot, dusty walk, so there was that.

The gravel of the drive broke up here and there into tufts of malnourished weeds. It continued past several buildings, each about the size of a modest, one-floor single-family home, each painted a boring and uniform shade of light tan. A carved wooden sign off to the right read TODAY'S EN-LIGHTENMENT in sun-faded letters. She hitched the backpack over one shoulder and listened to the stones crunch under her newly purchased hiking boots.

The chicken watched her approach. Ellie could hear nothing now save the far-off droning of some humming machinery and hoped it was an air conditioner. Three rough buildings, each about the size of a high school gymnasium, were lined up on her left, and two were on her right, with another two or three irregularly spaced beyond them, forming a loose horseshoe around this central drive. A door opened in the most distant one, and two women and a man emerged. Ellie could just hear the murmur of their voices as they spoke to each other with cheery animation, and then they disappeared into the next building. One of the women had looked in her direction, but if she'd seen Ellie, she'd given no sign, her body language neither concerned nor startled.

The chicken followed Ellie past the buildings. These bore placards, clearly delineating the first building as one, so that the ones on her left were one, two, and three, while the ones on the right were the meeting hall and then the gym. At the back, off to the left, Ellie spied a small sign reading OFFICE and headed for it. A burst of laughter rumbled from inside the meeting hall, amid the unmistakable sound of cutlery tapping against porcelain. That and a whiff of tomato sauce in the air told her she'd arrived at lunchtime. Her stomach rumbled in response to the idea. Air travel hadn't been the same since they'd stopped serving meals during flights.

The office consisted of a squarish aluminum trailer. A path of packed earth, perpendicular to the drive, led to two different two-story buildings and a barn on the right. To the left, about five hundred feet away, sat two small sheds without windows. Part of the vacant land between those and the office had been used as a campfire site, with a scorched oval of earth a good five feet in diameter beneath a tangle of blackened twigs. A second chicken pecked at the burnt branches, and somehow the sight of the second prompted some burst of envy or insanity in the first. It abruptly rushed at Ellie, as if intending to take a chunk or two out of her calf, and she dashed up the three wooden steps to the office door with unseemly haste and flung it open, startling the young woman inside.

"Well! Hello," said the too-slender woman. Her light

brown hair appeared to have been hacked off with a pair of garden shears. Her T-shirt had lost its shape and her only jewelry was a string of wooden beads around one wrist. She held a manila file folder in one hand and stood at a copy machine. The rest of the office had a construction-trailer lack of décor but seemed clean and bright, with shiny folding chairs and clean carpeting. "Can I help you?"

Ellie promptly forgot about the avenging chicken. It was showtime. "I'm Ellen Barr. I'm here to . . . um . . . join the program?"

The woman blinked, then looked around, as if Ellie might have brought someone along who could translate. "Where did you come from?"

"Cleveland."

"No, I mean . . . we usually pick groups up at the airport— Well . . . I guess it's not important." She seemed extremely unsure on this point, not so much nervous as hapless. She put the folder in a filing basket, changed her mind, and set it on the desk, outside the filing basket. Then she rummaged through every drawer in a filing cabinet before extracting a box of Winchester twelve gauge, number nine and a sheaf of perhaps five papers stapled together. She dropped the box back into the cabinet and plunked the papers onto the desk surface. She ignored the dusty laptop beside them, its cords snaking across the floor to an outlet without a switch plate.

Ellie waited.

"Have a seat, please. I'm Angela. Sorry, I should have said. Oh, would you like a water?"

Ellie would, indeed. She dropped her backpack on the floor and dragged a folding chair to the side of Angela's desk. There were only two such desks, in opposite corners from each other. A set of homemade shelves took up a third corner, with items ranging in type from toilet paper to bottled water to a dollar store–type pink plastic basket with FIRST AID written on the edge in marker. The fourth corner had a card table covered with folders and cardboard boxes, with more stacked beneath it.

Out of habit, Ellie scanned the room for cameras or any particular security. Nothing, save for a typical locking knob in the office's metal door. The two windows had minimal latches, no wires, no apparent alarms. Crime wasn't an issue in the middle of nowhere.

The young woman pulled a bottle out of a mini-fridge and asked if they'd begun an account for Ellie, who said no. Then she began filling in the blanks on the new client record pages, writing down Ellen Barr's name, address, occupation, next of kin. How had Ellen heard about the place? Some woman she'd met in passing at a party had simply raved about Today's Enlightenment.

When working undercover, Ellie liked to keep her fictional backstory full of convincing but unverifiable details. She had chosen a name very close to the real one of Elizabeth Carr; if someone called her "Ellen" or "Ms. Barr," the common letters would alert her brain to react. The intimidating Agnes had also created a basic online history for her, a few social media profiles, messages posted in two professional online communities, and a job history complete with her new name listed in company directories. Ellen Barr had spent the past six years as a biologist testing food safety. Ellie and Agnes hoped that sounded dull enough to prompt only a few polite questions, which her scientific background would help her to deflect.

"How will you be paying?" Angela asked her now. The website made it clear that Today's Enlightenment was not a charity. The coursework and counseling, not to mention room and board, cost more than a balcony suite on a small ship cruise for the same amount of time.

Agnes had also obtained a quite legitimate credit card (with an excellent payment history) for the completely illegitimate personhood of Ellen Barr. *If I ever need to flee the country, I am first going straight to Agnes.*

Ellie handed it over, noticing as she leaned forward a series of small holes in the surface of the desk. Three on the side and two on the top, about three or four millimeters in diameter. Perhaps from that number nine bird shot. "What happened here?"

"Huh? Oh, the holes—I have no idea." Angela spoke absently, flipping back and forth through the new client record, as if not sure it passed muster. Ellie let her focus on her work.

Each hole came at the end of a dented trough, which started at a taper and widened until whatever had skimmed the metal finally punched through it. The holes and troughs were all the same size but randomly spaced apart, which made her think of the typical damage from a hail of bullets, though these were small enough to come from shotgun pellets or BBs rather than actual bullets. The tapers, or leading edges, indicated that the force had come from her own direction and had been aimed slightly to her left. She could use the troughs' elliptical shapes to calculate an angle of origin, if she needed to. But, of course, she didn't need to.

Visually following the obvious trajectory, Ellie could not see corresponding holes in the wall behind Angela's work area, though the surface was littered with too many attached flyers, funny memes, photos, and sticky notes to allow much inspection. She scanned these for mention of Devon or even a handy scoreboard of clients but found nothing of the sort.

Paperwork completed, Angela went on to explain the basics of the place. Clients were provided both group courses and individual counseling with their assigned coach and sometimes other counselors, including Galen, the head counselor. Ellie would be given a bunk in the freshmen quarters. Clients were generally divided into groups depending on their level of progress, and Galen—well, all of them—had fallen into the habit of nicknaming the groups as high school classes. The freshmen were the newbies. After coursework and individual counseling, usually a matter of weeks to months, clients moved into the sophomore group.

Months?

Sophomores were expected to know the drill and pick up more of the contributory work at the ranch. Everyone did contributory work to maintain the place and also to engage in mental rest and a reconnection to their roots as physical beings. Work included cleaning, laundry, cooking, and working in the gardens.

"Then juniors and seniors, I suppose?" Ellie asked, not sure if that seemed fun or juvenile.

"Yes. Though there aren't any seniors at the ranch right now. And like in high school, no skipping classes. If you're not properly devoted to this process, then it's not going to be able to effect any change in you. Oh, and don't bother Mrs. Coleman."

"Who's—"

"She lives in a big house up the mountain. It's gorgeous," Angela confided in a moment of girl-gossip weakness before snapping back to crisp and professional mode. "Her family was quite wealthy, and she lets us use this land, but she's very private and doesn't want visitors. She's so kind, and we promised her no one would trespass. Does that make sense?"

"Leave the recluse alone. Got it."

"Great. I see you only have a backpack. Did you come prepared to stay awhile? I mean, is there anywhere you're going to need to be? Work, children, somebody's wedding? Because there's no set schedule—"

"As long as it takes. I am completely free."

"Great! That's so exciting."

"Not the word I'd use, but I'm trying to see it that way."

This led to Angela's next question. Leaning forward, with

her elbows on the worn desktop, elfin chin in one hand, as if Ellie's were the most fascinating story she'd heard in ages, she asked, "So, why *are* you here?"

Ellie told her the truth. Not about Billy Diamond and the Locard, of course, but about how her mother had been killed, supposedly in a car accident, and how her father hadn't cared to be a father and had left her in the care of her mother's family.

Then she shaded out of the truth, letting Angela believe that growing up with various members of her extended family had been traumatizing, when it had really been loving and outrageously supportive. Now, Ellie told the young woman, "Ellen Barr" had been laid off for no good reason and thought perhaps these unresolved issues were holding her back from success at work—not to mention in interpersonal relationships. A self-help retreat felt like her last chance to get her life on track.

This story made poor Angela produce more cold water and declare her personal happiness that Ellie had decided to join them. Then the young woman bundled her out to see her new home.

The mountain air hit Ellie with fresh clarity, despite its warmth, as they stepped outside. The sunlight dazzled, making the buildings appear bleached of any color. Perhaps to combat this monochrome, someone had formed a small flower bed in front of the office: green stalks with leaves but no flowers spotted its soil. Someone must water it daily, because the rest of the ground seemed hard and absolutely dry.

With lunch hour over, more people were outside, always in groups of two or three or more, and Ellie scanned them, searching for Devon. They seemed to range from early twenties to late sixties and across all racial and body-shape categories. Most appeared cheerful. No signs of discomfort, a tense face, turning away from others, fidgeting, flushed skin. But no sign of a young beauty with long blond hair either.

Angela ushered her into the building marked one, the first one she'd passed on her way in from the road.

This was the detail Ellie expected to be the roughest of the "sort of roughing it" part. The freshmen bunkhouse consisted of one large room with twin beds lined up along the two long walls, each bed with a wooden frame and a thick-looking mattress, a blanket and pillow. The exterior door they'd entered by didn't even have a lock. Apparently, the honor system ruled.

Each bunk had its own nightstand with a shelf and a cubby underneath and a surface bare of clocks or reading lamps. The beds were all neatly made, and personal items on the stands immediately identified the occupied bunks. That was about it as far as décor went, but the windows made the place bright, and it smelled only of a faint disinfectant. Not bad, though Ellie had recently bought her first home and ached to spend every day renovating, not to return to Girl Scout camp living.

"Men and women in the same house." Angela watched Ellie's face for signs of a major freak-out as they stood in the center of the floor. "You saw that on the website, right?"

"Yes, I did."

She puffed out a breath of relief. "Good. We simply don't have the facilities for different houses and certainly not for private rooms. Some people are only here for a single course and check out in a day or two. Some go and come back. We needed the most flexible arrangement. That's the women's restroom and showers at that end, and the men's are at this end. Thought I should warn you since we never did put up a sign. Use whichever fits your identity."

"You say *we*. Have you been with the, um, program since it began?"

"No! I wish! No, I came here looking for help, like you have. I didn't know where to go or what to do with myself. I needed help to find my path, but now I love it so much here, I'm not sure I'll ever want to leave!"

"So you graduated? Through the sophomore and junior and so forth—"

"No!" This time it came out as nearly a groan, and she ran her fingers through the cropped hair. "I have so much farther to go. I'm not . . . I'm hardly a poster child for anything. I haven't been able to . . . but I didn't want to give up on my future. I had to keep working harder on it! Then Galen needed help in the office, so now I . . ." The wattage of her smile flickered, then came back brighter than ever. She turned it on Ellie full force. "I can help people all day, every day. This is the perfect place for me. I know it will be for you too."

"Um," Ellie said. She hoped Angela wouldn't be too disappointed when Ellie didn't stay the course—literally. She needed only a private conversation with Devon, and then it would be back to DC and her new puppy, new house, and new job.

But Angela smiled at her hesitation. "I know it may all seem a bit overwhelming at first. The first few days after I got here, all I could think is, *What am I doing*? But you're taking the first step to make your life exactly what you want it to be, and you have to give yourself full credit for that." She laid one hand on Ellie's arm. "So many people, most people really, never do that, never even attempt to assess and repair their existence. They're afraid to even try. So by coming here, just by walking up that drive, you've taken the biggest step of all! It's so great. And we—I'm using the Queen Victoria and corporate *we*—are so glad you did." She stepped closer and wrapped her arms around Ellie in a brief but firm empowerment hug while Ellie puzzled out whether the expression for Victoria was the "imperial *we*" and whether "in the collective sense" might be more accurate.

But Ellie knew what she meant. Angela, not Victoria.

Ellie stashed her backpack in a nightstand along the north wall, one over from the next occupied bed but still with one empty bed-and-nightstand set from the men's room and the exterior door—spacing herself like an electron around a nucleus, as far from others as she could get but still in the right orbit. Like the building itself, the nightstand had no locking mechanism, but she didn't worry about that. She had brought only fifty dollars in cash, her Agnes-invented driver's license, and the one, now no longer empty, credit card.

Angela continued. "Afternoon sessions should begin in ten minutes or so. Sessions don't have to be done in order. Many clients take the same session two or three or four times before they feel they've mastered it, so it's no problem if the other clients have already been here for a while. Everyone is on their own schedule . . . so why don't we have you plunge right in, and in the meantime, I'll find out who your coach is and get you set up with them afterward?"

"By all means," Ellie said. "Let's plunge."

Chapter 6

The empty meeting hall/dining area, like the bunkhouse, appeared strictly utilitarian, with the industrial long tables and stackable chairs of a high school cafeteria. Only half of the building served as this open space. A hallway led to the separate rooms that occupied the other half of the building. Ellie's nose again picked up faint smells of the lunch she hadn't had.

She followed Angela into the other half of the building, past two closed doors and three large conference rooms, and entered the last. It held three rows of simple desks with chairs on only one side, facing the front of the room. No windows, to keep the majesty of nature from distracting the clients. About fifteen people had already taken seats and hummed with smiles and enthusiasm.

Angela spoke clearly, raising her voice over the bustle. "Hi, everyone. This is Ellen."

As a group, they said hello, as if at a twelve-step meeting, turning their smiles and enthusiasm on Ellie. She summoned up a pretend amount of both, returned the greeting, and slid into an empty seat at the end of the second row.

Angela bent at the waist to tell Ellie that she'd find her after class to finish getting her "set up" and that she shouldn't worry about a thing. This made Ellie wonder if she should have figured out something to worry about. "The notepads and pens are here for you, so use as many as you need." She pulled one of the thin pads of lined paper and a pen imprinted with TODAY'S ENLIGHTENMENT from a scattered pile on an empty desk and positioned them in front of Ellie, note-taking clearly not optional.

Then she patted Ellie's shoulder and walked away, the school aide dropping off the transfer kid. She paused in the doorway to chat with a blond woman, this one only slightly older, with hair past her shoulder blades and an overfull manila folder in her hands.

The man seated next to Ellie, thirtyish, with a scar on his cleft chin, introduced himself as Barry and shook her hand, as did the rosy-cheeked woman in front. The older lady next to her glanced over her shoulder, stated her name as Margot, and went back to writing the date and *Emotional Response* at the top of her pad.

The blond woman shut the door. She gave Ellie a friendly smile but then dove right into teacher mode. "Today is a very important step on your journey. All your days here are, yes, but today we're really going to focus on your inner responses to data. Maybe how you feel defines who you are, but let's face it, you're not really here to 'find yourself.'" She gave the last two words an exaggerated breathiness, and most of the class laughed. "You're here to figure out exactly what you want the rest of your life to look like, and how you are going to make that happen. Am I right?"

The class murmured agreement in a low, unintelligible rumbling, like distant thunder.

She prompted someone to volunteer an explanation of what perception was—the rosy-cheeked woman did—and spoke of categories of perception. The first seemed to be general perception, or learned information, such as chairs are for sitting and to start a car, you turn a key or push a button. The second whole category apparently consisted of stuff humans forgot or deleted because they were bombarded with information nearly every minute of every day. "If we didn't immediately toss the unnecessary and irrelevant stuff, our heads would explode." More laughter.

The third category was stuff humans perceived but changed in their heads, improving it, rejecting it, mentally repainting our friend's room in a more suitable color or picturing ourselves becoming an airline pilot and jetting off to Europe every week. This drive gave human beings their creativity and ability to push boundaries.

Ellie's fellow students took copious notes, faces furrowed in concentration. Ellie spent the time rehearsing what to say to Devon once she found the girl. It sounded as if Billy expected her to not only locate Devon but also to reconcile her to her father, and Ellie had no idea how to do that. Her own father had walked out the day after her mother's death. If he showed up or sent an emissary, would she be interested in reconciliation?

Hell, no.

Though Billy hadn't physically abandoned her, perhaps Devon was feeling some similar resentments. Feeling like she existed only as an appendage to his fame. Tired of being a satellite in his orbit.

Perhaps they could bond over similar parent-child relationship issues. When Ellie had worked undercover, it had helped her to find one thing in each target with which she could genuinely identify. A love of dogs, a favorite singer, coffee with cream. It helped. Even when the person in question ran a criminal organization responsible for over a dozen murders in the past year alone.

So when the instructor told them to write down three things that made them happy, three things that made them unhappy, and why, Ellie wrote about her father. The talking points might come in handy when she found Devon.

The hour-long class expired before she had to speak aloud, to her relief. The rest of the class promptly stood and said in unison, "Thank you for guiding us to find our own roads."

Another protocol Ellie would have to learn if she wanted to fit in.

Then they began to file out. Ellie realized she had no idea where to go next, but the blond instructor rescued her, lying in wait at the front for the rest to leave.

"You're Ellen. I'm so glad you're here. You should be really proud of yourself for taking this step. Most people never do, don't even want to know what they are and what they want, much less what they're willing to do to get it."

"Uh . . . thanks."

"I'm going to be your coach during your time here. You've had a tour?"

"I've seen the bunkhouse."

"I'll walk you through the rest of the property, and we can talk. I have so many questions, and I'll bet it's been a long time since anyone's asked, or since you've even asked yourself, am I right?"

"Um—"

"Here we learn to devote ourselves to ourselves first, because it's not until you know yourself that you can devote yourself to others." She laughed at Ellie's blank expression. "Never mind, I'm sure that sounds like gobbledygook to you right now, but you'll see what I mean. I'm so excited to take this journey with you." She stretched out a hand. "My name's Devon."

Well, Ellie thought, that was easy.

Chapter 7

Devon looked well; in fact, she looked great. Her fair skin glowed, her trim shape hovered neither above nor below normal weight, and she seemed at ease in her position of some authority. Mature for her age, just as Billy had said.

The first checkbox on the to-do list for this job had an *X* in it. The next two boxes were somewhat optional: find out why Devon had frozen out her father and where Carlos Freeman had gotten to. That might take longer, but this leisurely tour was a good way to start. They strolled up the packed dirt path while Ellie gave a condensed version of how her husband had left her for another woman, which was true, and how she'd lost her job, which was not.

The "fields" turned out to be exactly that, rows of corn, beans, and soybeans. Thirty or forty people worked among the plants, picking the produce or pulling weeds or scattering something Ellie took to be plant food. She recognized a few of her new classmates. The sun felt warm, but a constant breeze kept it from getting too hot.

Devon introduced a building tucked behind the gym as the publishing office, which printed up all the questionnaires and classroom worksheets. From what Ellie could see, the work included glossy brochures and what, in a glance, seemed to be direct mail advertisements. Nine people sat at a long table, stuffing these into envelopes. It seemed an old-fashioned approach to advertising, but then a physical item that someone could hold, set down on their counter, and come back to later might have more of a click-through rate than an unsolicited email in a spam folder, easily deleted without a glance.

Upon exiting the envelope-stuffing room, Ellie nearly collided with a dark-haired man, who steadied her with one hand on her elbow.

"Galen!" Devon nearly shouted. Then she recovered and turned to Ellie, the surprise giving way to a tense, bright excitement. "This is our head, the man who designed this ranch and its program."

Ah. The amazing Galen. Child Cornell graduate and Tibetan meditator. Pied piper of daughters. Ellie took the time to study him before responding, and he did the same to her.

He had brown hair with glints of chestnut throughout and eye color to match. High cheekbones over a hint of dimples. Enough muscles rippling under the skin of his forearms and neck to keep him from being girly but not enough to intimidate. He stood with his feet not together but not splayed—not submissive, but not intimidating either. Completely comfortable with himself and his surroundings.

"And you're Ellen," he said, holding out his hand. When she took it, instead of shaking her hand, he covered it with his other, pressing it between warm flesh. He leaned closer, never breaking eye contact. "But that's too formal . . . You've got a lot more Wild West, pioneer stock in you than that. I'm going to call you Nell."

"Actually, no one—"

"I'm so glad you're here."

"You and everyone else I've met," Ellie blurted.

He laughed, and it lit up his face in a way that made her think whatever else might be going on in Devon's mind, her eyesight remained twenty-twenty.

"I'll let you finish settling in, then. We'll talk later, maybe tomorrow. I want to make sure this program works for *you*, Nell, specifically, so that it changes the rest of your life until you can live every day to the maximum of your potential," Galen said. "I know there are parts of you," he added conspiratorially, gazing with great concentration into her eyes from a distance of perhaps six inches, "that have not yet been tapped."

"Good to know."

He strode away, perhaps aware—perhaps not—of the way Devon stared after him.

Then she moved briskly on. They walked past two buildings under construction—one a slab with four upthrust beams of wood and one just a slab—with teams of men and women hammering nails into studs with such professional attention that Ellie asked if they were contractors. Devon said one had been a construction manager and now supervised his fellow attendees. They were building a bunkhouse for seniors—seniors in the grading system of the program, not an indication of age—and more classrooms.

"Very impressive." Amazing what one could accomplish with free labor.

Ellie peeked into a cavernous barn that held the planting equipment, a chain hoist, and a rusting pickup. Outside its walls sat tables for sorting produce. Chickens scratched in a loosely fenced coop off to the side. Then a parking lot, with perhaps fifteen cars tidily lined up on patchy weeds and earth. She couldn't tell if the plants had grown up around them or if the greenery predated the vehicles. Devon said they even had a few beehives farther up the path, but she needed to end the tour to give Ellie time to change for yoga.

"Though if you don't like yoga, you can study in the classrooms or spend extra time in the fields."

"It's fine. Actually, I'd been looking forward to the yoga."

Devon gave her a hug, sinewy arms wrapping around Ellie's shoulders but leaving space between the rest of their bodies. "Good! It's so important to keep the body in line with the mind. But we have a lot more to talk about, you and I. Not just the job and the recent divorce but your inner journey to this point."

Ellie pretended enthusiasm and wondered when she'd have a chance to call Rachael.

Devon left her at the bunkhouse to change and find her own way across the drive to the gym.

The hollow building had plenty of floor space since the only workout equipment consisted of two treadmills, one of which had a handmade OUT OF ORDER sign taped to its console, and a weight bench without any weights. Netless basketball hoops had been mounted on opposite walls and had dark smudges on the wood behind them, but there were no balls that Ellie could see.

But the yoga mats were piled high, and each person selected their own to form a tidy grid across the floor. Ellie calculated how many people were present. Approximately ten mats wide and eight deep . . . less than the stated population, but as Devon had said, there were alternative activities available.

She really *had* been looking forward to the yoga, not only to stretch out after the plane trip and long car ride, but also to have twenty or thirty minutes without someone chattering at her for the first time since her arrival.

This didn't pan out—even yoga was co-opted to serve the mission, because the instructor promptly said they were to focus on improving their observation skills.

"Unless they hurt, you probably haven't been aware of your toes or your kneecaps or the bones in your wrist all day. So much happens to us and around us every day, and we ignore it. Think how much more effective we'd be if we could open up to being aware of these things. In this way we unlock that potential of our minds," the whip-thin older woman explained.

In child's pose, Ellie murmured an apology to her neglected kneecaps, breathing deeply of air tinged with mildew-scented rubber.

Dinner came after yoga, served buffet style back in the meeting/dining hall. Bare-bones salad, mac and cheese, and hot dogs—a lot of carbs and fat—but by then Ellie was hungry enough to blow off the food pyramid for one night. Ellie carted her tray toward a table in the middle, but a woman from the front row of her class appeared at her elbow, carrying her own tray. "Ellen! Hi! I'm Audrey. This way." And since Ellie had no better ideas, she went that way.

She took a seat across from the rosy-cheeked woman, who asked how she liked yoga, and Margot, who, now that she didn't have to turn around to do it, fixed Ellie with the look third-grade teachers gave to girls suspected of passing notes. She asked what Ellie thought about everything so far.

"I'm not sure yet." Which was completely true.

"You're going to love it here," Audrey stated, and a woman to her left backed her up.

"It's already changed my life," a man next to her said. "I just wish they had better food."

Having discovered the general mushiness of the mac and cheese noodles, Ellie agreed aloud.

Audrey adjusted her tank top, showing off tightly toned biceps. "I used to manage a Kohl's, and I hated it. Having to herd a bunch of twentysomething cats . . . I'm meant for something much more important than that. Galen led me to see that, and I'm never going back. Not to my old job, my old bedroom, my old life. Or my parents."

Ellie recognized most of the people around her as bunkmates and classmates, which she realized were one and the same. Fellow freshmen. Did they have to sit at the freshmen table? She didn't see any signs.

A woman mixed her salad in with her macaroni. "I wish my boyfriend would get it. But I don't think he ever will. He's too wrapped up in his friends and his games. It's as if he wants to stay in high school forever."

"How did you come to be here?" Ellie asked Margot. She skewed a bit older than the rest of the group, well into her fifties. Graying curls hung in her eyes, and her shapeless T-shirt bore a picture of the Eiffel Tower.

She stabbed shreds of iceberg with a listless fork. "Don't really know. The kids got married, they're off chasing careers, and friends of mine went on a cruise in Europe. I sat on my patio, adding up how many toilets I've scrubbed, and it seemed like too damn many. Next thing I knew, I was telling my husband he can scrub his own toilets, write his own checks, wash his own laundry, and remember his own mother's birthday. Then I got in the car and drove out here."

"Good for you," the rosy-cheeked woman said, but uncertainly, as if it might not be so good. She struck Ellie as chronically hesitant. But then she'd had enough backbone to break away and come to the ranch to work on it, so good for her too.

"We've left our pasts behind," Audrey said, which didn't seem to follow. But perhaps it did to her, because she reached across the table to grasp Ellie's hand, which had been resting next to her bowl. "We're all here to grow in ways we didn't think possible. I believe every one of us will unpack our vast and unique potential during our time here. I'm sure you will too. You only have to believe it."

She gave the hand a squeeze, and Ellie squeezed back, trusting her sincerity if not her assessment.

Yet a term erupted in her mind. *Love bombing.*

Ellie had had to infiltrate a somewhat inept cult one time and had learned something about the protocol. A new recruit was instantly surrounded by people who had only the recruit's best interest at heart and knew just how to serve it, unlike the nasty old world of clueless and uncaring friends and families. It was impossible to resist such a welcome when most everybody felt overworked, underappreciated, and miscast in the role of their lives at some point. At those points one looked for answers, and this new group, with its charismatic leader, appeared to have them.

She removed her hand from Audrey's, but gently. Today's Enlightenment wasn't a cult; it was simply capitalizing on the American obsession with self-improvement and success. Devon had certainly not been kidnapped and brainwashed. It seemed she'd found a rewarding career outside her famous father's shadow.

A man sitting a few seats from Ellie said he had managed a tech company in Silicon Valley but had grown to hate it. "I'd gotten off track somehow but didn't know what to do about it. Galen came out to do an in-service for the employees and said he was willing to take on investors. The company said no, but I said yes!" He watched Ellie expectantly, as if this had been a punch line.

"Investors?"

"In the ranch," he explained.

This made sense, Ellie supposed. The operation had probably grown over the years to its present capacity, getting too large for one man to run on a shoestring. "Is this a for-profit concern, the, um, Today's Enlightenment?"

"Profit is the last sort of concern around here." Audrey almost sounded angry at the insinuation, and two others repeated the same thing in different words.

Margot said, "If he's making any money off us, he sure doesn't spend it on clothes."

No one responded. A few squirmed uncomfortably, as if she'd made an inappropriate joke . . . but if she felt censure, it didn't seem to bother her any.

Finally, Audrey said in a resolutely cheery voice, "Time for evening sessions!"

Ellie and her fellow clients bused their trays, made a trip to the bunkhouse to freshen up, and as a group plunged back into the all-consuming task of turning themselves into the best persons they could be.

Chapter 8

Devon set her empty plate on top of the income sheets. She'd carry it over to the kitchen later; only reusable tableware was used at the ranch, nothing disposable. Better to wash dishes than contribute to a landfill, even if it used a little water and energy to do so. There was very little waste generated at the ranch—no place for it to go, since they were too remote to have regular garbage pickup. Organics went into the compost, with the rest burned in the fire pit.

She slid the income sheets from under the plate and prompted her computer back from sleep. Time to pay bills. Ranch bookkeeping stayed fairly simple—income flowed in from the clients, who paid for the courses, plus a bit extra for room and board, with only a tiny bit more variety in outgo. No staff member received wages, as she knew only too well; they were paid with a free place to live and more counseling. But, of course, there were utilities, taxes, and operating expenses, covered by client fees and deposits from their benefactor—the old lady on the hill, as Devon couldn't help but think of her.

Frances Coleman's money came from gold, the Colemans

having been one of the families that struck it rich in Bodie, California. Now Bodie was a literal ghost town, a state park accessible only by three miles of dirt road, but its mines had produced over thirty million dollars' worth of gold and silver during the late 1800s. Frances Coleman's family had managed not only to hang on to their share but also to grow it. Mrs. Coleman had danced in Paris, scaled mountains in Argentina, snorkeled in Tahiti, and outlived two children and three husbands before pulling a Greta Garbo and withdrawing from the social whirl. She had built a sprawling cabin nestled into the side of the mountain, and from her wide front porch, she could see the entire valley.

How Galen had talked Frances Coleman into building the ranch for them, Devon would never know. But then Galen could talk pretty much anyone into pretty much anything, so. . . . And she probably enjoyed having them there. It must be a comfort to see other humans when she looked out her window yet not have the obligation of interacting with them. Mrs. Coleman had cleaning staff in once or twice a week, and a visiting nurse made weekly stops, but otherwise she seemed content to spend her days reading books and watching television and sipping her way through her considerable wine cellar.

At first, Mrs. Coleman had let Galen squat on her land while she slipped a few bucks into the Today account as if he were a favored nephew. Later, however, she had decided to formalize the arrangement with some real money. Perhaps she had felt wings of mortality beating the air. Perhaps she had finally accepted that her missing daughter would never return. Her son was definitely dead and buried in a graveyard outside Reno. Mrs. Coleman kept a picture of the grave marker over her kitchen sink, something Devon found either really sad or really sweet or really, really odd.

Devon had gotten to know the old woman pretty well by delivering jars of honey from their own bees. Mrs. Coleman always insisted she stay for tea, and even though Devon couldn't stand the stuff, she'd listen as Mrs. Coleman—Frances, she insisted—regaled her with tales of Cannes festivals and corporate takeovers and Grand Canyon hikes. They'd sit at the kitchen table, a weak description for a slab of mahogany at least four inches thick and surrounded by a room that was a re-creation of a kitchen in a French country inn.

Devon craved these visits—not the tea but the peace—like Mrs. Coleman craved their honey. Being surrounded by the sturdy walls of your own space, satisfied with your own personal history, comfortable in your own skin, that was what she saw in the older woman, who had torn through her life with determination and appetite and a lack of regret. *This is how I want to live. Who wouldn't?*

But Mrs. Coleman often wanted to know how the ranch fared and how the new building's construction had progressed. She had dropped a large lump of money into an IOTA, an Interest on Trust Account. The lump belonged to her but could be accessed by Galen, acting as the ranch's attorney. He had gone to law school somewhere between studying medicine at Cornell and physics at MIT. Devon didn't know if he had ever actually practiced, though it didn't matter, as he must have taken and passed Nevada's notoriously difficult bar examination to get a state license. Having that license made the whole process okay with Mrs. Coleman's own lawyers and the state of Nevada.

This backing enabled Today's Enlightenment to buy the land. The deposits from the trust provided the money to pay the mortgage and the new construction. If Mrs. Coleman decided to revoke the trust, they'd be screwed.

Devon never saw any statements from the trust, as Galen had said the statements went directly to Mrs. Coleman. That way she kept an eye on her own money.

But those interest deposits had been dwindling, each amount less than the month before by about 6, sometimes 7 percent each month. Devon thought maybe Mrs. Coleman had backed off. Income off a trust, assuming the amount *in* the trust account didn't change, shouldn't vary. The prime rate didn't fluctuate *that* much. The only solid reason for the interest to decrease steadily was that the principal was decreasing.

Mrs. Coleman might have the money invested with unscrupulous or uncaring financial advisors. Devon would suggest Galen have a gentle chat with the old lady, just to be sure no one was taking advantage of her. Galen was so good at finding the flaw in one's foundation.

The door opened with a blast of warm air, and Tim came in, a bit grubby. He must have been working in the bean patch.

"Morning," she said. "Afternoon now."

"Yeah."

She had no idea what that meant, but then her greeting hadn't exactly been a greeting. More like a statement of fact. She had to get better at saying what she meant. Galen always got on her about that.

Tim, meanwhile, carefully wiped his shoes on the mat inside the door. All his actions appeared careful, as if he consciously chose and executed each one, no matter how small. Today's Enlightenment doctrines in action. No wonder Galen always had Tim somewhere close by; he appeared and vanished all over the ranch without warning, a human surveillance system. Devon had no idea how long Tim had been at Today or what his story might be, and had never asked. Perhaps he'd been with Galen since the leader's beginning at a student center at MIT, or perhaps Galen had found him out here in the Wild West, working as a ranch hand or as Ms. Coleman's driver. Sometimes she wondered, but she never asked.

Whatever his origins, Tim seemed to have no résumé, no job title, no official duties, and no more salary than the rest of them, but one and all accepted him as the voice of Galen in Galen's absence. Now the towering young man, all wiry sinew and sandy blond hair, approached her desk. "I need some petty cash. Galen wants me to go get more nails."

"Now what's he building?" She pulled out the tin cashbox, which was never locked, from her lower desk drawer, also never locked. They didn't worry overmuch about security at the ranch—sure, some client could stroll in and root around until they found the cash stash, but then they'd have nowhere to go and nowhere to spend it.

"Something for challenges," Tim said.

Her hand froze over the bills. She remembered her own challenge all too well.

"How much do you need?" She chose not to notice the tremble in her voice. *Everything is a choice. We choose to give memories power over us.*

"Ten bucks ought to do it." His voice had slid from gravel into granite. Had he noticed her weakness?

She handed him two fives. It hardly seemed worth the gas to drive to town for such a small purpose, but she didn't point that out. If Galen thought the nails were important, they were important. She buried herself behind the desk as she replaced the cashbox, and avoided looking at Tim until she heard the door close.

Chapter 9

The air outside the dining hall hit Ellie like a slap. She hadn't realized how sharply the temperature dropped in this mountainous region, with no humidity to retain heat once the sun disappeared.

Devon led the class again that night, with a lesson about bravery.

"Now, since we know here that the only thing holding you back is you, you need to recognize that we fail because we expect to fail. We see perfect, heroic people on TV, and we know that that's not us. So, it's success, and not failure, that frightens us. If we *do* succeed, what then? How do we maintain it, grow it, deserve it? We're paralyzed, and we feel stupid for being paralyzed, and it's all because of fear. All negative emotions are a result of fear."

Ellie checked out her fellow paralytics. Audrey not only took furious notes but also stopped now and then to scowl at any neighbors who weren't. Margot ignored this and wrote nothing, staring straight ahead with her chin propped on one hand. Ellie couldn't tell from her blank expression whether she sniffed BS or felt stunned with insight. Barry's head nodded at the end of every sentence.

Ellie wrote the date and *fear* at the top of the page and inwardly admitted that the word had figured prominently in her life as of late. Sure, there had been a serial killer out to get her and then the incident in the Gulf of Mexico, but physical fear didn't seem that important once it ended. She had more potent fears of failing to meet Locard-level standards, of never finding out exactly what had happened to her mother, of finding out exactly what had happened to her mother and the truth being worse than a car accident . . . all the way down to her new kitchen sink springing a leak. If Billy Diamond's daughter could tell her how to deal with all that, then she should listen.

Devon continued, "They might be large or small. Maybe you're afraid to do a headstand in yoga. Maybe you're afraid of snakes. Maybe you're afraid you're losing your mind. But large or small, only by facing and conquering them will you recognize your own strength. You have your worksheets in front of you. I want you to list your three biggest fears. Then list *why* they're your biggest fears."

She paced between the desks as people began to write. "And I'm not talking about vague, universal fears, like getting old or something happening to your children. I mean concrete, physical things or events that trigger your fight-or-flight response, that make your brain freeze and your heart go into triple time."

Ellie thought, then wrote in clear block letters: *1) claustrophobia, 2) public speaking, 3) heights.* Then she realized that the first should be "enclosed spaces" instead of "claustrophobia" but figured Devon wouldn't ding her for inconsistent word usage.

After a short couple of minutes, Devon picked people at

random to read their answers. A young man with too much facial hair balked when she said his name. "Do I have to? It's kind of personal."

Gently but firmly—perhaps she'd learned to handle balky males by keeping her father functioning all these years—Devon said, "Personal is why we're here. If you can't share yourself in an intimate group of people who are in the same lifeboat as you, who are here to accomplish the same goal, then you're never going to be able to do it out there in the world."

Other students nodded encouragingly.

He hesitated so long that Ellie thought he might refuse, but with the weight of the group on his shoulders, he gave it up. "I'm afraid I may be a cross-dresser."

Devon said, "Oh." Plainly, this was not what she had expected, but she recovered and asked what made him think that.

"Because when I put my girlfriend's . . . when I'd put my girlfriend's laundry away, I wanted to try some things on. Not, like, her underwear or anything, but some of her blouses. And tanks. And her jeggings. Anyway, that's it."

"Thank you for being so honest with us. We all need to take a lesson from you, because if we can't be honest down to our very bones like that, then we're wasting our time here. Margot. What about you?"

"Scrubbing more toilets."

Devon chuckled, though she didn't seem too amused. "We've all heard about your toilets, Margot. But what do you really *fear*?"

The older woman procrastinated by picking up her worksheet and looking at it, then said, "Drowning, tornados, and spiders."

"Interesting. Why?"

Like the young man, she hesitated before speaking. "I almost drowned in a lake when I was five."

"How did that happen?"

The rest of the class waited in utter stillness, well aware that they were about to hear something painful.

Margot traced one stubby finger along the desk's laminate. Ellie felt sorry for her. Margot wasn't the type to pull punches, not even with her own pain. Especially not her own pain. "We'd rent a cabin on Lake Mead for a week every summer, back when you could do that without taking out a loan. Not always the same cabin, depending on when we went and what was available. And cheap, of course. One year we got one that was directly on the water and had a little dock out back with a rowboat. My father would let me practice using the oars while it was still tied to the post, so I could only go out about seven feet, but . . ."

"You were five?" someone asked.

"It was a really small boat," she said, in her father's defense. "Anyway, one night after dinner I ran down to the dock to feed the rest of my corn to the fish. This made my fingers sticky, so I knelt on the dock to dip my hand in the water."

"And you fell in," Devon suggested.

"Not exactly. My sister pushed me."

A collective gasp from the room.

"Why?" someone asked.

Margot gave her a quick scowl. "Because she was a *kid*. Kids do things like that. And I could swim . . . sorta . . . Problem was I hit my head on the boat on the way down." She fingered her scalp and gave an unconvincing chuckle. "Still have a little scar." She stopped there.

"So who pulled you out?" Barry asked.

"My dad. He'd been smoking on the back porch, anyway.

He said I just coughed and woke up. It wasn't like I'd stopped breathing or anything."

"Maybe you didn't, but I just did," Devon said, earning nervous laughter from some of the students. "How awful! It would have been impossible to forgive your sister for that. She might have killed you."

"Of course I *forgave* her," Margot said, the scowl flashing again. "She was seven years old, and I was halfway over the edge. It would have been impossible for any little kid to resist. *I* wouldn't have."

Devon spoke gently. "Even as a child, she knew what she was doing and made her own choice. We all have to take responsibility for our actions, and that means holding other people responsible for theirs as well. Did your parents often leave you unattended like that?"

"I wasn't unattended. My father was right on the porch."

"But you were knocked out by the boat. You don't know how long you were in the water."

"It didn't hurt me." Margot squirmed in her chair at the memory, as if struggling to hold on to it under the flood of this fresh perspective. "I got a mouthful, that's all."

"Are you sure? You were quite little to be at a water's edge all alone."

"I wasn't—"

Devon didn't pause. "That's the biggest betrayal of all. When someone we're counting on isn't there for us. That's even worse than the direct betrayal by your sister."

Margot opened her mouth in another protest, but Audrey spoke first. "So her sister—"

Devon's tone silenced both of them when she said, "Everything we learn as a child is the foundation of our thoughts as adults, but we learn those things through a child's perspective." Apparently, no one other than Devon was to comment on Margot's experiences, including Margot herself. Ellie watched her for signs of chafing. "Unfortunately, that perception continues to filter incoming information, so we're absorbing an adult world through the foundation of a child. We have to acknowledge our past, shed it, drop it in the dust behind us. Along with anyone and anything that keeps us there."

But where did this leave Margot? Stuck in the mold the adults at the time had created when they no doubt demanded she forgive the sister who had nearly killed her? Or was she reasonably assuaging any lingering resentment with the knowledge that all children do foolish things? And which did Devon think preferable? Ellie had no idea what their takeaway should be.

Devon did not seem as sweet and malleable as Billy Diamond had implied. Perhaps he didn't know his daughter as well as he thought. But perhaps the young woman had blossomed, gained a warehouse of confidence since striking out from DC.

Margot said nothing. She stared straight ahead again, her mouth set in a straight line, neither agreeing nor disagreeing. But under her desk Ellie could see one foot jiggling in agitation. The feet, Ellie had learned in Rachael's course on deception detection, were the least schooled part of the body. We spend a lifetime training our faces not to betray us and maybe to keep our hands still, but the more we travel downward on the human form, the more honest our flesh gets.

Meanwhile, Devon moved on to Barry, who feared heights—his face paled when he even mentioned the subject— and a middle-aged woman named Ling, who hated fire.

"Ellen."

"What?" She had been lulled by the soft cascade of words

and had been hoping that the class would again run out of time before Devon got to her. No such luck. Apparently, evening sessions could go longer than afternoon slots.

Devon asked, "What is your biggest fear? And why?"

As always, the class listened, each person's complete attention focused on the speaker. In this case, Ellie.

"It's, um, enclosed places. I'm . . . Sorry, I don't usually talk to a group . . . but, um." Ellie cleared her throat and pushed on. "Like Margot, it's a childhood thing. My grandmother's house had this closet in her bedroom that had a second door opening to the living room, heavy wood doors with glass doorknobs and those little wing-nut dead bolts in each one. Why, I can't imagine . . . maybe to hang coats from guests who came in through the front door, without having to build a second closet. I don't know, but it fascinated my cousin Maureen and me. We'd walk through it, through the living room, the dining room, back up the hallway, and into the bedroom, and through it again, over and over."

She went on. "One day—I was about seven—during one of our circuits, when I went out into the living room, Maureen shut and bolted the door behind us, but I didn't notice. When we circled around again, I went into the closet from the bedroom, and she shut and locked that door as well. So I was in the pitch dark, with my grandmother's clothes and coats pressing in on me on all sides, but I didn't know what anything was, because I couldn't see it, and I couldn't breathe. It all smelled like mothballs. I still gag at the scent of mothballs."

"How long were you in there?" Devon breathed.

"It felt like forever. My grandmother was out working in her garden. I don't even remember who opened the door and let me out. I only remember a vague light and crawling and then finally reaching fresh air."

"Wow," Devon said. "So now you have a problem with closets? Enclosed spaces?"

"Small spaces," Ellie agreed.

"Airplane bathrooms?" a woman toward the front asked.

"Won't touch them," Ellie admitted. "I hold it."

"Must make overseas flights uncomfortable," someone joked.

"I had a therapist—" a woman next to Audrey began, and Audrey frowned her disapproval.

"That's a good point," Devon said firmly, though no one had made one. "The problem with therapy is it dwells on the past, and that changes our perception of the past and therefore might change our future in ways we didn't expect and don't want. It's better to forget the past. Take the present and future and change *them*, make *them* more complete."

"How?" Ellie asked. Despite herself, the concept sounded interesting.

Devon said simply, "You'll see. You need to shed what's holding you down before you can grow and move up. All these old fears and faults and preconceptions are the things we protect, we hold on to, because we use them to define ourselves. 'See, I told you I couldn't do it, because of *x* or *y* or this other thing that happened to me.' What we're going to do here at Today's Enlightenment is help you build a new internal infrastructure of *yourself*, so you can gravitate to that strength instead of hiding in your fears."

"You're talking about self-fulfilling prophecies," Ellie said.

This time Devon's brows didn't crease at the interruption. "That's an old-fashioned term for it, but something like that, yes. Everyone chooses their own responses and behaviors. If all of you get *one* thing out of your experience here, it should be to learn that we must take responsibility for those choices at all times and in all circumstances."

She let that sink in, then ended the class. Ellie gathered up the few notes she'd made, ready to take a shower and crawl into her bunk, even though she had firmly *not* looked forward to the communal aspects of her time here. But between the flight and the drive and the tour and the barrage of words and the three-hour time difference and the stress of being there under false pretenses, Ellie no longer cared about the lack of privacy. She wanted only to close her eyes.

However, they had more to do.

Chapter 10

Rachael was standing at her kitchen sink, washing up a few things she didn't want to put in the dishwasher, when her mother bustled in, full of enthusiasm for a book by Grady Hendrix and a new wine that book club host Maisie had discovered.

"Mama," Rachael asked after the detailed description of hunting a Southern vampire had run its course, "do you remember a lot of Isis's clients?"

Loretta grew quieter at the thought of her younger daughter, now dead for nearly two years. She cracked open the wine bottle—Maisie had gifted her the half-empty bottle—and poured a glass. "She'd tell me about some of her jobs when she'd come by. I know they had money, because some of their ideas were plumb crazy, but she'd say, 'Hey, if they want to pay for it, I'll find mini-lights in the shape of aardvarks and a band willing to dress like zombies.'"

Rachael had heard similar comments when the two women intersected. But she hadn't paid much attention. Resentment had continued to linger over Isis and her "wild days": staying out all night, returning drunk, skipping classes, flunking classes, totaling cars, abandoning college, getting picked up by police on (admittedly minor) charges, like public intoxication, and displaying rampant hostility toward everyone with whom she shared blood. Her excuses had skirted the edge of plausibility, with just enough detail to convince, provided one didn't look too closely. Rachael believed Isis-related stress had ushered in the cancer that took her father's life.

Maybe the pain would have faded away in the bright light that was Danton. Rachael had spent more time with Isis during the month of his birth than she had in all the previous year. However casually Isis might have taken her own life, she'd been dead serious when it came to her son. Once back on her feet, the baby sleeping through the night, she threw herself back into her work but never failed to make a doctor's checkup or a playdate. For Danton's first birthday, the premiere party planner celebrated at Rachael's home, just the three women and an exquisitely decorated cake, which the baby dug into with both hands. Rachael's husband was, of course, working, and Isis didn't bother to bring one of her many boyfriends. Rachael thought her sister had finally learned what to cherish.

By Danton's second birthday, Isis was dead.

A knock on the door at 3:00 a.m. was never a good thing, and this one proved no exception. Cops had found Isis's identification in her purse and had gone to her home, where, true to form, she had left Danton in the care of a sweet, capable college student certified in first aid. The student had shown them Rachael's business card, taped to the refrigerator, with the number to call in case of emergency.

Cops couldn't afford the kind of parties Isis threw, but every officer in the city knew Rachael, the district ME. A team had made a beeline to her house to break the news as gently as possible . . . which had never been possible.

The murders were unmysterious. Though she had learned

not to take them seriously, Isis had retained her bad taste in men. This last one had been no exception. A mountain of a guy with a history of small drug charges, he had stopped at an ordinary convenience store in a non-sketchy part of town, a place to which cops paid little attention because they didn't expect to need to. With Isis waiting on the sidewalk, an altercation occurred—over what, they never learned. The seller shot both the buyer and the witness, Isis, then ran inside, presumably to shoot the only other witness, the store cashier. The cashier had seen the entire drama unfolding through the store windows and had pulled the owner's Beretta from beneath the counter. He shot the seller point-blank in the chest—a lucky shot, since he was trembling from head to toenails at the time. Even luckier, the drug seller was so discombobulated that his own shot went awry and passed well over the cashier's right shoulder.

Video cameras both inside and outside the store verified this version of events, according to police. Rachael could have demanded a viewing if she chose to. She didn't.

Rachael often wondered if she should have wanted the killer to stay alive. She would have liked to look him in the face, to hear his paltry explanation for why he had been forced to defend his honor or his turf or his street cred at that particular moment. She'd like to know if he knew the man with Isis that night, if their beef had been long estab-lished or they'd only just met. Nothing had yet changed hands—the boyfriend's wallet remained in his pants, the baggie of fentanyl-laced heroin was found in the seller's back pocket—so it must have been a haggle over price.

Maybe it was better this way. She didn't have to waste time plotting to get her hands around his neck. The case was closed, over, done, and there was nothing to do but look for-ward. All that mattered now was Danton.

It seemed pointless to get interested belatedly in her sis-ter's career. But she couldn't help a small fire of curiosity, fanned by the irresistible oxygen of celebrity. "Did she ever mention Billy Diamond?"

Loretta thought hard, one palm covering her forehead, but said only, "Isn't he a singer?"

"Yes."

"No. Why?"

Rachael explained about the rock star's daughter.

"No, don't remember Isis talking about him. But she only came by once in a while, until Danton was born. I can remember she told me about a birthday party for a Supreme Court justice's eleven-year-old granddaughter that required four horse trailers and a guy with a shovel to follow them around to take care of the poop."

"Manure."

"Which is poop. And an anniversary party for a director of the Smithsonian. She tried to talk him into doing it *at* the Smithsonian, but he said he worked there all day, didn't want to play there too. And I remember she did a wedding for a congressman and said she'd never do another one, because he wanted it on a barge, sailing down the Potomac. The weather was bad enough, but the bride's idea of 'romantic' couldn't be done without CGI."

Rachael laughed. Isis and her whip-smart humor. It made one forgive all, even her pervasive and imaginative lies, over and over. Until it didn't. "But no rock stars?"

"Like I said," Loretta repeated, "she only came by once in a while."

Chapter 11

Devon guided the class to the publishing office so they could stuff envelopes for what turned out to be two hours—more activity meant to be therapeutic as well as productive. Ellie murmured her surprise (and dismay), prompting Audrey to explain how physical labor gave one's mind a rest and got it back in touch with one's body. Having an activity after class helped the lessons and insights sink in.

Audrey, Ellie could see, had been the kind of kid who ruined the curve for everyone else.

Besides, Barry added, as if it made perfect sense, it had gotten too late in the day to work in the fields. The dark came faster at the ranch since the sun set on the other side of the mountain and left the land in shadow by late afternoon. Obviously, he had accepted that doing nothing, relaxing, watching—Ellie had not seen a television in the entire camp—reading, chatting were not options. She wondered if he and Audrey were competing for an unseen Most Committed to One's Personal Journey Award.

After some settling-in chatter, the group stayed mostly silent; Ellie heard only the sounds of paper being folded and brushed and then piled on top of others in faint, secretive whispers. The quiet did feel restful—mentally, at least—so perhaps Audrey had a point. Or perhaps Ellie was plain worn out.

At last, the slight Angela arrived to tell them to stop, and the group moved out into the now quite cold night. Even though Ellie wore a jacket, the chill managed to get to her bones, but at least it kept her awake long enough to walk to the freshman bunkhouse.

As the rest of the class went inside, Ellie pulled her phone from her pocket. The hour marking a conservative bedtime in DC had already passed, but Rachael had made her swear to call the second she had an update.

So she dialed. . . .

CALL FAILED.

Ellie tapped the CALL button, and the tiny machine attempted to redial.

CALL FAILED.

She finally looked at the top of the screen and saw the utter lack of bars. And in case that didn't sufficiently explain the situation, the phone spelled it out: NO SERVICE.

She really *was* in the middle of nowhere.

How could there be any place in the modern United States without cell service? Was that even possible? She bounced up and down on her toes, watched her breath materialize and then evanesce in the air.

"There's no cell towers out here," said a voice to her left.

She jumped a foot is a cliché, and not even a very sensible one, as a foot is not that terribly far. But an apt one in this case, because Ellie ended up about half a yard to her right, gravel crunching under her feet, without knowing how she got there.

A young man stood in the dark as straight and still as a totem pole. He had come around the back of the building, over the dirt and weeds, a much quieter approach than over the noisy gravel. Ellie could barely see his face but managed to recognize him as another freshman in her class.

He said, "It's not your phone. No one gets service out here no matter the carrier."

She sucked in what breath she could. "Oh. Okay."

"If you have an emergency, go see Devon in the office. She can usually send an email or something."

"Okay. Thanks."

"You're welcome."

He moved past her.

"I'm Ellen, by the way."

"Yes, I know." Which didn't sound a bit creepy. "I'm Tim."

"Nice to meet you."

He nodded, then disappeared around the side of the building before she could ask anything about his position at the camp or what he did for Galen. Ellie remained standing in a cold, dark, twenty-mile-wide valley without cell service.

Her city-girl self fumed. Seriously? How could there not be a tower somewhere . . . ? With all that open, flattish land, the signal should travel. . . . She ground a few molars.

The gravel seemed to crunch loudly enough to wake the citizens of Topaz on the other side of the mountain, so she moved along the edge of the long drive, where the stones tapered into dirt. Even the chickens had gone to bed, swallowed by the dark, and none followed her. Other than the swish of her legs, she heard nothing save for the occasional cricket or whatever noise-making bug they had in the desert.

Ellie stopped to turn all 360 degrees, taking in the moonlit alien landscape. She could see liking it here, the quiet, the openness, the crisp air. The serenity soothed her after the craziness of the past few months. Maybe this place could do her some good while she did her job for the Locard.

She reached the road, a smooth strip of dark in the night. One bar.

The call went through—triumph at last. Rachael answered

on the third ring, her voice low and groggy. She woke quickly once Ellie began talking.

"Wait, what? You're breaking up. Devon is fine?"

"Seems fabulous. She's a counselor here. I haven't had any personal conversation with her yet."

"Any what?"

"Personal conversation," Ellie said more loudly, then glanced toward the bunkhouses. Sound could carry well under these circumstances: crisp air, no intervening structures. She'd better avoid saying Devon's name out loud lest her classmates figure her for a spy. "She hasn't mentioned her father yet, but I haven't had a chance to work on it—"

"But she's okay?"

"Better than okay, I'd say."

"What about Carlos?" At least Ellie assumed that was the question, since all she heard was "Carlos."

"No one's mentioned him yet."

"What?"

Ellie turned her back on the buildings and cupped her hand over the receiver. "No one's mentioned him yet. Did Agnes find some more pics for me? I'd like to confirm—"

"Okay, just—" Rachael began, as if she hadn't heard Ellie's question.

Then nothing. The screen kept ticking off seconds, showing the call as continuing, but Ellie could hear nothing but the crickets. She said the standard things people did when they were left with empty air. "Just what? Are you there? Can you hear me? If you can hear me, I can't hear you."

CALL LOST

She dialed to reconnect, but nothing happened. The phone rang, then showed a connection, but without ringing, and then the connection was erased without explanation. It even stopped reporting CALL LOST, assuming she could figure that out on her own.

Oh well. She had gotten all the information she had so far over to Rachael, and that was the important thing.

Ellie hiked back to the freshman bunkhouse and kept going, veering off the main drag and around the other side of the building, to the outer edge of the ranch. Tomorrow she would chat up Devon and assess her current state of mind vis-à-vis family members and ex-boyfriends.

Ellie enjoyed working undercover. It gave her a chance to be someone else, someone who hadn't been orphaned at four and then passed from household to household. She loved her life and her past, but she also loved plotting out a new persona, giving herself the parents and childhood friends and experiences that she wished she'd had. As long as the case didn't involve kiddie porn or biker gangs, she could have a little fun with it. And maybe this one would teach her something useful about efficient time management or well-defined career goals.

So far, however, the ranch underwhelmed. The freshman bunkhouse still had its lights on, and they ruined the moon-glow view of the valley beyond the north wall of the bunkhouse, which looked exactly like the south wall. Beyond it, a field of some kind of crop. All the buildings crouched a couple of feet off the ground, elevated with blocks of concrete. Within the gap underneath lurked vague shapes, which Ellie took to be plumbing, electricity, and heating elements. Sophomore bunkhouse, same view—building, crops. From her angle on the ground, she could see only the ceilings inside and caught the occasional glimpse of a person near a window. She didn't try to see any more, since Ellie didn't intend to add *voyeur* to her résumé. Junior bunkhouse, same setup. She noticed they had already passed lights-out and wondered how many people there were in each group. At dinner the occupancy of the tables had seemed roughly equal. But no seniors? Did no one ever "graduate" from this program?

At the end of that row, Ellie came to the office. Past that, to her right, would be the publishing office, the construction site, the house where the staff lived, and the large barn.

The door of the office opened, and Angela stepped out. Lit by the open doorway, she stood there, talking quietly with Galen. There didn't seem to be anything particularly romantic about the exchange until he put one hand on her cheek and caressed it. Even from thirty feet away in the dark, the adoration on Angela's face shone like a beacon.

He leaned forward, but not for a kiss. He said something to her that caused her expression to change. The outline of her body had been soft, but it now stiffened, and the adoring look became uncertain and a bit sad.

Another caress and he shut the door, leaving her on the step. Ellie plastered herself against the wall of the junior bunkhouse like a cold war spy, now cursing the moonlight that had lit her way.

But Angela didn't see her, busy staring at the now-closed door, until she finally gave up and walked away, with a disconsolate slump to her shoulders. Ellie waited until the sound of her footsteps faded before emerging onto the path and moving toward the office.

To the side of the window that was behind Angela's desk, she could see tiny glistenings on the building's exterior, like pinpoints of light. What was that? Bits of paint, glue, snail tracks, dew reflecting the moonlight? She stretched out her arm and was barely able to reach the lowest one, and then she felt a prick to her skin. With piercing jagged edges turned outward, a hole in the siding covered, she assumed, on the inside by those notes and flyers, and these thin enough to let a bit of light through. Something had exited through the hole, possibly one of the pellets from the presumed shotgun blast that had put the holes in Angela's desk. So, barring one hell of a coincidence, the damage to the desk and the trailer were of a piece.

Huh.

Angela hadn't flickered an eyelash when Ellie had pointed out the holes in the desk, so the damage held no bad connotations for her. Perhaps it had been an accidental discharge or a drunken mishap, one that hadn't concerned the staff enough to bother patching the holes. The desks had appeared to be secondhand; maybe the trailer had been purchased secondhand with the furnishings inside and the damage had nothing to do with Today's Enlightenment at all.

But if it did, then who had had a gun, and why had it gone off? And, most importantly, had the shot hit anyone? The cheap carpeting in the trailer had seemed new. Could there be bloodstains underneath it? And where was the gun now?

Carlos, at least, had not been shot. Therefore, the holes were curious, but not relevant to Ellie's tasks.

She continued off to the darkness to her left before Galen could exit and stumble upon her. The next two buildings seemed to be sheds, small, windowless, no lights, padlocked. She stepped up to each of them and could hear a hum of machinery in one. The other, nothing.

Ellie had expected the path to end there, but it kept going, winding through the gathering weeds, passing over the river as a low bridge. It moved up into the mountain, barely distinguishable from the deepness of the trees around it, and there it disappeared into the waiting maw of the forest, a trap of blackest black. This must be the drive to the house up there. Ellie wasn't crazy enough to tackle mountain climbing in the dark or to surprise a recluse who didn't want visitors, so she turned around and returned to the freshman living quarters.

Her bunkmates had already turned the lights out, but the sickly fluorescent glow from the respective facilities at each end let her gather her stuff and use the now-vacated bathroom. It smelled of a strong disinfectant, and she passed a

young woman walking out with a bucket of cleaning supplies and a heavy pail of dirty water. Ellie didn't recognize
her and didn't ask why she'd been cleaning so late at night.
No doubt there would be some kind of reason—there
seemed to be a reason for everything done at the ranch.

Ellie took a shower under a stream that had lousy pressure
but decent heat and finally crawled into her bunk. The mattress felt lumpy and worn, but at least the blankets were suf-
ficient. In the dark she wondered why Devon had stopped
calling her father. Tomorrow she would find out.

Then she slipped into a deep and dreamless sleep.

PART II

SHOWING THE WAY

But a powerful attraction drew me, rooted in an instinctive quest for self-knowledge and a recognition that I needed some discipline in my life. . . . It had to be provided by a very special person, like David, a man I was beginning to feel I could trust with my life.

David Thibodeau and Leon Whiteson,
A Place Called Waco: A Survivor's Story

Chapter 12

Five o'clock came early, but likely there was no other way for 5:00 a.m. to come.

The clients breakfasted on oatmeal. Ellie had been hoping for a little protein, maybe some bacon and eggs, but no such luck. Afterward, after the coffee had settled, she expected to head into a class about self-actualization or positive thinking or some such thing, but instead they trooped outside in the predawn light for a crash course in joists.

The assignment that morning was to assist the construction crew in laying the floorboards in the new building. Two by two, the newbies would grab the ends of a long plank in the barn and tote it over to the foundation footers. At least Ellie thought that was the correct terminology. Her brain functioned better in sunlight.

The planks were cold and rough. Ellie had been sensible enough to wear her coat to breakfast and also sensible enough to pack gloves with it, but some of her classmates had arrived in summer, when the air was warmer. They had to work with bare hands and light jackets. Terse Margot, the fiftyish toilet-cleaning hater, cursed at every splinter. Ellie asked Devon what construction activities had to do with life planning.

Of course, a child raised by musicians had a somewhat New Agey answer. "Hard physical work reconnects us with our bodies. There's so much distraction in the world today that we lose touch, literally, with our flesh and blood selves. And it's a way to see results from effort. Effort doesn't have value. Only results do. Concrete results are a boost to your self-esteem."

"I always considered my self-esteem pretty healthy."

Even in the dim morning light, Ellie could see the young woman mentally raising an eyebrow. "You're here because you've lost confidence in your decision-making abilities. We need to get your self-esteem back on track."

She had a point. People came here to put their lives in Galen's hands, so it didn't seem unreasonable to go where those hands directed them. It wasn't Devon's fault that Ellie's goal was a fib. "Will you and I have another coaching session today? I have a lot of ques—"

Devon had been watching a big guy, who seemed to be the construction manager, and interrupted Ellie with, "I would love that. We'll try, but please excuse me right now."

Galen had appeared on the scene, awake and chipper in a light jacket, but then he had Angela in tow, with a mug of coffee. Ellie could have gone for a second cup herself, preferably in a Georgetown café, with a digital copy of the *Post*.

Galen made a beeline for the construction manager, and Devon made a beeline for Galen before Ellie could point out that they should at least provide work gloves for their clients.

She moved over to pick up another plank, making sure her route took her past their little knot.

"Going to need . . . rafters . . . Can't do that without . . . ," the construction manager reported, his words constantly lost amid the shots of the nail guns used to secure the floor-boards.

"I'll tell Tim to . . . ," Galen said. Devon stood next to him, with Angela, as always, in the background.

Ellie picked up the end of a plank from the stack, providing slightly *Three Stooges*-like action as she pulled on it. Her illogical path forced her classmate Barry to fishtail about, and he nearly knocked over the slight Audrey.

"Going to need this made too," Galen said, handing the construction manager what looked like a piece of paper that had been ripped out of a spiral notebook.

Whatever was written on it seemed to confuse the construction manager. The paper fluttered in his hand, a butterfly in the throes of death. "Uh, okay. Why—"

"It's for challenges."

The man asked nothing further.

Galen added, "Have it done by tonight. Everything else on track?"

"Yes," he said fervently and unconvincingly. "Yes."

Then Barry's tugs grew demanding, and Ellie had to move on, reflecting on how Galen's influence extended beyond women. Men seemed eager to please him as well . . . but then he *was* the boss. Making the boss happy had always been a gender-neutral desire.

Two bruises and an errant splinter later, Ellie went to school.

That morning's class focused on value. At least as far as Ellie could tell, because *her* brain focused instead on cell towers and Wi-Fi signals. Devon said again that effort had no value in and of itself, that ball teams weren't given trophies because they trained extra hard. They got trophies because they won games. Once they internalized that they would automatically get more efficient in their work, they realized that spending more time on a project did not make it better or them more admirable. If they could get the same thing done in ten minutes instead of twenty, all aspects of the situation would improve. So they needed to stop multitasking themselves into complete incompetency and get in the habit of doing one thing at a time as if their lives depended on it.

"Start small," Devon told them. "Practice drawing as many squares as you can for a ten-minute period, but neatly, with even sides. Or toss up a marble and catch it. Anything, so long as it requires concentration. Then make the periods longer. You'll soon find yourself in the focus habit."

On her notepad Ellie doodled arrows piercing the dark centers of their targets and reassessed her own secret focus. She had established that Devon was fine and healthy and even thriving and had conveyed the same to Rachael to pass on to Billy. Number two, if she could convince Devon to contact her father—open up communication even in some small way or at least let him know that she hadn't called, only because of substandard cell service—then Ellie's work there would truly be done.

Carlos's death remained a mystery, but it was not one for Ellie to solve . . . officially. As no one had mentioned him, she had no way to segue into the topic of a man she shouldn't know of—a common problem in undercover operations.

She had begun to draw question marks instead of arrows when the door opened and Galen strode in.

A charge crackled through the room like static electricity, stirring hair follicles and knocking Devon off the desk she'd been half sitting on. The headmaster had come to grace the class with his personal guidance . . . though the headmaster looked more like a mischievous boy, with locks of dark hair falling in his eyes and a smile hinting at dimples, come to share not a lesson but a really delicious prank.

He asked what they'd been talking about, then told the group to pull their little desks into a circle. Chair legs scraped against the unpolished floor, and the movement got the blood flowing again, whereas the early morning and the warmth of the room had been causing Ellie's eyelids to droop.

If this abrupt usurping of her class annoyed Devon at all, she didn't show it. Instead, she hustled to Galen's side and spoke quietly to him, though he did not appear to listen. When the circle had been completed and the circumference tidied as much as they could engineer in the small room, he sat in an empty chair. Devon had no seat. In order to fit, the circle extended to both sides of the room, and she couldn't get to the few empty chairs at the back of the room without climbing over desks and people. She opted to stand, her back against the blank whiteboard.

"I'm sure Devon has been telling you all about setting your goals and making sure your work has value, right?" Most of the clients nodded. "You've been talking about doing things with intensity. You can learn to increase your intensity at will, so you'll experience life more fully. We'll teach you to take your natural fight-or-flight response and channel that into a new physiology to find yourself with more stamina for the long term of any process."

Masterful delivery, but Ellie could feel her eyes start to cross.

As if he'd heard her thoughts, he said, "But I'm jumping ahead. Let's go a bit slower. You're all here because you want to change your lives, want to start achieving your goals instead of consistently failing."

Consistently seemed a bit harsh.

"You're intelligent people. I know from your paperwork that you all have good educations, decent backgrounds. By all rights, you have carved a coach out of the pumpkin of your lives and hooked up a team of strong horses, all set to go charging toward your goal. You flick the reins. But the lead horse is going north, and the one behind it turns west, and the one next to him just wants to stand still and eat clover for a while. So guess what? Even with that decent coach and those fine animals, you're not going anywhere."

Breaths of amused agreement puffed around Ellie.

"You think, This isn't working. Why not? Why did I only have a pumpkin to work with? Why do these horses suck? I did everything right, and still . . . At that point you're halfway to being a remora, a parasite depending on other people to take care of you and help you out. You *deserve* to be helped out, because you did everything right. I hate to use clichés like 'self-fulfilling prophecy,' but things become clichés because they're true. For example, we're all sick as hell of hearing about self-esteem, but that's because we've tried to mutate it into some sort of cure-all, when it's really a very simple truth. Self-esteem grows from producing a result in this world, as when you laid part of the floor of the new building this morning. You put forth work, and you produced a result. You feel good, even if a bit sore."

More chuckles.

Devon stood as still as a statue, her gaze boring into the back of Galen's head. Ellie couldn't be sure she even breathed. Divorcing her from this place wouldn't be easy; so far, Ellie didn't see a strong reason why Billy should even try. Aside from the lack of communication devices, Galen and Today's Enlightenment seemed harmless and even helpful.

"The result is our reward. When we receive a reward without having caused the effect, it seems a whim of the universe, and this actually lowers our self-esteem. Getting a pat on the head that we know we didn't earn makes the world seem random and ourselves powerless. This is why the whole self-esteem movement with children has backfired, why constantly heaping praise on kids only makes them more insecure. Children aren't stupid—they know when they've produced value and when they haven't. We're not stupid, either, and we have to stop treating ourselves as if we are."

Ellie felt a little ping of recognition, as when someone put into words what one had known all along.

"So here's the secret, people. Here's what we're all about." He ducked his head an inch, conspiring to share this holy grail. "You chose that pumpkin. You chose those horses. You chose not to get out of the driver's seat and put the blinders on their bridles. Every behavior and reaction you've ever expressed has been *your own choice*, and you need to take responsibility for those choices, every single one, every single second of every single day. It's all yours, on you, and up to you."

Huh, Ellie thought. *That's it? You made your bed, now lie in it? Or we've had the magic ruby slippers all along, all we have to do is believe it?* This was the same "power of positive thinking" that had been written about since the turn of the last century.

"You all know that," he went on, again reading her mind. "You've known it all along. But it takes more than knowledge. It takes more than figuring out what your goals are and writing them on a piece of paper. It takes *commitment*. I'm sitting here and asking you to commit to reaching your goals, commit to a program to reach those goals, and work on that program every day. It's a big step, one that you can't take lightly. If you're not all in, then you're wasting your time here—and mine as well."

He spoke quite solemnly, but a lump of worry coalesced in the pit of Ellie's stomach. What exactly constituted a commitment, if an internal promise or even a pinkie swear did not? His "commitment" sounded more specific, and more ominous.

But then he veered off into a discussion of choices again and the importance of surrounding oneself with helpful people and not more "remoras." "Remoras are the parasites. They're all warm and fuzzy and great pals when things are going badly for them, because they want your help. They love to be sick because that immediately obligates everyone around them. The rest of the time they're cold and uninterested in you. Result people like you, your internal state remains the same no matter what's going on in the world around you. 'Resulters' are stronger, more stable, but if they're covered in those sticky remoras, they can be slowed down or stopped."

The room remained silent, save for the frantic scratching of Audrey's pen against her paper. Many others made the occasional note as well. Ellie drew another arrow without knowing what it pointed at.

"I don't mean the term 'remora' in a bad way—we have all sucked up to someone we don't like, because they have something we need, or exaggerated our sniffles into a cold to get our spouse to leave us alone to watch the game." Amused noises around the room. "But when a person makes it a consistent habit, you need to get out from under them. The biggest remoras in our lives tend to be our family and friends. Your significant other treats you like the maid, your parents are positive you'll never amount to much, and the kids focus on your wallet. Friends only want you to pick them up from the airport and retweet their selfies. If you express a goal or a desire, they will leap up with reasons why it can't be done. If you want to grow even the *littlest* bit, you need to shut the door on them and set the bolt."

In a mild form, this seemed a valid self-help point. Say you announce at the kitchen table that you've put in for a management position. Your aunt may declare you're not management material, because she still sees you as a ten-year-old who always left their bike out in the rain. There could be good reasons to ignore your friends and family, all of whom have their own hang-ups and ideas and don't even know what your company does anyway.

Or have been using you as a personal assistant/all-around gofer to your rock star father since you could walk.

But Ellie had been trained to look for threats and couldn't stop her mind from going there. Anything good could be taken to an unhealthy extreme. Without the stability of a network of family and friends, these clients had no choice but to depend upon their *new* friends—the established members of the group, like Devon. Those members' actions were lauded and accepted, so the recruit's frame of reference was replaced by new mores and standards. Then, no matter how destructive these new standards became, there were no others to go back to. The bridges had been not just passed over but also dynamited. Worst-case scenario.

Best-case, a client ignored his aunt and put in for the management position anyway. Galen's advice sounded mild and valid and reasonable.

But Ellie's cell phone wouldn't work, and neither would anyone else's.

Galen had gone on to combine these two ideas and say that they needed to make their commitment to each other, to people who understood what they wanted to do and would support their decision to do so. And to him. "I truly want you to succeed," he told the group, making eye contact with each person in the circle, one by one. "So if you won't do it for yourselves, if you can't muster the discipline to take what we're teaching you here and follow it to the letter, then do it for me."

"Absolutely," blurted Audrey.

"I will," Barry said. "I've had it with my life up to now. I'm going to be CEO no matter what." He repeated the last three words with enough intensity to give Ellie a chill. These people weren't casually reading *I'm OK—You're OK* on a beach somewhere. They hummed with an intensity of purpose that should have warmed her.

Should have.

Galen said, "Today is your commitment ceremony. You're going to restate your goals and declare the date by which you intend to accomplish them. We're going to go around this circle. We'll start to my left, here, with Drew." He clapped one hand on the shoulder of the very young man next to him, who paled so sharply Ellie thought he might faint. "Each of you will publicly commit yourselves to that goal. Then you will tell us the worst thing you've ever done, the biggest secret you've kept. It has to be something that no one else knows and something that will significantly hurt you if revealed, either legally, financially or emotionally—because this is serious, people. This will only work if you go all in, one hundred percent. If you can't, then you are not committed, you are not serious about changing your life, and you will never reach your goals. And you can leave now."

A tiny gasp escaped someone; Ellie couldn't tell who. But around the circle, eyes had widened, and faces had gone still. A dark-skinned man to her right began chewing on a nail. A young woman with unnaturally red hair twirled her pen through her fingers and visibly started when it slipped and made a clink against the desktop.

"Devon," Galen went on, "will take a video. Everything you say will be recorded and saved."

Devon straightened, but casually, the only person in the room not concerned by this turn of events. She had seen it before.

"This," Galen intoned, "is not a drill."

Nervous chuckles. Ellie had missed the goal-setting class, so she scribbled a short list among her arrows as unobtrusively as she could.

Devon took the time to make people move so she could get her camera tripod and miniature video camera—retrieved from a desk drawer, so clearly oft-used items—around to the back of the room. Ellie could hear her behind the row of desks, no doubt making sure the young man's face showed clearly in the video.

Thrown onto the hot seat without warning, Drew's voice

cracked as he spoke about cheating on his college entrance exam. He had gone to a small religious college, and it would probably revoke his diploma if it knew. His parents would be horrified, and many friends would turn their backs, friends he would need to open a bank in his town. Owning a bank, he confided in an aside, was the only way to make money in banking.

When Drew finished, Galen patted his hand and congratulated him for having the courage to take this step, not only for himself but for all of them as well.

The young woman next to him, whose name Ellie didn't catch, told of a one-night stand with her sister's boyfriend, the same one her sister later married. "She'd never forgive me . . . and my parents would be devastated. I think they think I'm *still* a virgin."

The confessions continued. One had driven drunk and taken out a few mailboxes only a block from his own home, then had slunk out of the neighborhood during the wee hours of the following morning and driven the car a hundred miles away to get it fixed.

Margot had been the executor of her mother's estate. The will had specified that it be divided evenly between Margot and her sister, but instead, Margot had invented receipts and looted jewelry to boost her share to more than three-quarters. "She was living with some bum and feeding a serious Jack Daniel's habit. I knew giving her money would only speed up the cirrhosis."

"But it's not your place to make your sister's decisions for her. And you betrayed your mother's trust to do so," Galen pointed out. He didn't ask if this might have been revenge for the "pushing into the lake" incident, but then he might not have known about it, and Devon didn't make a peep. "Plus, it was completely illegal."

"Yes," she said. Though, true to what seemed to be her form, she didn't sound sorry or even concerned.

"And your goal is?"

"To get a divorce."

"When?"

"Filed by New Year's Eve."

"Of this year?" He watched for every loophole.

After a slight hesitation, "Yes."

"And you know if you do not accomplish that, a copy of this video will be sent to the Maricopa County district attorney?"

Her face seemed carved from steel, but Ellie saw her throat move in a gulp. She was among a hundred or so clients at the ranch, yet he had managed to name, from memory, the place where she lived.

"Yes," Margot said.

Barry told of smashing a door on the loading dock one morning when he'd left his key ring on his desk and locked himself out, then saying nothing and letting the supervisor think it had been the cleaning crew or maybe a vandal. He could kiss the CEO slot goodbye if his company ever found out.

Barry, Ellie thought, had the determination to achieve his career goals. Now, if he only had the talent. She didn't think Galen could teach him that.

The woman next to Ellie told of a brief affair with her child's fourth-grade teacher.

Then Galen turned to her. "Nell."

Chapter 13

Sure, Rachael could have accomplished the same thing with a phone call—she hadn't really needed to make a return visit to the rock star's mansion, with its eclectic cast of characters. But to be fair, she had tried, and the great man hadn't answered his phone and neither had anyone else. She hadn't wanted to leave a message, with no idea where Billy's phone might be or who might pick it up. Nothing at the estate seemed particularly secure or organized. She wondered if Devon had been the one who saw to that.

Besides, with nothing exciting planned at the Locard and DC traffic cooperating for the most part, why not take a drive? To a famous rock star's house? Whose music she'd been listening to her entire life?

Well, hell. If one couldn't go a bit fangirl over Billy Diamond . . .

As before, no one answered her knock, though a few more cars littered the driveway. And as before, she turned the knob and went in. But this time she found her way blocked by a man the size of Mount Olympus but without the visage to match. Apparently, Rachael had been wrong about "not particularly secure."

"Who're you?" he demanded, arms crossed, his back to the ornate center table, where the roses had lost many more petals.

She gave her name. "I'm here to see Billy."

His scowl cleared up. "Ah. You're the forensics lady."

"Um . . . yes."

"Good. Come with me." He turned and started up the wide marble steps. "Sorry about checking. With this new tour coming up, a lot of his fans have been . . . What's the word? Rejuvenated. Like you add water to something that's dehydrated, and it puffs up and comes back to life. Know what I mean?"

Rachael hustled to keep pace with him. "Not really."

"Well, he's been living the quiet life out here in the middle of nowhere."

The nation's capital was the middle of nowhere? Granted, when it came to the music industry, it wasn't New York or LA. . . .

"But with all the recent attention, now we've got people hopping the fence to ask for an autograph and girls leaving their panties on the porch. Found a guy trying to climb into a second-floor window last night. He says he wanted an autograph, but I'm not so sure. I think he thought he'd be some kind of cat burglar, until he couldn't get the window open and fell off the ledge." The memory made him chuckle.

"Have you worked for Billy a long time?"

He hit the top step, his large foot slapping against the marble hard enough to echo across the lobby below. They seemed to be in a different wing than before, in a shorter hallway with more elaborate décor, including a six-foot-tall marble statue of a griffin in one corner. All doors but one stood open, with various conversations emanating from some or all, voices murmured and sometimes raised. Someone some-where sang a heartfelt rendition of "Hallelujah."

He said, "I don't work for Billy. Newton hired me."

Newton, the "Don't call me Newt" manager. "Recently?"

She didn't even know why she asked, but regardless, he didn't seem inclined to answer. He stopped outside a closed door and turned to size her up, his gaze sweeping her from head to toe, which might have felt creepy if it wasn't done with such professional disinterest. "You aren't carrying any-thing, are you?"

"Like . . . a gun? No."

"No, no. Like fenty, Rit, Addies." He searched her face and apparently saw nothing but slight confusion. "Pills, bottles, even pot. Especially anything with an alcohol con-tent. Newton's trying to straighten him up and not having much luck. This is a big house, and he's got hidey-holes all over it."

"No," she assured him. "Not carrying anything."

"Good." He twisted the doorknob and entered but con-tinued speaking, possibly to himself. "That's right, you're the *forensics* one. Hey, Bo. Where's Billy?"

He directed this question at a young man with an electric guitar, who stood near a window, peering at pieces of sheet music pinned to a music stand. Rachael thought it might be the same young man who had been lying on the couch dur-ing her first visit to the house, the one a girl had been speak-ing to so earnestly. But now that he was vertical and minus the girl, she couldn't be sure.

He said, "In the can."

Rachael's guide gave a quick stare at a closed door on the other side of the room before moving closer to Electric Gui-tar Boy. "Oh, for—You didn't give him anything, did you?"

"Nah."

The large man invaded the kid's personal space, stopping

six inches from his face, with only the guitar in between them. "You sure? Because you're high now, aren't you?"

"Yeesh, no! Back off."

"Do you want to make any money on this gig? Because people ain't buying those tickets to see you, mate. They never heard of *you*."

The guitar player's lips became a hard line, the lower one turning out just a hair.

"So if you want to get anywhere, *he* has to stay on this planet, got it?"

"I didn't give him nothing! It's my stuff. I took it before I got here, okay? I needed something to get through this! All *you* have to do is check the door and windows and beat people up. I have to actually make *this*"—he waved at the sheets of music—"sound like something."

They glared at each other, and then the guide or guard or whatever he was turned and left the room without further comment. The guitar player strummed a chord, affecting nonchalance.

Rachael did as well, strolling around the room, careful to step over the electrical cords and around the music stands. The room appeared to be a minimal rehearsal space. No drum set, no amplifiers as tall as her head. No sax or synthesizer. Nothing but the two guitars for some intense practice or maybe a composition session.

Or reassurance. The walls were ringed with professionally framed concert posters, so many they seemed at first glance to be a colorful wallpaper.

Upon closer inspection, she found they moved from left to right in chronological order. A faded rectangle in the northwest corner proclaimed SONIC AGE AT THE FIRST AVE, MINNEAPOLIS. A small line at the bottom read WITH SPECIAL GUEST CHIMERA. Rachael had only to glance over her left shoulder to see, as if with L'Engle's tesseract, how far Billy

had traveled since those early days. The last poster adver-
tised Chimera at the Hollywood Bowl, a Thanksgiving Day
concert two years past. The band's logo, a stylized beast
with the body of a lion and the tail of a snake and some extra
animal heads thrown in for good measure, was depicted
about to chow down on a terrified turkey. If they'd had a
special guest band to open the show, the poster didn't mention it.

"They should never have broken up," the guitar player
said.

She turned. "Why did they?"

He plucked another string. "*I* dunno. I wasn't there. But
Far told *Rolling Stone* that he finally got fed up with Billy's
shit, and Tarrie told BuzzFeed that Far had been trying to
steal his wife for fifteen years and finally succeeded, and then
Far told *People* that Tarrie was delusional and—"

"What does Billy say?"

Perhaps miffed at being interrupted, he twisted a tuning
peg one nanometer more before answering. "He says they all
got old and fat." Then he confided, "I did give him one
snort. Just so he could work. He needs it to work."

She moved closer and could see what had alerted the
guard. Though standing near a bright window, the young
man's pupils remained dilated. Of course, Rachael had long
been familiar with the "sex, drugs, rock 'n' roll" mantra of
being a musician. A boyfriend had once insisted she watch
Long Strange Trip, and she remembered thinking that the
dozens of lovable members, crew, and friends of the Grateful Dead must have been consistently unsober for twenty or
thirty years. But by now, she thought, that stereotype had to
be more myth than reality, especially for one who'd managed to make it to Billy's age.

Or maybe myth became reality in Billy's house. "Is he
having trouble working?"

"Kinda."

She had no idea what that meant. "How long have you been in the band?"

"*This* band? About a year."

"How long have you known Billy?"

He threw her a look, as if she might be stupid. "About a year. Before that, I was with Best March. You've heard the bass line in 'Killer Food'? That was me. They were okay guys, except the drummer. He couldn't keep time worth shit, so the label finally cut off our studio hours. Label never gave us any support at all. That's why I—"

The bathroom door opened, and Billy emerged, wiping his hands on skintight jeans. "Isis! I—Oh, no, sorry. You're Rachael, right? The other sister."

She didn't know what to say to that. Fortunately, she didn't have to. Billy stopped, stared at her, shook his head so hard his ponytail flicked from side to side, and regrouped. "What's up? Did you find her?"

Since he didn't seem concerned about discussing the matter in front of his bass player—and being a parent, she knew reassurance would be his top priority at this point—she did not hesitate. "Yes. She's fine."

Relief caused him to deflate like a soccer ball with a rip in it, and the skinny man didn't have that much bulk to lose. And for one moment, he was still and calm.

Whatever else Billy Diamond might be, self-absorbed star, wild man of rock, possible alcoholic, possible drug addict, he did love his daughter.

"Who's fine?" the guitar player demanded.

"Nunya," Billy snapped. "Nunya business. Go away. I mean, yeah, beat it for a bit. Just give me ten minutes. Twenty."

The young man gave one massive eye roll, hiked the neck strap over his head, stalked over to a formerly white velvet divan, and then set the electric bass down with elaborate care, laying it to rest as if it were a china doll of Sleeping Beauty.

Then he walked out.

Billy let out a little groan. "Ohmygawd, bass players. They are *so* sensitive. Is she still at that spa or ranch or whatever?"

Rachael passed on what little Ellie had been able to tell her.

Billy paced as he listened, nodding vigorously. "What about the boyfriend? What happened there?"

"No one's mentioned him, and Ellie couldn't ask without alerting Devon."

"What? Oh, like then she'd know I sent you. Yes, you *cannot* let her figure that out. Do *not*. That's *so* important."

Clearly, the sensitive bass player was a model of sobriety compared to Billy. Rachael watched his eyes quiver in repetitive, uncontrolled flickers from side to side. Nystagmus. The condition could result from many ophthalmological and other physical conditions. It could also result from intoxication, though whether the cause might be drugs or alcohol, she couldn't immediately tell.

"It's too bad about Carlos. He was a nice kid. But nothing I can do about that." He plopped down on the divan, narrowly missing the bass guitar, as if suddenly tired. "As long as Devon's all right. Did she say when she's going to come home? I can't believe she'd miss the kickoff concert."

Rachael repeated the very limited information. "I'll let you know what else Ellie can establish."

"Good, good. Are you coming tomorrow? I can get you a ticket. I'll get you a backstage pass! Isis used to love coming backstage. She did some of her best business there. Hardly surprising."

The slight slur made Rachael wonder if Billy would even remember this conversation tomorrow. "For parties?"

"Absolutely! So many parties. Isis got us the best stuff.

Never stiffed me. So many people like that you can't trust, you know?"

"Like what kind of people?" asked the Black woman.

Perhaps her tone alerted him, penetrated the rosy haze he'd stepped into. His expression changed from melancholic to apprehensive to confused in quick succession, as if he couldn't remember himself what he'd meant. "Like . . . party . . . people."

She put him out of his misery. "Party planners?"

"Yes! Yes, that. I'm so relieved about Devvie. But I have to stop calling her that. She thinks it's juvenile." He bounced up to walk in an aimless little circle as Rachael watched. She had so much experience with mood-altering substances in tissues, in blood, in gastric contents . . . not so much in living people. It wasn't her job to protect people from Billy, or Billy from himself.

It was her job to find out not how people lived but why they died.

"When Isis was killed . . ."

Billy stopped in his arc, swaying gently in a nonexistent breeze.

"Did you know the man with her?"

"Carson?"

"I thought his name was Kevin Destina."

"It was?" Despite the chemical influences at work, he seemed sure of this point. "It could have been. But everyone called him Carson."

"Why?"

He laughed as if that were a silly question. "*Nobody* uses their real name."

"Did you know him well?"

"Long time. Yeah, long time." He started playing the bass guitar. She recognized the first strains of "Flower," an uncharacteristically slow and pretty song of Chimera's.

"He and Isis were together a long time?"

"Oh yeah. Never saw one without the other."

"Do you think it was serious?" Rachael didn't know why she asked, or why she'd never asked before. It had seemed normal—preferable—not to know any of her sister's friends. She'd gotten too used to keeping Isis and her whole life at arm's length. Other than Danton, of course.

"Serious?" Without pausing his fingers over the strings, he stared at her, then shook his head. "No, no. They didn't *date*. Carson worked for her."

"Worked? Doing what?"

He went into the chorus, his fingers dancing across the strings. "Muscle. People like her always got muscle."

Rachael pictured Destina—she could conjure up only a vague image of his large, still body lying on the convenience store sidewalk—lifting large boxes of tablecloths and party favors. A handy assistant, but why would he and Isis be together on that last evening, when she didn't have an event? Why would he risk his job by doing a drug buy in front of his boss? "Was he a heavy drug user? Or more occasional—"

"Carson? Nah." He finished the song with a flourish.

"Then what was he doing at the convenience store, buying drugs?"

"Prolly getting ripped off." Billy set the guitar to his side, then stretched out beside it, spooning it on the narrow divan. "I think I need to take a nap now."

The bass player returned in time to hear these last words. "No, dude! We need to work. You know, rehearse? Concert? Your big, triumphant return?"

"Nunya." Billy's eyes had closed.

"*Dude*! Get *off* my *strings*!"

Rachael found her own way out.

Chapter 14

"I—" Ellie began and found her own throat dry. "I'm sorry . . . I really . . . I can't talk in front of a group."

"This isn't a group," Galen said in a kindly tone. "This is your family. And it's okay. This can count as one of your fear challenges."

Whatever that was . . . Then she got it. He referred to one of the fears on her list—enclosed places, public speaking, heights. Like Margot's home county, he had committed them to memory.

Ellie took a deep breath and began. "About seven years ago, a few things happened at once—we moved to a new house, we won a car, believe it or not, at a town carnival, and my husband lost his job. We sold our old house, but still, we had a lot of expenses with the new one, plumbing repair and then the furnace went out. And on top of that, we had to save up enough money to pay the taxes, because the car we won had to be reported as income. We were drowning under it all."

Sympathetic glances all around. She avoided Galen's steady gaze, playing up her nervousness to match the tone of the room. If she wanted Devon to open up about herself, she had to get the young woman emotionally invested in her first. Any con artist—or undercover operative, a similar creature with a different objective—worth their salt knew that.

"My husband worked on finding another job, but he wasn't interested in taking anything less prestigious in the meantime. I got desperate enough to take a second job at McDonald's. At night. I'd work from about seven p.m. until we closed at two. Then I'd sleep for maybe four hours, get up, and go to my regular job." She didn't mention that her regular gig was in law enforcement. The less emphasis on that, the better. "In retrospect, it was kinda stupid. I exhausted myself, and the little bit of money hardly made a blip on our radar."

Galen kept her on track. "So what happened?"

Ellie let her shoulders slump. "By two o'clock in the morning, there would only be two of us there. And one night, we got robbed."

She felt, rather than heard, the small but collective gasp among her classmates.

"He couldn't have been more than eighteen, some kid . . . They never did catch him. Came in with a scarf around his face like Jesse James. The gun in his hand shook like he had palsy, but the gun itself was very real, so I opened up the cash register. I'd been closing that night with a little girl named Serena, who had immediately yelped and run into the back to shut herself in the cooler and dial nine-one-one.

"As I pulled out the money, I heard a siren close, right up the street. The kid got so scared that he screamed and ran out the door. But I knew that siren had nothing to do with us— Serena couldn't have even dialed the phone that fast. So I'm standing there with these bills in my hand, completely alone in the middle of the night."

"Ah," Galen said, guessing where she'd go with this.

"Yes. I emptied the cash register drawer into my pocket.

Then I stepped over to the other register and did the same. I buried it all at the bottom of my purse—I was into the big tote bag style then, so it wasn't hard—got Serena out of the cooler, told her everything would be okay, and waited for the cops to show up."

Ellie glanced up from under her lashes, surveying the circle of her classmates. Barry stared with something like horror. Even the rosy-cheeked woman didn't look too sympathetic. The young man who had started them off wanted to know how much she'd gotten. Devon continued to film, her face impassive.

Tough crowd.

"And you never got caught," Galen said.

"No. Never even suspected. Management was terribly kind, offered follow-up counseling and everything, which only made me feel worse. I didn't get much," she told the young man who'd asked. "About three hundred and twenty dollars. It paid a couple of bills that month."

"What about cameras?" Margot asked. "You ever tell your husband?"

"They hadn't worked for months. And no." The question made her wonder if the ranch had any cameras. She hadn't seen any, but that didn't mean they weren't there.

"What would happen to you now," Galen asked, "if this came to light?"

Ellie thought. "Legally, nothing. The statute of limitations on theft would have passed years ago. My husband has already dumped me, so his opinion doesn't matter. But I'd never get another job that involved any level of trust."

"I see." Satisfied that the consequences were dire enough to ensure Ellie's dedication to the program, he moved on to the man next to her.

Confession was cathartic. Everyone showed relief when they finished their tales, and a sort of peace as they sat back and listened to others. Their secrets had been carried for years, sometimes decades, and a burden shared was a burden lifted. That each of them had just handed someone a loaded gun and told them to point it didn't seem scary. It was only a simple, direct way to cement them to the straight and narrow path to their goals. Confession would be the blinders on their bridles, and the room hummed with the energy of hooves warming to the race.

Ellie wasn't so sure.

When everyone was done—except for Tim, who was not present that morning—Galen thanked them all for their honesty. "You've taken a huge step on the road to your new lives. I can promise this is a turning point for every one of you. Now that you've committed, truly dug in and invested in yourselves, you have only to learn the system, conquer your fears, and define your steps before getting everything you could possibly want."

That seemed a tall order, but Ellie could feel the confidence of her classmates, a magnetic field of determination.

"Now," Galen said, "a little bit of labor to get the blood flowing again, and then we'll break for lunch."

That field stayed intact, and no one groaned. They were more than ready to harvest crops or carry planks until the sun set on the other side of the mountain.

Galen waited at the door as they filed out, with a word of encouragement for each and every client, greeting them by name, touching their shoulder or their elbow. With her seat at the back of the room, Ellie trailed out last.

"Nell." He grasped her hand, held it in both of his. "Let's talk."

Chapter 15

Galen directed her to a seat at one of the tables in the meeting/dining hall. A young woman mopped the floor along the far wall, swirling the mop around with a desultory back-and-forth motion. An older man washed the windows, spraying on a solution before wiping it off with a cloth. They were both well out of earshot.

Ellie wondered if Galen had somehow detected her reason for arriving at the ranch. Had Devon recognized her as an agent of her father's somehow, her radar honed by years as a celeb's kid?

"Sorry to take you away from a chance to get outside this morning, but I haven't had a chance to do any one-on-one work with you yet."

"That's okay." And what did one-on-one work entail?

He gazed at her as if focusing his full attention, so Ellie returned the favor, mirroring his posture, leaning forward slightly, with both hands on the table, a stance designed to put people at ease. He had wavy hair that fell past his chin, a five o'clock shadow over dimpled cheeks, and long lashes framing brown eyes with flecks of gold in the irises. She couldn't guess what he saw when he looked at her.

"Devon's given me the basics of your story, but why don't you tell me why you're here?"

Was he giving her a chance to confess? But his expression radiated nothing but interest.

"Clearly, you're working through your own ethical lapses," he went on.

"Yes," she admitted. "As you heard this morning."

Without blinking, he said, "I don't mean your pilfering from the cashbox. I mean never telling your husband that you'd lost interest in him. Your marriage had died a long time before he figured it out and sought connection elsewhere, hadn't it?"

A tingling started at the base of Ellie's neck and spread up and over her scalp. Her throat closed up. How could he possibly know that?

He kept up the deep gaze, as if he'd heard the question aloud. "You're not remotely upset about your husband's affair—"

Her ears began to burn. "I said I *understood*—"

"You're relieved as hell that he took care of it for you, that he had the courage that you lacked. Good girl Nell, always following the rules. You didn't have the guts to break out of the mold society formed for you—and that's okay." He gave her hand a reassuring pat. "Hardly any of us do. All those nonsense rules get programmed into us, some by others, some by ourselves in order to maintain our own preconceptions and fears. Here we help you *deprogram* yourself so that you can live in honesty, not only with yourself but with everyone around you."

"But it's not okay." She spoke without thinking. "Marriage is always work. Just because I screwed up and married the wrong guy—"

"As you have to accept responsibility for your own choices, others must do that as well. Your husband made his own decisions."

Her head swam. *We're all responsible for every choice we make, yet we're not responsible for how those choices affect others?* It felt as if he had assigned her the blame and then taken it back, all in the same sentence.

Did it even matter? She was there undercover. She wasn't here seeking absolution for screwing up her life.

A sly voice way back in Ellie's head whispered, *There's no reason you can't do both.*

"As for your career," Galen went on, "we need to examine whether you have the strength to make decisions for other people when you haven't been able to make them for yourself."

This she found confusing. "I don't make decisions. I only determine what the food quality is."

"But the evidence is speaking through you, so your level of honesty is extremely important."

Evidence? Had he found out who she was?

"So what you do here will help you decide if you can go back to doing that or not, or if how you handled your marriage tells you who you are. If we can't achieve our goals with honesty and integrity, then those are the wrong goals. That's what Today's Enlightenment is all about."

Her brain sighed with some relief. Galen's takeaway: Ellie had, mentally and emotionally, checked out of her marriage years earlier but hadn't informed the one person who needed to know. She had *not* been living with honesty and integrity, despite what she'd told herself.

"I know this is a lot to absorb all at once, but we're here to help you through it." He clasped both her hands in both of his, again leaning forward over the table. She caught a whiff of spice-scented shampoo or maybe aftershave. "It's going to be all right. You're going to integrate your own mind until everything becomes crystal clear, both your own motivations and other people's as well. Once you've mastered that, there won't be anything you can't do."

He squeezed her fingers, not uncomfortably but hard enough to drive the point home.

"You came here to learn how to live, and I'm going to teach you how. Everything about you is going to change, Nell, change for the better. When you're done here, you'll hardly recognize yourself."

That could be taken two ways, but she chose—one *chose* everything in one's life, apparently—to think of it in a good way.

But his words also implied that she needed to be there for a while. Perhaps forever, or at least as long as Billy's funding held out. And Ellie didn't agree with that at all.

Devon sat at the scratched secondhand desk in the corner of the trailer that served as her office, writing the videos she had just collected to DVDs for storage. She had learned to record each person as a separate video so that she didn't have to go into a video-editing program to separate them. Each video went onto a blank DVD, labeled with the person's name and the date. They were stored in individual hard plastic cases and kept under Galen's bed, in a metal trunk with a padlock, to which only Galen had the key. All of which seemed a bit silly since if someone wanted to retrieve their collateral, they had only to break the glass in the entry door of Galen's little house, reach in, turn the knob, find the trunk, and walk away with it. Sitting miles from civilization kept the clients nicely isolated from outside influences, but it also limited how secure they could really get. If they were in a city, she could keep the DVDs in a bank's safe-deposit box or at least reinforce Galen's bedroom door. It surprised her that he'd never installed cameras.

At least not that she knew of. She damn sure hoped there wasn't one in his bedroom.

Burning completed, the DVD drawer popped open, and she slid another blank into the incredibly delicate little disc writer, reflecting that the isolation worked both ways. Someone might abscond with the trunk, but then they would have to carry it for miles along the road or strap it to their back for a steep hike over the mountain, at least until they could pry the padlock off and collect their own item. She wouldn't want to be weighed down by such an object when Galen turned Tim loose on the trail. The idea made her shudder.

Rachael stifled a groan when her phone rang for what seemed like the forty-seventh time that morning, then quickly answered after noticing the Nevada area code. Perhaps Ellie had borrowed someone else's device, since hers had such poor reception.

"Hello? Ellie?"

"Dr. Davies?" A man's voice, tired and with the tinge of an accent she couldn't place.

"Yes?"

"Dr. Rachael Davies?"

"Yes. Who is this?"

"Well, hi there." Unhurried but not unfriendly. "This is Peter Steinberg. I'm the ME over here at the Washoe County regional office. You called me about a Carlos Freeman?"

"Yes! Thank you so much for getting back to me."

"Welcome." A slight pause. "What's your interest, if you don't mind my asking?"

Rachael told him everything, minus Billy's actual name.

She told him about the Locard—he knew it, of course—and trying to locate a client's daughter at Today's Enlightenment. Steinberg had never heard of the place, which Rachael took as a good sign. It meant deaths at the ranch were not a common thing.

She could hear the soft clicks of a keyboard in the background as she talked. He might be calling up Carlos's file or ordering lunch from DoorDash, or perhaps Dr. Steinberg was searching her name as he spoke, checking up on her background. If so, whatever he found made him willing to discuss the case over the phone.

"I haven't quite settled on a cause of death yet," Steinberg admitted. He spoke in a relaxed manner, pausing now and then to . . . smoke? Sip coffee? Rachael didn't know and didn't care as she jotted down notes. "Most likely drowning. Plenty of water in the lungs. But I've still got tissue sections coming, and tox."

"Good job getting usable fingerprints. That couldn't have been easy after all that time."

"That was a fluke—we got lucky. *And* we've had a cool summer, so the water temp stayed pretty low coming from Tahoe. His body got chewed up in all sorts of ways, but in *spots*. Know what I mean? He still had a shoe on his right foot, but his left foot . . . Well, fish are eatin' that somewhere. You know much about dams?"

"Let's assume I don't," Rachael said, "because I don't."

Steinberg chuckled. "Yeah, me neither. Derby is a diversion dam, meaning it don't generate electricity. It's just there to siphon off water from the Truckee River that otherwise would have gone into Pyramid Lake, so that there's more water in the river for the farmers. See?"

"Okay."

"But lowerin' the level of Pyramid messed up the population of cutthroat trout, and they almost went extinct. So in addition to the diversion, there's a fish ladder installed just past the dam proper."

"A fish ladder," the city girl repeated.

"It slows the water down and has sections so the trout can make it upstream without completely exhausting themselves. The cutthroats are stream spawners, see. Like salmon."

"Oh." Salmon leaping upstream, she got. She'd seen beer commercials.

"What this means for your young man is, first, he shot through the barriers at the diversion point and then got caught up in fast water going to the fish ladders, and then the ladders themselves. Of course he can't jump from box to box like a trout, so he just stayed in the first box, with his body repeatedly slammed against a concrete wall. Scraped off a lot of skin. Yep. Lot of skin."

"I see. Is he missing any parts?"

"The left foot, like I said. A couple of fingers. One ear's pretty sheared away, as well as almost all his ventral torso. His innards were beginning to fall out, only the ribs holding them in. The left kneecap was nowhere to be found, but the right knee didn't even have a scratch . . . Random, that's what I mean."

"The skull?"

"Still on him. A few postmortem lacerations."

"No bruising? Fractures? Signs of foul play?"

More tapping. "Meh. Intact, except for what the concrete scraped off. No weirdness, no fractures. Nobody popped a cap into his brain, if that's what you were thinking. What *are* you thinking?"

"Nothing, yet. Just seems odd that a healthy kid is suddenly dead for no apparent reason."

"That's not so odd. Happens all the time."

"Um, really?"

"People think a river is like a lake, which is like a pond, which is like a big puddle. If it's not the vast ocean and a tidal wave, it must be harmless. They don't know how cold and how fast and how quickly it can take you right down." He paused. "He underestimated his opponent."

"I'm sure you're right," Rachael told him.

But which opponent? Mother nature or someone all too human?

Chapter 16

Lunch consisted of limp green salad and antipasto dripping with Italian dressing. Ellie doubled up on the greens and tried to pick the bits of protein from between the tomatoes and olives. Conversation stayed minimal. The attendees were mildly tired out from an hour of picking beans while the chickens chattered in their pen, and no one wanted to discuss the morning's lesson. It seemed impolite to bring up others' past indiscretions, though Ellie caught several "I can't believe you did that" glances from across the table. Some were directed toward her. This didn't bother her, since she had never worked at McDonald's. Adam had never lost his job, and the couple had never won a car. I should be so lucky.

Quiet except for one young man who, now that he had begun, couldn't seem to stop talking about his entrance exam transgression. "But it was algebra, and I'd never been able to get that x and y stuff. Who actually uses algebra in real life, anyway?"

Those around him murmured uh-huhs and let him talk.

After lunch Angela led them over to the gym. She seemed even more nervous than she usually did, though from worry or excitement, Ellie couldn't tell. The two emotions might be indistinguishable when it came to Angela. "This will be a big step in your progress," she told them, prancing along the gravel. "Some of you, I mean. We can't get everyone done today. But eventually everyone will complete theirs."

"Their what?" Ellie asked.

"Their challenge." She puffed her breath out, walking fast enough to form a trot. "Part of your training here is to over-come your fears. They are a huge factor in what holds us back from our goals. We need to push through those fears, conquer them for all time, and discover the strength within ourselves before we can really begin to change our lives."

Straight out of the company text, but the words landed on Ellie's ears like pinpricks, representing only the tips of the iron spikes to come. Yesterday they'd spoken of fears. Today they would be asked to face them. She wondered what form her "challenge" would take. Making a speech before the entire contingent?

Yoga equipment had been put off to the side. The ceiling of the gym had been built more than high enough to accommodate basketball games, with the center beam two-plus stories up. Now she noticed that a pulley had been installed in its center. A rope was draped over its wheel, both ends reaching the floor.

Devon and Galen waited for them.

"Barry," he said, his voice echoing slightly around the chamber.

Ellie's tall classmate took in the rope, the pulley, the height of the building. She watched the blood drain from his face, sink through his capillaries, and run for cover to some inner organ where it might not be noticed.

"You said you were afraid of heights. You can function in

buildings over two floors only by staying far away from any window. You drove three days to get here because you can't get on a plane. That's what you said, right?"

Standing next to him, she could hear the gulp. "Yes."

"CEOs have to be fearless, Barry. A major company isn't going to elect a leader who can't hold a meeting on the tenth floor and has to take the slowest mode of transportation everywhere he goes. So that's going to end, stop, today. Come here." He swooped up one end of the rope and held out what dangled from its end. A contraption of straps and buckles and Velcro. A harness.

Barry seemed frozen. He stared at that harness as if it were a living thing composed of snakes and barbed wire.

Angela, nearly as pale as Barry, put one hand on his back and one on his arm. "You can do this," she told him quietly. "Mine was bees, and he got a hive for me to put my hand in. I thought I was going to die, but I didn't get stung, not once. Galen will keep you safe, and you'll see that there's *nothing* to be afraid of, after all."

Ellie took a few steps forward, the better to see the loose half of the rope, which trailed along the wooden floor and ended near their group. It seemed new and in good condition. So did the pulley contraption, though she couldn't see exactly how it had been attached and hoped its massive bolt hadn't been simply screwed into the wood.

The beam held up the lid of this cavernous building, she told herself. Surely it could support the weight of the average grown male.

Perhaps they wouldn't hoist him at all. Maybe his simply agreeing to the trial would be enough.

Ellie doubted it.

Barry had moved to the center and was holding his arms out stiffly, as if he were a live totem pole. Galen personally strapped him into the harness, pulling the buckles tight and carefully lining up the Velcro closures. Barry gave a shudder at each one, his skin shrinking from the nylon belts as if they burned. Ellie doubted Galen could teach Barry what he needed to achieve his career goals, but clearly, as long as the possibility existed, Barry would do anything Galen asked. *Anything.*

"This will be great for him," Audrey said, though for once she didn't sound completely sure.

"Wait," Barry said.

Galen said, "No procrastination allowed. That's a bad habit you're here to break, just like this heights hang-up."

"No. I'm going to throw up."

He tried to move away, and the rope slithered past the group, almost tripping a young woman who accidentally straddled it. But even with one loose end, the volume of rope had enough weight to restrict his movements. He made it only halfway to the exit before he ran out of slack, held in place like a toddler with a leash or a mime pretending to fight a snowstorm.

But he had been heading not for the exit, but rather for a large garbage can positioned just inside the doorway. Devon hustled past him and grabbed its handle, then scraped it along the floor to bring it to him at the precise instant he could hold back no longer. He bent forward and lost what sounded like his entire meal into its depths.

"Maybe it wasn't a good idea to do this right after lunch," Ellie said aloud.

"Better he get it out now than up there," Galen said with satisfaction. Driving a grown man to puke in fear did not bother him. Or perhaps he felt it would all be worth it, since this fear of Barry's truly crippled him. And it *was* better for all of them if he lost his lunch while still on the floor.

Barry straightened and wiped his mouth on his cuff. Devon waited to make sure he had finished. When he turned back to the center of the room, she dragged the garbage can to the exit and even took it outside, with an expression of utter distaste.

Barry stood before Galen and said, "Okay."

Ellie didn't particularly like Barry, but in that moment she felt like a witness to true bravery. *You go, pal. You deserve to win this.*

"Ready?" their leader asked the room at large, grinning widely. "Okay. Everybody, pick up the rope. When I say go, you pull. Barry's life is now in your hands, right? He's trusting us. He's trusting you. Don't let him down—literally."

With a decidedly greenish cast to his paleness, Barry waited for them to pick up the rope. Ellie put her hands around the deep blue threads, trying to catalog all her misgivings about this venture. Barry had to weigh about two hundred pounds, but fifteen people should be able to control that. If they ran out of floor space, they'd have to hand over hand it. But what if they all moved their hands at once and he began to slip? If the rope began to run, it could burn—once again they were working without gloves—and if some of the crew fell out from injuries, it could overload the remainder. Letting Barry down might be more precarious than hoisting him up. She doubted any of them were experienced hoisters, herself included.

Ellie tried to quiet her qualms and squeezed the rope with both her hands. The class, as a unit, began to walk backward. Audrey was the first in the line, a bad placement given her size; the angle of the rope as it descended from the ceiling could lift her right off her feet. Tim had reappeared, and he and another largish man had positioned themselves behind Audrey, and then came Ellie. She felt one of her classmates at her six, his arms brushing hers.

The slack quickly disappeared, and Barry's feet stopped touching the floor. He gave one short, strangled cry as he dangled, gently swinging, the harness positioning him so that he had no choice but to gaze downward. It might have been fun if his terror hadn't infected nearly all present.

He looked ridiculous, but no one laughed.

They kept moving. Ten feet off the floor.

What if the rope got tangled in the pulley? Did the ranch have any equipment that could reach that high? It must, for the pulley to have been installed in the first place, right? Though the original buildings could have been built by contractors, who took their equipment with them.

Twenty feet.

"How you doing, Barry?" Galen called. When the man didn't answer, he repeated his question.

"O-okay." Ellie had never heard a grown man's voice quaver. He grasped the front of the harness with white knuckles.

"I sure hope he got all that lunch out," said one of the men in front of her.

The ranch must have insurance. Did Galen's carrier know about these activities? Would Barry's medical expenses be covered if the harness failed or the rope broke or it slipped too quickly away from them and he broke his spine?

Though the last scenario seemed unlikely. With that many people on the rope, it moved easily. Many hands did make light work.

Thirty feet.

"How about now, Barry?"

Barry had worn light gray slacks that day, perhaps having packed for more of a business meeting–type program. This turned out to be an unfortunate choice, since all of them could clearly see the dark stain form in his crotch.

"He's pissed himself," one of the men said, unnecessarily.

Someone burst out, "What's he going to do to the rest of us?"

If Galen heard, he gave no sign.

A scuffle sounded from the back of the group, and someone called, "We've reached the wall. We can't back up any more."

"Hand over hand," someone said, and they adjusted themselves to shorten the rope that way. Audrey did indeed rise up off the floor at times, but she gamely hung on, using every ounce of strength she had to bring the rope under control. Ellie could smell sweat, and it wasn't all hers.

Galen continued his attempts to engage Barry. "How's it going now? Look around. It isn't all that terrifying, is it? You're not hurt. You're not in pain. We're all here with you. There's nothing to be afraid of, is there?"

Finally, mercifully, Barry reached the top, the knot of rope at his back colliding with the pulley. *Don't let it tangle*, Ellie prayed silently.

"Stop," Galen said. "Hold it right there."

Ellie hung on, shoulders and biceps straining. She didn't need to; the group had more than enough weight to hold him in place. But despite her mind's analysis, her body completely believed that the man would fall to his death if she let the threads slip even a millimeter. Her fingers began to tingle. What would happen if they went numb?

"Open your eyes, Barry," Galen demanded, voice more strident than before. "Look at the floor beneath you. Look at us. Look at me. You're staying up there until you talk to me."

Ellie watched the man dangling from the ceiling over the broad shoulders of the man in front of her. A few glistening drops fell through the air. Ellie couldn't tell if they were saliva or urine or sweat.

Barry squinted, then slowly opened his eyes. His gaze darted around the gym in panicked sweeps, which eventually slowed.

"How ya feeling, Barry?" Galen called.

He said okay in the same quavering voice as before, but then cleared his throat and repeated the word.

"You're high up," Galen pointed out.

Ellie saw the man gulp before he answered with a yep, but remarkably, some of the color had come back into his face.

"But you're not dead."

"No."

"You're not hurt."

Barry murmured something we couldn't hear.

"What was that?"

"The harness is a little tight."

Galen laughed. "Better than loose, right? You're handling it."

"Yeah." Barry spoke as if he'd discovered something very interesting. "Yeah."

"Let go of the harness."

That wasn't so interesting. Barry's hands tightened all the more.

"They're not holding you in, Barry. The buckles are all in the back. It doesn't make any difference where you put your hands. It won't make you any more or less safe. It's your insecurities making you feel that way, and you're here to conquer your insecurities. They can't hold you back anymore."

He continued in this vein until Barry's fingers loosened and his hands dropped entirely. Slowly, he spread his arms out.

"There you go, like Superman. You've become Superman! Now, keep them out as we lower you. Don't let the insecurities flood back in for any reason. I see those hands move, you go back up."

Ellie questioned the psychology of using the trip to the ceiling as both a triumph and a punishment—didn't one cancel the other?—and also grumbled that she may not be up for another trip. Behind her, someone muttered agreement.

"Don't be a wimp," the guy in front of her said, with the hint of an East Coast lilt.

"Awareness of physical limitations is not wimpiness," she told him, in no mood for schoolboy machismo. "It's being a grown-up."

He spared her an argument when Galen spoke, telling them to let Barry down. The classmates inched forward, literally, as in moving an inch at a time, leaning back against the tension and planting their soles as flat as possible to avoid slipping. They lowered him to the floor like he was an angel in the school play. He kept his arms out until his feet were firmly planted. Then he stood there in his wet pants, a small but distinct smile on his lips.

"How do you feel?" Galen asked him. The rope fell to the floor, and Ellie rubbed her sore palms together.

"Good." Barry seemed stunned and relieved and amazed and proud. "Really good."

"You did great. You're not going to be afraid of heights anymore, right? Business meeting on the tenth floor, in a boardroom that's got floor-to-ceiling windows?"

The smile widened. "Bring it on."

The rest of the group gathered around to voice support, while keeping a healthy distance from whatever it was that had dripped onto the floor.

"Team-building hike up a mountain? Maybe even get on a plane . . . ? Good job. You can go change," Galen told him, and Barry didn't hesitate, moving through our group, with many claps on the shoulder. Galen waved at the wet spots on the hardwood and told Devon to clean them up.

For an instant, Ellie saw Devon's brows knit with anger and the same disgust she had shown for the garbage can full of Barry's vomit. Then she turned away and headed for a door near one corner of the gym. It seemed the young woman wore a number of different hats at the ranch . . . but with a small staff, most likely each one covered a great variety of tasks. Feed chickens, set up a two-story pulley, run group therapy sessions.

Galen clapped his hands and said, "Next, Margot."

After the words sank in, all of them turned as a unit to stare at their unlucky—or lucky, from Today's point of view—colleague.

She glanced up at the ceiling.

"No, no," Galen clucked. "No harnesses for you. You're not afraid of heights, so that exercise wouldn't do you any good. This is all about you, specifically freeing you from your personal fears. Only that way can you be free to achieve."

Ellie saw the woman's throat move and her lips compress. She remembered what fear she'd told them about.

So did Ellie.

Chapter 17

Rachael knew she'd been unusually quiet all through dinner. Even Danton, her adorable tiny toddler, had to keep patting her arm to direct her attention to his adorable tiny antics. Her mother, who'd had more years to inure herself to Rachael's obsession with work, shot her only a few considering looks in that way mothers had. Rachael let her assume the Locard had her thoughtful. No sense bringing up worries about her late sister, no sense revisiting the many pains of the past where Isis was concerned.

But once Danton had been bathed and put to sleep with a bedtime story and a hug and a kiss, and Loretta was sitting up in her bed with *The Great British Baking Show*, Rachael made her way to the stuffed closet in the baby's room.

The weeks after Isis's death had been full of shock, grief, and myriad court appearances to ensure that Danton would be coming to her home and no one else's. Rachael's husband had moved out, and her mother had moved in. The party-planning business had dissolved with the filing of a single piece of paper. The trappings of Isis's adult life—the very expensive wardrobe; the utilitarian and underused dishes, pots, and pans; the wall art, which Rachael found too jarring—were quickly dealt with. Rachael and Loretta cleaned out her sister's tidy penthouse in a weekend, sold her car, shoved anything that might be sentimental or relevant to Danton in the nursery closet, and looked to the future. Rachael had to get back to work, and both she and her mother had to adjust to structuring their new household around a human being who couldn't yet walk.

So the boxes had sat. Rachael had packed them herself and did not expect to find any earth-shattering clues now. Isis hadn't been a great one for sentiment, and she'd moved around a lot during her wilder youth. She hadn't kept her second-grade report card or a pressed corsage from the high school prom but *had* kept a box of photos, a ticket stub from a scary movie at the Cinemark Egyptian, and the speckled sundress that had been her favorite at the age of ten. Rachael had tossed in one box party-planning receipts, forms, ledgers and USB drives, in case there were tax issues or items needed to close the business completely.

Now she pulled this box out, hefting the bins around it in a near-silent version of a Jenga Giant game, always alert for a hitch in Danton's breathing. He slept well, but if disturbed . . . best that didn't happen. And she didn't want Loretta to find her either. Rachael didn't know what she might find, but knew she wouldn't like it. No sense distressing Loretta yet again over the antics of her younger daughter or forcing her to take sides between the two girls.

Like most parents, Loretta couldn't help defending her child even when all evidence supported the case against her. Rachael's complaints had been met with disapproval and instructions to be more empathetic or more understanding, as if Isis had some disability she couldn't control, as if she couldn't help staying out all night or skipping school or riding without a helmet on yet another boyfriend's stolen motorcycle.

The child in Rachael still rankled at the unfairness of it.

Rachael told that child to disappear. Her time was past; Rachael was mature now. If there was something about Isis that Billy wasn't telling her, she would face any truths on her own without further un-rosying her mother's memories.

With the awkward light from her phone's flashlight app, she delved into the contents of the box. The uppermost pile was made up of tax forms, which Isis had filed quarterly, as required, listing herself as both the company's president and employee. An old-fashioned green ledger, with jotted dates, names, amounts . . . Was it a backup in case electronic files went kaput? And an external hard drive with unknown terabytes of storage. Isis had had a laptop slide into the Potomac once and afterward had become fanatical about backing up files.

Brochures of venues, DJs, caterers, printers, bounce house renters, people she would have hired for clients to provide a turnkey party. All the brides or proud parents or execs would need to do was show up.

A small stack of invoices, itemized expenses, for the most recent jobs. It didn't take long to find one for Billy. Isis had listed four tents, copious amounts of liquor, five bartenders, something called a "Mediterranean menu," and two DJs. Did professional musicians really hire DJs for their own parties? Did they insist that only their own music was played? Probably yes, and maybe no. Who wanted to work at their own party?

The total bill had come to just under 650,000 dollars. But that didn't surprise Rachael as much as the date on the form: Thanksgiving Day two years ago. Chimera's last concert at the Hollywood Bowl.

A day to be throwing a party, certainly. But how could said celebration—or memorial service—be thrown at his house when he was in California?

She read the invoice again. Date of party . . . Rachael checked her calendar app. Yes, that had been Thanksgiving that year. Location: the same address Rachael had visited that day. Billing address: same.

Maybe Billy had played the evening concert, immediately jetted across the nation, and gone straight into party mode. All-nighters would not be unusual in that milieu.

Maybe the celebration had been for his crew, family, and hangers-on who didn't attend the concert. Throwing a party he wouldn't be going to sounded like a very Billy thing to do.

Maybe someone had noticed the date conflict and changed the day of the party, and Isis hadn't updated the invoice.

It was curious, but nothing more.

Danton stirred in his toddler bed, made a cross between a sigh and a snore. Rachael muffled the glow of her flashlight in her lap, willing the boy not to wake. After a long minute of silence, she went back to work, paging through the sheets as silently as she could. More invoices, some for Billy, one with a prominent senator's name on it. More tax forms, some bank statements. Rental agreement for the penthouse. Nothing seemed strange to Rachael. Other than that one errant date, it seemed like the dull detritus of an ordinary business.

Rachael didn't know what she was looking for, and knew she didn't know. But . . . she knew who might.

She dropped the stacks of paper back into the file box, where they landed with a whump. Almost immediately, Danton let out a grunt, fidgeting under his blankets.

Oh no, no, no. Go back to sleep, baby. Snooze under your

Binky in that adorable toddler bed from Restoration Hardware, which I put together myself with nothing but a Phillips screwdr—

A full-blown wail.

Oh, *hell*. Now she'd done it.

Chapter 18

Margot's challenge required a field trip.

Ellie thought that since she hadn't seen a lake on the property, there would be no way to re-create Margot's childhood incident, but apparently, the river would suffice. East of the bridge to the recluse lady's house, the river widened to span thirty feet, moved fast, and created a series of tiny rapids along the base of the mountain. The rushing surface made it difficult to see the bottom in a few spots, but surely it couldn't be deep enough to drown somebody. Like Barry, Margot wouldn't be in any actual danger.

Would she?

But to judge from the stack of towels Audrey carried, the victim would definitely be getting wet.

Said victim, for her part, walked next to Galen at the head of the pack with a grimly determined cast to her face. Margot would be described by younger coworkers as "a tough old bird," and neighborhood kids probably found her intimidating. She might be firmly into her middle years and with no ambition beyond having her own designated bathroom, but she would be damned before she'd let these young people dismiss her because of her age.

Or perhaps she wouldn't back down just because she was Margot.

Galen reached the water and stopped, then turned to the class. Ellie had been sticking close to him and stood only a few feet away.

"Here we are. We are going to release Margot from the burdens of her past, from the guilt and shame and anger and sense of betrayal—or rather help her release herself."

Margot didn't seem remotely convinced, of either the disease or the cure.

He beckoned to one of the two guys who had been in front of Ellie on Barry's rope—not Tim, but the other one, whose name was Andre—then took Margot's arm. All three of them walked out into the water without further explanation or regard for anyone's shoes. Margot hesitated at her first wet foot but pushed on. The currents lapped hungrily around them.

Ellie crouched down to feel the water, wondering if it really came from the melted snow of mountaintops. It flowed over her palm, still raw from the rope trick. Not freezing cold, but definitely below pleasant-swim temperature.

The river must have magnified the stones along the bed, foreshortening the visible depth, because the group reached waist level—chest level on Margot—by ten feet from shore.

Galen spoke. He and Andre each grabbed one of Margot's arms, and Galen put a hand on her head. Then they pushed her under the water.

It happened so quickly that Ellie gasped, along with a few others. She could only hope Margot had sucked in a deep breath just before the plunge, but that could be hard to do when the body was still reeling from the shock of cold water.

Then they stood and watched Galen drown a woman.

Ellie began to count. How long could someone hold their

breath? The average person maybe two minutes at best. More to the point, how long could *Margot* hold her breath?

Ten. Eleven.

Her hands came out of the water, grabbing at the forearms that held her. Grabbed and held—not quite struggling, more like steadying herself. The knuckles were white, but that could be due to the cold.

Or so Ellie told herself.

Fifteen.

Her feet kicked, the splashes blending with those of the water as it churned past her.

Twenty.

As Ellie's lips were forming the words, Galen spoke them. "Let her up."

They hauled her upper torso into the air, and she coughed, hair soaked, mascara running. Ellie breathed again herself, as deeply as if she'd been the one under the river's surface.

Then Galen shoved the woman's shoulders down, and they submerged her once more. Ellie didn't even have time to take a breath first, and she hadn't been coughing. This time the hands fought, yanking on the arms of her captors, her feet kicking hard enough to muffle the rapids.

Ten. Fifteen.

This time Ellie did shout. "Let her up!"

"She has to do this," Audrey said, with dead certainty.

Ellie snapped, "How would *you* know?"

The class seemed to agree with Audrey. "This will be freeing," someone behind Ellie said. "It will take away the fear forever."

The water chilled Ellie's kneecaps before she realized she had waded into it. Her feet felt as if she'd stepped into a vat of ice cubes, and even in her haste, she thought, *I'll regret this later,* since she had brought only one other pair of shoes. But she didn't slow more than the water demanded as it covered her thighs, her crotch. The icy water kept her from drawing breath—yet she managed to scream, "*Let her go!*" as Margot's arms became lethargic and her hands slipped from her captor's forearms. Her wrists, her fingers collapsed into the water and sank.

Ellie had nearly reached them when two arms grasped her from behind, then lifted her until her feet struggled as uselessly as Margot's had. The submersion also slowed her kicks as she tried to take out his knee. Without a pause, her shouts switched from demanding Margot's release to demanding her own.

Ellie had watched Margot drown, and now she would be next.

But the man did not dunk her in the river, and Galen and his henchman then pulled their victim upward. Margot appeared limp and lifeless, for one horrible moment devoid of any life. Then she shuddered and coughed and gasped and coughed again.

Ellie stopped screaming.

The men who only a moment before, to all intents and purposes, had been trying to kill Margot now held her gently upright, and Galen patted her back with a firm hand. He asked how she felt. Dripping curls hung in front of her face, but she shook her head up and down.

"Great job!" he crowed, and they dragged her toward the shore. The classmates cheered.

Ellie's captor turned her in that direction, and she bobbed along for a few steps before he let go, sliding his arms away from her torso and moving back. When she turned, he stood in the river a few feet away, as if waiting to see if she might slug him, a possibility she, at least, had not ruled out.

Tim, of course. He said nothing, only watched for sudden movements. Ellie couldn't find any words murderous enough and instead splashed her way to shore, her hands balled into fists.

"You are reborn," Galen was saying to Margot, as if this had been some sort of baptism, "into your new life, without fear and without regret. You arrived here as dumpy Marge, and I've turned you into resilient, vital Margot. You can move on."

Ellie neared them, to see this new reborn Margot for herself, and Galen turned to Ellie. "There's our little Saint Bernard. You soaked yourself for nothing."

"You were drowning her!"

"Does she look dead?"

And indeed, Margot's skin bloomed with excited color as Devon wrapped a blanket around her and Audrey blotted her hair with a towel. Andre, a nice-looking if imposing guy of about thirty, used another towel to wipe the last vestige of mascara off one cheek.

The rest of her classmates glanced at Ellie and away again. Awkward that she had injected herself into the drama . . . or maybe awkward that they hadn't. Probably the former, now that the drama had turned out to be make-believe.

Galen said, "This was her journey to take, not yours. You had no right to interfere."

His tone stayed level, but his face did not, and he held her gaze until everything around her blurred. Ellie had the sensation of seeing one vision while everyone else saw another, as if he could slip the mask up for Ellie while the others saw only a calm, wise guru gently scolding a child.

Ellie crossed her arms, her blood too high to yield.

"You got wet for nothing," he said again. "And you made poor Tim soak himself as well. Let that be a lesson to you. Stay on your path, and let others stay on theirs. Perhaps if you remain out here and let the sun dry your clothes, that will sink in."

With that, he dismissed her and put his arm around Margot. Ellie watched the woman's face, waiting for support, gratitude, or even just empathy, but Margot's expression remained shocked and slightly grim and utterly blank. Ellie had gone to bat for her, but Margot hadn't needed or, apparently, wanted her to.

Galen began to lead the group back toward the compound. If conversation sprang up, Ellie didn't hear it. No one wanted that gaze turned on them.

But when Ellie picked up one foot, Tim appeared again, now in front of her—how *did* he move so quietly?—and held up a hand like a traffic cop. "You'd better stay out here for a while, until he cools down."

Cool had already set in. Despite the sun, her wet clothes felt icy against her skin, the steady breeze snatching any body heat away as soon as it peeked out of her pores. Her shoes were sodden, and trickles ran down her legs. Even worse, she knew the now-soaked stiff rectangle in her back pocket had been her cell phone. "*He* cools down? What the hell is this place? I doubt anyone signed up to be tortured."

"Injuries teach you to be strong. That's what my dad always said." He stepped closer, obviously not worried about any punches of hers. He had at least six inches and a hundred pounds on her and no idea she'd been trained at Quantico. "And you have no idea what you're talking about. Because you *did* sign up, so you're going to want to bury that attitude six feet under if you don't want to wind up floating face down in this same river."

"Is that a *threat*?"

"It's a piece of advice, and you should take it. Because it won't be Galen holding you under—it will be me. And you don't want that."

Ellie could only stare, amazed he could issue a prosecutable threat in such a matter-of-fact tone in broad daylight in an open, exposed place. Horror movie dialogue on a stage set for touching sagas.

"Look," he added, as if *he* were the reasonable one, "give them about twenty minutes for the wet people to change. Then they'll all go back to the classrooms, and you can sneak into the bunkhouse and get some dry clothes."

Then he walked away as well. He had threatened her life and then advised her not to catch cold. Ellie felt dizzy.

You don't know what you're talking about. Was he right? She shivered from more than the chill. Did she have this all figured wrong? Galen wasn't a sadistic control freak? He was a counselor utilizing the same "face your fear" thought process that had been around for a century, expressed as exposure therapy, reframing techniques, the Outward Bound program? Barry and Margot, at least in the short term, seemed to have not only survived but also thrived, emerging from the fire with a new self-confidence.

Whereas Ellie had arrived only to spy on a grown woman for her overprotective father, and so far, she hadn't even managed to do that to any extent. She still had no real sense of Devon's emotional well- or ill-being, and even if she did, she could find no way to relay that information back to her father. Especially since she'd likely destroyed her phone.

In the meantime Ellie had been left in a patch of desert with squishy shoes, shunned by the only other humans within a five-mile radius.

She turned in a slow 360, taking in what she could see. Definitely no humans. Not even an errant chicken.

Then, on the other side of the water, higher up the mountain, she saw the edge of a structure built into the trees, glass panes twinkling through the branches. It must be the house of the ranch's benefactress, Mrs. . . . She worked to summon the woman's name.

The house was the "big, gorgeous" place that Angela had gushed about. It had to have a phone. And Ellie had some rare unsupervised moments to check in with Rachael and tell her the investigation would take more time. On the surface all seemed well in Devon's life, but there were undercurrents still hidden and possibly dangerous.

She walked upstream and crossed the river where it grew shallow, just above the rapids, balancing on rocks as best she could. The bridge sat on the other side of the compound, and she didn't want any more attention. Better if all of them believed she still sat on the riverbank, contemplating her poor life choices, when instead she splashed over the rounded stones to the opposite bank.

She couldn't get any wetter, after all.

Chapter 19

Devon stood outside their bathroom in the little house, holding the towel. Holding the towel was one of her many jobs. Steam wafted out, a spot of moisture in the dry valley air. Maybe it would help her skin. She had run out of her good moisturizer months ago. If only she could talk Galen into giving her internet access just long enough for her to order a few things from Amazon. Selections in Topaz were limited, and Reno . . . Reno might as well be on another planet. She tried to calculate how long it had been since she'd been in a town with more than one gas station.

He'd thrown his wet clothes over the back of the chair, no doubt swelling the wooden slats as the clothes dripped onto the carpet. Only Galen's bedroom had carpeting. Other tenants in the house—like herself—made do with bare floors.

She could see from the wet jeans that Galen had collected the mail before plunging into the river. Only Galen could get the mail—one of his many rules. He'd tried to tell her it was against federal law for anyone other than him, the director, to open mail addressed to the ranch. If so, millions of corporate secretaries were violating that law every day, but whatever. She suspected instead that Galen intercepted written pleas to come home from the clients' loved ones, but if it satisfied his need for control, fine.

Though now the mail would stick together in one sodden mess, and messes invariably got dumped in her lap. She threw the towel over her shoulder, listened for the water, and eased the bundle out of the pocket.

One envelope, already opened. Her attention perked up when she saw the bank's name in the upper left corner. The wet pages were delicate, requiring care to unfold while she remained alert to any change in the sound of the running water behind the door. The shower continued to run.

Even with the pages made confusing by their sodden near transparency, she knew what she was looking at—the trust account. Not the ranch's account, but the main trust account, from which their monthly income derived. The statements for which Galen had said went straight to Mrs. Coleman.

The total balance remained huge, but the statement—a quarterly summary—showed bimonthly withdrawals. Transfers to another account. Fifty thousand dollars for each transfer.

No wonder the interest payments to the ranch had been decreasing . . . because the principal had been as well.

But where had it gone? The statement noted '*Internal transfer to account number*' and so on.

Maybe Mrs. Coleman thought a gradual decrease would be a gentle way to ease the ranch into self-sufficiency.

Maybe someone was siphoning off funds to their personal account. . . . And there was only one person who could.

She realized the shower had stopped.

He emerged from the marble-clad bathroom in a cloud of steam, wetting the carpet further and letting her get a long look—which she dutifully took, plastering a wide smile of admiration across her cheeks.

Here I am, a human towel rack. Look at me, not at the wet clothes and the envelope that's now falling out of the pocket, with a crease in it that it didn't have before.

He took the towel from her hands.

Devon tried to suck in a breath without letting it show. "That went well. Two real breakthroughs."

Of course her cheer didn't work. "Who does that bitch think she is?"

"She was just scared. She feels stupid now." Actually, Ellen hadn't looked sheepish at all, more like suspicious and pissed as hell, but Devon saw no upside to saying so. "She won't do anything like that again."

Galen toweled himself dry, carefully rubbing every inch of his skin with the butter-soft towel. He had five, specially imported from Italy, and Devon had to launder them herself, along with his clothes. "You better believe she won't. Jumping in like that! Attacking us like *she's* going to take over, like *she* knows what people need. She hasn't listened to a word I've said!"

We've said, Devon mentally corrected. She hadn't moved, needing to wait until he'd finish with the towel so she could drape it back on its rack, keeping his gaze in her direction and away from the wet clothing on the chair. "It's not the first time someone's overreacted during challenges. It always turns into a really good teaching moment for them."

"Like Carlos?"

The name fell as both a memory of the past and a threat to the future. She'd almost rather talk about the trust account.

Carlos and his two years of psychology courses, which had made him think he was some kind of genius. Carlos and his gentle eyes, which made you feel warm and accepted, even more than Galen could, because Carlos never turned that warmth off. It didn't disappear when people stopped watching. Sweet, weak Carlos.

The guy had faced his own challenge—a live snake—without too much drama but had objected when Galen made Angela put her hand in the beehive. Galen had been giving the group the usual pep talk about having to overcome their fears in order to become resulters, and Carlos had gone off.

For once, his bearded, zen-calm face had scowled, and unaccustomed to long speeches, he had stumbled over his words. But he'd managed to launch into a history of places like Today's Enlightenment.

"Those words mean nothing," he'd said to Galen's face in front of an entire group of sophomores, who were waiting to see if Angela would be stung. They all heard him. The entire valley could hear him, provided there were any humans *in* the valley besides them. "And you're not the first to use them."

"Change always requires work—" Galen began as the tips of his ears turned red.

"You haven't invented any new way for human beings to function," Carlos stated flatly, then turned to his classmates. "He's simply repeating what people before him have been talking about for a couple of centuries now. José Silva came up with Silva Mind Control in the nineteen forties. It was supposed to teach you to be more energized, need less sleep, have more intuition, and heal yourself of any ailment."

Galen kept his voice level, but Devon could read between the lines of his tightened jaw. "You're not the first to resist change. You won't be the last. Angela, there's the hive. You can't progress with your goals if you don't integrate all the parts of your personality. That includes your fears."

The young woman took a step closer to the buzzing insects but hesitated as some curious bees danced around her face. The rest of the group watched without, it seemed, breathing. Devon thought the air had been sucked out of the valley.

Carlos didn't stop. "This *isn't* change. That's my point. L. Ron Hubbard said he'd cured himself of blindness—he hadn't—and talked about 'suppressives' and 'clears.' Keith Raniere's NXIVM had a bunch of modules like these classes and talked about parasites and producers, like Galen's remoras and resulters." The young man took a deep breath and spoke in a more reasonable tone. "I'm not saying you've done anything wrong, Galen, but you certainly haven't produced anything new."

Galen's voice fell like marshmallows on a sundae. "Angela. You realize that if you don't complete all sections of the program, you forfeit your collateral."

This prodded her into motion, and she moved up to the white beehive. The insects had lost interest in her looming form, but the amount of them grew denser the closer she got. Her face turned deathly pale, and maybe she forgot about Carlos and Galen as the hive and its occupants became the only thing in her sight.

"Collateral is another sick little game you learned from NXIVM," Carlos spat out.

Devon felt herself go as pale as Angela, each word like a punch to her solar plexus. *OMG, will there ever be hell to pay for this later.* It would take days to calm him down.

But except for the ears, Galen remained the very picture of serenity. He slipped into damage control without further ado. Rebellions spread like wildfire—if one person resisted the training, more might follow. "All right, Carlos. Obviously, there's some disconnect here . . . Let's do a private session, just you and I, so we don't hold up the rest of the class."

Angela plunged her hand into the hive and held it in a frozen spread-fingered sprawl without touching the honeycombs on either side of it. Devon couldn't see inside the box but knew what must be happening. The bees would climb all over her fingers, looking for pollen, and would give up when they couldn't find any. She had to hand it to the kid. She wouldn't have thought little Angela had the guts.

The shoulders of both men slumped. Galen's in relief. He had won.

Carlos's in disappointment . . . perhaps in Angela for not backing him up, perhaps in himself for failing to convince the rest of the group. When Galen beckoned to him, he went. It seemed as if the young man had decided to give the program another chance—the program he had traveled far and paid heavily to join.

His classmates never saw him again.

The young man, his belongings, even his records, receipts, and video, all disappeared. Galen told Devon, "I pointed out that he came here to get advice and then refused to listen to it, like a spoiled child, and that I wasn't about to waste any more resources on a moron. He packed up his things, and I called a car service. The tool had the nerve to ask for a re-fund!"

No bad reviews were posted on social media, no visits from cops. It seemed that whatever Galen had said to him, or whatever deal he had made, had shocked Carlos into silence.

But after that, a few people did not sign up for another session, and two more left before completing the first.

And now here was Ellen, wanting to leap in like a super-hero, with no idea how much she might be screwing things up for other people.

Devon, for example.

Her boss said, "This has ruined my day. Maybe this whole week. I'm going to need a release."

Oh, hell. "Ellen isn't like Carlos. She didn't challenge the *idea* of challenges."

"Great grammar there, *sweetie.*"

"You know what I mean."

Oh, that was a mistake. Never express impatience . . . certainly not exasperation.

"Yes," he said. "I need a release. I'm way too tense."

He handed her the towel, sat down on the bed. Dead center at the foot of it. And waited.

"I have afternoon sessions to set up," she said.

"Let Angela do it."

She hung up the towel, leveling the sides over the rack. "She doesn't have enough module four experience."

"It's just one day. Come on."

It would do her no good, should the freshmen pepper Angela with questions she couldn't answer, to remind him that this had been his idea. No good at all.

She moved over to the bed.

Chapter 20

Ellie reached the other side of the river, but only by resoaking both legs. She hoped the shoes wouldn't be completely ruined. They'd have to spend the night in front of whatever delivered heat inside the bunkhouse. . . . She'd been so tired the night before that she hadn't even noticed. Forced-air heat? Radiator? Potbellied stove?

The real estate on the opposite bank had no gentle spread but immediately tilted upward into a forest of towering trees and brush-choked earth. Pine cones lay abandoned amid protruding roots and rocks of every size, from gravel to jutting boulders, and all at a 20 to 30 percent incline. Ellie used saplings to pull herself along, the thin trunks flexing, refusing to provide security, and snapping away quickly when released. Birds chirped their protests, and she heard the occasional rustle of a squirrel or a chipmunk or what she hoped was a nonbiting animal.

Once out of the sunshine, her wet clothes sucked away body heat with a vengeance, and the clammy chill became more noticeable. At least the movement kept her blood moving.

A lot of movement. Walking up the practically vertical side of a mountain turned out to require a lot more exertion than she'd expected. But soon she happened on a trail of sorts and followed that off to her left.

Trail, however, overstated it. More of a narrow sliver of hard-packed dirt, no more than six inches across at its widest spots, snaking around the trunks and over the roots of the mountain's occupants. But as the only sign of human habitation, she devoured it hungrily. At one point it dead-ended into another equally narrow line of dirt, with a wooden post denoting that the trail she had been on was called "Hy" and the other "Jp." This information seemed less than helpful. The marker also told her that the elevation was 4,120 feet.

Ellie had spent a lot of time among the trees as a child, exploring their many secrets in quiet peace . . . but not while soaking wet and working a secret mission to rescue an aging rock star's child. She turned to her left, taking Jp down the mountain instead of up, and in no time at all, the trail took her close enough to glimpse her goal through the trees.

The house didn't look like a city dweller's image of a mansion. Two stories of rough dark wood. A sprawling porch along the entire front of the house. No yard to speak of, no grass to cut, only the same leaf- and needle-covered dirt that she'd been traversing for thirty minutes. This made the house appear as an extension of the forest, part of the trees and earth, instead of a human invasion of this wild kingdom. It also saved a great deal in landscaping costs.

The home and its small clearing were deadly silent. Ellie couldn't see a light or hear any sound of movement or activity or life.

She approached a back corner of the house, where she found a door level with the ground, a lovely construction of burnished wood and glass panels. It seemed very elegant, old world, and utterly insecure for a woman living alone so far from help. Break one small panel and you could reach through and turn the knob in perhaps two seconds.

She wondered if the owner had had visits from the clients before. The woman must feel kindly toward the ranch if she let them use her land, and it *was* the middle of the day, business hours, when a knock at the door shouldn't seem either threatening or too intensely annoying. Show up pre-bedtime, like during her previous night's ramble, and Ellie wouldn't blame the owner a bit for greeting her with a shotgun blast.

A nacre button was recessed into the door frame. After running through what she planned to say—*So sorry to intrude, but I'm staying at the ranch, and I really need to borrow your phone for one brief call because mine would not work, and it'll take sixty seconds and I'll be out of your hair, promise*—she pressed it.

She peered through all those glass panels as she waited. The granite and walnut kitchen inside was twice the size of any she'd ever been in, with copper-bottomed pans hanging over the center of a marble-topped island and, beyond it, a table heavy enough to withstand the building's collapse. Ellie didn't know if Nevada had earthquakes, but if one occurred, she would want to hole up under that sucker.

No humans appeared. Ellie heard only the whispering rustle of the leaves overhead in the slight breeze and lots of birds.

Perhaps the bell didn't work. She knocked, carefully hitting the wood and not the glass, shifting her weight in her sodden shoes. The climb had drained off some of the water, so she only scattered drops instead of leaving a puddle, but her clothes were still plenty wet. A puff of wind reminded her that it was fall in the mountains and that she stood in the shade.

No signs of life.

Ellie knocked again, on the glass this time, striking it as hard as her hand and the panel could take. Maybe the rich woman had gone on a tour of Europe. Maybe she'd gone to the grocery store. Maybe Galen had killed her and stuffed her body in the woodpile.

Unbidden, Ellie's hand fell on the knob. It turned.

The door swung open on well-oiled hinges.

Definitely not safe for a woman living alone so far from help.

"Hello?" she called, then called again, louder.

Nothing.

And then she saw the phone hanging on the wall.

An old-fashioned heavy plastic model with a cord and everything, the solid item that a phone used to be when people had only one in the house. A dark green color to coordinate with the kitchen's accents, and push buttons instead of an actual dial, seemed the only concessions to modernity.

Ellie shut the door behind her and moved over to the phone. She'd given propriety her best shot, and it hadn't helped, and all she wanted to do was make a damn phone call. She'd be in and out before anyone noticed, if there was anyone there *to* notice.

She put the receiver to her ear.

Nothing. Not even static, certainly not a dial tone.

A voice behind her said, "That thing hasn't worked in years."

Rachael and her filing box stood at the door of the Locard's resident forensic accountant. Desiree LaVoie had been a voodoo priestess in a former life, or at least that was what she told people. Rachael had never been sure if Desiree meant it as a joke or not. The slender Haitian transplant seemed to have a sly sense of humor.

Desiree looked up from her desk and the papers scattered across it, where she'd been jotting notes on a legal pad. "Yes, boss? What can I do for you today? *Grenadia?*"

Rachael turned down the fruit juice with some reluctance—she needed to make this meeting as efficient as possible. She had never before used the Locard's resources for her private business and needed to get this done before she changed her mind. "No, thank you. I actually have a personal favor to ask."

Desiree blinked in surprise, but said only, "Of course. Please sit."

Instead, Rachael came around behind the old wooden desk—one of the holdovers from the Locard's former life, when it had been a private boys' school—and, after a moment's hesitation, set the box on the floor. Invoices and statements and handwritten summaries covered Desiree's desktop from end to end, and it would be rude to plop her box atop the legit work. "This is a little hard to explain."

"Take your time."

Rachael took a seat in one of the three guest chairs that she and the director had personally shopped for. Forensic accounting represented one of the Locard's steadiest sources of private clients, as there would never be a shortage of embezzling executives and heirs disgruntled with their share of the estate. Such well-heeled guests should be made comfortable during the hours they would need to spend with Desiree going over each fact and figure.

As concisely as she could—which wasn't very—Rachael told the woman about Isis, the business, Billy, his habits, the concert date, the party invoice. She showed Desiree the party invoice, told her about the poster.

Desiree fixed that clear-eyed gaze upon her and asked in her lilting accent, "What is it that you are looking for?"

"I don't know—that's the problem. I just . . . see an inconsistency, which needs to be explained."

"Why?" Desiree asked unexpectedly.

Why, indeed? What difference did it make? Isis was dead and gone. Let her lie in her grave in peace. What was Rachael trying to prove? That her largely estranged sibling had never stopped being the "bad" sister? That Rachael had been justified in not forgiving and forgetting? "Can you tell if this was a legitimate business?"

The forensic accountant had perfected her poker face over the years. "You don't believe it is?"

"I don't know. I don't have any reason not to think . . . looking back, I don't . . . It . . . it wasn't a brick-and-mortar business, of course. She didn't have inventory or supplies, other than a few brochures. All services, printing, catering, venues, would be contracted out. Isis only put all those things together, so physically . . . But there would be paper, at least, wouldn't you think? Not just invoices but also estimates, communications, the bride's requested colors and songs. I didn't think about it at the time. We weren't thinking of much at the time, only grief and Danton."

Her voice had grown agitated, so Desiree's came as a calming balm. "Perhaps she kept only electronic copies, shredding all others once the event ended."

Rachael grasped at this. "That's exactly something Isis would do. Her laptop and drives are in that box as well. You may need Agnes's help if she encrypted her files."

"Of course. Leave it with me."

"Thank you, Desiree." They exchanged a few rounds of Desiree saying it was no problem and Rachael expressing her discomfort at asking for such a favor, and on company time no less, until Rachael realized that if she really cared about company time, she had better get back to the work she'd been paid to do, and rose to leave.

Halfway to the door, Desiree called after her with the question Rachael had been studiously avoiding. "Are you sure you want to know what there is to find?"

Perhaps she wasn't kidding about that voodoo priestess thing.

"No. Not sure at all."

Chapter 21

Ellie whirled around in a most ungainly way.

The lady of the house stood next to her kitchen table, as slender and frail as the table was thick and heavy. She wore wool slacks and a satin blouse topped with two different cardigan sweaters, her silver hair pulled back in a haphazard braid or bun, Ellie couldn't tell which. Her skin had a pale, translucent glow, and faded blue eyes studied Ellie. She did not, Ellie saw with relief, carry a shotgun.

But Ellie would be expelled from the premises even without firearms, because she was déclassé, because she was rude enough to enter the house uninvited, or because any grown woman tramping through the woods in soaking wet clothing had to be completely deranged. "I'm so sorry. I'm from the ranch. I rang the bell, and then I knocked. I knocked twice. I just wanted to use the phone, and I couldn't tell if anyone was home, and the door wasn't locked, and—"

"I heard the bell," she said. "But I don't move as quickly as I used to."

"No, of course not. I mean, I should have been more patient and waited. I'm so sorry Mrs.—" Ellie could not remember her name.

She didn't seem particularly fascinated by Ellie or quite ready to throw her out, either. "That's quite all right, my dear. You're from the ranch? Today's Enlightenment?"

"Yes! Yes, I am."

"Oh, that's—Are you *wet*?"

Ellie looked down at the drops she'd scattered on the deep red ceramic tile, then shivered in the well-insulated house. "Yes. I'm so sorry—"

"My goodness! You must be chilled. Would you like some hot tea?"

Manna, quite literally, in the desert. "*Yes*. A thousand times yes."

The woman put the water on to boil and went to retrieve some bath towels after Ellie turned down her offer of a dry outfit. It would have been sensible to accept, but between the day's events and the altitude, the ex–FBI agent already felt otherworldly enough without wearing the manor lady's clothing. Blotting her pants with towels would have to suffice.

They sat on stools at the island, since Ellie didn't want to risk getting water spots on one of the table's matching chairs. The woman poured tea into a delicate china cup with a saucer and added honey from an adorable pot in the shape of a beehive. No cream or sugar, but with temperature more important than taste right then, Ellie didn't quibble.

The woman climbed onto another stool spryly enough and faced Ellie. "So, you're staying at the ranch. Going through their program?"

"Yes. I arrived only yesterday."

"And you've already been dunked?" She seemed to find this amusing, which was good, Ellie supposed. She wanted her hostess to feel at ease and not to tell Galen that a crazy lady had broken into her home. "You *are* making quick progress."

"Do dripping people often show up at your door?"

She answered seriously. "Oh, yes. Not dripping, but hikers come by. And occasionally patients wander up here, or Galen brings them."

Ellie didn't comment on the "patient" term. She needed to tread carefully, hoping to gain more than a phone. "It's very kind of you to loan them the land."

"Oh, that's no skin off my nose. It was just lying there, baking in the sun, anyway, and the Colemans have always maintained a strong social commitment." She leaned forward with a conspiratorial air, meaning her words as a joke, and said, "We try to use our powers for good."

Coleman, that was the name. Her posture bespoke girl-hood training, and Ellie flattened her spine to keep up. Not that she stood a chance of looking regal while wrapped in two different towels. "Did you grow up in this house?"

"Goodness, no. I was a city kid . . . well, at first. We lived in Manhattan, then Westchester County. Then I got married—the first time—and he worked in Chicago, and after that . . ." She waved her hand, as if detailing her location history would take too long or would require too much effort to recall. "They were all gone by the time I came here. I forget which of my parents or uncles bought this land way back . . . but I walked around this mountain and decided this is it, this is where I need a house. I felt ready for quiet, so I sold all the other ones. I used to travel quite a bit. I got too old."

Ellie exclaimed something, made some sound meant to imply that "old" might be too harsh a judgment. Mrs. Coleman, though thin, seemed in good health. "It's beautiful, the house. Do you have children?"

The lines in her face deepened, but she spoke calmly. "My boy was killed."

"I'm *so* sorry. That's terrible."

She added more honey to her tea. "But I have a daughter, as well. Her name is Theresa. She's . . . Let's see, how old is she now? She was born in fifty-eight, yes?"

"That's wonderful," Ellie spoke with sincerity. "Does she live nearby?"

"No, goodness! She's in . . . Bolivia." Ellie's expression betrayed her surprise, and the woman laughed. "Yes, it's quite a ways. She's in the Peace Corps. Rejected all the money and the fancy homes and argued with her stepfather about unions and argued with me about health care all the time. She wanted to help people."

"How nice. A friend of mine joined the Peace Corps—"

"She comes to see me often, though. She was just here last night . . . no, the night before."

Ellie hadn't heard any cars moving about, so perhaps it *had* been the night before, prior to her arrival. The only roads in or out of the ranch went past the bunkhouses, but then she'd been occupied in the classrooms and dining hall and publishing office. For all she knew, a major convoy had passed through. "That's quite a trip, from Bolivia."

"I suppose, yes. But we've always been great travelers. That's why my great-great-grandfather trekked all the way out here to Nevada. Have you been to Bodie? It's exactly in the middle of nowhere."

"I've heard of it." Ellie got down to her purpose for the visit. "I did need the phone, to check in with my job. Your landline doesn't work at all?"

"More tea?"

Ellie didn't really want the Today crew to come looking for her; they might, once they felt she'd stewed long enough. They might think she fell in the river and launch a search party. Or they might find her at Mrs. Coleman's, annoying Galen further. She'd gotten the impression from Angela that keeping the clients off Mrs. Coleman's doorstep was a requirement, though the old woman had certainly welcomed Ellie right in. Either way, she wanted to keep this visit on the q.t.

But she also needed a way to communicate with the outside world. *Now.*

"Yes, I'd love another cup, if you don't mind. I'm not keeping you from anything, am I?"

"Not at all." She puttered with the boiling water, then added fresh tea bags to the cups. "I'm completely retired from any real work these days. I still have my charities and keep an eye on the accounts, keep in touch with the few friends still alive."

Ellie tried again. "Your landline—"

Mrs. Coleman paused on the way back to the table, carrying a full cup and saucer in each hand, concentrating hard to keep from sloshing any tea. Ellie felt guilty for distracting her. "My what?"

"Your telephone."

She glanced over at the corded telephone on the wall, as if she'd forgotten its existence. "Oh yes. It hasn't worked in years."

Ellie let her set the cups down before speaking again, then thanked her for the hot liquid. The towels had blotted away much of the water, and she felt almost partially dry, the damp fabrics not as plastered to her skin as they had been. "Do you have a cell phone? Or a satellite phone?"

Filmy blue eyes gazed at her over the rim of the china cup.

Surely a daughter savvy enough to be still working in the Peace Corps at, what, sixty-three—perhaps she was an administrator, worked in DC, and oversaw Bolivia or, Ellie chided herself for her ageism, was still building aqueducts in the Peace Corps at sixty-three—*surely* such an intrepid child would have a way to stay in touch with her physically isolated mother. A sat phone wasn't out of the question. Dial-up VoIP access wasn't out of the question. A signal booster on the roof wasn't out of the question.

Please tell me something *isn't out of the question.* "How does your daughter call you?"

"Call me?"

"Yes."

"Theresa was never much for talking on the phone. Even when she was a girl, she didn't spend hours yakking like other girls. When I was in high school, oh my lord, I used to—"

Ellie leaned forward, sloshing the cooling tea in her cup. "Do you have a way to get in touch with her?"

She found this understandably odd. "You want to talk to Theresa?"

Ellie made herself set the cup down, afraid that she might absently use it to gesture with and soak them both. Then she forced a smile she didn't feel. "I'm sorry, no . . . I want to talk to *my* family, but I don't have a phone. Do you have a computer I could use? Internet access? If I could even send an email . . ."

"Oh yes. I have one of those things."

Ellie gasped with relief. "Could I possibly use it for a minute? Just send one email."

"It doesn't do that."

Ellie blinked. "Do what?"

"It doesn't have the modem or the weefee or whatever. It's too easy to get hacked, my dear. Robbers can get in there and take all my accounts. Best to stay off it. Besides, the monthly fees were ridiculous. I only use it for balancing my books and typing letters."

She spoke with authority, bursting any idea that she had mistaken the question. Ellie couldn't comprehend living in such isolation without Google to keep her company, but if Mrs. Coleman didn't feel any real need for it, then she didn't.

Ellie went back to the phone idea. "When your daughter calls, what does she call you on?"

She put off answering, stirring more honey into her cup, with a tiny furrow between her eyebrows. "Call?"

Maybe she wasn't such a good daughter. Maybe she visited often enough to make phone calls unnecessary. From *Bolivia*, though? "If there were an emergency, what would you do?"

"What emergency?" She asked this as if Ellie were impertinent for suggesting such a thing.

"If there were. Say I broke my ankle and needed an ambulance. What would you do?"

She raised one eyebrow. "Dear," she said with the gentle tolerance of a veteran schoolteacher, "you are hardly *my* responsibility."

"No, of course. I know that. But somehow there is no cell service, and I haven't seen a phone yet. So my question is, do you have a telephone? Of any kind?"

She allowed a tiny sigh to escape the patrician nose, only that one crack in her elegant patience. "Well, of course I have a *phone*—"

"Could I *please* borrow it? Just for one very short call, I promise. I wouldn't ask if I weren't desperate."

"But I couldn't let you *use* it."

Full stop. Ellie's mouth gaped, and some voice deep in her head had to tell her to shut it. "What? Why not? Are you charged for long distance?" She probably was. Older people tended to get the less inclusive cell plans—

"It would set your recovery back."

Ellie picked up the teacup, going for a casual look, and tried to pull this conversation back from the land of the absurd, into which it had tumbled. "Mrs. Coleman. The ranch isn't for drug rehab or any other substance abuse or any sort of addiction, really. It's a career development retreat, that's all. The only reason my phone won't work is because it got wet." *And because I can't get a signal to save my life.* "I don't have any 'recovery' to worry about."

Mrs. Coleman smiled and nodded and didn't budge. "Of course not, my dear. But Galen's told me all about the program, and I've had very strict instructions not to indulge anyone who might turn up. You have to heed your internal disciplines, or you're not going to get anywhere."

That sounded like Galen, all right. "Mrs. Coleman. Not being able to make a phone call is *not* part of developing our internal discipline. Galen has never ever said we couldn't make phone calls."

"Everything outside this ranch is holding you back—"

Being cold, wet, hungry, perplexed, and extraordinarily frustrated began to reach an apex, and Ellie could feel that internal discipline pulling out of her grasp, as if it were covered in oil. "No, this *ranch* is holding me back!"

"You'll be fine, dear. You'll come out stronger on the other side, you'll see, and be amazed at how powerful you can be. But we have to choose the path that will take us to success."

Ellie's mouth slipped again at this fortune-cookie piece of nonsense. Then a shadow covered the doorway to the rest of the house, and Galen stepped through it.

Chapter 22

Ellie started so violently that she sloshed tea over her thigh, though without much real effect. The pants hadn't dried, and the tea had cooled.

"Quite right, Frances. That's exactly our goal." He spoke to her, but he looked at Ellie, dark eyes appearing darker in the shaded sunshine of the kitchen. He had changed from his wet clothes—lucky him—and now looked like a Gap model in worn jeans and a heavy T.

He moved over to them more quickly than Ellie was ready for, his tread vibrating up from the floorboards. She created a barrier with the cup and its saucer, showing him how she was a sort of invited *guest*, not an invader, and Mrs. Coleman *liked* her.

"Angela said Mrs. Coleman had a phone that the ranch could use . . . if necessary." Best to keep the "emergency" requirement out of it. Wanting to report to Rachael would not qualify.

His hand landed gently on the old woman's shoulder. "Frances is so committed to the success of every client that she has trusted us the land we're on. We really can't abuse her goodwill. It's very rude."

He had to hear Ellie's teeth grind. "Using a phone for a few minutes is hardly abusive. She's been so kind." This she directed at Mrs. Coleman, who smiled and patted her hand. "And I'm . . . not comfortable with being kept here incommunicado."

He showed his dimples, grinning, as he shook his head in patent disbelief. "No one is keeping you here. The ranch doesn't even have a fence, and it's not my fault your cell phone doesn't work. It's a common problem in these remote areas. Come on, let's go. You've taken up enough of Mrs. Coleman's time for one day."

"Oh, I don't mind—" the old lady began.

His voice firmed, a hint of the iron under the velvet. "Nell isn't here to have chatty visits or to take advantage of your hospitality. She's here to reshape her life, and that's hard work." As he spoke, he wrapped one hand around Ellie's upper arm and pulled her off the stool with a mild tug. She half expected him to crush her bicep, make her gasp in pain to teach her the errors of disobeying, but he didn't. Only a slow, inexorable drawing forth until she set the teacup back on the counter and finally gave up. A good side kick would take out his knee, or a chop to the throat to crush the windpipe . . . but that seemed a bit extreme, and besides, curiosity had overtaken anger. How had Carlos come to drown in that very wet river? Was Devon conspiring, brainwashed, or simply in love?

Besides, an unexpected demonstration of mixed martial arts would startle Mrs. Coleman.

Ellie thanked the woman for the tea and allowed Galen to guide her out the same door she'd entered. The servants' entrance, perhaps . . . but then her old shoes *were* still a bit muddy.

Once outside, Galen allowed a suppressed irritation to

show as he stomped along the drive. "Mrs. Coleman is our benefactor. She's done great things for this program, and in return, I make sure she's not pestered by our group. If clients constantly bang on her door, wanting things, she might decide to throw us out for good."

"Angela said—"

"Leave Angela out of it! This was your choice, not hers."

Ellie stopped and pivoted, made her stand under the trees, curious to see how sensitive to disobedience he might be. "I simply want to make *one phone call*! You have, what, over a hundred people here? You mean to tell me they're all going without phones, texts, and emails? That you have no way to call an ambulance if, say, Barry slipped his harness and broke an ankle? Your insurance would never allow it. You do *have* insurance, don't you?"

Seen from a distance, he would appear completely relaxed, hands at his sides, legs loose. But up close every tendon in his face had tensed like a rod under the skin, and Ellie could smell something sour on his breath as he leaned in.

They stood alone in a vault of tree trunks and foliage; Ellie couldn't even see the ranch from there. And they couldn't see her. She might never leave these woods; her body might be left only a few yards off the path, never to be found. No one would even know where to start looking.

But she refused to step back even an inch.

For all the good it did, because Galen went on, "Barry didn't fall. Margot didn't drown. Cell phone reception is not the problem, Nell. It's only one more way for you to avoid the fact that you *have* no one to call. Your husband dumped you. Your mother died on you. Your father dumped you. Your job dumped you. Stop looking to them for validation, because they've stamped you *reject*."

This would have been harsher had it not been true.

Ellie's chest felt as if she'd taken a blow to her diaphragm. Ten years of marriage and Adam *had* left it on the curb for pickup like a set of worn-out clothes. . . . His leaving didn't disturb her nearly as much as how easy that leaving had been for him.

Once an orphan, always an orphan, looking to a job to replace her family, fulfill a function mere employment wasn't designed to do. . . .

"This is why you're resisting, Nell. You want a reason to disregard everything we say or do in this camp. I see it on your face during the training sessions. You don't want to admit that you need our help to change, because you don't want to admit that you need to change, because you don't want to admit that your choice of paths has led you to a dead end."

Then, suddenly, any tension had left him, and his voice wrapped her in its warmth. "With all that to process, it's not surprising that you're acting out. Believe me, you're not the first and won't be the last. It's okay. I'm going to guide you through it. We'll do this together."

Unexpected tears pricked her eyes. Was she really feeling this? Had this ridiculous "bad cop, good cop all rolled into one" mind trick really gotten to her?

"*There* you are."

Devon emerged from the tunnel of leaves, panting a bit from the long walk. She said to Galen, "I'm glad you found her."

To Ellie, she said, "We're ready."

Chapter 23

He graciously allowed Ellie to go into the bunkhouse to change clothes, with instructions to be back in the gym in five minutes. She ignored that on principle, taking time to prop her soaked cell phone against her meager pillow on the far, far off chance that it might come to life. It would be Murphy's Law to get a signal after the fuss she'd made. But Murphy's Law dictated that when you wanted Murphy's Law to work, it didn't, and the screen stayed dark. Her thumb itched to press the POWER button just to see what would happen, but she figured any electrical shock would fry any diode struggling to revive.

She dug some fresh clothes out of her backpack and headed for the bathroom, where she purposely used all her remaining five minutes on a shower.

When Ellie emerged, the same young woman she'd seen the night before exited a toilet stall, carrying a bucket with brush handles sticking out the top. She started on the sinks, sprinkling scouring powder over the first, then taking a grout brush to it. Her hands were reddened; the fingertips raw.

Ellie began to pack her shoes with paper towels. "You work a long day."

The young woman glanced up and away again, mumbling something like yeah or uh-huh.

"Do you live around here?" Perhaps civilization wasn't as far off as it seemed.

She wasn't chatty. "I live here."

"On the ranch?"

"Yes." Her tone described how that should be blatantly obvious to all but the brain dead.

"Oh. Do you work for the ranch, or are you a client here? If you don't mind me asking."

She clearly *did* mind but answered anyway. "I'm a sophomore."

"Oh. You're in the program here."

"Yes." She started on the second sink, possibly to hide an eye roll.

But Ellie wasn't done. "I just got here yesterday morning, so I'm still figuring out the system. Why are you on cleaning duty? Is that routine?"

It probably was. Ellie had already been put to work on mailing, construction, and farming, so why not janitorial and housekeeping services? All part of the cleansing aspects of physical labor.

"It's sanction."

Ellie gave that word a moment to make sense, to no avail, while the young woman rinsed scouring powder down the drain. "What do you mean, sanction?"

Either she felt embarrassed to talk about it or she wanted Ellie to get out of her way so she could finish, and the words came out in a rush. "I didn't complete my tasks, and I took one of Esai's cigarettes."

"You stole a cigarette?" Okay, pilfering, but—

"No, he gave it to me. But I'm supposed to be quitting smoking. I *did* quit. So I can't backslide."

"I see." A new kind of smoking cessation program. Not that strange. Ellie pointed at her hands. The young woman probably thought rubber gloves were too old-ladyish, but when you were scrubbing other people's toilets . . . "Don't you want to wear gloves when you do that? All the soap can be really hard on your skin. I know. I worked as a hotel maid during college."

Dark locks fell over her eyes as she shook her head. "It's not allowed."

"Not *allowed*?" Anti-smoking or no, this went too far. "But it's not healthy to be working around toilets with your skin all cracked like that. There's so many illnesses that . . . when there's a direct route to the bloodstream . . ." Nightmares from Microbiology 101 swam through her head.

"I won't get sick."

"You can't be sure of that. There's—"

"*No* one gets sick. It's all a weakness trap. Are you done?"

She had finished all the other sinks, and now she and her bucket waited for Ellie's.

"Yes. I—I hope your hands heal quickly."

The young woman turned her back to sprinkle powder over Ellie's abandoned sink.

Ellie returned to her bunk and spread her now nearly dry clothes over the footboard. Perhaps her sanction could be laundry duty. Ellie had interfered with Margot's challenge and had browbeat Mrs. Coleman over the use of her telephone—surely a punishment loomed in her future.

Maybe it should. She just hoped it wouldn't be scrubbing toilets without gloves.

Really, that was over the top. Effective personality fine-tuning or cruel quack psychotherapy? Such lines were murky and in the eye of the beholder.

Ellie hustled out of the bunkhouse.

Unplugging the clients from phones and the internet had seemed to be a power play until she began to think it might be a good idea. Now, after meeting the bunkhouse maid, Ellie felt herself swinging back.

Did Galen's little project produce broken drones or success-focused adults? Was he a healing guru or a dangerous control freak? And which would Devon turn out to be?

Ellie wasn't going to leave without an answer to those questions . . . no matter what it took. Not only for Devon's sake, but for Angela's and Barry's and Margot's and the former nicotine addict turned housekeeper's.

The heavy push bar on the gym door created a clang that echoed through the open space. Ellie's classmates had gathered in the center, and each one turned at the sound to watch her walk in—disconcerting scrutiny that instantly set her heart pounding. This felt like being called to the principal's office multiplied about a hundred times.

It didn't matter that she was a trained agent and had grappled with killers on more than one occasion. She still squirmed in embarrassment and, yes, fear.

As she got closer, she could see the expressions—of worry, nervousness, somber concern—and one or two narrow-eyed, oddly satisfied leers of anticipation, most notably on Audrey. Tim and the other muscle-bound one, Andre, waited with arms crossed. But before Ellie could interpret all this information, her gaze fell to the object behind them.

On the floor seemed to be a platform of some kind, made of unfinished plywood, perhaps a foot high and rectangular, the ends disappearing behind people's legs.

"Ah, Nell," Galen said, greeting Ellie as if he hadn't seen her all day. If her tardiness annoyed him, he gave no sign. "It's time for your challenge. You're obviously having a hard time adjusting to the goals you've set for yourself and the means to achieve them. I think this will jump-start your mindset. Your fear of change is paralyzing you. Everything in your life has been altered, and this has overwhelmed you. But if we can get you over one fear, you can begin to conquer them all."

His words, calm and reassuring and terrifying all at once, ran together in her head. A light arm went around her to guide her forward, and his other hand held hers. He pushed Ellie, more or less, but so softly that she didn't resist—and there would be no point anyway. Where would she run?

Her strangely quiet classmates parted like a silent sea, and the linoleum angled the sunlight from the windows into her eyes. It took some squinting to notice the shape of the pine box on the floor.

It was a coffin.

An Ellie-sized coffin. A few pieces of cloth had been tossed inside, and a lid was propped against its far side. Her heart began to thud against her ribs.

Her claustrophobia.

To cure her claustrophobia, Galen intended to put her in a coffin.

Devon stood behind it, watching her with sober eyes.

Ellie's feet stopped again—she couldn't help it. "You don't have a closet in this place?"

"If we're going to do it, we're going to do it right," Galen said. His arm slipped from her shoulders, but he kept holding her hand. "We have to go to the extreme end if you're going to remake your life. Half-hearted measures won't do."

Ellie ordered her face to conceal any terror. Whether it obeyed, she couldn't be sure. "What's the plan?"

"You get in, and you stay in until you're no longer afraid. Think of it, Nell. Right now you can't even stomach airplane restrooms. If you can handle a coffin, then you can do anything. You can handle getting a new job. You can handle saying goodbye to your husband. You can wake up every day knowing you're as strong as you'll ever need to be."

Ellie failed to see how conquering claustrophobia would solve every other problem in her life, but by now she knew not to bother arguing. Still, she wasn't really worried until Barry, wearing a malicious grin he didn't even try to hide, held up a nail gun, an oversized, rounded thing of hardened black and yellow plastic.

They weren't going to just close the lid and let her go the honor system route of staying inside the coffin. Galen intended to make *sure*. And once she was enclosed, helpless, then what? Send her down the river like Moses? Like Carlos?

Bury her?

"No," she said.

"This is necessary," Galen said.

"No it's not. I quit."

"Fear is a vested-interest emotion. You don't want to let go of your fear, because you don't want to change. That's all it is. But without change, you'll never get anywhere—"

"Fine, I won't. I'll stay a failure, and you can keep my fee. I don't care."

"But *I* care, Nell," he said, and his fingers had tightened like a vise. "I told you I wouldn't let you fail, and I won't."

"No!" Ellie pulled away. Or rather *tried* to pull away.

Tim, Andre, and Audrey each grabbed a limb and, as Ellie continued to struggle, lifted her bodily to set her down inside the coffin. It was not a comfortable process. She tried to wrestle her arms out of their grasp, but fingers dug into her flesh, and all at once her previously stonelike classmates burst into a churning, shuffling mass of agitation that murmured and spoke with various intensities. She heard one man laugh and two different women ask if this might not be truly necessary.

Once they closed the lid, she would be completely out of options. She would simply have to endure whatever tortures Galen felt she deserved.

They shoved Ellie, not gently, into the box, and she thumped her spine and the back of her head against the bottom. Her view of the ceiling became a mural of faces, some worried, some clearly excited, some curious to see if she would speak in tongues. Nubs of the rough plywood poked her legs and shoulders and bit into her scalp as they held her down, working hard, as she kicked and pushed. Even worse, they hadn't planned out their process and had put her in upside down, so that the slightly bowed-out section meant for shoulders actually fell at her calves.

Ellie knew she may have screamed. She definitely shouted. She told all assembled that this was stupid, illegal, and easily considered torture. That they shouldn't fall for Galen's crap, that they were idiots for falling for Galen's crap. In light of the situation, these comments likely did not help her case.

Ellie grabbed an open edge of the coffin with each hand and pulled herself upward like a pesky corpse, then refused to lie back even as they positioned the lid and the bare wood ground against her knuckles. She could glimpse Barry at the ready with the nail gun as he frowned at the inability of those around him to stuff her hands and feet back into the box. Each limb would be placed inside, but as soon as they let go to retract their own fingers, she'd pop it back out again. Ellie wasn't *about* to make it easy for them.

Then the lid slammed her in the forehead hard enough to force several splinters into her scalp, and without thinking, she freed one hand to put it to her face. That shifted her leverage enough that they shoved her feet in and lowered the lid edge onto her other hand. Ellie would have liked to think they weren't purposely intending to smash her fingers in order to make her let go, but that was what happened.

The last two faces she saw before the light disappeared belonged to Margot and Devon, both of whom were standing there without participating, faces somber and concerned. But not, apparently, concerned enough to do anything about it.

As soon as the lid was lined up with the coffin's edges, she heard thumps. When she pushed against it, nothing happened, save scraping the skin off her palms. Ellie felt pretty sure some of her classmates were sitting on it. Good thing it had been properly placed—if one side fell in under their weight, she could have instant and serious bodily damage. Then she heard a much louder thump, which rang in her little space and annoyed her eardrums. Barry had finally gotten to use the nail gun.

More thumps followed on the opposite side. Not taking any chances, Galen must have armed two people with nail guns. Ellie would be sealed shut too quickly to do anything about it, even if she could stop her classmates from using her as a bench.

Not that she didn't try. She spread her palms flat against the inside of the lid and shoved, steadily opening her elbows to exert as much pressure as possible. When this produced nothing, not even the slightest shift, she gave in to her rage.

Heedless of her splinters and scrapes, Ellie pounded the lid with both fists. She couldn't get a lot of momentum going, as she swung her clenched hands through maybe twelve inches of space minus what her shoulders took up, so this effort had no more impact than pressing had. But it relieved a small amount of frustration.

A very small amount.

Barry wasn't much of a shot with the nail gun, because one nail, then another, missed the side wall by at least a half inch and poked through into her little space. But too many made it into the wood, securing the lid all too well.

The thumps stopped, and the sudden quiet silenced her. Nails stopped turning her container into an iron maiden. Without a thought, she kicked and banged. She had no more room for kicking than she did for hitting, and it produced the same effect: none. At first, she demanded to be released, but this quickly devolved into simple wails of animal fury.

Ellie wondered how long she should keep that up. She wondered how long she *could* keep it up.

In movies people in coffins—when they were still alive— always worried about their oxygen supply becoming depleted. But Ellie wasn't in a real coffin; she was inside a hastily built stage prop, and a sliver of light showed from at least three seams. Suffocation would not be a danger.

Ellie let her kicks slow. If she rolled over, perhaps she could turn the whole thing on its side, though the not perfectly rectangular shape might make that harder and the result questionable. She had the wild image of rolling herself down a staircase so that the box broke apart—though her skull might break as well, and in any case, there were only three steps outside the distant door, which she'd never fit through.

Her movements slowed, and now Ellie noticed the smell. The rags or cloths in the box were tangled around her feet. Perhaps they were meant to cushion her head, but her head had wound up at the wrong end. As if he'd pulled them from a corner of the barn or a supply closet, the cloths had sort of a musty, dusty smell, that stale smell that cloth got when it rested too long in one place.

Exactly as the old dresses and fur-edged coats in one's grandmother's closet might smell.

He had even thought of that.

Ellie gave up. She stopped moving, stopped yelling, and waited.

What if they *did* throw her in the river? What if they *did* bury her?

That, Ellie believed, she would not be able to handle. That would be truly terrifying, not to mention potentially, oh, *fatal*. That would really scare her.

Because so far Ellie was not really scared. Angry, yes, but not scared.

Because she was not really claustrophobic.

Chapter 24

The story Ellie had told about her grandmother's closet was true in essence. She and her cousins *had* played in it and occasionally had locked each other inside (until the one outside got bored), but never as a frightening thing. The closet was a delicious feast of the senses, a delight of touch and smell awakened in the absence of sight, a place to confide secrets and whisper plans.

Ellie had invented her terror, knowing a damn sight better than to tell Galen any *real* fear of hers. It had seemed a good bet that some experience like this could be lurking up the road in the name of "therapy." Ellie might not be an expert in cults, but the research done for an earlier undercover job had warned her that gathering information about a convert to be used against them later on was a standard cult technique.

Of course, it was also a standard *therapy* technique—examining your childhood traumas and working through them. The possibility remained that Galen was, in a perhaps misguided way, trying to help her.

She was not yet sure of that.

But Ellie had decided one thing: if she wanted to get close enough for Devon to confide in her, Ellie had to get with the program. She had to stop arguing, stop resisting. She had to become the damn poster child for the success of Today's Enlightenment.

And she had to make it convincing.

One more series of pounds and kicks hurt her toes and scraped the edges of her fists. One fist felt wet; the splinters must have drawn blood. She shouted, "Let me out!" as loudly and piteously as she could.

Galen's voice, close, came through a gap in the wood. "Stop and think, Nell. No one is hurting you but you. You're creating your own pain."

"I can't breathe," she moaned, though she could.

"Yes you can. It's not airtight. It's just a box, Nell. Nothing is hurting you."

Except the splinters and the bruises on her arms, where his goons had grabbed her, and the scrape on her head, where a piece of plywood had slammed into it, but yes, other than that, she was perfectly comfortable nail-gunned into a coffin.

"It's only your thoughts that are harming you. It's your thoughts that are keeping you locked into your fears like a jail cell. It's a silly childhood experience that is curtailing your adult life. Do you want to keep giving it that power?"

His voice mesmerized with its soothing, steady cadence. And if Ellie really were claustrophobic, everything he said would make perfect sense. She stayed still and listened, wondering how long to wait before capitulating, and what she could say to make him, all of them, believe it.

"Tell me, Nell, do you want to give the memory of your cousin's betrayal power over you?"

Again, she noted, he rephrased one's experience in words designed to turn that one against family and friends. "No."

"Do you want to give your ex-husband power over you?"
Get the gist. Get with the program. "No."

"Do you want to give your absentee father power over you?"

"No."

"Do you want to give your cousin power over you?"

She had got the rhythm now and made her answer louder. "No!"

"Who gave them that power in the first place, Nell?"

"I did."

"Should we let you out now?"

Was this a trick question?

"Should we let you out?"

"Okay." Ellie figured that was neutral enough to show her command of her fear. Sounding terrified or full of false bravado might extend her stay in the pine box.

"Are you ready?"

Ready for *what*? Again, she tried to stay noncommittal. "I think so. Yes."

A thump sounded near her feet, and then another, and then came the ringing sound of metal striking metal. Then the screeching cry of pieces of wood being pulled apart as they began to remove the lid with a pry bar. Ellie sucked in a huge breath of oxygen and relief. It was all very well to tell herself she wasn't *really* afraid, but still, you couldn't get much more helpless than when nailed inside a box. She thanked her lucky stars that maybe Galen had thought burying the thing would be too much work.

The sliver of light as the lid began to lift seemed like a tangible lifeline she could grab with both hands, and she tried. That only got her another bump on the head, so she counseled herself in patience and stayed supine until the man with the pry bar had completed the task and her classmates had set the lid aside.

Galen himself held out his hand. She gave him hers and played the part of Venus rising from the sea, resurrected from her tomb. Her classmates burst into spontaneous applause, which should have seemed sweet. Audrey appeared transfixed.

Devon watched her with a vague concern, Margot with a vague curiosity, and Ellie couldn't help a surge of resentment at the woman's inaction after Ellie had both soaked and embarrassed herself to help her. But then Margot *hadn't* drowned and thus could assume Ellie wouldn't be harmed either.

Barry seemed a bit disappointed and glanced at her crotch. Ellie wondered if Galen had encouraged her to change into fresh clothes so that if she *did* pee her pants, it would be more noticeable.

Ellie stepped out of her box, visibly ready to be a new person.

"You see now that fears are illogical, boogeymen invented by others to keep us in our place, and by ourselves to keep from having to change and grow," Galen said.

He waited, and she realized that it hadn't been a rhetorical question. "Yes. Yes, I do."

He let go of her hand and made a sweeping gesture around the group. "This is for all of you. You're trapped inside boxes of your own making, and you don't have to be. You can break out of them at any time."

Technically, Ellie hadn't had that option, since he'd neglected to drop a pry bar inside the coffin along with the musty cloths, but she didn't interrupt.

"Your fears and your habits and your obligations and your beliefs are your coffins, and despite what you think, you can leave them behind. You can reduce them to ash. Would you like to reduce your coffin to ash, Nell?"

"Um, sure." Again, she examined the question for road mines. "Yes."

"Then pick it up. Pick it up," he said, first to her and then to the group.

Ellie grabbed a side and tried to pull, but even quarter-inch plywood was heavy in that size. A few classmates joined in, and in an instant, they had hoisted the thing up to their shoulders, easily bearing the empty box. The wood chewed Ellie's raw palms anew with its tiny rough splinters.

The last few people picked up the lid, and Galen led their little procession out the double doors and up the center drive of the camp. The day had slid into late afternoon, and with the sun sinking toward the other side of the mountain, the valley lay in partial shadow. The air felt cool on her fevered skin.

They followed Galen toward the river and then to the left, to the side of the office where a patch of scorched earth and charred branches awaited fresh fuel. Two chickens milled about, still somehow fascinated by the ashes. Obviously, the statement about burning their psychological coffins had not been figurative.

They set the coffin in the approximate center of the fire area, over the scorched earth and the remains of burnt wood. Two of the larger guys turned it over and jumped on the long edges until the pieces broke apart. Galen had the rest gather sticks and twigs from under the trees near the river for kindling. A stump off to the side had a small hatchet protruding from it, and Barry took that to the plywood for a bit before giving up. He gave Ellie a smile and offered it to her, as if it might bring further catharsis, but Ellie could only remember his enthusiasm with the nail gun, and her fingers itched to bury that hatchet in his skull. Her expression must have given her away because Barry's eyes widened, and he hastened away to stow the weapon somewhere far from her reach.

Devon had gone into the office and returned with a bottle of lighter fluid, which she sprinkled at random over the pieces of caved-in coffin and kindling. Then she gave Ellie a pack of matches and told her to do the honors.

With a healthy respect for fire and how careless work with lighter fluid could cost one in eyebrows and fingertips, Ellie tossed three matches before one caught, the liquid igniting and infecting the wood with flame. She thought the fire might fizzle out as soon as it used all the fluid, but the plywood burned better than expected.

Ellie had not seen Angela throughout this event, but now the young woman showed up with a bag of marshmallows. Clearly, this had been planned, since Galen did not look surprised, nor did he ask for an explanation. The sweet kid presented the bag to him with a face aglow and spoke with enthusiasm and animation. Across the fire from them, Ellie couldn't hear what either of them said, but Galen's lack of either enthusiasm or animation for Angela or her words or her marshmallows caused those feelings to be wiped from her face as if swept with an eraser. He didn't seem at all angry, yet Angela recoiled as if she'd been struck. She turned and walked back to the office, stumbling from either the terrain or her emotions.

Only five or six feet away, Devon had also watched this, frowning. Ellie couldn't guess if she was mad at Galen for his treatment of Angela or at Angela for her obvious fawning over Galen. Maybe both. Maybe she really hated marshmallows.

But Galen turned to his clients with a huge grin and told them to find "a good stick" to roast the candies. In her new, converted mode, Ellie dutifully poked around in the weeds until she found a somewhat straight twig that would suffice. She broke off the end to create a sharp point and returned to the fire.

"How are you feeling? Do you feel great?" Audrey asked,

with such happy glee that she bounced on her toes. She even hugged Ellie, her wiry arms crushing Ellie's shoulders, her heart beating firmly against her ribs. She held Ellie for too long, her body warm. Or feverish.

"Yes, really good." Meaning: It did feel *terrific* to be out of that stupid box. Ellie watched it burn with satisfaction.

Two beetles dashed from the conflagration, one skimming over the toe of her shoe, and she saw why the chickens hung around. They pounced on the fleeing arthropods.

As the other clients searched for sticks and dug in the bag for marshmallows, Margot stood next to her with one already nicely browning. She gave Ellie a friendly smirk but said nothing.

Ellie took the opportunity to give her fellow novitiate a quick but deep gaze. "One hang-up-laden student to another, how are you doing?" Subtext: *No hard feelings*.

Margot stared into the flames. "Fine."

"Really?"

Smoke twirled into the air, and the shifting winds threw some in their faces. She coughed and said, "I'm not sure. I'm still . . ."

"Assimilating? Me too. I think it's going to take a while to process."

The white fluff at the end of her stick burned in a bright flame, but Margot didn't seem to notice. "Part of me wants to strangle everyone here, starting with the beloved guru himself. But part of me thinks, I survived that. I did it. The world does look a little different now. Maybe I'm overdue to tell a bunch of people I know to go . . . well, go. Like I'm a computer and I've hit RESTART."

A breakthrough—and other than her story for the class, the most words Ellie had heard from her at one time. Perhaps she'd become an ally, after all. "Huh," Ellie said aloud.

"I kinda feel the same. Maybe I've learned something really valuable. But maybe I'm just telling myself that to make up for the fact that I let a bunch of people lock me in a box."

"Yeah. Like that." She studied her marshmallow, now incinerated beyond hope. "Damn, I'm going to have to start over."

Margot walked off to claim another from the dwindling supply.

The coffin continued to burn with purpose. Uninterested in marshmallows without chocolate on them, Ellie used her stick to poke at the ground beneath the edges of the fire. It gave her a reason to avoid eye contact, as she was not quite ready to discuss her entombment with the very people who had done the entombing.

Something glittered underneath the burning twigs. A flat yellow metal disk about the size of a quarter, in the roughly triangular shape of a guitar pick. Ellie crouched for a better look, which only got her a gust of smoke in the face. When the wind shifted again, she scraped the disk free and let it cool against the dirt before picking it up.

The shape of a guitar pick, but too thick to use as such. Like most teenagers, Ellie had dabbled. Unlike most teenagers, she had dabbled on a very basic acoustic guitar that Aunt Katey had picked up at a garage sale for five dollars, hoping at least one of her two daughters would become a musical sensation. After competing to see who could produce the most obnoxious sounds, neither of her cousins had ever touched it again.

Ellie rubbed the object clean with the inside edge of her pants leg, revealing a silver framework inset with cloisonné. The colors on half its face had blistered into a distorted jumble, but the design had originally been of some sort of dragon or maybe a lion. She flipped the item over, observed the other side.

"Nell!" Audrey stood nearby, calling her name for, apparently, not the first time. "Ellen! Tell us what you've learned."

Ellie straightened up, dropped the trinket in her pocket, and blinked the smoke out of her eyes. "Learned?"

"From your experience. You pushed through your fears! Now they will have no power over you ever again!" Audrey waited expectantly. So did all the other classmates, holding their sticks over the dying fire—everyone except for the two big guys, who were quietly confabbing off to the side. Galen and Devon watched her as well.

"Learned?" *Poster child*, Ellie reminded herself, *poster child for success*. "I learned that fear is all in your head, and you can conquer any of them if you believe you can. I know now that all my geeking out over the recent knocks I've taken is just that—geeking out. My future won't be anything I can't handle, ever. I can make my own circumstances."

Audrey literally clapped her hands, and Barry beamed behind her. Maybe Ellie's hatchet impulse had been unfair; maybe he honestly rejoiced at her progress. Surely Audrey seemed to feel genuine happiness for her. Another classmate exhaled with patent relief, and most of the remaining clients smiled and nodded.

Not so successful that you don't need them, though. "Of course, that doesn't mean I have any *idea* what to do next! I still have to figure out what I want my life to be."

That drew even more vigorous smiles and nods.

"To that end," Galen said, "time to get back to work on yourselves. Celebration time is over. And we're out of marshmallows."

Assorted chuckling, and they moved back to the main walkways. No one seemed particularly concerned about the fire and the last bits of burning coffin, but unless the wind really picked up, the weeds should be safe. At least Ellie hoped so. Obviously, many campfires had been held there without incinerating the place.

They went in to dinner, yet more pasta with a bland tomato sauce and limp salad. Ellie wondered if these choices were made to be cheap or if the cooks were working off a sanction and noodles represented the extent of their repertoire. No one complained, however. Her classmates were either too hungry or had eaten too many toasted marshmallows and weren't hungry at all.

Ellie wasn't, either, but for different reasons.

Chapter 25

That evening's class dwelled on ethics. Ethics, Devon explained—she and Angela handled the lecture, Galen having disappeared before dinner—meant living with honesty and consistency. They should treat everyone around them the same, with the same expectations and the same responses.

True that, Ellie thought. Provided one left room for kindness.

To live in and be 100 percent effective in the present, they had to divorce themselves entirely from blame, lies, and justifications. Those were the ways one manipulated oneself into believing what one wanted to believe instead of what was real.

Angela passed out worksheets so each client could write down someone they had blamed and for what, a lie or exaggeration they had told and why, and a behavior that they practiced that they knew was unhealthy but didn't want to change.

Listing someone to blame was easy for Ellie. Her ex-husband. For the lie, she wrote of deducting a haircut as a business expense, since it had been just before doing a series of training lectures for new staff. No one in the class would know that both the job and the salon bill had never existed, and her answer filled in the blank spot on the worksheet. Maybe—*maybe*—some of Galen's techniques were legit, but that didn't mean she felt ready to give them any real piece of her life.

As before, they were prompted to read their answers out loud. Devon asked Angela to set an example, and though the young woman didn't seem too happy with the idea, she dutifully produced a ready smile. "I blame my parents," she read aloud, her tone wavering with each word, "for my complete lack of self-esteem. I lied when I told Galen I had nowhere else to go. I kind of do, but I wanted to stay here."

"Manipulation," Devon said, "is always the goal of lies. That seems like a no-brainer, but if you remind yourself of that when you're tempted to tell one, you'll see how falsity leads you into a death spiral." She paced at the front of the room, languidly stepping back and forth, reminding Ellie of a lioness on a very hot day. Their chairs were still in a circle, making it difficult to walk toward the back. Devon stopped to drape one loose hand on Angela's shoulder. "Go on."

"My persistent behavior is . . ."

Ellie expected her to say, "Chasing unavailable men," since they were being so honest. But she didn't.

"I use my weakness as an excuse to fail at my goals."

"Such as?" Devon prompted.

"I . . . I didn't get my reports written up, because, well, because I didn't, but I said that I didn't, because I had to stack boxes in the publishing office until midnight. I also didn't get the grocery list written, because I spent too much time on my hair—"

These sounded like very venial sins to Ellie, though, on the other hand, did they have Angela to blame for all the carbs at mealtime?

Devon cut her off with a pat on the shoulder. "We have to

forgive each other for failure. But forgiveness with integrity means the punishment is fitting, appropriate, and consistent."

Punishment? For a late report?

"You're frowning, Evelyn. What are you confused about?"

"I'm not confused. It's just . . . 'punishment' sounds so condescending. Like treating people like children."

"Because we *act* like children," Devon insisted. "That's the point. The attitudes and habits and assumptions we formed as children are still controlling us every day, even though we lacked knowledge and perspective when we formed them. But fine, call it consequences instead of punishment. Every action triggers a reaction, right?"

Ellie agreed half-heartedly.

"Good." Devon began pacing again, as if energized by her progress. "We need to put our motivation front and center and discourage procrastination. Nothing keeps us moving forward like a knife at our back."

That sounded a bit harsh . . . though, again, true.

Next, a young man blamed his brother for wrecking his motorcycle. The brother had borrowed it without permission and gotten in an accident. The brother had been thrown clear onto the grass, with only scratches and bruises to show for it, but the bike had been totaled. Forgiveness, Devon and the class decided for the young man, included taking precautions, such as never letting his brother near his possessions again and, in fact, keeping contact with such an irresponsible remora to a minimum.

Solutions or other plans never seemed to involve family or friends. No matter the issue, they were mentioned only as something to avoid, like Margot's sister or her ex and Barry's mother, who had suggested that he try a different company. Ellie would have thought, if this were some sort of twelve-step program to a better person, that making peace with loved ones would be part of the process. Forgiving past grievances, apologizing for past mistakes, that sort of thing. But instead, the focus stayed, with laser-beam intensity, on themselves.

Perhaps that was the point of taking full responsibility, and perhaps it was an acknowledgment that there could be quite valid reasons for cutting someone out of your life, but Ellie remembered again that isolation was the number one priority of any cultlike group. The last thing they wanted was one's mother or best friend pointing out that that group of people you had joined sounded kinda crazy.

Every time Ellie began to think Galen and his group might actually be on to a way to help people, a detail like this gave her pause. Nothing, *nothing*, not all the plywood coffins or mountain ranges in the world, would keep her from her aunts, uncles, cousins, dog, or the Locard.

All very well, but Ellie needed a plan. So while Audrey spoke of telling a fiancé she was a virgin, Ellie figured out what she would do as soon as the lights went out.

By the end of the day, Rachael had nearly talked herself into believing that her concerns about the business records had simply resulted from a late-night flight of overactive imagination and that she shouldn't have bothered Desiree with it. She barely knew the woman, really. Desiree had always been brilliant and kind and reliable, without exhibiting any real openness. Whatever she had gone through to reach and establish herself in the United States, whatever or whomever she had had to leave behind, she didn't say, and she didn't encourage Rachael to ask. If Desiree needed to keep people at arm's length for her own reasons, Rachael would not argue with that, even if it precluded any deep friendship.

But she didn't call the woman and tell her to forget the whole thing.

Besides, Rachael had been neatly distracted with class rosters for the following week's training sessions, organizing the notoriously absent-minded ballistics instructor, finishing the next year's budget proposal, setting up the next stage in her own research project to determine the signs of skeletal remains exposed to copper pipe, and trying to get Ellie on the phone. Honestly, how could any place on the planet not have cell service in this day and age? And was that all it was, the distance from cell towers or mountains blocking the signal? Or could there be a more worrisome reason?

On cue, her phone rang. Not Ellie but Desiree, who said she had completed her examination. Rachael trotted upstairs to the woman's office with unseemly haste.

Agnes, their digital forensics whiz, sat in one of the guest chairs. The file box from Danton's closet rested on the edge of Desiree's desk, which had been cleared of its previous flurry of work, and that flurry was replaced with small, perfectly spaced stacks of papers. This frightened Rachael. Such effort seemed to indicate bad news, the organized rationality needed to convince a family member of a very uncomfortable truth.

"I did need Agnes's help," Desiree began without preamble. "As we had thought, your sister kept nearly all her records electronically. She had her receipts, client forms, invoices, and the like in folders by date and client name."

"Oh," Rachael said, taking a seat. Exactly what they had suspected. The corset squeezing her lungs loosened a few laces. "And the bank statements? The ledger?"

"They are consistent with each other."

"And there's nothing that appears . . . unbusinesslike?" Rachael asked, feeling silly about her wording.

"There is nothing to indicate that your sister's income was not legitimate."

Rachael's shoulders relaxed for the first time in days, something she hadn't noticed until now.

Then Desiree ruined it by continuing. "Simply looking at the ledger and statements will not tell you whether the activity is legitimate or not."

Rachael stopped relaxing.

"One major indication is if personal and business funds are comingled. That is a red flag."

"And are they?"

"No. Isis charged her clients a flat eight percent of the party's overall costs. Deposits to her bank accounts varied but were not unusually large. She most likely collected some as cash and deposited the rest."

"Okay."

"A lot of cash," Desiree added. "And the party on the concert date is still a mystery."

Agnes said, "Billy did play the concert. There's videos of it all over YouTube. Of course, there's nothing to say he had to *be* at this party at his house."

"Okay," Rachael said.

"But that's not the problem," Agnes went on.

The laces began to tug.

Desiree spoke gently, her delicate accent a contrast to Agnes's blunt statements. "We examined each vendor. Monteleone Catering. Starling Music and More. Motown Bakery. And so on." She paused.

Agnes forged ahead. "They're fake."

Somehow Rachael kept breathing even as her brain stumbled. *"What?"*

"They don't exist. I combed the internet, state business databases, court filings. Nothing. Take Billy's party. Twist of Lime Entertainment Staffing billed twenty thousand for rented bartenders. The closest thing to that name I could find was a Twist of Fate Art Gallery on M Street." Rachael opened her mouth, but Agnes anticipated the objections. "Maybe they're out of business. Maybe they're a new business and records haven't caught up even yet, or they didn't last long enough to *be* listed. Maybe they're subsidiaries of larger concerns. But *all* of them?"

Rachael clung to strands of hope. "Isis's best friend in grade school was Marika Monteleone. Maybe it's a small family venture, a boutique? Not even a formal business?"

Agnes shot that down. "The address is fake too. All the addresses are wrong. Starling Music is supposed to be at 3300 Forestville Road, but that's actually a convenience store and has been for the past ten years. Motown Bakery is at 25 Parrish Lane in Mitchellville, but addresses there are five digits."

They'd had a dog named Motown, Rachael remembered and wanted to cry.

"Most of the clients don't exist either," Desiree went on, her voice gentle. "The names, the home addresses cannot be found. Some can—a senator, an assistant to the minority whip, a professor at George Washington U. They are real people."

Agnes said, "But six of them, out of eighteen, were traveling or doing something else on the day of their supposed event, according to their social media. Perhaps the rest really were having a gender reveal party on a Thursday night or whatever, but we can't tell. Then there's the invoices and forms themselves. I examined the metadata. Isis ran this business"—here Rachael could hear the slight hesitation, the unspoken quotes around the word "business"—"for almost five years. Invoices during the first two or so were actual scans of pieces of paper. By five years, they weren't scans but the original documents, in Word or Excel. All the metadata is there. They were created once, saved, and never modified. The fonts became uniform. The Client Needs form with details like what kind of flowers the bride wants or if the quinceañera girl has any food allergies, stayed identical for each file over the past two years."

Rachael didn't recognize her own voice, too flat, too lifeless. "She got lazy."

"At first, she created the paperwork and scanned it. As time went by without audits or questions or interest, she cut and pasted and saved. If the IRS got curious, she could produce records."

"On paper," Desiree said, "Elite Events was a small business, its forms were filed on time, and its taxes paid. The IRS rarely audits concerns like that."

Rachael's insides no longer felt tight. They had relaxed from a different kind of relief, one born of hopelessness. Desiree had asked her if she really wanted to know, and now she did. A can of worms had been opened, and the worms would now spread as far and wide as they could crawl, but she could not stop that. All she could do was protect her mother and Danton from the scourge.

"There doesn't seem to be a real party-planning business," Desiree said, stating the obvious in a deeply empathetic voice. "But we can't tell you where her money *did* come from."

"I can make a guess," Rachael said.

Chapter 26

"Work" that night entailed two hours in the publishing office and then another hour processing vegetables by cutting green beans and shelling peas. Ellie kind of liked shelling the peas, enjoying the feel of the crisp pods bursting open to reveal the round green things full of living cells, even as the humans all lingered on the edge of flat-out exhaustion. Talk stayed minimal; no one had the energy.

Finally, at midnight, they were allowed to turn in.

The temperature had fallen into the forties. But on the plus side, her phone teased her with occasional flashes of life. Could it have survived its immersion in the river? Ellie tried to calculate exactly how long her back pocket had been underwater and not just damp. As her classmates/bunkmates showered and got into bed with deep sighs, Ellie pulled on her coat and gathered her scarf and gloves as well. Lastly, she retrieved some cash and a mini-flashlight from the side pocket of her pack, but the flash wouldn't turn on. She had loaded it with brand-new batteries, but now the glass was splintered and the bulb was dead. The flight must have been rougher than she'd noticed.

Ellie had no illusions about how dark the desert would be once she was away from the lights of the ranch, but she'd already checked the moon—nearly full—and that should at least keep her from falling off the road. She wouldn't try the hike over the mountain to the town of Topaz. Even if she stuck to the cleared, wide path under the power lines, it seemed foolhardy, though her stomach perked up at the thought of nachos or fresh fruit or whatever that bastion of civilization had to offer. No, Ellie planned simply to walk until she reached a signal. That might *be* all the way to the town, hence the cash. Just in case. Even a vending machine would be welcome at this point.

She slipped out the door with a single glance behind her. Her classmates took no notice. With luck, they would think she went out for a smoke or some such vice and would fall asleep before they realized she had never come back. Assuming they'd even care.

Ellie crunched over the gravel to the drive, checking the ranch for signs of activity, anyone prowling, checking faces, remembering names. If anyone caught her, she could say . . . well, the truth. They couldn't *stop* her.

Though they had managed to do so for roughly thirty-six hours so far, a voice in her head pointed out.

Had it really been only that long? Ellie thought back. *Yesterday I arrived, joined my class, met Devon, got a tour, did yoga, had dinner, talked about fears, worked in the publishing office, and tried, unsuccessfully, to find a cell phone signal by walking around the ranch in the dark. Today I worked on the new building, confessed to sins and crimes in class, had lunch, hoisted Barry, drowned Margot, met Mrs. Coleman, was shut in a coffin, had dinner, talked about ethics, shelled peas. Yep, thirty-six hours.*

Lights in the gym distracted her. It hadn't been lit during her midnight ramble the evening before. She wondered if

Galen was working in there, devising new tortures—sorry, *challenges*—for her fellow classmates. Was she truly in the clear, or did they each have to do more than one challenge? Would she have to be strapped into Barry's harness or give a speech to an assembly to combat the other two fears she'd listed? No problem if so, because she'd lied about them too.

Ellie detoured, drawn by the portent of the glowing gym windows. *Forewarned is forearmed.*

She tried to make her footsteps light as she approached— no easy task on gravel. Since each building sat on a raised platform, the windows were too high for her to peek inside. She climbed three steps, where the door's glass revealed the empty but well-lit room and Angela, alone.

Barry's harness still dangled from its rope and pulley, and Angela was struggling with the carabiner that secured it. She had probably been assigned this cleanup task, to neaten up the place for the next day. Had anyone else mentioned a fear of heights? Ellie thought a woman had—perhaps Audrey or the girl with the maraschino-red hair.

Angela freed the harness and let it slip to the floor, the thick, empty carabiner swinging free. Then she took the other end of the rope and dragged it over to the broken treadmill. Ellie meant to turn away, leave her to her task and get on with her own, but couldn't take her gaze from that nylon snake twining around the young woman's ankles. Angela looped the loose end around the front post of the treadmill, under the monitor and handrails. She pulled and adjusted the rope until both lengths of it descending from the pulley appeared taut and the carabiner swayed gently through its arc about seven feet off the floor. She tied several knots to secure the anchored end.

This seemed odd.

Angela picked up the weight bench, staggering a bit with its bulk, then seemed to check and rethink the distance to the harness. She set the bench back down with a thud and moved to the northwest corner of the room, out of Ellie's sight. She reappeared a moment later, carrying a folding chair.

Ellie did not like this.

Stepping onto the chair, Angela pulled the rope through the carabiner, forming a loop. An easily cinched loop.

I do not like this. Ellie's body reacted before her brain caught up, and she turned the latch to open the door and spilled inside.

"Angela!"

Angela fell off the chair, overturning it, and its clattering protest echoed through the room. But she hadn't yet put the rope around her neck, and used it now to regain her balance over shaky feet. Her face had never seemed paler, the chalky cast of the already dead, or her eyes larger.

"What are you doing?" Ellie demanded, unable to keep the harshness from her voice.

"I . . . I—"

Ellie reached her before she even figured out what to say. *Calm. Sound calm. Calm and soothing.* "Angela. What are you doing?"

The young woman stared at Ellie. Then her face screwed up like a baby's and disintegrated into sobs. She sank to the floor in a puddle, crying wretchedly into both hands. Ellie sank, as well, and stretched one arm around her. Ellie had worked around people under great stress, but suicide attempts were a different category altogether.

After the racking sobs had finally mutated into a snuffling misery, Ellie asked what was going on.

"I can't do it!"

"Do what?"

"*Anything.*"

Good thing they had all night. "Angela. What do you mean? What can't you do?"

"*Anything.* I'm terrible at *everything.* I haven't fixed any of my failings. Galen says I'm making him sick."

"Well, that's a mean thing to say."

"No, *literally* sick. Like he has been having stomach pains because of my negativity."

"Hold on. Don't move." Ellie rubbed her shoulders and then made a very quick trip to the tiny kitchenette at the end of the large room. She checked cabinets until she found a towel—or maybe a rag, though she couldn't be sure, but it smelled clean enough—and doused it with water. All that took less than sixty seconds, and yet she nearly ran back to Angela in the center of the floor, not wanting to turn her back on her for even that short time.

Ellie plopped down next to her and held the cold, wet cloth to Angela's face. The young woman sighed.

"Honey," Ellie said, "people's attitudes can't make other people sick. Unhappy, maybe, but not physically sick."

"Yes they can." Angela shook her head, clearly disappointed but not surprised by Ellie's lack of faith. "That's why we have to avoid remoras, because they'll drag us down into their habits and failures every chance they get, so they won't be lonely. But that's just it!" The agitation had ebbed, but now it flowed anew. She rubbed the wooden beads around her wrist as if they were talismans. "I keep doing everything wrong! *I'm* the remora, and I'm dragging Galen down."

Ellie shifted her weight on the unforgiving floor. The gym had few seating options—the weight bench, some folding chairs, bitter and uncaring sentries. A battered futon had been pushed into one corner, but Ellie didn't want to break Angela's confessional mood by suggesting they move. She patted the young woman's back and rethought her approach. She would not win a direct argument here. "Honey, I'm new here. I don't quite understand a lot of things, so you need to spell it out for me, because you are undoubtedly the most enthusiastic person I've met at this ranch. What *exactly* did you do wrong?"

She pushed tear-dampened hair out of her face. "Okay. I ate some of the noodles at dinner, and I was supposed to eat only salad. I yawned during class this morning."

Ellie badly wanted to interrupt with, "Wait, wait, wait," but she bit her tongue between her teeth. If she pooh-poohed Angela's agony, the young woman would stop talking altogether. . . . Ellie had learned at least that much from interrogations over the years. If the subject was talking, let them talk.

"Nobody at home sent me more money. I tried to stay at the bonfire, when I was supposed to stay away from him for a while to quench my obsession with attention. I got the mail, when I know that's Devon's job, but I forgot because I was trying too hard to get approval. I forget things all the time, when I'm supposed to be able to remember *everything*."

She began to squeak again as she spoke, so Ellie interrupted the crescendo. "I'm still trying to catch up here. Why are you supposed to eat only salad?"

Angela blinked, as if she'd already forgotten she'd said it. Either that or she was wondering why Ellie couldn't figure out such an obvious answer. "Because I weigh too much."

"You? You're a perfectly normal-sized girl! You don't have an extra pound on you."

"I have three. And there's too much fat here, and here." She pinched the extra skin on her tiny belly and taut thighs.

Ellie chewed her lip, having also learned never to argue about diet with a female. "Okay, I'd like to know who told you that, but let's go on. What about yawning in class? We *all* yawned in class. Days here are pretty long. I've been here less than two, and I'm already exhausted."

"But you're a new group. You haven't learned all Galen's insights yet. He knows each of us better than we know ourselves, and can teach us how to know, too, if we let him."

This stymied Ellie, or perhaps she was more worn out than she realized. "Uh—"

"You'll learn in the later classes that if we focus on our desires, our goals, and get in the habit of feeling enthusiastic and energized about them, we can develop a trigger, a word or sound that will bring back that energy and enthusiasm whenever we want. So our energy can never flag unless we want it to."

"As handy as that would be, we're still human beings. And physical bodies need food and rest and maintenance."

"Not really. Most of that is psychological. So I shouldn't be tired ever . . . but I'm tired *all the time*."

"So the people in the upper classes, the ones who have taken more lessons, they don't ever sleep?"

"Less and less."

Ellie tried to keep the disbelief from showing. Every minute she kept Angela talking was another away from the noose. But they couldn't talk forever. Would the young woman rush right back into its arms, or find some other method, the moment they parted? Should Ellie tell someone? She didn't know if Angela had a friend anywhere in the camp. Galen would be the obvious choice, but it seemed equally obvious that he'd only make her insecurities worse. "I see them going to bed about the same time as we do. Their lights are out now." Ellie jerked her chin toward the windows.

Angela ignored this. "If my dad would only send me some more money, that might make it okay."

"How so?"

"Money is a representation of effort, so it would be another way to show how hard I'm trying. Giving is a form of trust, and money is given. So without it, my progress is stuck, and I can't demonstrate trust."

Ellie's head felt as if someone had stuffed it with cotton. Maybe boiling weeks of instruction down to a few sentences simply couldn't be done with any coherence. And maybe someone had fed this young woman a trough of hogwash. Ellie chose her next words carefully, aware that each could go off like a grenade.

"Tell me about the bonfire."

That was all she needed to say. Angela's eyes swam and overflowed again.

"I can't help it," she wailed into a wad of paper towels. "I love him."

Ellie didn't bother to ask who "him" might be.

"He's the most amazing man I've ever met! I knew the minute I saw him on the quad that he was going to change my life. I'd been so boxed into my life at home that I felt suffocated every day, like I was swirling down a drain and no one ever noticed. Then Galen was there and told me that I could help to change other people's worlds, so I came here. But first, I have to change my own, and I *can't*."

Hopeless wail.

"Because you yawned?"

The wrong thing to say. *Don't shut her down.* But Angela writhed, in too much agony to care. "He said I have to stay away from him unless he calls me until I learn to stop being so *lazy*. I'm supposed to be stretching myself, and instead of inventing my own energy, I'm hanging on to him and sucking all his away. I haven't gotten any closer to being a resulter. I'm more of a remora than ever!"

Find a path through this tangled lexicon, Ellie told herself. "Let's step away from the terminology for a little while. As I said, I just got here, so I don't know a lot of the terms. But what is it you actually want to *do*?"

With a loud sniff, the young woman paused for thought. Angela had been in the trees for so long, she'd forgotten why she had entered the forest in the first place. "I want to stop living other people's lives for them while ignoring my own. I want to . . . do something to help people. I thought maybe

I'd work with children, like be a gym teacher or maybe a nurse in an elementary school. And I'd like to get married and have my own house and children." She said this last part quietly, perhaps trying to picture fitting that life into this world.

"And why is that so impossible?" Ellie asked.

Angela didn't answer.

So Ellie did. "Because there's no room for your own job and your own house and your own children on Galen's ranch. Maybe that just tells you that it's time to go."

"But I don't *want* anyone else. I want Galen!"

"Then why don't you go home for a while? Just a visit. That will make him realize how important you are to him." Ellie didn't believe this, but time away from this place could reorient Angela to the real world, break the mass hypnosis.

"I can't go home. I can't bear the thought of being away from him."

Ellie hugged her again, as a way of easing into her next question. "Have you slept together?"

A *sniff* and a shy nod. "Yes. But it was only to help me work on my body issues. If I can't trust someone else with my body, then I won't be able to trust myself."

Ellie bit the inside of her mouth.

"But he doesn't love me!" She blew her nose into the sodden towel. "It was only three times. And only to help me."

Sure it was.

"I am supposed to leave all the conventional obsessions about sex and flesh behind with my other old habits . . . but I couldn't help it. He's all I think about. But Devon is the right one for him. She's strong, like him. And you know what? We're the same age practically! But she's so much more mature than I am. She's a real resulter."

"Angela, listen to me. Those are just catchphrases. Galen is pushing people's minds around and saying it's therapy, from someone with no training, degree, or license."

"Oh, but he does! He went to MIT! He . . . he's studied, like . . ." The words faded into a sniff. Two tears continued to travel down one cheek, marking their territory.

It was not really possible to talk someone down from love-sickness, but Ellie had had some experience with her cousins and even an aunt. Applied logic usually got them over the worst of it until the pain faded, though their dramas had never been this extreme. Ellie felt like *she* was the one providing therapy without a license, training, or the slightest clue.

But she had to do something to keep Angela away from that noose.

Picking her way with caution, Ellie went on. "Some things disturb me. First of all, don't ever—*ever*—let anyone tell you they know you better than you know yourself. Second, when they begin by telling you you're special and wonderful and then begin to list all the things that are wrong with you, then they always intended to tell you what was wrong with you. They only told you the good stuff first to get you to listen. Telling us to forget our families, changing our names, like calling me Nell, changing Marge to Margot . . . You know who also did that?"

The moisture magnified Angela's eyes. She shook her head.

"Charles Manson."

The girl's mouth opened, closed, opened again. "Yeah, I was . . . but it *does* work," she argued, though arguing for Angela meant offering a soft protest in a barely audible whisper. "He's helped lots of people. He helped *you*. You said he cured you and you would never be afraid again."

Ellie hadn't said anything of the kind, but that didn't matter—it was what Angela had heard. And she had heard what she expected to hear, that Galen was benevolent and all-powerful.

"I, um, exaggerated. A lot. My claustrophobia was never

actually debilitating . . . I talked it up more than I really felt it." Angela didn't seem to be tracking. "In truth, getting locked in that box was terrifying—not to mention dangerous, and if I had a heart condition or some real mental health issue, it could have been disastrous—and I guess I wanted to convince myself that it hadn't been for nothing. For sure I didn't want him to do anything *worse* to me. So . . . I overplayed my 'seeing the light,' or whatever you'd call it. My epiphany."

No response. Angela didn't seem able to process this.

Fabulous. Ellie's playacting to get close to Devon, who didn't seem to need or want rescue, had been one more pebble on the scale tipping Angela to suicide. Ellie had, accidentally and with the best intentions, gotten not only herself but also someone else into murky depths way over their heads.

Time to push off the bottom.

"Angela. Look at the facts here. You came here for a little bit of life coaching, and now you're about to kill yourself. *Kill* yourself." Ellie made the word as harsh and *real* as she could. "That cannot possibly be a good outcome for Galen's program. Maybe he's helped some other people, but he certainly hasn't helped you. So he's not all-knowing and all-powerful."

QED, Ellie thought.

"But that's because of me, because of my weakness."

"It's because he doesn't really know what he's doing! He's thrown together all the self-help, 'power of positive thinking' precepts into a soup kettle and served them up. Believe in yourself. Define your goals and work toward them every day. Don't let others drag you down. Simple—and true. But what's really benefiting people is getting away from their daily routine and having the peace and the time and the emotional freedom to think about themselves and their desires for a little while, that's all. Not any special magic that Galen is doing."

Lovesick or true believer or both, she wouldn't give it up. "You've been here only two days." She spoke harshly, which, for Angela, meant she sounded like a kindergarten teacher reprimanding a toddler for a minor playgroup infraction.

"That is true. But you've been here for a while—and you were about to end your life. You were about to *hang* yourself in the most public place on the ranch. Obviously, all is *not* perfect here."

Angela looked up at the ceiling, from which the noose still hung. Her eyes swelled with water once more as she thought this through, picturing the scene. Her body would have commanded the instant attention of anyone who stepped inside the gym. It would have been visible through the windows to any person walking by. She hadn't even turned out the lights—to the contrary, every one of them blazed, making the gym a beacon for miles across the valley.

She hadn't wanted to die. She had wanted only to give Galen and his program the ultimate finger.

"It was still all about me." Her voice seemed like an echo, devoid of hope or even life. "I was *still* just trying to get attention."

"The people whose attention you want aren't worth this pain. They certainly aren't worth your death."

But logic, Ellie's default position, neither comforted nor interested. "I haven't grown *at all*!"

Angela no longer had the strength even to cry. Ellie gave up the talk therapy—at which she clearly sucked—and pulled the young woman to her feet. Then Ellie guided her over to the worn futon in the corner, walking her slowly there like she was a sick child. The young woman collapsed onto the threadbare upholstery in a semi-fetal position, facing away from Ellie, eyes staring at nothing.

Ellie perched on the edge of the futon to stroke her hair. "Angela? Do you have any friends here at the ranch you'd like me to get? Any you'd like to talk to?"

The tiniest shake of her head, not easily accomplished in that position.

"Would you like me to call your parents?" Okay, Ellie hadn't completely forgotten her goal of a working phone or her suspicion that the staff had some method of communication with the outside world.

A whisper, but a firm one. "No."

"Do you want to go to bed? Where do you sleep, Angela?"

"With the sophomores."

"Oh. Why—" The middle bunkhouse. She couldn't even graduate to the juniors. Because she was a basket case or because the hope of a promotion made her work harder?

Angela answered the question Ellie hadn't finished. "I'm supposed to help them. Like Audrey with you. But I haven't helped anyone."

"What about Audrey?"

"She's a junior," Angela murmured, eyes closed. "She's with you guys to help you. I was supposed to get her bed, but Galen gave it to Marie."

Well, well. Not only had her oh-so-helpful classmate drunk the Flavor Aid, but she'd also bought stock in the factory. "How long has she been here?"

"Dunno . . . two, three years."

Years. For a career development program? "And those two big guys? Are they in my class to 'help' us too?"

She yawned, having resigned herself to hopeless-cause status. Next, she'd be eating carbs. "Andre and Tim? Yeah."

Very interesting. When half asleep, Angela turned into a fount of information. But in the next instant, her breathing slowed and the fount went dry. Sheer exhaustion had finally caught up to her.

Ellie stood. She didn't dare leave the young woman alone. She might have staved off suicide for the present, but she had no way to know how determined Angela might be. If she woke alone, she could easily talk herself back into it.

Ellie untied the loose end of the rope from the broken treadmill, then pulled on the harness/noose end until the other end snaked over the pulley and fell to the floor as Ellie jumped out of its way. One loop caught her on the shoulder with a slap, but nothing too painful. Now Angela could not possibly string the rope up again without help. Neither could Galen.

Ellie coiled the rope neatly, lugged it over to the open supply closet, then placed it inside after retrieving a half dozen yoga mats. There were no towels or old uniforms or anything else that could be used as blankets. She turned the button on the knob and closed the door, locking it. If the keys could not be located, yoga might have to be cancelled the next day, but at least Angela could not take that rope and find another handy beam under which to do herself in.

Then she found the thermostat for the room and kicked the heat up a little. If that month's electric bill made Galen unhappy, so be it.

She covered Angela as best she could. Lying on a dirty futon, with nothing but yoga mats for comfort . . . No young woman should sleep that way. Neither should Ellie, but she made herself a bed on the floor next to the futon and sank onto the thin foam. All the positive thinking in the world could not keep the body from eventually crashing.

Her search for a cell phone signal—assuming the phone even rallied—would have to wait. While Devon did not seem to be in immediate danger, Angela quite definitely was.

All life-change gurus throughout history have evidenced certain similarities, such as the habit of keeping inductees overtired, through constant activity, physical labor, no down-time, and insufficient sleep hours, and undernourished, with minimal food lacking decent nutrition. Their own "insider" lingo is designed to make established members feel exclusive and newbies feel a bit stupid and therefore less likely to ask questions. Newbies are kept in line by established members, who act as the eyes and ears of the leader. A leader, whose word is law, can make or break any member who falls out of favor. Interfere with him, oppose him in any way, and you might find yourself nail-gunned into a coffin.

Angela, my dear, you and I are inside a cult.

With no way to tell anyone, and no easy way out.

Chapter 27

Devon undressed and went into the bedroom; she had a bed in the small building meant for staff, but no one dared to ask why she rarely used it. She flicked out the light as she walked in. Some nights she put on a cute teddy or at least a silk nightshirt, but tonight she was naked, too tired to bother. It didn't matter anyway. The end result would stay the same.

Galen lay under the blankets. He stirred slightly at her approach, to her complete lack of surprise. She no longer bothered to hope that he might be asleep any more than she bothered to put on mascara before entering the room.

She slid in next to him and briefly pressed against him at every point to warm up, making a comment about how cold the nights were getting. Then she got to work, running her hand around his chest, making a large circle down to his thighs, across, back up again. This was as subtle as foreplay got or needed to be. She suppressed a sigh. Express discontent or, worse, boredom to a man once, and he'd never forget, never forgive. Nothing in Galen's philosophy spoke of forgiveness, quite the opposite. People with "unhelpful" attitudes were to be put out and forgotten.

She thought about that sodden bank statement. If Galen was embezzling the trust account funds—correction, *since* Galen was embezzling the trust account funds—her schedule needed to keep pace. The very delicate dance needed its tempo updated.

She'd stopped paying the slightest attention to what she was doing, but it didn't matter. Routine, in this context, reigned. No kinks, no fetishes, no threesomes, nothing out of the most *ordinary* ordinary. Quantity definitely trumped quality in his estimation, and for that, she had always been grateful. Knowing when to be grateful for the status quo and when to push for a change had always been one of her better qualities. Along with patience. She had lots of patience.

For her plan to work, it had to be unbreakable. And if Galen's greed had foreshortened his future as a guru, it had put a knife to the throat of hers as well. She needed to act quickly.

But before she could do anything, she needed him to go to sleep.

She climbed on top of him, kissing his oily face and neck. His hair smelled of a strange perfume, and she wondered what Angela did for him, whether her desperation might be a turnoff or a turn-on. Devon had done her best to suggest without suggesting that Angela was too soft, too unstable, that she could be a problem, but Galen clearly enjoyed poking the kid to watch her jump.

The job got done. She didn't bother faking enjoyment— he didn't care, and she had never been a great actress. She wondered idly why men took offense at that idea. If some chick cared enough to go through all that effort just to salve your ego, why would you complain? Count your blessings, jerk. Know when to be grateful. Know when to push for more.

She slid off and rested beside him, one hand lightly on his chest, making herself count to thirty. Just because she didn't fake a climax didn't mean she'd risk the insult of bolting for the shower the minute he let go. *One thousand twenty, one thousand twenty-one—*

"Who's got challenges tomorrow?"

"You didn't schedule any for tomorrow. You wanted to raise the walls on the new bunkhouse, remember?" *Go to sleep.*

"Yeah."

Sleep. One thousand twenty-eight—

"But we should do some. Tough ones. Ones that will put the fear of God into Nell, so she learns not to question me."

He really meant "the fear of Galen." Devon almost giggled, and bit the inside of her cheek.

"Go back over their questionnaires. Get some ideas."

"Now?" She tried to sound reluctant about it, having to put on clothes and boots and dig the key to the office out of his pants pocket.

"Yes, now." As if that should be obvious, and it was.

"Okay." She summoned a bright tone. *That's a great idea, and I only wish I'd thought of it myself.* If she ran those words through her brain, it got easier to put them in her voice.

But this time she didn't have to fake it; instead, she couldn't believe her luck.

She threw on clothes, boots, brushed her hair, and found the key. Then she got a flashlight from the tiny kitchen counter. She didn't need to reread the clients' "fears" answers; she remembered them well and had already thought of a few ideas that would satisfy Galen's bloodlust.

Right now she had a different task in mind.

She flicked on the office lights. Devon moving around the office during the last few hours of the day would not be remotely unusual, but Devon skulking around the office, using only a penlight, would be very much so.

Inside the top drawer of her desk rested a plastic pencil tray. She ran her fingers along the underside until they encountered a key secured with a square of duct tape. She plucked this out without spilling the pens and pencils. Then—tape back in place, tray back in place, drawer back in place—she did a visual sweep of the office to see if there might be anything else she should do. She saw nothing and left the light on in case Galen glanced out his windows. Unlikely, since he would have been asleep before she left the house, but the precaution couldn't hurt.

The night had turned cold, as they all did at this time of the year, and she used the walk along the path to smell the night air and mentally practice responses to any questions that might arise. She would have them ready, and they would sound natural. Consistency, as Galen often reminded them, constituted honesty.

Devon continued past the outbuildings and crossed the river. The woods at night used to freak her out, an East Coast city girl, but by now she'd gotten accustomed to them and even appreciated the deep darkness under the trees, the tiny rustling sounds of animals on their nocturnal jaunts, the whisper of each leaf as it wondered who dared to walk among them. But she didn't look at it, either, that darkness. Stare into the shadows between the trunks and shrubs, and you could see all sorts of things: weird shapes, wavering movements, formations that almost looked like something or someone, a threat, a devouring entity. She kept her gaze on the gravel, the path to the Coleman house, using the penlight once the forest canopy blotted out the moon.

The old lady didn't have motion-sensitive lights, afraid that animal activity would keep them flashing on and off all night long, but she did have two small, not very effective floodlights mounted on opposite corners of the house. Devon didn't want to wake Frances if she'd already retired, but the woman was something of a night owl, often up until the wee hours and then asleep until lunchtime. One could do that with no job, children, or husband to look after. Devon couldn't wait for that to be her life.

Six steps led her up to the porch. The windows on her left revealed gorgeous rooms ever so dimly lit by residual light from somewhere in the house. To her right, past the porch railings, black nothingness. She kept her footsteps light, even though the old lady wouldn't notice them. Her hearing had deteriorated along with the rest of her body, poor thing.

Devon peered into the main foyer; the formal living room; the drawing room, or what she guessed might be called the drawing room, whatever the hell a drawing room was, anyway; and the smaller, cozier room at the south end of the house, across from the kitchen. One small table lamp had been lit, and she saw Mrs. Coleman. She'd fallen asleep in her armchair, a book on her lap, an empty wineglass on the doily.

Devon continued along the porch to the kitchen door. The knob didn't turn. Mrs. Coleman hadn't drunk enough wine to forget to lock the doors last night. But no matter, as she'd given Galen a key, of which Devon had made a copy on one of her increasingly rare visits to civilization. Devon also kept the lock well oiled—the ranch showed its appreciation for Mrs. Coleman's generosity by providing free home maintenance.

She entered the kitchen, then relocked the door behind her. She might have ignored the black nothingness, but that didn't mean she had forgotten about it. Then she walked into the south room and sat on the edge of the coffee table, in front of Frances Coleman's chair. She laid one hand over the blue veins that corrugated the back of Frances's bony fingers and said in a near-whisper, "Hey."

The eyelids flickered, opened. Blinked. She saw Devon, and the wrinkles in her face creased into radiance.

"Theresa," she said over an exhaled breath.

"Yes, Mother," Devon said. "It's me."

Chapter 28

Devon made two cups of tea, using the most ornate bone china cups she could find because it made her laugh to use such expensive things, then carried them back to the armchair. She didn't turn on any more lights.

"How have you been?" she asked Mrs. Coleman.

"I'm all right." Which meant she wasn't, but she was both too ladylike and too unconventional to be a complainer. It would take another few minutes before she would consider confiding how her aches and pains had been making her so *forgetful*. "Are you back to stay now?"

"Not quite. There are still a few things I have to take care of in Bolivia."

"That awful place. I don't know why you've been there so long—Don't sit on the coffee table, dear."

"Sorry." Devon moved to the other armchair. Better, anyway, with the lamp in between. She had been startled the first time Mrs. Coleman had confused her with her dead—presumably dead—daughter, and had been filled with pity the second time. By the third, a plan of sorts had formed.

It happened usually at night, when the older woman was

tired and the past crowded in around her brain's defenses. "Sundowning," the experts called it, or "late-day confusion," which often affected those with Alzheimer's or other forms of dementia. It seemed to be Mrs. Coleman's only symptom of any infirmity. Tomorrow morning she might meet Devon on the path and know exactly who she was. She often told Galen to "tell Devon and that nice Angela I said hello."

But late at night, different story. A bizarre story, since Devon looked nothing like stodgy, dark-haired plus thirty years older Theresa. Devon had found a photo of her in Mrs. Coleman's bedroom and had promptly hidden it between books in the spare room. Best to let Frances's mother love and wishful thinking rule without distraction.

"You always put so much honey in it, darling," Mrs. Coleman said of the tea and laughed. "You're going to rot my teeth."

"I'm sorry. Anyway, I'll be back here soon. You know I have to see to my husband's legacy, the orphanage he built there."

"Yes, of course. Such a pity he—" She stopped, not quite able to remember what the pity was.

"Was killed by the rebels," Devon supplied.

"Oh, yes. I remember when your father died. I felt as if the floor had collapsed under me."

Devon made her voice as sweet and thick as the honey. "I know. I know."

A tiny furrow appeared between Mrs. Coleman's brows. "You were only a tiny baby when—"

Devon gently interrupted. "Because of my husband, I mean, being married. That's why my last name is different now. You did remember to tell the lawyer that when you changed the will, right?"

"Yes." Spoken immediately, but not with conviction, the expression in her eyes worried.

"Can I see it?" Devon asked. "You did change it, right?"

A long pause.

Devon stifled an impatient breath. "Mother. You had the lawyer come three days ago. I—" She almost said, "I saw him," but stopped herself in time, since she couldn't have if she had been deep in a South American forest.

The small, stuffy attorney had driven up and disappeared into the house for an hour. Devon had watched from her office, peering from the window behind her desk. Her stomach had churned with the agony of not knowing whether Frances Coleman told him that her errant daughter, Theresa, once expelled from any heiresship by her willful absence, had returned with a new name and a contrite manner. Or if Frances forgot all about it.

Devon hadn't been able to do anything to guide the process, of course, in the fear that even during the day Mrs. Coleman might jump to introduce the lawyer to her "daughter, Theresa," when the lawyer knew Devon on sight. And she had not had a chance to check on the outcome of this vague, variable plan until now. For all she knew, Mrs. Coleman could have declared Galen her damn beneficiary.

So now she kept her voice low but insistent. "Mother. I have to have something to come back to. Where is your will?"

The cup rattled against its saucer. "I know I put that somewhere."

"Where, Mother?"

"Oh! With the pearls. That's right."

"Pearls?"

"In the safe."

That made sense. Where else would one keep a last will and testament, and why wouldn't a house this grand have its own vault? "Let's look at it."

"Right now?"

"I have to show that I have a secure situation to come to," Devon said. "Or they won't let me be discharged from Bolivia." It didn't matter that this made no sense. Reality had long since ceased to be of concern.

"All right."

Devon grabbed the cup and saucer before Mrs. Coleman could drop them. She'd wash them and return them to their designated spots in the cabinet before she left. Or perhaps it would be best to leave them on the counter, to convince the daytime Frances that the nighttime Frances really had had a visit from Theresa, that her daughter really had been resurrected. Or would it confuse matters to cross the two worlds? She'd wait to see if the will had really been changed, if Frances's nighttime visitor had survived the harsh light of day.

She followed Mrs. Coleman, who was now moving with more purpose, up the wide staircase to a bedroom larger than the entire one-floor house Devon shared with Galen. Mrs. Coleman had a safe in her bedroom, of course, because where else would rich people keep their valuables but close by, to cuddle like a teddy bear? Devon half expected a painting to swing out and reveal a built-in combination lock, but the safe turned out to be a freestanding tower only a bit skinnier than the average refrigerator. It was nestled in the closet, next to the old ball gowns, denim shirts, boots, and a full-length fur coat. And had been bolted to the floor, Devon noticed.

The combination might cause a problem. If Mrs. Coleman couldn't even remember that her daughter had died—though whether had she died or simply had never returned, no one seemed quite sure—how on earth would she remember a three- or four-number combi—

The chicken bone–like fingers with the perfectly shaped nails twirled the dial as if she'd never mentioned arthritis, clicking through first this way and then that so quickly that Devon kicked herself for not paying closer attention to the stops.

Then she pulled up on the handle, a heavy-looking bronze latch. Nothing happened.

Devon let the air out of her lungs.

Undeterred, Mrs. Coleman twisted the dial again. Somewhere inside the door, a shift occurred, and the door swung open.

"Wow," Devon couldn't help saying.

Mrs. Coleman gave that devilish grin. "It's your grandmother's birthday."

The safe didn't exactly turn out to be the cave of Ali Baba's treasures. It contained only a stack of velvet cases and shiny boxes, a small painting of what appeared to be a toddler playing on a beach, an alligator purse with worn straps, a haphazard pile of buff-colored folders, and an even larger pile of bound volumes of different sizes and colors. Ledgers? Diaries? Devon couldn't guess and didn't care anyway. She cared only for the topmost folder, which Mrs. Coleman now withdrew, opened, and passed to Devon.

"Here it is! I told you I didn't forget."

Devon held her breath, would have said a prayer if there existed any god who might sanction her goal, and read the document in her hands.

"I, Frances Coleman, being of sound mind and body, leave the entirety of my estate, including all foreign investments and properties, to my daughter, Devon—"

The daughter part might raise some eyebrows in the probate system, but it could be explained as a term of affection. Her *spiritual* daughter. Her emotionally adopted daughter, whatever. Let the eyebrows waggle. Devon would find a way to explain it.

She flipped to the next page and noted not only Mrs. Coleman's spidery signature at the bottom but the scrawls of her attorney and a witness, Lou May Tunney, the cleaning woman. Very official. And if the attorney had a copy, he would have filed it with the county, or whatever it was an attorney did with a will, right? Totally real. Incontrovertible. There would be nothing anyone could do about it. Nothing Galen could do about it. Done deal.

"Thank you, Mother."

But Frances had been distracted by a blue satin dress hanging a foot away. "Look at this one. You always loved this dress. I wore it to Cannes one year when we took you, and you said I looked like the Blue Fairy in *Pinocchio*."

"You did," Devon said. "That was a magical time."

"That's just what you said then!" The old lady beamed at the memory. "You said the plane was magic because it made us fly like birds. And this one . . . you remember this pink silk? You wore it to your senior prom."

Devon put the will back in the safe and gently reined in the reminiscing by reminding Mrs. Coleman to lock it. Devon didn't poke about the velvet boxes or ask about the painting—there would be plenty of time for that. All the time in the world.

Nor did she ask about the combination. It shouldn't be that hard to find out Frances's mother's birth date, and even if she couldn't, who cared? If the lock had to be drilled out, that would only make Devon look more innocent, right? She had no idea dear Mrs. Coleman had become so fond of her.

She helped the old lady get out of her trousers and blouse and into a worn flannel nightgown, then tucked her in and turned out the light. Then she bid her good night as sweetly as a real, loving daughter would a real, caring mother— something Devon had never had—and tiptoed down the stairs, the woman already asleep and snoring behind her. Devon didn't bother to hide the grin that lifted both cheeks until they hurt. A huge hurdle had been leapt. A long bridge had been crossed. Her vague plan had become written in stone—or at least in a legitimate legal document, which was even better.

She'd never have to ask her father or Galen or the government or anybody else for anything ever again. She'd be *free*. For the first time, really, truly free.

Once the next phase had been completed.

PART III

HEATING THE WATER

None of us knew that his teachings, which promised to make us leaders, were actually making us followers— his followers. His disciples. He wanted us to worship him.

Sarah Edmondson (with Kristine Gasbarre), *Scarred: The True Story of How I Escaped NXIVM, the Cult That Bound My Life*

Chapter 29

Early morning pinpricks of light forced Ellie to wake the next morning, cocooned inside the smelly yoga mats. First, she groaned. Second, she opened her eyes.

Angela had disappeared.

Third, Ellie sat up so quickly that her head swam. The futon sat sullen and abandoned, the yoga mats slumped to the floor, and her own agitated breaths were the only sound in the vast room. How did that young woman get up and out without waking her?

Ellie neglected to restack the mats before she checked out the small lavatory—really the only separate room in the building other than the supply closet, which remained locked. Angela wasn't in the building.

That was all right, Ellie told herself, as long as wherever she *was*, she was still alive.

Ellie moved outside and stumbled down the few steps. Already high above the horizon to her left, the sun stabbed her eyeballs. The long days had worn her out, so this particular morning, when she needed to be on the ball, instead she'd had a ridiculously long lie-in. Her mind may have needed the sleep desperately, but her body didn't care for where it had been accomplished, and she ached in strange places.

No people, no movement, save one lone woman trudging into the junior bunkhouse. Leftover breakfast smells wafted from the kitchen. Ellie would be in trouble for missing breakfast, the morning class, the bed check, and the roll call, or however one might classify her absence from the group. She didn't stop to remind herself that as a legal adult, she could miss all the meetings she wanted. What could they do? Dock her pay? Instead, she recalled that Angela had said she had a bed in the sophomore bunkhouse.

Ellie hustled across the way, refusing to think about how much her stomach really did care about food and the consequences of missing the narrow window in which meals were served, and how much her brain cared about sanctions and what she'd do if Galen insisted she scrub toilets without gloves. Probably walk over the mountain to Topaz, if necessary, and tell Rachael to tell Billy that his daughter was fine and that if he wanted more, he could fly to Nevada himself.

The sophomore bunkhouse, like all the buildings, had no lock on its door. The furniture was arranged exactly like in the freshman version, each bunk with its assigned nightstand, rinsed-out clothes drying over the footboards. It also seemed more crowded than the freshman quarters, as every bunk area was lined with possessions.

The occupants moved without pause and with a barely constrained hurry in and out of the bathrooms, stowing toothbrushes and hair clips and legal pads full of notes. No one noticed Ellie at first, but as she passed the men's room and a few beds, a tall woman with very close-cropped hair peered at her face and said, "You're not supposed to be in here."

"I'm looking for Angela," Ellie told her. In the absence of posted and announced rules about other people's bunkhouses, and with no security and no door locks, they were all one big happy family, right?

"She's not here."

"Have you seen her this morning?"

She squinted at Ellie and frowned to show how baffling she found this inquiry.

A man at the next bunk stopped to listen to this exchange before dropping his two cents. "You're not supposed to be in here."

"Says *who*?" Ellie demanded, but rhetorically, because she gave up on them and went into the women's restroom along the far wall. Two older ladies bustled past her; one did a double take at her unfamiliar face but apparently decided not to pile on.

The sinks were empty, and one toilet and one shower were occupied. Ellie leaned her hips against a basin and waited, pondering her next move should neither occupant turn out to be Angela. Where would the young woman have gone? Where could a determined suicide find the means? There were plenty of trees in the forest, but would there be rope? Of course, she could use a belt or an electrical cord from among her own items or could scrounge around for something suitable in the barn. Ellie should probably check the barn next. Would there be firearms anywhere on the property? She had no idea what Nevada's gun control laws entailed, but such a remote property would probably have long guns in case of rattlesnakes or bears or coyotes.

The toilet flushed, and a thirtyish, heavyset woman with a lazy eye and an unflattering bob emerged. Like some of her bunkmates, she gave Ellie one piercing glance before deciding not to ask.

But Ellie did. "I'm looking for Angela. Have you seen her this morning?"

The woman washed her hands, keeping an eye on Ellie in

the mirror during the process, then finally consented to say no. The shower stopped. Ellie switched her gaze to its curtain while the woman used the cover to scamper out the door.

Ellie continued to wait. If Angela had pills or access to pills, she could have used them the night before, but she had wanted the theater of the rope and pulley, had wanted to be outrageously visible to all and sundry. But today she might want to deny herself the drama as an act of self-discipline and slip away quietly in her bed.

Razor blades and knives. Very few people used anything other than safety razors to shave, but the kitchen had to have at least a few sharp knives, and the barn would have box cutters. Lots of blood would be equally dramatic. More painful, however.

The door unlatched, and she really hoped Angela would exit.

No such luck. A petite fairy of a woman with wet black hair came out, took one look at her, and fled into the main room before Ellie could even part her lips.

Ellie followed, panic settling in her throat. Where *was* she?

The bunkhouse restrooms had no doors. Each of them had only a gap; then a short wall beyond that blocked this center gap from the view of the bunkroom. Still inside the restroom and hidden by the barrier wall, she heard Galen's voice. "Stand!"

An agent's instinct to avoid detection froze Ellie in place. She didn't move. She didn't even breathe. *Stand?* What did that mean?

"Are you *listening*?" he demanded from somewhere in the outer room. He hadn't sounded that harsh even while trying to drown Margot or while nailing Ellie into the coffin. She set one silent foot in front of its partner to peek a wary eye at the only section of space she could see from that angle, pressing her face against the rough divider wall so hard that her cheek began to go numb.

The sophomores stood at attention, ramrod straight. Only four were visible from her location, but they seemed to be standing in rows, equally spaced from each other. Backs to her, they faced the wall with the entrance, the east wall, so she guessed Galen stood there. Tim, the young man who had startled her the first night, wandered into view, pacing about and keeping an eye on the formation. Ellie snapped her head back, out of sight. It was a ladies' room. He wouldn't violate the universal rule and enter a *ladies'* room, would he?

Ellie berated herself for even thinking it. Universal rules didn't apply on this property. There were no rules except Galen's.

What to do? She felt 95 percent certain that she could take Galen to the floor without breaking a sweat. He had a few muscles, but nothing in his movements suggested any real training.

But she wasn't there to take Galen down. She had come to find Devon, had found her, and now owed it to Billy to at least try to get her the hell out of there now that she suspected just how malignant Galen was. But cult busting had to be done carefully. If she openly opposed Galen, his followers would rise up. If she tried to drag Devon away that very morning, the rock star's daughter would dig her heels into the desert dirt and refuse to budge.

Devon would have to see the truth for herself. Maybe Ellie could help guide her to the exit; maybe she couldn't. But she had to give it a try.

Which was all very well and good, but at the moment it left her hiding in a ladies' room.

She set this extreme internal embarrassment aside to listen. Galen continued, "I know what you've been doing. I know what you've been thinking. You're getting tired, you're getting weary, you're sick of the food, and you want to go home and watch TV and stay in your pajamas all day!" His voice developed a singsong cadence, cutting and slashing with violent mockery. "'It's too *hard* to change, Galen! I can't *handle* it. I'll just stay a parasite and blame it all on genes or Mommy or because the boss doesn't like me.' He doesn't like you, because you're a *loser*!"

If he meant this speech to be motivating, Ellie wasn't feeling it. And it didn't seem to perk up the few people she could see. All of them kept their unwavering gaze on the floorboards.

"You, Jeremy," Galen boomed. "You've been here eight months, and you're still a sophomore. You know why? Because you're not progressing. You're not growing. Do you know what growth is?"

The unseen Jeremy mumbled something Ellie couldn't catch.

"What is it?"

More mumbling.

"Louder!"

Jeremy raised his voice and enunciated when he said, "Growth is an increase in self-esteem that involves expansion and work."

"And?"

"Expansion and work and, uh, increased possibilities."

"What does that mean?"

Mumbling.

"Pain to create expansion and an increased range of possibilities. All this time and you can't even handle a basic definition! What am I supposed to do when you can't even get that down? Are you trying at *all*? Or are you just coasting, the way you've been doing your entire life? You can't coast through this, Jeremy."

Work is pain to increase expansion? What did that even mean? And why did these intelligent adults, who had come here for *career development*, put up with being screamed at as if this were their first day at Camp Lejeune?

Why didn't anyone protest?

Ellie fought the urge to walk out, look Galen straight in the eye, and tell him he was very much full of shit. The temptation was overwhelming . . . but every undercover operation got to a similar point. Interfere and blow your cover? Or let the chips of violence fall where they may?

"Since you're not expanding in any way, shape, or brain cell, we'll go back to the basics, Jeremy! Delia, what does 'basics' mean?"

A woman spoke softly, hesitantly.

"I can't hear you!"

She spoke louder, but Ellie still couldn't make out the words.

"No, he's not going to work on the flooring! That's what he's been doing and, apparently, learning nothing! Time to get the walls up. And since you're trying to soften the blows to Jeremy's lack of progress, Delia, you and everyone else in this bunkroom are going to do nothing else today but put hammers to nails on the new building. Nothing else! No lunch, no dinner, no drinks, no going to the bathroom, no taking a smoke or resting your lazy little asses in the shade! I want the walls up and the roof on by *sundown*."

Ellie didn't know much about construction, so this demand could have ranged anywhere from routine to difficult to completely impossible.

Still, no one protested. No one even questioned him.

And neither did Ellie. She focused only on how to get out of that building without attracting Galen's notice. No back entrance existed, so she would have to wait until they left . . . but Angela was out there somewhere. She couldn't have gotten far; she couldn't have woken up that much earlier than Ellie, as exhausted as she'd been. Could she have?

"Do you *think* you can disrespect me like this? Just *ignore* everything I'm trying to teach you? Spread your parasitic ways to your colleagues and keep them down in your cesspool of failure so that you won't have to be alone? Do you?"

"No," his target croaked. "Yes, I mean—"

Ellie had to get out of there and couldn't wait until Galen finished eviscerating poor Jeremy. The ladies' room had a frosted window at each end of it, a regular old double-hung with a latch in the middle. While Galen's voice rose in condemnation of two others whom Jeremy had corrupted with his germs of sloth, Ellie gripped the latch and slid it to one side. Then she pushed upward on the lower sash.

Creaaak.

She froze, certain that like a character in a trite madcap comedy, she would turn and find the entire sophomore class crowding into the ladies' room to see who on earth was trying to escape out the window. Nothing—*nothing*—about her situation felt remotely comedic.

Utter silence from the next room.

Then a sound came, like the flapping of one relatively soft surface against another, a broom on a rug, a flag in the wind. A hand across a face.

More silence. Then it came again.

Slap.

What the hell was going on?

A more solid sound, followed by what had to be the expulsion of breath after getting sucker punched. Someone was getting *hit*.

Then the soft movement of dozens of feet as the group shuffled, and without thinking, Ellie used the noise as cover to shove the window sash up all the way. A gust of desert air tumbled in, with wisps of cool left over from the night and wafts warming up for the day ahead.

The sill sat at about chest level. Ellie spread both palms over it and pushed off the floor with her toes. The sound in the main room didn't pause. Scuffling, grunts and, above it all, Galen's voice proclaiming that he didn't have time to waste on time wasters—none of them did—and that if Jeremy and his ilk didn't shape up, they'd be doomed, were probably already doomed, to a lifetime of remora-ism. But it wasn't Galen's message that made Ellie turn away from the window and return to her post at the wall to the ladies' room.

What if they actually killed him?

When last she'd checked, the sophomores had been lined up with their backs to her and, she assumed, with Galen facing them. If Ellie showed even a lock of hair, he'd see her. It sounded like there was too much activity for anyone to look in her direction, but it would take only one less-violent type standing on the sidelines to notice a shadow by the wall to the ladies' room and sound the alarm like a possessed victim from *Invasion of the Body Snatchers* . . . an apt analogy, because these were pod people if ever there had been.

Ellie dropped to the floor and hazarded a peek from there, hoping that the group of legs and feet would hide her. And she made it fast, snapping one eye past the edge of the wall and then back again.

The group no longer stood in neat rows but had gathered in a rough circle around the man she presumed to be Jeremy. Galen faced him, kept up the invective and, during her second quick glance, slapped Jeremy's already reddened face. A short guy to the side followed up with a punch to Jeremy's gut, shoving the flannel shirt into his midriff with a visible depression. Jeremy whooshed air and bent forward, at which point a woman hit him on the back of his head, bringing her balled fist down like a hammer. Without loosening her fingers, she pivoted and backhanded the chin of a taller woman, knocking her face to one side. The woman didn't react, didn't protest, didn't even raise her arms to defend herself. Ellie guessed that she was one of Jeremy's coconspirators in the crime of indolence and failure.

The debate of the undercover operative: What was more important to stop? A crime that might occur in the future or a crime that was occurring right now?

But was this a crime? These people—even Jeremy—were adults and voluntary participants. The fifteen or twenty people taking part out there had listened to Galen, their leader, until his word became law, prophecy, the only truth they knew, and thus they had no choice but to obey him. If Ellie tried to stop them, they would only turn on her. That justification had been used before, during, and after every conflict since the beginning of time, but that didn't mean it wasn't true. Or accurate. Or sensible.

Assembly beatdowns were not new or even unusual in unhealthy group structures. From the group of friends in grade school who decided they were mad at one particular girl and let her know, to the project managers who decided not to share research leads with the guy from Marketing, because he might be dating the boss's daughter, all the way back to when others in the cave didn't let Ugh have any of the mastodon, because he had too conveniently forgotten his spear, community censure had always been a part of human life.

In many ways it could be a good thing. If the disapproval of peers kept one from littering or from letting one's dog dig up the neighbor's flower beds or from sleeping with one's coworker's spouse, then it produced a healthy outcome for all.

But it could become extreme in isolated societies. Jim Jones directed members' smackdowns at prayer meetings when the accused's behavior didn't meet his standards. Members of Scientology were punished by confinement, malnourishment, and humiliation for months to years at a time. Using the Biblical quote about not sparing the rod as an excuse, radical Christian cults, such as Word of Faith, Word of Life, The Move, and Grace Road, beat members. And always as a group activity.

Even if this wasn't the first time Jeremy had been on the receiving end of this treatment, he probably wouldn't leave the group. He had been led to reject his family and friends in favor of the new "family," and he no longer had anyplace else to go for social companionship, support, or even education or income. So he'd stay. They'd all stay.

It made sense from a cult leader's point of view. The ability to command such beatings cemented the leader's authority. Getting the members to join in made them coconspirators, and so they would be unable to spill the beans to outsiders without implicating themselves. And above all, the beatings made the remaining members more motivated than ever to obey, concede, fly under the radar, lest they become the one standing alone in the middle of the room. Galen's activity was, sadly, nothing new. Disgusting, but not new.

Ellie got up, went back to the window, and pushed herself up onto the windowsill. She twisted around until her hips were outside the window and then slumped until her legs and feet slithered out as well, still hanging on to the sill. She no longer worried about the gang inside hearing her or discovering the open window. It would probably do them a world of good to realize they'd been witnessed.

Might not do *Ellie* any good, but she no longer cared. She was going to get Billy's daughter out of this place. If Ellie couldn't convince her to leave, she'd grab her phone and maybe Angela for good measure and hit the road to Topaz or as far as it took her to get a cell phone signal. There may not be much Billy could do, ultimately, about Devon, but if

Ellie could expose Galen's tactics to the world at large, at least it might save future clients from a trip to Hell Ranch. Only light could take down a guy like Galen, only brilliant, streaming illumination that burned and exposed.

She dropped to the ground, only a few feet down. Straightened.

And felt a hand clasp her shoulder.

Chapter 30

"What were you doing in there?" Devon demanded. She carried a bundle of whitish clothing under one arm and gripped the handle of a five-gallon bucket with the other.

Ellie had run fresh out of plausible explanations. "I was looking for Angela."

"Angela?"

"She said she has a bunk there."

"Oh, yes. But why aren't you in class?"

Ellie ignored the question. "Do you know where she is?"

"Angela?"

"Yes, Angela! Is she . . . Have you seen her this morning?"

A small line appeared between Devon's perfect eyebrows. "Yeah . . . I believe she's teaching your class. If you were working on the proper module, you'd know exactly where she is. We choose our progress, and we choose our lack of it. What do you need Angela for anyway?"

"To . . . tell her I'd be late. I thought you'd said Galen didn't allow lateness."

"No. You'll have to wait in the hall until they break."

This settled, Devon turned to walk away. But Ellie was

lighter on her feet than that and kept pace beside her. "Why aren't *you* teaching the class?"

"I have other work to do."

Ellie gave her best imitation of a sincerely eager child. "Like what?"

"I'm tending to the bees this morning. There's the classrooms. You'd better go—"

"That's fascinating. Angela said her challenge involved a beehive. My nephew used to raise bees. I'd love to see the hive."

Devon didn't hide the impatience in her sigh as she stopped and faced Ellie. "You really should be learning the module. That's the training you're paying for, you know."

"I know." And she waited. Ellie very rarely lost a staredown.

People began to spill out from the front of the sophomore bunkhouse. They walked mostly in silence, Galen among them, Tim bringing up the rear. Galen had his arm around a limping Jeremy and was rubbing the man's shoulder in either encouragement or concern. A woman had red marks on her face. Everyone in the group appeared grim.

Except Galen, of course. He talked easily, gently comforting, then noticed the two women. "We're heading over to the new building! Nell, my dear, why aren't you in class?"

"Devon's going to teach me about bees."

"All right." Bestowing permission he hadn't been asked for, he didn't pause before he spoke, carried along in the sea of sophomores. Tim passed by, giving her a long look that was probably supposed to mean something. A warning not to make his day more difficult?

Thus committed, Devon said, "This way."

They walked well past the new building, where Galen shouted enthusiastic instructions to the worker students. No one appeared to share this enthusiasm, but Ellie knew that had nothing to do with weariness. Each seemed lost in thoughts of guilt or fear. Guilt at what they had done and hadn't done, and fear that they would be next.

She considered telling Devon what she had witnessed, but the young woman seemed preoccupied. Besides, it wouldn't come as a surprise to Devon or anyone else who had been around Galen for a while. He didn't hide his philosophies or his methods.

Angela, obviously, had survived the night—a great relief—and now stood in a room, surrounded by others. Ellie didn't know what else to do for her. The sensible thing would be to tell her colleagues that she might be a danger to herself and that they should remain hypervigilant about her condition. Ellie couldn't be with her every minute, but surely *someone* could, as there seemed to be very little privacy at the ranch.

But Ellie feared that would make things worse for Angela. Even if Ellie didn't reveal her reasons, how could anyone miss Angela's slavish devotion to Galen? The embarrassment might tip her over into the abyss. Ellie also didn't know what sort of "sanction" might be applied. If sneaking a smoke put one on midnight bathroom duty for days or weeks, what would a suicide attempt garner?

Devon led her down a path past the barn, past even the erstwhile parking lot, where cars baked on the hard earth as their wheels grew flat and the daily dust blotted out the windows. To her left, the mountains shot upward, and Ellie could hear birds tweeting from inside the dense foliage, competing with the sound of the river. To her right, the crops grew silently, no one working between the rows right then. At her feet, large stones and patches of too-stubborn brush dotted the dirt walkway.

"Does that ever flood? The river?" she asked Devon, remembering Carlos's cause of death.

"It gets high in the spring, when the winter snows are melting. But it never reaches the buildings, so far as I know."

"How long have you been here?"

She blinked, surprised at this interest. Or perhaps the sun got in her eyes. "A while."

"Lots of happy clients? Do graduates ever come back and speak to the current, um, students?" Ellie stuck to their own terminology.

"Not often, but we are rather remote."

"Have you been through the whole course yourself?"

Devon laughed unexpectedly. "Me? No, to be honest. I did a bunch, but then Galen needed an assistant director, and somehow, I . . . didn't finish."

Five white boxes sat in a neat row. Ellie heard the humming, low and insistent, and was now close enough to recognize the dark specks on the boxes as individual bees. There were no other structures in the clearing, and the river ran at least sixty feet away and down a slight incline. This probably kept people out of harm's way and the hives safe during the spring floods. A wooden pallet rested just off the path, a very clean metal canister slightly larger than a five-gallon bucket next to it. The canister had a crank on the top and a valve at the bottom. Two quart-sized mason jars with lids and what looked like a metal watering can, but with smoke coming out of the top of it, also sat on the pallet, as did a large marble mortar filled with deep green leaves, a pestle at its side. A bee or two floated by.

Devon suited up before wading in. The whitish bundle of clothing became baggy pants and a coat, thick gloves, and a wide-brimmed hat with netting that covered her face and neck. She opened the top of one box and pulled out what looked like a furnace filter, but Ellie could see the waxy honeycomb inside. The bees buzzed around Devon but didn't seem particularly upset. She selected three of these filters and placed them in a five-gallon bucket at her feet. Then she picked up the bucket and began to walk back toward Ellie. The bees stayed with her, wanting their comb back.

Ellie waited, with no desire to get any closer to those teeming hives.

When discussing fears, she had totally lied about claustrophobia and, in fact, rather *liked* heights. Public speaking didn't bother her a bit, either. Lecturing to groups of new police officers, nurses, forensic science students, and other scientists had happened to be among her "other duties as assigned" and was the first one to be dumped on the new guy. She'd had to learn, and quickly. Then, of course, there had been years of courtroom testimony, where she not only had had to speak in front of a room full of individuals highly invested in the proceeding but also had had to respond to attorneys who felt it their job to make you look incompetent at best and corrupt at worst. Compared to that, *any* public speaking engagement seemed a cakewalk.

No, Ellie's *real* fear had always been bees. It wasn't a phobia or anything, but as a child, she had lived barefoot during the warm months and would invariably step on a bee at some point. Her life had been idyllic enough that a beesting seemed the absolute worst. As an adult, she knew to avoid bothering bees and they'd avoid bothering her, but still.

So Ellie stayed where she was. "I have some concerns."

Devon brought her bucket to the pallet. Bees flew past Ellie's face, no longer in a lazy, floating way. They seemed to have a few concerns themselves. She did not move.

Devon ignored this opener, pulling off her hat. She took one of the honeycombs out of her bucket and began to pry away the wax coating with a wide-toothed metal comb and scrape the gunk on the side of the bucket.

"I just witnessed something very strange in the sophomore bunkhouse."

"Really?"

"A group smackdown. Galen and the group of clients actually *beat* someone named Jeremy and maybe a few other people, but mostly Jeremy." Ellie found her hands were still trembling with fury and frustration, and so she stuffed them into her pockets. "Like a mob. An *angry* mob."

Devon appeared unshocked. "Physical sanction. It *is* part of the program."

"Beating people? Seriously? That falls under the category of *career development*?"

"Yes. Galen says it reestablishes the mind-body connection and creates new awareness. I—I know it sounds strange . . ."

Ellie's hands curled into fists, one closing over something hard in her pocket. "*Strange*? It sounds bizarre. Not to mention illegal."

Still unimpressed, Devon said, "Physical sanction is mentioned in the admitting paperwork you signed."

But who reads the fine print? "Assault is a crime, and a contract to commit it is invalid."

"Then how is boxing legal?"

This, Ellie had to admit, seemed like an excellent question. She took her hands out of her pockets. "So this is actually part of the therapy or program or training, or whatever you want to call it?"

"No. Only as a sanction, for people who are truly resistant to change. I'm sure you won't . . . I mean, Galen tailors everything to the client's personal circumstances."

Meaning: *He probably won't beat up a girl like you.* Ellie did not find that comforting. She fingered the guitar pick–shaped metal disk still in her pocket, since she'd had the pleasure of sleeping in her clothes. Then she held it out to Devon. "What's this? I found it at the edge of the firepit yesterday."

Devon's expression, which hadn't been pleasant to begin with, darkened to a deep scowl. If Ellie had planned for the item to bring back memories of her father onstage and the kindly roadies and maybe the thrill of being on the road,

clearly, it did not. The memories evoked were not happy
|at all.

And when Ellie turned the metal piece over, revealing
Chimera engraved on the back, Devon's frown only deepened. Not from sentiment or melancholy but from anger. At
the father who had used her? Or the boyfriend who had
abandoned her?

Either way, she didn't feel the need to confide. "I have no
idea." With that, she seemed to dismiss Ellie and turned her
full attention to the bees and their honey.

With the pale wax cleaned off, the combs gleamed with
heavy dark honey, and each fit into a frame, which propped
them upright in the metal canister. The three frames were
evenly spaced, and when she fitted the top with the crank on
the canister, Ellie saw why. Devon spun them inside this
centrifuge, pumping hard enough to explain her toned biceps.

The work seemed to calm her, and in a calm, rational tone,
she delivered the party line. Physical sanctions were part of
the program, where appropriate. The possibility of sanctions
was mentioned in the entrance paperwork. Jeremy chose to
be here and could leave at any time.

Devon finished up the spinning and turned to the mortar
and pestle. With the pestle, she began macerating the deep
green leaves, along with their stems and a few bud-like
growths. "I don't know what you want me to tell you, Ellen.
Do you want to get your life on track or not?" The sales-
man's spin. "Don't you want to make more money? Don't
you want to get your clothes cleaner, your children health-
ier, your spouse happier?" Phrased to make it seem as if you
had free choice when there was only one rational answer.

What Ellie wanted was for Devon to wake up and leave
this place with her. Galen had a propensity for violence,
and if Ellie rocked the boat, he might take it out on Devon,
her counselor. Therefore, Ellie had her own reasons for want-

ing Devon out quite aside from her father's worry. Margot and Barry and Angela would have to figure things out on their own.

Ellie sidestepped her question, instead asking what the mortar contained. "What are you doing?" Was it some kind of food for bees? What did bees eat, other than pollen?

"This? I'm infusing some honey with basil. You know you're free to leave anytime you like, Ellen, if you don't feel this program is for you. But you've only been here a few days. You have a problem with commitment, don't you? Bailing on things when they get hard." As she spoke, she scraped the mashed leaves into one of the mason jars. Ellie thought they might be from the flower bed in front of the office, because she hadn't noticed an herb garden anywhere.

"I've never had a commitment issue before," Ellie couldn't help pointing out, thinking Devon should try the latent print examiner certification test if she wanted to see hard. "Are *you* okay with Galen's methods?"

"They work." Ellie couldn't tell if the younger woman avoided her gaze because she didn't really believe her own words or because Ellie and her philosophical objections didn't truly warrant great attention. She wiggled the heavy metal canister over to the edge of the pallet so she could fit the glass mason jar with the crushed greenery under the valve.

So far there did not seem to be penalties—"sanctions" in ranch lingo—for being blunt. So Ellie was blunt. "Has he ever hit you?"

"Once or twice, when I was dithering," Devon admitted with a complete lack of concern as she opened the valve and let the thick golden liquid slither into the mason jar. "It was good for me. It shocked me back into the present, instead of getting lost in the jungle of what might be or should be." She straightened up and finally looked directly at Ellie. "Don't worry. Nobody's going to beat you up. All your fears are puppets of your old habits and preconceptions because they don't want you to become aware of them and change them. The only person you're battling right now is yourself. But we're here to help you do that."

All Ellie heard was, "Blah-blah-blah. We don't have a problem here."

She would never be able to talk Devon into leaving. But perhaps she could do the next best thing.

It would be necessary to play the poster child awhile longer. Ellie shut up until Devon had replaced the honeycombs in the hive, removed the protective suit, and checked it carefully to be sure no bees still clung to it. Ellie helped by carrying the steel canister back to the barn—carefully, since parts of her hands were still sore from her internment in the rough coffin the day before—while Devon piled the remaining items into the five-gallon bucket and tucked the suit under an arm. Two chickens appeared from out of nowhere and followed them, probably hoping they'd filled the bucket with mashed corn.

"I'm sure you're probably right," Ellie said as they walked, then edited out the qualification. "I'm sure you're right. I am resisting any future changes in my life because it gets more difficult to adapt as you get older." Thirty wasn't exactly older, but it probably seemed so to a young woman Devon's age.

"It shouldn't, though. It should get easier, because increased experience gives you increased confidence."

"It should, but it doesn't always." They reached the barn, where Devon stowed the equipment on some primitive shelves and hosed out the bucket. She hung the now-clean bucket from a hook on the wall and took to rinsing the steel canister.

Ellie tried again. "I'm sure your parents must worry about you. I know I would if my daughter was here and I was back east instead of vice versa."

Devon hung the washed canister on the wall, as well, and the valve dripped water on the dirt floor below. Then she turned off the hose, picked up the mason jar with the infused honey, and headed for the exit, not bothering to check that Ellie kept up with her before speaking. "Our families are perfectly capable of getting along without us. We tell ourselves otherwise only to salve our own egos."

"Surviving is not thriving. There's no reason career success has to preclude loving relationships. I'm sure your dad would appreciate a call. We could go together to find a signal." By this point Ellie had to trot to keep up with her. Devon wanted to be rid of her, and how.

Devon marched past the staff quarters and turned up the main drive. "If you walk up the road far enough, you should reach a cell tower."

"But there has to be a way—"

"Here's the classrooms. You'd better wait in the hall until they have a break. You're not allowed in once class has started."

"I know, but—"

Now she did gaze at Ellie directly, blue eyes narrowed in a face as harsh as a human Barbie doll's could appear. "You're showing a surprising lack of commitment, Ellen. I expected more from a professional woman like you."

With a firm grip on her jar of honey, she turned on one heel and walked away. After going twenty feet or so, she glanced back over her shoulder, and Ellie dutifully bounded up the three steps to pull the meeting hall door open. A murmur came from the classrooms down the side hall, but the main chamber stood empty.

She darted to a window. Pressing her temple to the wall, she was able to catch a sideways glimpse of Devon's form moving at a brisk walk. When it disappeared around the junior bunkhouse, Ellie went out the door again. The ranch wasn't a place where one could sneak around, bathed as it was in blinding sunlight and lacking any handy fences, shrubs, or even vehicles to hide behind. But she did the best she could, moving past the bunkhouses while making her footfalls over the gravel as light as possible. Ellie didn't know where they were headed or why—only that Devon's little craft project had waved a bloodred flag at her subconscious.

Chapter 31

Rachael ate her lunch at her desk, hardly a new phenomenon, but instead of reading a book or writing up her research as she ate, she scoured the internet for mentions of DC parties, Billy Diamond, and her sister's name. She didn't know exactly what to look for, and it felt a lot like procrastination.

Her phone rang. A robust "Good morning!" spilled out of the device, and she recognized the voice of Peter Steinberg, the Reno-area medical examiner. "Or afternoon. I can never remember if you're two hours different or three."

"It's one here. How are you, Doctor?"

Happily, he didn't care for the small talk, since she wasn't in the mood for it anyway. "Found something else on your Carlos Freeman. I said I still had to go through the tissue sections? Well, I found something in his heart slices."

He chose that moment for one of his maddening pauses, to smoke, sip, or just enjoy the dramatic effect. She opened her mouth to prompt him, but he went on.

"Piece of lead. It got wedged behind the papillary muscles. That's why I didn't see it at first."

"A bullet? He was shot?"

"Nah, it's barely two millimeters round. It's bird shot, if anything."

"So he was shot?"

"Nope. The heart was intact. The pericardium was intact."

"Was it an old injury?"

"No scar—at least on the heart. I'm thinking the thing was bouncing around in his bloodstream from an injury someplace else. Maybe in that left leg, which is largely missing. Up the femoral vein to the inferior vena . . ."

"So he was shot?" she repeated.

He paused again, but maybe to form his summary. "That pellet got into his heart somehow . . . but it didn't kill him. I didn't find any non-fish- and non-river-related injury. Maybe he was shot in the leg or some other spot, which the river ripped apart before we found him, or maybe some neighbor peppered him with bird shot for pickin' his apples when he was ten and this thing's been swimming through his system ever since. Seemed pretty clean, though. No real deposits formed."

"It might explain why he fell into the river," Rachael said.

"It might. *If* it happened at the same time, and not last year or last decade . . . If you find out anything like that, you let me know, right?"

"Absolutely. What about tox?"

"Clean as a choirboy's. The hair showed some drug use a year, year and a half ago, but that's it. Your man had been livin' healthy for a while now."

"Not healthy enough to save him."

She thanked Steinberg for his time, and they signed off with mutual promises to get in touch should anything interesting arise. Rachael pressed the HANG-UP icon on her phone and immediately tapped on Ellie's number.

The connection did not ring, only sent her directly to voicemail. There could be a number of reasons for that. Ellie could be attending, or pretending to attend, as it were, one of the sessions. She might have the phone on silent for the duration of her work there. She might have left it behind in a coat pocket. But it was annoying.

Not worrisome, she told herself. *Just annoying.*

She left a message. "Possible shotgun wound in victim's left leg—not at all confirmed. COD still drowning. Tox clean. Call me when you can."

Then Rachael sat back, her lunch forgotten, and told herself not to worry.

Devon continued up the drive, toward the river and Mrs. Coleman's house. Ellie approached the office, becoming immediately visible to anyone inside it, but didn't care. Next to the rickety steps, the plants of Devon's infusion thrust up from the ground, their healthy green leaves erupting from the dirt in slender ovals with a pointed tip.

Ellie moved around to the back of the office and crouched behind the cold skeleton of the bonfire. She planned to make up a bad excuse about checking the remains of her coffin if caught. A few of its planks, thinned and gutted from the fire, were still distinguishable from the tree branches and construction leftovers. Flies buzzed her, and a beetle charged her shoe, as if to warn her off its property.

Across the river, Devon paused at the entrance to the forest, where the land began to slope sharply upward, and turned to look behind her. Her gaze swept past the burnt wood and Ellie without pause. Ellie waited.

The beetle made another run at the toe of her sneaker before pausing to think better of it, though a caterpillar-like creature—the same insect in its larval state—came to back it up. They were carpet beetles, capable of burrowing into all sorts of things, like grains, meats, and other food stores. These were probably hungry since burnt wood provided little nutritional value. They were also *not* her favorite things, bugs . . . another personality trait she had purposely not shared with the leadership of Today's Enlightenment. Ellie could easily picture Galen tossing a few of these carrion eaters into the coffin with her.

"Stay away from the crops," Ellie hissed at them before hopping up and trotting along the riverbank, following her erstwhile mentor into the woody depths.

Devon had effectively disappeared, but Ellie soon caught up with her just as she reached the Coleman house. She went around the back, so Ellie hugged the outer rim of the front porch, moving as hastily as she dared. Its elevated surface hid her as she avoided twigs and leaf piles, anything that would make noise under her weight. Nearing the end of the porch, she heard the unmistakable sound of a key sliding into a lock, then turning. Devon's footsteps trailed inside, and after exactly two seconds Ellie poked her head out to view the kitchen door area. Nothing. The door had been closed but not pushed all the way shut.

It occurred to Ellie that her goal had become impossibly muddled. She had come to check on Devon and maybe convince her to call her father, not to spy on the young woman. But Devon didn't want rescuing, and what she had put in that honey wasn't basil, so Ellie needed more information before she could decide what to do next. She pulled herself up onto the wraparound porch, scraping her body between the floor and the lower rung of the porch railing. Wriggling out of windows, doing pull-ups with sore hands on a rustic veranda . . . This trip was turning into a much more physical job than she'd imagined. She liked it.

Ellie plastered herself against the wall to peer through the window and saw Devon at the sink, washing out a cute beehive-shaped honey pot. Or rather she ran the water at a trickle while she dumped the contents of the honey pot down the drain. She'd cut classes to let herself into Mrs. Coleman's house in the middle of the day only to do a little housekeeping?

Ellie doubted that very much.

Devon glanced toward the inner doorways every ten or twenty seconds—probably checking to see if the homeowner had heard her activity and come to investigate—but not in Ellie's direction. Once the ceramic pot had been emptied, she placed it on the counter without further washing, picked up the small handheld strainer she had pulled from a drawer, and poured the new honey from the mason jar into the beehive-shaped pot. The strainer caught the macerated leaves.

Devon stopped for what seemed like a quick internal debate, staring down at the strainer in her hand. Then she dumped the leaves back into the jar, using one fingernail to scrape the greenery off the mesh. She wiped a few drips off the ceramic pot with a paper towel, replaced the perky lid—which featured a porcelain bee grinning out from the center of a daisy—and put the pot back on the center island. She rinsed the strainer, stowed it neatly in the dishwasher, picked up the now half-empty mason jar, and stared around the kitchen.

Ellie tiptoed along the porch and around the corner, crouching well below window ledge range, in case Devon checked the rooms before leaving.

She needn't have worried. She heard Devon trot down the few steps to the packed earth and step around the back of the house, her feet crunching loose leaves and twigs. Either she didn't worry about Mrs. Coleman hearing her or even looking out a window or she was in a hurry to get back to the ranch. Possibly both.

Ellie kept her steps light as she walked to the kitchen door. She hadn't heard Devon relock the door, and indeed, the knob turned in her hand. Perhaps Devon meant to return shortly, though the kitchen door had been open upon Ellie's previous visit, so perhaps security didn't weigh heavily in anyone's mind at the ranch.

Ellie stepped inside and glanced into the adjacent room. Empty. She could again glimpse the view through the front windows. Through a frame of trees and branches, the valley and the larger ranch buildings appeared serene and gentle, picturesque. From a distance.

She listened for Mrs. Coleman, her maid or nurse or handyman if she had one, anyone else who might be in the house. Silence. She might not be home, or she might be napping or reading a book or quietly moving about in a remote part of the house. It didn't matter. Ellie knew what she had to do.

She took the honey pot and poured Devon's contribution down the drain, aided by a bit of hot running water, just as Devon had been. Unlike her, Ellie washed out the pot with more water and some soap, then rinsed it thoroughly. Then she blotted it dry with a paper towel and explored Mrs. Coleman's vast pantry. She found an unlabeled mason jar filled with golden fluid but opted instead for a half-empty commercial product. She refilled the pot, put it back in its place just as it had been, returned the honey jar to its spot on the pantry shelf along with Devon's now-empty mason jar, and did one last survey of her surroundings—again, just as Devon had—to be sure she had not left any evidence of tampering.

Right then, Ellie heard a scrape upstairs, as if a chair had been pushed back. A simple, everyday sound that set her heart jackhammering in a panicked flutter. At the same time she felt relief at the sound—Mrs. Coleman, alive and well.

And with luck, she would stay that way.

Ellie nipped out the door but first turned the lock in the knob and checked to be sure it caught. She had already foiled part of Devon's plan . . . might as well be thorough.

Ellie opted to go back the way she'd come, along the less noticeable path in front of the house. If anyone noticed her, she'd give them the "I'm looking for Galen" excuse. No one at the ranch would question why someone would seek out

Galen. Each of them would assume *everyone* wanted to be around the guru every minute of every day.

It might even be a good thing if Devon saw her. It might discourage the young woman.

Yes, the goal had shifted in the past half hour. She had come for some family intervention, then had decided to save Devon from Galen. Now, it seemed, she had to save Devon from herself.

Because the plants that grew in front of the office, the ones with the long, slender leaves and the stems that Devon had picked and said were basil, were not basil. Ellie wasn't much of a botanist, but she knew a bit about hazardous greenery and foxglove had always been her favorite. It had a cool name and bright bell-shaped flowers, with each cell chock-full of digitalis. The plants in front of the office had no flowers, but only because they had been planted recently, perhaps during the past spring, and foxglove didn't flower in its first year.

Digitalis, used in some heart medications, made the heart beat stronger by increasing the calcium in the heart's cells. It slowed the signals from the sinoatrial node, alleviating arrhythmias, which could be a lifesaver to someone with congestive heart failure. But given to someone with a relatively normal cardiac system, digitalis could increase the heart rate to a dangerous level and precipitate a heart attack. It could kill easily and quickly, all while the flowers bloomed prettily in the garden, making foxglove a favorite of mystery writers from Agatha Christie on down.

She crossed the low bridge over the water and took the shortcut along the riverbank, heading back to the ranch and not at all certain what she would do when she got there.

Ellie could be wrong—again, botany, not her forte. *Maybe* the "basil" leaves were an exotic form of basil or some other herb, and Devon regularly supplied Mrs. Coleman with infused honey, though in that case, why throw out an almost full jar? Maybe the leaves were foxglove, and Devon *thought* they were basil and wanted to leave Mrs. Coleman a surprise and was planning to ask the older woman later if she had noticed anything new in her tea. Maybe Devon had experimented with the infused honey in her own tea, found it to be a mild energy drink, and thought the older woman could use a pick-me-up, Devon being young enough to disregard complaints about the frailty of old age and ready to believe that it really *was* just a frame of mind.

Mrs. Coleman hadn't seemed all that robust to Ellie—in decent health, certainly, but not so strong that a dose of digitalis could be taken without consequences. It could precipitate a heart attack in someone of any age, so it certainly wouldn't do the elderly Mrs. Coleman any good.

But Devon's focus, her grimly aimed work, did not smell of a cheerful little gift to Ellie.

Ellie *could* be wrong, yes, but she didn't think she was. Which meant she would have to find a way to tell the very wealthy aging rock star that his daughter had just tried to murder someone.

Then, crying out with an abrupt peal that could have easily pushed Ellie into cardiac arrest herself even without the aid of digitalis, her phone rang.

Chapter 32

"Rachael? You mean this thing actually works again?"

"What thing?" Her boss's voice sounded faint and somehow staticky, but enough words came through to make sense.

"This phone! It got, um, wet. I haven't been able to get a signal since the last time I called you."

"Why not?" the city girl asked.

"Don't know, but I'd better talk fast before it fades." But how to summarize? Her words faltered. "Things are weird here—very weird."

"Devon okay?"

"Yeah. About that—"

"Are *you* okay?"

Other than being nail-gunned into a coffin, but that would take too long to explain. "Yes."

"Carlos may have been shot with bird shot. It probably didn't kill him, but it may be why he ended up in the water. Anyone there handy with a shotgun?"

"Don't know. I've seen the ammo but not a gun."

"Blood trail by the water? I know it's been weeks—"

"Haven't seen anything interesting." Ellie paused on the bridge over the river that had carried Carlos away, and gazed at the remains of the bonfire. Carrion beetles would be interested in any human tissue . . . including blood. Not to mention the bits of flesh that a shotgun blast, even with bird shot, would produce at close quarters. "But then I haven't been looking."

She started to leave the bridge, hoping to use the afternoon light to examine the riverbank more closely. But the phone gave a sharp crackle, and she stayed where she was. Trading information took priority.

"Still may be nothing," Rachael admitted. "What were you saying about Devon?"

Ellie took a breath. "That I think she's trying to kill Mrs. Coleman. The benefactress here. Elderly, very rich."

A long pause. No doubt Rachael was rearranging those words in her head, waiting for them to make sense.

But of course they didn't. "Coleman."

"She's a somewhat reclusive woman who supports the ranch."

"Why would Devon want to *murder* her? She's Billy Diamond's daughter. Why would she care about money?"

"She wouldn't. But Galen would."

"Galen. That's the, what, leader there?"

"The guru. This is a cult, and Devon's been converted up to the roots of her hair. Kinda makes sense. She broke away from her father's influence only to replace him with another high-maintenance man. She will do anything he asks, and clearly, that includes murder. I think I've managed to foil her for now, but I have no way to know what other booby traps she might have set up for this lady . . . Coleman is her name. We may need Billy to come out here. Do you think you could get him on a plane? Like, right now?"

No response. Not even the hissing, staticky sound.

"Rachael?"

CALL LOST.

Fabulous. Ellie redialed several times, without effect. She had no idea how much Rachael had heard. She could only hope it was enough.

In the meantime, Ellie remained solo, unarmed, and incommunicado.

The brush and roots and stones snatched at her shoes with every step along the riverbank. Ellie had just witnessed an attempted murder and was legally obligated to report same. She should call the local police, even if it took a hike over a mountain to do so, but what would she tell them? She had already destroyed all the evidence. Devon could just say, "Oops. I thought this was chamomile," or some such thing. If Devon had already gotten rid of any remaining murder weapon, it would be only Ellie's word against hers.

She could confront Devon. Best-case scenario, the young woman had honestly mistaken foxglove for basil and had the "oops" defense. Worst-case, she gave the "oops" defense and then found another way to get the poison into Mrs. Coleman . . . and maybe cooked up some extra for Ellie as well. Even worse case, she and Galen might decide that Ellie hadn't made progress with her emotional issues and that they needed to nail her inside a box again, this time for good.

Finding physical evidence of the attempted murder seemed unlikely, and evidence of the possible murder of Carlos, even more so. He had been gone for weeks, and perhaps the carrion-eating carpet beetles had developed a taste for marshmallows.

The area around the bonfire could not seem less suspicious. The ranch had no grass to speak of, only a sparse covering of weedy plants. No ripped-up drag trails or freshly dug hollows that might be a grave. The river lapped at the stones and dirt along the bank, reminding her of childhood days in Ohio and West Virginia. She saw nothing that—

Another beetle, down by the bank, and a tuft of green with rather pretty blue flowers pushed to its side. But then the whole freshmen class had been milling about the fire only yesterday, so those things meant nothing.

Until she glanced to her left and saw a wavering flash of purple under the water. Careful not to wet her only pair of dry shoes, she stooped for a better look. A left Air Jordan, deep purple, was wedged under a flat stone, one lace drifting back and forth with the current.

Carlos had been wearing purple shoes. An uncommon color for footwear. Certainly two people at the ranch could have the same taste in footwear.

Or perhaps it hadn't been the fish ladder that ripped Carlos's left leg to shreds.

Hardly conclusive, she told herself. The young man could have walked into the water there at the ranch and disappeared under its waves, despondent after Devon switched her considerable devotion from him to Galen. Or he'd simply decided to go wading on a hot day and misjudged the current. An expensive pair of shoes to ruin, but he'd hardly been poor.

Regardless, she needed to collect that. She needed to photograph it in place and then collect it. She snapped a photo with her phone, but she had no paper bag or secure storage area in which to put the shoe after recovery. She would have to leave it in place, consoling herself that if it had stayed there for three to six weeks already, it wouldn't go anywhere soon.

She hoped.

Meanwhile, if Carlos had gone into the water here, almost directly behind the office, it made Ellie very curious about the tiny holes in the tin building's wall. She needed to get inside that trailer.

For once, the tendency of cults to keep their members busy, busy, busy worked to her advantage. She could hear voices and the ringing of the nail guns from the construction site, and her own colleagues were almost certainly boxed up in the classroom, learning how to focus on their goals. She moved up the side of the office trailer, head bobbing up and down as she both kept an eye out for other people and checked the ground for clues to Carlos's fate. But she saw only another beetle.

The miniscule holes in the siding of the front exterior wall were visible in the bright sun, but still there were only four, with perhaps a fifth too high for her to touch. Around two millimeters, the same size as number nine shotgun pellets—and the same size as plenty of other items, right? Though why any of these would have punched through the office trailer, she could not guess.

She climbed the few steps and opened the door, praying, *Don't let anyone be in here.*

Anyone wasn't. The one-room office sat silent and empty. It hardly appeared to be the scene of a bloody confrontation.

Ellie got to work. Now that her phone had returned to life, she photographed the desk, the damage to its surface and side, the wall beyond it. She located the holes, then gently removed some of the taped-up notices, reminders, and calendar. Sunlight streamed through the tiny perforations, illuminating them well.

So okay, Ellie thought. *My theory is that someone shot off the still-unlocated shotgun with the bird-shot shells from the file cabinet. But did that shooter hit more than the desk and wall?*

At close range—and the tight quarters made it impossible to be anything but—even bird shot would do considerable damage to human flesh. Carlos would have bled. Maybe not much if only a few pellets hit him, profusely if the shots were direct.

From the shape of the indentations on the desktop, she could tell in which direction the pellets would have traveled:

from somewhere between the door and the desk, toward the wall. She dropped to her knees and studied the floor. She had noted the cleanliness of the industrial indoor-outdoor carpeting on her first visit. Now the pristine fibers could have a more worrisome history.

She needed to find out what lay beneath the fresh décor. At the junction of floor and wall, she pulled up on its fibers. The bare floor of the office was metal, like the walls. The carpet had not been tacked or glued down. She pulled it back to get a look, but the backing was both stiff and weighed down on both sides by the desk chair and the filing cabinets.

She got her fingers under the edge and yanked. It caused a wrinkle in the carpeting but exposed about four inches of metal floor.

It looked completely clean. No dried blood pools or handprints. She could smell nothing but new synthetic fibers.

Ellie crawled over to the desk on her knees and snatched a banker-like desk lamp off its surface. Pulling its chain, she took a moment to angle it toward the exposed floor without blinding herself and could soon see the clean metal. Mostly clean metal. If she looked *very* closely, she could see what seemed to be swirl marks where someone had cleaned up something dark. It could be blood, and she felt a pang at the thought of brainwashed little Devon mopping up her ex-boyfriend's blood while Galen stood and watched.

Of course, it could be dirt. Or a pesticide. Or something the metal had been treated with to make the carpeting stay in place.

She needed her crime scene kit. She needed phenolphthalein and an OBTI test, but they were twenty-seven hundred miles away.

She'd have to improvise. The pink basket with first aid supplies still sat on its shelf in the corner, and Ellie yanked it toward her, moving her lips to this unusual prayer: *Please have hydrogen peroxide. Please have hydrogen peroxide.*

The basket overflowed with bandages, antiseptic creams, aspirin and every type of alternate painkiller, tinctures for sunburn and bug bites and, yes, the standard brown plastic bottle of cheap hydrogen peroxide.

Next, she pulled a paper towel off a loose roll on Devon's desk and helped herself to an unopened bottle of water from a case under the card table. She tore two one-inch square pieces from the paper towel, wished she had latex gloves, then realized that really wasn't too important right now—

And then the door opened. She had been too absorbed in her task to listen and hadn't heard the footsteps on the wooden steps outside.

Angela stared at Ellie, crouched on the floor next to her desk, with the carpeting peeled back. She said nothing, but her mouth hung open in surprise.

"It's an experiment," Ellie told her. "Come here and hold this carpet out of my way."

Angela shut the door and did so. Angela was a young woman who so desperately needed direction that at this point she'd take it from anyone.

Ellie didn't give her a chance to reconsider. "Did you know Carlos Freeman?"

"Me? Yes, yes, of course I did. What—"

Ellie dampened the first square of paper towel and used it to wipe the possibly stained floor. Then she set the square on a clean paper towel and shuffled along the edge of the carpeting, using the desk lamp to study the floor. "He have any conflict with Galen? Or Devon?"

"Yes, he . . . he loved Galen at first. But when Galen was telling us about not needing sleep, Carlos said this other guy said the same thing in the nineteen forties, and how L. Ron Hubbard said he cured himself but he didn't. He'd say stuff like that. Carlos was a psych major. What are you doing?"

Ellie had done the same wetting and wiping with the second square of paper towel when she found an edge of the floor that seemed clean. "I need a control sample. I bet Galen didn't care for the challenge."

"He got real mad. He didn't act like it, but you could tell. Especially when Carlos said that calling ourselves resulters and how the people holding us back were remoras was stolen from Scientology and that sex cult."

"I remember." Ellie now had both squares on the clean paper towel and used the cap of the peroxide bottle to pour a few drops of the liquid onto each square.

"Yeah, had a bunch of modules like these classes. He said Galen was just rehashing derivative concepts. It's the only time I've seen Galen really *angry*. He didn't . . . he didn't know what to say."

"When did you get new carpeting in here?"

Angela blinked at the change of topics but, true to form, worked to fulfill the request. "I don't know. A few weeks ago? A month? I walked in one morning, and the old one was gone. What are you *doing*?"

Ellie peered closely at the square she had used to clean the steel floor nearest the desk. The dirty spot on the small square of paper towel had foamed up under the hydrogen peroxide. Tiny bubbles had appeared over the darkened area. The square with the sample collected four feet away, her control sample, merely looked wet. "I'm testing for blood."

"*Blood!*"

"It's not confirmatory. Other things can react with peroxide, animal tissue, plant tissue. What did Galen do then?"

"Huh?"

"When Galen and Carlos had an argument."

"He and Carlos walked away. Carlos decided to leave after that. *Why* are you looking for blood? Whose blood?"

"Did you see Carlos leave the ranch? Or did Galen just tell you he left?"

"Galen told . . ." A look crossed her face, bafflement slowly turning to horror. "You think this is *Carlos's* blood?"

Then the door opened again, and the man himself entered, Devon on his heels. They both stopped short to gaze at Ellie and Angela on the floor. The edge of the carpet slipped from Angela's fingers.

"Oh shit," Devon said, more to herself than to Galen. "She knows."

PART IV

ALL IN

"You would say to yourself, 'Why didn't you do anything? Why didn't you speak out?'" Eltringham later remarked. "You see, I was a true believer [. . . .] None of us did anything."

Lawrence Wright, *Going Clear: Scientology, Hollywood, & the Prison of Belief*

Chapter 33

With DC residents hypervigilant about any change in the beleaguered traffic system, the owners of the Snapple Sports Arena had been forced to move farther and farther away from the city center before they could obtain the necessary construction permits. Therefore, the arena, the perfect place for loud, crowded events that no one wanted in their backyard, had been built in the swamps outside Dentsville, Maryland. This worked to Rachael's benefit as, unlike with Billy Diamond's estate, she could drive there without having to go through DC. And this was one concert she didn't intend to miss.

She arrived two hours early yet still waited in a crawling line of traffic to get into the venue. Most of the fifty or so thousand fans would be sitting on the first-come, first-served grass and wanted a good spot. She paid the outrageous fee to park, also on grass, grumbling to herself how society had begun to crumble once event planners realized they could charge people not only to attend the event but also for the privilege of leaving their car in a poorly lit vast space exposed to any element that cared to visit.

The line to get into the arena also crawled, largely because all those grass-sitting early arrivals had thought to bring their own provisions, a nice meal of chicken wings and beer to have while lounging on a blanket under the late afternoon sky, or maybe even a thermos of coffee or brandy to keep them warm on that blanket once the sun dipped. But this idyllic image had evanesced thanks to the arena's "no outside food or drink allowed" policy.

Rachael handed over the ticket Billy had given her and moved on, wondering absently whether the policy had come from the same people who had thought to charge for parking. Forcing concertgoers to purchase all provisions from the company store had to give quite a fluff-up to the bottom line. Then she wondered if rock band fans were, statistically speaking, the type to throw bottles and cans at the stage. The arena might turn a blind eye to a Mendelssohn fan carting in a magnum of Dom, calculating the much lower odds of that bottle being chucked at the cello player.

Then she shook off these frivolous things and focused on what she would ask Billy. She had so many questions but needed to prioritize. Time would be short. And she didn't have time to wait behind the people arguing over the contents of their cooler.

She found a security guard—no trick, since there were at least six working the entrance gates—and flashed her pass. He took it, glanced at it, unimpressed to the point of ennui, and handed it back. "What's that supposed to be, ma'am?"

"It's a . . . oh." She had handed him her Locard Institute ID. "Sorry, not that. This." And she pulled out the laminated card Billy had made Newton give her. It hung from a purple lanyard and glowed a brilliant shade of coral. It said a number of things on it, but Billy had summed those up as "This will get you anywhere."

"I see," the man said, without any change of expression. "Come with me."

She followed him past the heavy lines of concertgoers, feeling their resentful gazes as she slipped past the turnstiles. She disappeared into the trees, still behind the security guy, using a small unmarked trail. If the guard turned out to be a serial killer, her body might go undiscovered until the spring thaw.

But they emerged on a hill overlooking the venue, an oversized, half-moon-shaped, dirty-white structure opening to a wide, grassy slope. A crowd had already settled there and was relaxing and enjoying the last of the late-day sun before the cooler night air swept in. A crush of colors and styles and shapes, ages and genders. Some fans walked around with canes, and some were clearly dragging their parents, too young to attend by themselves. Billy had not lost his universal appeal.

The stage loomed as they drew closer. Roadies wheeled amplifiers larger than themselves around, and an unseen crane lifted one on top of the other. Three men on a suspended catwalk, which didn't look sturdy enough to hold them, twisted, adjusted, and banged on blinding lights while screeching commands to an unseen engineer to "test B-four, C-six" and the like. A woman with a clipboard argued with a man with a clipboard. Among the chaos, a man and a woman in jeans and T-shirts sat on folding chairs near the middle of the stage, plunking one note after another on two acoustic guitars.

"How can they hear to tune?" Rachael wondered aloud.

The security guard surprised her by answering, "Years of practice."

She hadn't seen this couple at the mansion. "Are they in the warm-up band?"

"Nah. They're roadies." They reached the side of the structure, where a well-worn brick path led to a single door in the wall. "Part of their job is to tune all the instruments before every show. Most roadies are better musicians than the guys they work for. But . . . for whatever reason, personality, life choices, they're not onstage, and Billy is."

"Are you a fan?"

"Of Chimera, yeah. Who wasn't? It'll be interesting to see what kind of stuff he does by himself."

Two separate sheds in the back were protected by chain-link fences topped with barbed wire—probably electrical and plumbing stations. The grass had long been flattened into dirt, with only a few stubborn blades here and there. Cigarette stubs and two abandoned water bottles completed the look. The security guard stopped at the door and looked around, no doubt to check for crazed fans who might use the opening to storm the backstage area. Then he waved his key card over the pad, and the heavy door unclicked. He held it for Rachael, and she entered.

It didn't look anything like the stage of her college drama club productions or the numerous auditoriums in which she'd lectured. In contrast to an open stage, she immediately saw that the back half of the structure had been built for security. The walls were concrete, and the doors were heavy steel. Inside this area, the pervasive noise from the stage became a dull hum—which probably protected the eardrums of those present when the concert got going. She stood in a room that was larger than expected and was painted an industrial white, with fluorescent tube lighting overhead, illuminating the space with a nearly operating-room brightness. Four rows of picnic tables sat in the center, some with occupants eating dinner, which clearly had come from the permanent galley kitchen against the opposite wall. Others bustled around, carrying wires and boxes, more guitars, and a small snare drum. No one paid the least attention to her, and the guard had already left. His job had been to deliver her to the restricted area, and he had. She would have to find her own way from there.

She stepped in front of the boy with the snare drum. "Hi. Where's Billy?"

Young enough to still battle acne, he scrutinized her just as the guard had, but with much less authority. "Are you supposed to be back here?"

She held up the bright pink pass.

"Oh. Third door on the right."

"Thank you." She counted doors from where she stood, and moved to the one directly across from the kitchen, knocked. No answer. She could hear someone talking inside and knocked louder. Same result.

She turned the knob and went in, with very little idea of what to expect from a rock star's dressing room except what she'd seen in movies.

This wasn't it. Another concrete cube with stained indoor-outdoor carpeting, an equally stained dressing table with the requisite light bulb–rimmed mirror, a rolling rack of clothing, an old-fashioned corded phone mounted to the wall. It smelled of sweat and stale pot. The three armchairs and a couch, if a bit battered, were very well cushioned, though Billy Diamond failed to lounge on any of them.

Pacing between the dressing table and the armchairs, he whirled around to greet her and nearly lost his balance. "*There* you are"—as if he'd been waiting for her—"and it's about time. Do you have my stuff?"

"Stuff?"

"Yeah, yeah!" He scowled at her, swaying on his feet until he almost lost his balance and had to shift them to maintain equilibrium. Then he rubbed both eyes with his fists like a sleepy toddler and gave her a sharper look. "Who are you? You're not Isis."

"No, I'm not, Billy."

"Oh yeah. You're the other one."

"You don't look so good. How are you feeling?"

"Like death." He added a few expletives between "like" and "death." "Newton's bossing me around like Nurse Ratched. He's killing me! I'm not going to make it through the first song!"

Rachael feared that might be true. Billy's skin glistened with a sheen of perspiration, and his cheeks had turned ruddy. His hands shook, and he would pace a few unsteady steps, then tire and stop, then pace again. He stumbled into the back of the couch and angrily pushed it away, nearly falling over backward from the effort.

And he hadn't asked about Devon.

"Billy. Let me take your pulse."

"What? Why? You don't need to do that. Just give me something!"

"Like what?"

"Like anything! Don't play dumb, Isis!"

"I'm not Isis!" This came out a lot harsher than she intended, but someone needed to take control of the situation. "I'm her sister, Rachael. Now, sit down and let me look at you."

"No." The toddler had returned. "If you're not going to help, then go away."

Mom voice. "I *am* going to help. *Sit. Down.*"

With a petulant glare, he obeyed.

She sat on the couch next to him and felt his wrist. It had been a long time since her patients had had a pulse, but med school and residency experience all came back to her. "You're suffering from delirium tremens. You have tachycardia—too fast, irregular heartbeat—and you're sweating, trembling, and keep mistaking me for my sister. You're in alcohol withdrawal."

"No shit."

"I can help you."

He brightened. "You got something? You got some

candy? Isis always had candy handy. Candy handy!" He giggled, the sound a bit nauseating.

Cocaine would probably help with the worst of the symptoms, but of course, she wasn't in the habit of dispensing illegal drugs. Unlike, obviously, her sister.

"But first you have to tell me what you paid Isis for. Because I know it wasn't to throw a party."

"We gotta lock the door. Newton pops in here, like, every three minutes." He started to get up, but she pulled him back down.

"What was Isis doing?"

"But it was. To throw parties, I mean. Isis threw the *best* parties." He giggled again, and Rachael wished he'd stop. "Guys would blow into town, and I could call Isis, and she'd be there in an hour with the best stuff. What do you have? Give it to me."

"She'd sell you drugs. She used the party business as a cover to launder the money."

"What do you *have*?"

"Yes or no?"

"Yes!" He collapsed back against the cushions. "You're her sister. How could you not know that?"

Rachael stood up and went to the dressing table, where, among the unopened makeup containers and a box of tissues and a short stack of Styrofoam cups, her gaze fell on a photo in a dented metal frame. A rare picture of Billy and his daughter, taken close enough to read the tattoo on Billy's neck. Dust caught in its cracks made Rachael wonder if he carried it around in his guitar case.

She plucked off the uppermost cup, turned to Billy, pulled a flask from inside her blazer and opened its cap. His eyes followed the movement of her hands with a desperation that made her feel dirty. And guilty.

When she brought it to him, he drained it in an instant and

held the cup out for more. But she had backed away, out of his reach. He seemed too weak to stand, but that could change in a flash.

"What kind of drugs would she sell you?"

He answered promptly this time. "Anything I wanted. It wasn't the quantity. It was the quality. I saw too many people die on fenty . . . but Isis always made sure what we got would be kicky but wouldn't kill us. It's not easy to get that kind of reliable product." A tremor shook his body, scrambling the last two words, but she got it.

He waved her closer. The transaction had been completed, so she needed to pay up. Watching him carefully, she took the cup and poured another shot of the expensive bourbon, which had been her father's. His gaze never left the cup.

But she didn't pass it back to him. "Who was Kevin Destina?"

He frowned. His eyes tried to focus on her.

"Carson," she added.

"Carson! Her bodyguard. Don't know how that little punk got the drop on him. Carson was *sharp*. He came up in Philly." He held out one trembling hand.

She didn't move. "What about the guy who shot them? His name was James Flinn. Who was he?"

The focus didn't become any sharper. "He was a little punk. Give that to me."

"Was it really a rip-off? Or was he gunning for Des . . . Carson?"

"I don't know! Geez, I don't know anything about *that*! Now, give that to me, or I'm going to pass out right here." The outstretched hand waved in agitation.

"Was Isis the target? Did he mean to kill her?"

"I don't know! That had nothing to do with *me*." As well as his drunken face could convey, he seemed shocked at the very idea. "I had nothing to do with her business. I was just a *customer*."

She handed him the cup.

Again, drained it in one swallow. He inspected the inside of the Styrofoam shape and tilted it back again, straining for every last molecule. "I heard about it from Pat. He's the sound engineer. We were playing in Minnesota. No, not there, but somewhere in those North states. Crappy little stadium, but it had good acoustics. Come on." He held the cup out. "Fill it this time."

She didn't, but she poured a good shot, then sat on the couch next to him. "About Devon."

He almost choked, swallowed. "What? She okay?"

"Last I heard, yes. But we think she's in some trouble. That place she's in is not a spa or a retreat. It's a cult. And Carlos may have been shot before he was drowned. She's in trouble, Billy."

"Make her come back here. I can't believe she's going to miss my first show anyway. I have a plane. Get her back here. At least she can make it for the second half? I'm going to do—"

"It's not that easy. Devon's in deep, and it sounds like she is in danger of, well, irreparable damage to her future. You need to go to her."

"I thought you sent this woman—"

"She doesn't know Ellie. She's not going to listen to her. She needs *you*."

He gazed at her in shock yet managed to pull the flask from her fingers in one nimble gesture. She let him; there was only a dram left in it anyway. "Like now? I can't. I can't possibly. I'm about to *play*." He poured the last of the bourbon. "Maybe . . . Tomorrow we have a show. Then we go to . . . maybe Thursday. That might be free. I'll ask—"

"Billy—"

The door opened, and Newton took in Rachael, the flask, the cup, and Billy in one instantaneous flash, during which

Billy drained the cup. "What the hell are you *doing*? I need him sober!"

"Withdrawal doesn't work like that," she said.

"I know! Hell, I've managed enough drunks. I've been working him down for weeks!"

"Still not enough. He'd have a seizure halfway through the first set."

Billy's manager hung on to the doorknob as if it would hold him up. The manic energy drained and left exhaustion in its wake. "What am I going to do?"

Rachael stood up. "I can help you. And after that, I want to talk to your sound engineer."

Chapter 34

Devon turned instead to Galen. "Who the hell told her about that?"

His gaze never wavered from Ellie as he spoke. "It wasn't me. That only leaves you. I doubt she's been having any heart-to-hearts with Tim."

"Of course it wasn't me." She considered Ellie and her bottle of peroxide without admiration. "Maybe his family hired her."

It never occurred to them to ask Ellie. She supposed that when deception became so pervasive, transforming lives so completely, they saw no reason. If every answer was a lie, there was no point in asking. "Not his," she said as she rose. "Yours."

"As if," Devon snorted.

"What is going *on*?" Angela cried.

Galen shook his head as if wounded by disappointment. "You've been a pebble in my shoe since you got here, Nell. Why? Who sent you to make my life difficult?"

"Looks like Carlos Freeman's life has been a little more

difficult than yours. Why did you kill him? Because he saw behind the curtain? He knew your act for what it was?"

"Galen?" Angela's voice trembled.

Finally, he looked at her, held out his arms. "Angel. Come here."

Warring emotions battled within her, evident in every halting movement. She wanted nothing more than those arms around her, and yet—

She went to him.

As his fingers touched her sleeves, Ellie burst out, "She doesn't know anything!"

Galen gave the young woman a gentle hug, patted her back. Then he took her face in both his hands and spoke softly. "Nell isn't adjusting to our system, but it's okay. We can work with her. We'll do a group intervention. Will you gather everyone up and have them go to the barn? Will you do that for me?"

"Yes." Relief sounded in her voice. She probably thought nothing bad could happen in a group. But Ellie knew better. At the door Angela paused, only for a moment, catching Ellie's gaze. Ellie gave a slight nod, and the young woman left.

She didn't want Angela disobeying Galen. Look how Carlos had ended up. But she prayed Angela had at least the gumption to find a working phone and call the friggin' police, although what could she tell them? The peroxide foamed?

Galen waited for Angela's footsteps to recede. Then, "Who are you, Nell?"

"I'm Ellie Carr from the Locard Institute in Virginia. We're a forensic research and investigation foundation, and"—she turned to Devon—"your father hired us to make sure you were all right after he hadn't heard from you in so long."

"That's a lie. My father doesn't give a shit about me." At Galen's cold look, she added, "Seriously! There's no way."

"If this goes south because—"

"No!" Devon insisted.

He grabbed Ellie's arm in one crushing grip, yanked her forward, splashing drops of peroxide from the open bottle she still held. "I suppose you're going to tell us the FBI and the National Guard are on their way."

She hadn't, but now that he mentioned it . . . "I don't know about the National Guard. But you got the part about the Locard being an institute, right?"

He reached around her, jammed his fingers into the back pocket of her jeans, and grabbed the phone. He'd probably seen its rigid outline from the door as she'd bent over the bloodstains. "And you'll call in the troops on this, right?"

"Yes. Go ahead. Check the call history."

He didn't check the call history. He dropped her Locard-issued iPhone to the floor and smashed one heel into it. The poor thing had survived a soaking, but the edge of his cowboy boot nearly cut it in half.

Devon grabbed Ellie's other forearm, and they hustled her out the door. Ellie didn't resist. Alone with the two of them was the last place she wanted to be.

"I was assigned to come here. I'm *paid* to be here. That means a host of people, from the director to my boss to the local police to the payroll clerk to your father, know where I am."

"I keep telling you—" Devon snapped.

"Look around, Nell," Galen said, pausing in their march but not easing his grip on her arm.

And she did. The sun had dipped behind the mountain, and the brightest stars were making their nightly appearance. The crisp nighttime air flowed, enough to feel but not enough to kick up the dust. The clients were inside the buildings, but sounds wafted over from the construction site. Two people exited the gym, unhurried, neither one Angela. With the river and mountain to her back, she could see for what seemed like miles in a three-quarter radius.

What she did not see was a convoy of police cars, a troop of FBI agents, or even Rachael with a baseball bat. No one was on their way to rescue her.

At least not in time.

"What's the plan here?" Devon asked him. "Why get everyone else? We hardly want—"

Ellie tried to yank her arm from Galen's grasp, didn't quite succeed, and splashed hydrogen peroxide across his face.

He gasped and let go of her, allowing her to do the same to Devon.

Then she ran.

Chapter 35

Ellie followed the river in the dusky moonlight, taking precious nanoseconds to pick her feet up and over the weeds and brambles and rocks that reached up to grab her with each step. The odds of outrunning Galen seemed pretty slim. He was taller and was in decent shape, but she could only hope that years of making others fetch and carry had softened him. She could also hope he didn't keep that twelve-gauge stored any place too accessible and that he didn't have other guns or ammo with a more predictable flight pattern and carrying distance than bird shot.

Somewhere to her right, the chicken coop exploded into sound, no doubt alerting all to her flight, but that hardly mattered now. Galen couldn't have lost sight of her already. Typical first-aid-kit 3 percent hydrogen peroxide might irritate the eyes, but it wouldn't cause any actual damage.

If he and Devon were pursuing her, she couldn't hear them over her own harsh breathing. The river's edge appeared and then the narrow stretch she had found earlier. Ellie didn't pause but jumped off the bank and started leaping from stone to stone without hesitation, hoping her instincts and adrenaline would let her dart from one to the next.

They did not.

She planted her left foot on one stone, but the other landed awry on the next, then slipped off the edge into the water. As before, the last space to the bank proved too far to leap, and her left shoe wound up soaked as well. She slipped on the mud and fell to that knee, her kneecap landing on a stone with a painful snap. She ran on before the pain even registered.

Voices rang out. The river wouldn't hold Galen up, unless he decided to be delicate about getting his feet wet. Ellie couldn't make out the words he shouted, and didn't try. Instead, she plunged into the trees, heading to the north, the opposite direction she'd taken before. Away from the Coleman house and toward the slash in the mountain she'd seen where the land had been cleared for power lines. She could follow that slash to the town of Topaz. Of course, that entailed climbing over the top of a friggin' mountain, but right then she didn't see any other choice.

The light of the full moon couldn't penetrate the canopy of tree branches. Vague impressions of light and dark gave way to pitch black, and she ran full tilt into a wall of rough bark, the trunk of some child of the kingdom Plantae. Stars orbited her vision, and she felt a trickle of blood on her forehead. The blow had probably reopened damage from the coffin lid. She would never make it through the woods like this—she had to slow down if she wanted to get to the cleared swath without a concussion.

Ellie stopped. The only sounds were those of crickets and other noise-making insects, birds, and frogs. Given time, she might have identified most, thanks to Aunt Katey's training in the hills of West Virginia, but time was the last luxury she had right then.

The trees breathed, air flowing out through their leaves. But she didn't hear Galen or Devon or anyone else.

Maybe he had given up. Maybe he had gone for reinforcements, either weaponry or humans or both.

Ellie began moving again, hands outstretched. She might not be Davy Crockett, but she had a very good sense of direction. The air had gone past cool to cold, and her exposed skin tingled from the chill. Her wet feet squished with each step, but the activity kept them from freezing . . . so far. Ellie wished she'd brought her gloves and really wished she'd eaten something that day. She wished she had a sat phone. And a Glock 40 with two extra clips.

She tried not to think about snakes and coyotes and mountain lions. And spiders.

Mostly, Ellie felt the ground beneath her as if it were a living thing, its roots and brush trying to trip her and its stones making her stumble. Then she took one step into the open air and fell. A bush broke her sliding descent by thrusting its branches into her stomach until she cried in pain, hopelessness brushing her mind. This was ridiculous—she'd never make it out of these trees, much less to the next town. A fall over even a small cliff could kill her. Ellie righted herself and flailed her arms, brushing away the loose leaves and dirt and unseen bugs, until she could feel the first pricks of panic bubbling up in her.

Then she saw a glimmer of light. It could be imaginary, but she thought she could pick out the shape of the tree trunk in front of her.

She also heard a voice. Voices. It sounded like shouting, but very far off.

Ellie moved toward the light like a blind person, not only

holding her arms outward but also feeling the ground all around her with her toes before each step. It didn't require as much time as she expected, and she managed to reach a clearing. It had been only eight or ten feet away.

The moon seemed as if it could light a football stadium after what she'd just experienced, and she stumbled into the clearing, singing hallelujahs in her head. She paused for a moment to check for lights, movement, and to listen for the shouts of pursuers. There were none. The voices were gone, provided they hadn't been in her head to begin with.

Ellie began climbing the mountain.

She stuck close to the tree line, otherwise she would be immediately visible to anyone watching from below. The moon might only *seem* as bright as stadium lights, but she wouldn't take any chances.

However, the cleared-out area ahead, which looked like a gently sloping meadow from far below, was not even remotely smooth or gentle up close. The level of the ground wavered like the convolutions in a brain, and she quickly wound up in one dip so deep that she had to climb with hands and knees and swing on a few protruding roots to get out of it.

Then she heard a growl.

A deep rumbling from an animal's throat, but not close. It seemed to echo around her, a loud sound muted only by distance. Then a scream, definitely human. Ellie thought it came from across the open area, perhaps from somewhere closer to the valley. From somewhere in that direction, anyway.

The growling grew sharply from a rumble to a roar, and the scream grew from fright to terror in zero to zero point one. It reverberated in the cold air and sliced through the trees. In a flash Ellie felt more fear for that unseen person than she did for herself, which she would not have thought possible.

Both sounds cut off at the same instant, and in the silence a cold sweat flooded her skin.

But she also heard shouts. Pinpricks of light moved down in the valley, more than Galen and Devon. Galen's clients were coming up, coming toward her. Now that her eyes had adjusted, she could see them as clearly as the stones at her feet and the streak of blood on her left hand, near a broken fingernail.

Ellie had two choices: she could be a clear target in the open swath or she could run around until she killed herself in the very dark woods.

A thumping vibrated the ground, and someone spoke in a low tone. Her pursuers were nearly on top of her.

Ellie retreated and, with the help of the moonlight, jumped back into the crevice she'd just worked hard to climb out of. She froze and tried to listen hard, as if such a thing were possible. She couldn't believe they'd nearly caught up with her that quickly, but of course, she hadn't made as much progress as her sweat and pain and panicked rushing should have guaranteed her. They were taking the hiking path with flashlights.

She waited.

Nothing. And then, as clearly as if she wore high-quality earbuds, Ellie heard, "Ow! I . . . Something smacked me in the face."

"Quit whining." That was Audrey, her sharp focus cutting through the air and the spirit at once. "If she hears you, she's just going to keep running."

"But what are we supposed to do with her once we find her?"

"Bring her back to Galen. She can't endanger all our progress."

"But how could—"

"Oh, what the *hell*, Barry! Could you *just shut up* and move?"

That subdued him, but not for long. "What *was* that? Was it a wolf?"

A third voice spoke. "Who did it get? Do we know?"

A fourth. "How would we know that? We've been out here together the whole time. What, are we supposed to become psychic too?"

Barry again. "But what was it? Are there more?"

Audrey answered in a gruff, impatient voice. "How the hell should I know?"

"We can't possibly find her out here, you know." The fourth voice, that of a young man, vacillated between frightened and whiny. "This place is huge. And if she doesn't even have a flashlight, how far could she get? She'll break an ankle or fall over a cliff."

True, that.

"You want to go back and say so to Galen?"

This silenced the young man, but Barry couldn't stop talking. "It was probably a coyote. I heard one howling out here once. Do you think it killed whoever it was that screamed?"

"Please stop talking," Audrey snapped.

As searchers, they were no great shakes—it seemed they used their flashlights to watch their own step instead of scouring the woods for her. The young man was right; they'd never find anyone that way. But Ellie couldn't afford to scoff; as a hider, she wasn't much better. She'd just been lucky.

So far. She waited until their voices faded before she moved.

Okay. So it wasn't just Galen and Devon who were looking for her; they'd mobilized the whole camp. And not just a core of true believers, or they wouldn't have included the hapless freshman Barry. What was her crime supposed to be? At best, they might say that she had had a psychotic break and needed help. At worst, that she had killed Carlos—a month before she'd even arrived here. But, hey, they already believed Galen had the qualifications to mess with their psyches, so why not stretch their devotion a little more?

To anyone below who was watching the open swath—and she felt sure someone would be watching the open swath—her dark shape would be visible climbing into, then out of the crevice, then into it again. But she didn't have a choice, and besides, those in the valley had no way to communicate with those up in the woods. For once, the communications blackout worked in her favor.

Ellie might have been prodded from her hiding space by whatever had just fallen on her shoulder. She hoped it was merely a clump of dirt that had been loosened during her descent, but it could easily be a spider the size of a baseball. She chose not to think about it either way and scrambled up the rocks as quickly as her aching muscles would allow.

Ellie had no idea how Galen had distributed the search parties, but he hadn't had time to get them very organized. She had to expect anyone at any time on either side of the open swath. She also had to assume that he could guess her direction and her goal—she'd want to get to the town to get help, to get to a damned *phone*.

She plunged back into the inky blackness that was the forest and stumbled forward until she felt the clear space of hard-packed earth that was the trail. To her right, up the mountain, she could catch occasional flashes of light from Audrey's and Barry's flashlights. Ellie moved to her left.

Following a trail in complete darkness was only slightly easier than crashing blindly through a heavily forested area in complete darkness, but even that slight bit made a difference. Her feet quickly learned to tell the difference between the narrow but bare dirt path and the leaf- and brush-covered not-path. Of course, said path still held plenty of obstacles: roots, stones, pine cones, and a log with the diameter of a phone pole, which she promptly fell over.

Then Ellie saw more lights.

Not like end-of-the-tunnel lights. More like oncoming-train lights.

Chapter 36

More pursuers behind Audrey and Barry, but perhaps they had made up time because they didn't waste their breath chatting.

Ellie had figured that in such a situation, she would get off the path and hide behind a tree until they passed. She should have the advantage since they were moving faster and their breathing and footsteps should drown out any noise she made. Plus, the flashlights would ruin their night vision, rendering her both inaudible and invisible.

In theory.

In *reality*, no one tree seemed likely to hide her full-grown figure. . . . These weren't the California redwoods. Her coat was black, so that helped, but faded blue jeans didn't quite blend into the environment. As long as they kept the light beams on the path and didn't wave them around, she should be good, but why would they do exactly that? They were looking for someone hiding in the woods, after all.

Ellie put one hand up to protect her face and moved off the trail, trying to step carefully, to avoid any more tumbles, and also quietly. She had to work fast, but sticks snapped like dry bones under her feet, calling out their pain in sharp cries.

Her knees knocked into another fallen log, and she tipped forward, her fingers brushing its rotted bark coating, before she recognized it for the godsend it was. Ellie hiked one leg over the log, felt the ground on the other side of it and, satisfied, slid over it before dropping to a crouch. With one hand, she tried to judge the relative height of her head and the log. Would she be completely concealed if they swept a flashlight over the log? It didn't seem thick enough. She'd have to lie on the ground, with the stones and the spiders.

Ellie stayed still and listened.

Soft thuds pattered along, telegraphing their threat through the earth. Looking down the mountain, she saw flashes twinkle in the trees, producing split-second silhouettes of trunks and leaves. They *were* sweeping the woods. Ellie clamped her chest to the ground, pressed her cheek into the dirt. Any rustle could give her away.

She heard them approach—*thud, thud, thud*—and her heart pounded in time, so hard it had to be audible from a football field away. Steps continued—*thud, thud, thud*—past her spot.

But only one set. It sounded like only one set. But there were two pursuers. She'd seen two separate lights in that quick glance, right?

Ellie had no idea what the path she'd covered might look like were she to view it with the aid of a flashlight. Maybe she'd left scrapes in the dirt and a wake of scattered leaves that gleamed like an arrow toward her direction. She'd be a rabbit cornered by foxes.

Maybe her forehead or perhaps a knee had left a trail of blood, wet drops scattered over foliage that shimmered and glinted in a clear progression, right up to her hiding spot.

She also had no idea—she had not had any time to explore—if the log lay flat on the ground. There could be a half-foot gap in one spot, where her jeans might now be clearly visible.

Lights glistened above her, shot past, as their flashlights played over the log, over her.

Her heart stopped.

"Anything?" Tim, of course. The "not a real" fellow freshman.

The light continued to flicker over her log, moving in quick waves from left to right. At any second she would hear the crunching of his feet as he made his way to her hiding place and turned the light into her eyes, would feel the mindless terror and abject humiliation as when she had played Spotlight as a kid and the "it" person had found her unwise hiding spot. Would he say something cute, like, "Well, what do we have here?" or simply grab her by her hair and drag her down the trail to her execution? She could take one of them, she felt sure. But two? Not so easy.

A sliding crunch, the reduction of a pine cone to mulch as he took one step off the trail. The air in her lungs ached to scream. The muscles in her legs begged to bolt.

Another crunch. "No." She couldn't tell if it was Tim's partner, Andre, or not.

He trotted after Tim and faded into silence.

Ellie didn't dare breathe or lift her head from the dirt for what seemed like a full minute but probably wasn't even ten seconds. Then she felt something wiggle under her temple and jumped up in revulsion.

The woods were pitch black once more. Ellie listened mightily, scanning for more lights. She could see bobbing flickers from Tim's flashlight and maybe Andre's, and this time she did wait a full minute before moving, climbing back over the slimy log and retracing her steps to the trail.

Ellie could continue up along the path and hope it led her over the mountain and eventually down to the town, hiding in the trees whenever a pursuer came by, but her odds of success were not high. She had managed it once only because of the luck of encountering a large and well-placed log, and so many things could have gone wrong.

But Mrs. Coleman's house, she estimated, sat only a thousand feet or so below her, back toward the ranch. A short, easy walk in the daytime, though one that might take her an hour in her present circumstances, but it was still simpler than the all-night trek to the next town, through deep crevices and wild beasts and people looking for her. It could be wishful thinking, with basic fear at its core, but doubling back might be a wise move.

It might also be a stupid, cowardly, fatal move.

Ellie headed downward, feeling her way along the path.

She didn't walk for too long—relatively speaking—before she saw a light ahead, a steady one, not from someone's swinging flashlight. She felt like bolting toward it but made herself step even more carefully, if that were possible. Lights meant people. And people might mean death.

Chapter 37

Ellie walked toward the Coleman house without a clear idea of what to do when she got there. Surely Mrs. Coleman would have the door locked at night. And Galen and Devon might be there, forming a war room. No, unlikely . . . Why would they go there instead of staying at the ranch, where all the clients would know where to find them for updates? They had seen her run into the forest, but a more logical move for her would be to cross the river again farther on and head for the road. It would be a longer walk to town via the road but an easier one, and Ellie might be able to hitch a ride. They would have spread some of their manpower out across the valley floor, sent some pursuers into the forest, and remained at the ranch to monitor progress.

They also wouldn't want their benefactress to know they'd had an escapee.

But Galen knew that Ellie had tried to talk Mrs. Coleman into allowing her to make a phone call once before, and that the most direct, least-trekking-involved option for her would be to do so again.

From within the trees Ellie watched the house for movement, wondering how far Mrs. Coleman would go. If the nice old lady patted her hand and regretfully told her she couldn't interfere with her treatment by loaning her a phone, what then? Would she believe her story of a murdered young man or think it had come from the fever dreams of withdrawal?

Ellie could force her way into the house—she'd be surprised if the older woman weighed a hundred pounds—but the last thing she wanted to do was push around sweet Mrs. Coleman.

However.

She had no other options.

Only two windows were lit up in the night, one on the upper floor and one in the lower front corner. There were two exterior floodlights on the two far corners, mounted just under the eaves and trained on the ground around the house.

Ellie came out of her hiding place and trotted over to the kitchen door. There she could peek through the glass panes at the room where, only a few hours before, she had dumped out Devon's poisoned honey. The kitchen sat dark and empty, the edges of the counters and the island only vaguely illuminated by leftover light from the room next door.

Ellie tried the knob. It turned. This meant that either Mrs. Coleman was as shockingly casual about personal security at night as she was during the day or that Galen and Devon had already arrived.

She pushed the door inward. It gave only the slightest creak as she stuck her neck into the guillotine of door and jamb.

Dead silence.

Once inside, Ellie shut the door behind her. In two steps she reached the wall phone and picked up the receiver— might as well check, just in case it had been miraculously restored to life at some point during the past day.

It hadn't.

Ellie padded silently—or as silently as she could, with only the slight squishing sound of her still-damp shoes to give her away—to the arched opening into the next room, the one with the light. It seemed to be the only lit room on that floor, and the long hallway was dark.

A table lamp with a fringed shade glowed merrily, an empty glass and a book underneath it. A chair next to it faced the windows, away from her, and a set of thin, frail fingers rested on the overstuffed arm. Mrs. Coleman. Asleep? Dead? Had Devon poisoned anything else in the kitchen?

Just then, Ellie could not risk finding out. She could not trust Mrs. Coleman not to give her away, even if told the truth. The woman doted on Galen; Ellie was the crazy ex-addict who kept showing up on her doorstep.

Ellie decided to borrow her cell phone without permission. Trespassing, entering, and burglary. After a lifetime of helping to enforce laws, she now broke several.

But Ellie could live with that. With luck, she would have the opportunity to live with that.

Now she only had to locate a five- or six-inch-long object in a strange house with at least ten rooms. It could be in a kitchen drawer or on a table by the front door or in Mrs. Coleman's pocket or stuffed in a closet. But as long as no one came knocking, she had time.

The house seemed extremely tidy—a huge break. Ellie assumed—hoped, really—that Mrs. Coleman was a logical and everything-has-a-place type of person, so she would keep her phone in a logical place. . . .

Just please, some place other than her pocket.

Ellie swept the kitchen, opening the uppermost drawers and poking around in the dim light. She checked the pantry even, but no love there. No phone, no charging cords, no adapters.

She did make her second most important find in the form

of a small but brilliant flashlight, which she did not turn on other than a quick click to make sure it worked. Surely someone from the ranch would check out the house, and the bouncing beam of a flashlight would give her away faster than a Klaxon. From the same junk drawer, she got a rubber band, then ripped off a piece of paper towel from its roll.

Ellie tiptoed up the hallway. The exterior lights allowed her to see the outlines of the furniture and the shape of most other objects. As she walked, she doubled up the paper towel and folded it over the glass of the flashlight, then secured it with a rubber band. It still might give her away, but with luck, the paper would diffuse the beam enough to make it less noticeable to someone outside the house. It would look like a night-light, albeit one that happened to move.

Ellie checked the front door but doubted anyone used it. No small table or stand had been placed nearby to hold mail and car keys and, oh yes, cell phones. She moved on. She would have also loved a car to borrow—okay, steal—but unless Mrs. Coleman's came with a cloaking device, Ellie had to guess that she no longer drove. The house didn't even have a garage.

She found jackets and shoes at the south end of the house, next to another glass-paneled door. A heavy, sensible, and no doubt designer-brand woman's handbag hung from a peg, and she hesitated. Poking around in another woman's purse violated every tenet of civilized behavior. . . . Ellie had just snuck into her home with less trepidation. But desperation won out. A purse seemed the most logical place in the world to find a woman's cell phone.

Papers, what felt like a datebook, lipstick, a powder compact, a mini-umbrella—which seemed odd for this climate—a container of mints that rattled, tissues, two small bottles . . . but no phone. Ellie made herself take the handbag off the peg and go through it again, slowly, trying to shift items to one side of each section as she worked through the morass of stuff with her diffused-light flashlight propped under her chin.

No phone.

She hung the handbag back up and checked the pockets of the three jackets and one sweater on the pegs. Nothing.

Kitchen, purse, office, bedstand. The likely places to keep a phone. Ellie hadn't found a desk and was out of rooms on the first floor. Time to head upstairs.

The stairs were carpeted and didn't creak much. She couldn't imagine how terrified Mrs. Coleman would be to wake from a nap and hear someone moving about overhead in a supposedly empty house. She might have a heart attack, and Ellie would complete the job she had thwarted when she threw out Devon's honey.

Or she might have a shotgun stashed in a downstairs closet for just such an emergency and would complete the job Galen had started when he chased Ellie into the woods. Everything about the situation sucked—for both of them.

The exterior lights continued to guide her through the upper floor, past three guest rooms, two baths, all of which seemed too tidy and sparsely furnished to be used much. Ellie skipped them. At the end of the corridor she found the master bedroom, made obvious by the rumpled four-poster bed and the open closet door. An overhead light illuminated the room well—oh happy day!—and sheer curtains covered the windows, so she stopped tiptoeing and made a beeline for the nightstand.

But Mrs. Coleman wasn't a millennial and didn't text in bed—only a tub of hand cream, a lamp, a Bible, and a box of tissues rested there. The matching nightstand had a matching lamp, unlit, and nothing else. Ellie checked the drawer of each for good measure, rummaged quickly through booklets, pens, and handkerchiefs. No phone.

The furniture did not match the more rugged ski-lodge look of the first floor. It was white with curlicued accents, what Ellie's grandmother used to call French Provincial. The set included a rolltop desk, open to reveal a clutter of papers and pens and bills and notepads and stationery.

And a cell phone.

On its charging pad.

Ellie's breath choked in her throat, and she was momentarily paralyzed. Then she crossed the few feet of carpeting between her and it, snatched the thing up, and pressed the HOME button hard enough to break it.

It didn't break. The screen glowed to life with a digital number pad and an instruction: ENTER PASSWORD.

Ellie tried not to use language that Aunt Rosalie would not approve of. But in this case, she muttered, "*Shit!*"

Okay, think. The phone had one flickering bar, so it got some sort of signal. Galen and his team were outside somewhere, looking for her and maybe getting eaten by coyotes. Ellie had time. She set the phone back on its pad.

Surely Mrs. Coleman would have written her password down. Mrs. Coleman would have a neatly maintained address book with an embossed leather cover, or maybe an account ledger, and would have duly noted her phone password. Of course she would have.

Ellie checked the two drawers and found a supply of greeting cards and colored markers but nothing helpful. She searched the desktop and the cubbies in its hutch, methodically moving from end to end, fingers clutching and probing in controlled chaos. It didn't have to be in an address book. It could be on the phone's receipt or manual or an index card or a flippin' store coupon, for all she knew. All the while Ellie fought down the rising fear that she had bet on Mrs. Coleman being a character from a novel, a dowager who had been raised to do proper, ladylike things, such as wear white gloves and write thank-you notes on scented stationery. But Mrs. Coleman would have read those novels in her youth, not lived them, and it sounded as if she had *not* been interested in being a proper lady during any decade of her life. She had roamed the globe and remained independent enough to live alone on a mountain. She could have a memory like a bear trap and might never have forgotten a password in her life. Ellie might be wasting time trying to find a way into a tiny electronic vault that was never ever going to let her in without the owner's permission.

She combed the entire desk without finding a piece of paper that said, *Phone pw*. Time to admit defeat. She had once processed a burglary in which the victim had kept the combination to the safe written on a piece of paper tucked into the pocket of a bathrobe hanging at the back of her closet. A simple system like that couldn't be beat.

Ellie picked up the phone, pressed the HOME button with forlorn despair. The number pad floated over a photo of evergreen trees. And then she saw it.

In the lower left-hand corner, the small word *emergency*. In her panic over the password, it had not even registered. Ellie had used her phone twenty times a day every day for years, and not once had she needed to see that word, and so she hadn't. Now she spent only a split second screaming over the idiocy of not having remembered that even a locked phone could still call 911, the only call she needed to make. Ellie pressed the word with her thumb.

A series of fuzzy clicks and she heard the beautifully melodious sound of a calm woman on the other end. "Ni . . . ne . . . wha—"

Then nothing.

No, no, *no*! Still not enough of a signal to communicate. But even the inadequate success buoyed her. Maybe if she went outside. If she went farther up the mountain or circled around and headed down to the road on the other side of the ranch, in the opposite direction to town, where they might not look for her. Somewhere, somewhere out there was a usable cell phone signal. All she had to do was find it.

Ellie slipped the phone into her pocket and turned to leave.

Galen stood in the doorway. "Breaking into an old lady's house, Nell. Not cool. I'm beginning to think Today's Enlightenment isn't going to be able to help

Chapter 38

Ellie stared. There didn't seem much else to do.

He held out his hand and asked for the phone.

Ellie declined to obey, crossing her arms. "Did someone get eaten by a coyote?"

"Not that I know of—yet anyway. What are you doing in Frances's bedroom, Nell?"

"What are *you*?"

"Following your trail. Are you going to come downstairs so we can discuss this like civilized people?"

For what seemed like the fourteenth time that day, Ellie didn't see another option. The upper floor had no exit, unless she wanted to jump out a window, and Mrs. Coleman hadn't left any handy guns or knives lying around her boudoir. "Sure. Be happy to."

Ellie started toward him cautiously, wondering if he meant to precede her, walk behind her, or just break her neck right there. Let him try. Without the muscle-bound set of Tim and Andre to back him up, Ellie still felt her chances in a one-on-one were excellent. But once she was within arm's reach, he only asked for the phone again. Ellie handed it to him and said, with a bravado she most certainly did not feel, "Take it. I already called nine-one-one."

He glanced at the screen. "No you didn't. No signal."

"Right." Apply a bit of reverse psychology, anything to keep his mind unsettled and jumpy. "Of course."

He waved an arm for her to go ahead, but she saw him take a second, worried glance at the screen. Apparently, he didn't have the password, either, because he didn't try to check the call history. But her heart sank to her toes, and she couldn't rally it. Nine-one-one would have returned a disconnected call, if they could. Either the signal hadn't been strong enough to provide them with the caller ID or now it wasn't strong enough for them to call back. And Rachael would be waiting for another report on Devon's activities, not convincing the FBI to get a warrant. All in all, the odds of the authorities arriving to help ranged from slim to absolute zero.

Ellie retraced her steps down the upstairs corridor, acutely aware of Galen behind her. Lights blazed at the bottom of the stairs, where Devon waited, arms crossed. In the dark Ellie had thought she moved like a ghost through the house, but with the lights on, she could see the faint but clear outlines of her muddy shoes against the beige carpeting. Devon might as well have left neon arrows pointing the way to her.

She noticed a reddening spot on Devon's cheek and wondered if it was man-made or if Devon had fallen while chasing her. If the latter, it might explain why she practically spat the words at her when she said, "Who told you?"

"About the blood trail from where you shot Carlos? Divots and beetles. Why did you kill him?"

Devon ignored her questions, only shook her head and muttered, "Couldn't believe it when I looked out the window. When I was slammed against the window." She gave Galen a dark look.

"Temper, temper," he murmured.

Ellie had nothing better to do than persist, and every moment they said things was a moment in which they weren't killing her. "So why did you shoot him? And why"—she nodded her head at Mrs. Coleman, who was making her way up the semi-dark hallway like a wraith—"are you trying to kill her?"

Devon scowled. Galen moved from behind Ellie so he could see Devon's face and frowned at the sight. Coming up between them, the older woman rubbed one eye. Far from having a heart attack from waking up to uninvited guests in her home, she stretched her mouth into a wide smile. Her eyes lit up, she said, "Theresa! You're back."

"What do you mean by that?" But Galen spoke to Ellie.

"Devon poisoned the honey with foxglove . . . digitalis. It causes heart palpitations and can easily lead to death in someone with compromised cardiac muscles. Like an elderly person."

"That's a complete lie." Devon spoke without the slightest change of expression.

But Galen, for all the exaggeration of his psychic abilities, knew her well. "Then what's she talking about?"

"Foxglove?" Mrs. Coleman said. "I used to have that in her garden in Charleston. Theresa, where's your coat? You shouldn't be running around in this weather without one."

"I'm fine," Devon told her, summoning a smile.

Galen would not be sidetracked. He asked Ellie, "What honey?"

She ignored him and focused on Devon. "Wondering why she's still breathing? Because I followed you here. After you filled that honey pot, I dumped out the honey and refilled it from a jar in the pantry. You don't have to explain to me why you tried to poison Mrs. Coleman. I'm sure it was because your boss told you to. But you should have the courtesy to explain it to her."

But Devon's boss only demanded, "Poison? What have you been doing?"

Devon told him not to listen to Ellie. That had about as much stopping power as a penny on the tracks to a passing train. For all his posturing, Galen picked up the gist at the speed of lightning.

In what seemed like genuine anger and confusion—maybe the first real emotions Ellie had seen from him—he blurted, "Why would you risk her kicking it before she signed the deed over?"

Mrs. Coleman stiffened in affront. "I *did* sign . . . well, not the deed. The will. But that's none of your business, young man."

Ellie began to wonder if she should back out slowly. The south door stood within reach. She shifted her weight, moved her right foot four inches closer to it. Not much of an escape plan, but better than nothing.

"*What* did you sign, Frances?" Galen demanded, iron in each word.

But Frances Coleman had more iron than all the Galens of the world combined. "I told you, that's none of your concern. I'm sure Theresa will look out for your little ranch after I'm gone. Won't you, Theresa? Galen, have you met my daughter?"

Ellie stopped moving toward the door in spite of herself. *Daughter? The one from Bolivia?* But of course, that couldn't be, and she knew it even better than Galen did. But to a frail woman desperate to see her child again—

"This isn't your daughter!" Galen exploded. He turned to Devon. "What is she talking about? What are either of them talking about? What have you done?"

"Nothing! She just—" Devon stopped and put an unconvincingly solicitous arm around Mrs. Coleman's thin shoulders. "It's late at night, and we woke her up. Let's get out of here and let her rest. We have more important things to take care of." She jerked one temple toward Ellie, as if he might have forgotten about the threat she posed.

Of course he hadn't. He sucked the fury back inside himself with one deep breath and said, his voice low and tight, "Frances, sweetie. Are you telling me this is your daughter? The one from Bolivia?"

The old woman's face, which had appeared nervously angry, now brightened into a broad smile. "Yes! I'm so glad you could finally meet. And she's not *from* Bolivia, silly. She only worked there for a while. With the Peace Corps."

"Of course." He glared at Devon, who seemed not to breathe, as if her lungs had turned to stone. "And you've changed your will to leave everything to her?"

"Yes." She drew out the word with reluctance. Frances Coleman would have been taught by her parents not to discuss family finances with nonmembers, even sweet boys she liked. But she had never been a shrinking violet either. "Yes. And as I said, she will take care of your . . . facility . . . after I'm gone."

Galen seemed to be gritting his teeth in order to keep smiling. "That's lovely. Except her name isn't Theresa Coleman."

"Not *now*," Mrs. Coleman admitted.

That was all she had to say to explain the situation. Somehow Devon had convinced Mrs. Coleman that she, Devon, was her long-lost daughter and rightful heir. Ellie didn't see how it could hold up in court, since Devon was decidedly *not* Theresa Coleman. And why had she done this at all when Billy had all the money she could spend? And if she had done it for Galen, why didn't he know about it?

"Frances, dear," Galen said, "would you show me your new will?"

Doting only went so far. "I will not. That's for family only."

Ellie edged another step toward the door.

"Of course. Please forget I asked. Well, we have a great deal of work to do tonight, so we will leave you to enjoy the evening. Oh, and here's your phone back."

A pained but outwardly polite scuffle ensued when Mrs. Coleman didn't want "Theresa" going out without a sweater. Ellie used the distraction to get her hand on the doorknob, but then the door opened, and Tim crowded into the foyer. His gaze blamed Ellie for the chilly and uncomfortable tramp through the woods.

"Where's Andre?" she asked.

He didn't deign to answer. The man towered at least four inches over everyone else; he outweighed her by a hundred pounds, all of it, apparently, muscle. He had a jagged scar on one side of his neck, and one of his fingers ended in a stub. When Galen headed for the door, Tim closed one massive fist around Ellie's right bicep. Escape would not be an option.

Chapter 39

Tim dragged her back into the chilly night, down the drive toward the river and the ranch. Ellie didn't resist. Plans had changed; now she needed to stick with Devon, despite the girl's murderous bent. Devon herself might be the next victim.

Behind them, Galen had a similar grip on his acolyte. "How did you pull that off? I can see her mistaking you for Theresa—once in a while she thinks I'm her dead son—but you actually got her to change the will?"

"Of course not! She's old, and she's a bit crazy. I told you about sundowning. They do this—"

"And then you slip her some poison so she kicks off?"

"You can't listen to *her*." Meaning Ellie, she supposed.

"Leaving everything to you. But probate court is going to know you're not her daughter. How did you think that was going to work?"

A breathy exclamation came from Devon, as if she'd been struck or her arm jerked hard, and Ellie craned her neck to glance behind her.

"Exactly. I didn't, because it wouldn't. She's just chattering, like when she talks about Kenya or her studio in the Philippines."

"And *then* what did you think you were going to do? Give it to me like a Christmas present? Was *that* your plan?"

This opening gave Devon a chance to admit her deed with a spin that would please him.

Take it, Ellie silently advised.

She didn't. "I had no plan. It never happened. She just gets confused sometimes. You know that."

If she didn't do it for Galen, then she wanted the money for herself. Because Billy had spent all his fortune? He seemed like the type. Or simply to have the funding to break away from him once and for all?

"Then why did this bitch say you tried to poison her?" Again, Ellie assumed the "bitch" part meant her.

They emerged from the whispering trees, plunged back into the moonlit valley, and crossed the bridge over the river.

"Because she's lying. She's lied about everything since she got here."

Not everything, Ellie thought. But she did not enlighten him. Ellie had come there to save Billy's child, not throw Devon under the bus to save herself.

"That's a damn specific lie. And you insisted on growing that foxglove stuff. I wanted daisies—"

I'm about to be murdered by a man who quibbles about daisies. Ellie craned her neck and glanced behind her again and interrupted. "Where are we even going? What are you planning to do?"

"You'll find out," Galen said.

"Your plan *should* be packing up and heading out to invent another résumé. I already called nine-one-one. They're on their way."

"Yeah, sure," Galen said. "Tim, take her to the barn. And

get everyone else back here. Who screamed before? Sounded like Mark."

"It was. Saw a coyote and panicked, but his squealing like a little girl scared it away."

Ellie struggled against Tim, but not seriously. She no longer wanted to escape. She needed to keep an eye on Devon. No innocent coed, but the young woman was still Billy's daughter and the Locard's client. And maybe a brainwashed teenager.

Maybe not.

Galen didn't hustle Devon away, however. The foursome trudged along.

Two people wandered up the path, walking with flashlights. Ellie did not recognize them, and Tim told them that the search had ended and that everyone needed to gather in the barn. That gave her something to think about. If Galen meant to murder her, would he want to do it in front of a hundred witnesses?

He might. He was, after all, a cult leader. He would want his followers to see his power over life and death—*her* life and *her* death. He would want them to participate, to make them coconspirators so that guilt and legal considerations would keep them silent in the future.

Or he might not mean to kill her. He might be planning another group smackdown, with her playing the role of Jeremy. Ellie would be beaten en masse.

But she would live. So, not so bad.

Unless, as often happened in group actions, things got out of control. Then bad.

Her eyes shut against the sudden light as Tim dragged her into the barn. Devon and Galen followed, and three other ranch members showed up shortly thereafter. Tim held her in the center of the packed-dirt floor, awaiting instructions. Directly overhead dangled the huge hook and chain hoist. Was Galen planning to lift her up to the ceiling like he had Barry, only without the benefit of a body harness? Maybe with a noose?

Out of earshot, Galen gave Devon some order, jerked his head toward Ellie, and then busied himself with the farming equipment.

Ellie's fellow classmates continued to trickle in, one or two or three at a time. She had no idea what communication system had summoned them, since she hadn't heard any sirens or even shouting. Maybe Galen really did have the psychic power to control their thoughts. Most glared at her, no doubt blaming her for their chilly, dangerous trek through the forest. Some seemed afraid, and others simply confused. But they all stayed in or near the open barn doors, keeping their distance, as if Ellie carried the plague.

"Devon," Ellie said as soon as she came near her. "We need to get out of here."

"Shut up." The woman glanced at Tim. The guy wasn't deaf, which left them no way to have a private chat. Unless Devon told him that Galen needed his help and that she would guard the prisoner.

She didn't.

So, with nothing to lose, Ellie pressed on. "He's never going to let you live to collect the Coleman estate. She's a strong woman in her way, and he won't be able to talk her into changing the will again. If you die, his problem is solved."

"She was never going to leave it to anyone who is *not* her flesh and blood. This way he can marry me, and then it will be his." She stated this firmly, but with a tiny, surreptitious peek at Tim. "Or if he doesn't want to do that, I can just quitclaim it over to him. The ranch will be his."

Clearly, Devon had rethought her options in the past four minutes and had decided to take the lifeline Galen threw her: It had all been for him. Her subterfuge had stemmed from her devotion to her master, and now she hoped Tim would report to that master how Devon had always had Galen's best interests at heart.

But Tim's stone face revealed nothing; he didn't buy it any more than Ellie did.

Ellie said, guessing, "You're also the only witness to the Carlos Freeman murder."

She didn't bother to deny either the murder or the witness part. "No, I'm not."

Tim's sphinxlike composure faltered at this. He stiffened, blinked, and gazed at Devon with sudden concern. In Tim-speak, he had burst out with a startled "*What*?"

The crowd had grown, and Galen trotted toward them with a rope in one hand and the oversized black and yellow nail gun in the other. Ellie had no time left and hissed, "Devon. You're in danger. If he's willing to murder me in front of a hundred people just to keep me from talking about some stains under a carpet, what do you think he's going to do to you to keep you from stealing this land out from under him?" Ellie ignored the fact that Devon had been willing to murder a kind old woman; it would only remind her that Ellie's death would benefit her as well.

"I would never keep anything from Galen." She enunciated every word, which only made them less convincing, not more. "I love him. I will never leave him."

Fifteen feet away now and closing.

"He's going to kill you too. He has no choice," Ellie insisted. "If you aren't willing to help me, at least help yourself. Get out of here and don't look back. Think of your father. He loves you. He wants you to come home. That's why I—"

Thoroughly startled, Devon croaked, "*What*? What the hell would you know about my father?"

"Don't listen to Nell," Galen said. "She's a proven liar. But it's something we're going to work on, isn't it, Nell?"

Gah. "You know that's not my name, right? You can pretend you're Charles Manson and she's Squeaky Fromme, or whatever floats your boat, but are you really going to murder me in front of one hundred or so people? You think not *one* of them is going to talk? Not *one* is going to come to their senses and tell the cops, make a deal with the prosecutors to avoid a conspiracy charge? Like Tim here, if he ever grows a brain?"

Tim tightened his grip until her arm tingled, as if he didn't appreciate her characterization.

Galen grinned. "Who said anything about murder? All I'm going to do, Nell, is help you face your fears."

Her mind went blank. What had she told him of her fears—

"You're going to make a speech."

Public speaking. That had been her third untruthful entry. The trip up the mountain had already dealt with the heights thing. In a moment of cautious relief, Ellie congratulated herself again for thinking ahead and lying her little heart out on all their questionnaires. "But, but what am I going to be talking about?"

He dropped the rope on the dirt and came close. She could smell the sweat on his skin and the onions on his breath. "You're going to tell your classmates how you're a delusional chronic liar, how everything you've said about me is untrue, and you've been working against the success of this ranch since you got here because you've been too afraid to change your old bad habits."

"Okay." It couldn't be that easy. "Then what?"

"Just worry about what you're going to say."

Ellie remembered that she should be filled with a new dread at this idea and dragged out her limited acting skills. "I . . . I can't. I can't talk in front of a group! Please!"

He put the nail gun to her cheek. "Oh, but we're all about conquering our bad, illogical habits here, aren't we?"

"Okay," Ellie whispered, afraid to move any more muscles in her face than were absolutely necessary. The terror in her eyes made him happy, and he rewarded her by moving the nail gun to her side. It slipped up under her coat with unwanted intimacy and nudged her skin. He took over grasping her arm, and Tim moved away, watching as if he were at a mildly interesting poker match.

Lacking a podium, Galen ordered Devon to stand in front of him, next to Ellie. This hid the nail gun from sight, since holding a weapon to her rib cage might make even his most ardent supporter wonder about the sincerity of her words. He could also pivot to aim it at Devon's body in an instant. A nail might not be a bullet, but it still wouldn't be a welcome addition to one's anatomy. Especially when the nearest hospital sat an hour away.

Ellie allowed herself one moment to marvel at the absurdity of the moment: she stood in the middle of a barn, miles from nowhere, with evidence of a murder she couldn't tell anyone about, clasped to the bosom of a madman and threatened with bodily harm unless she . . . made a *speech*?

This couldn't be happening.

And yet it was. In the crazy, upended world of men like Galen, it could.

Ellie tried to think of what to say. How could she fulfill his demand while also planting a seed of doubt in any minds not completely bleached? She could start with, "Um, Galen did not murder Carlos Freeman." Her classmates should have no idea who that was, but the people who had been there longer, the sophomores and juniors, in the ranch lingo, might know. "He also isn't practicing psychiatry without a license and endangering lives with his 'challenges.' And he isn't actually threatening my life to make me say this stuff. Best leader ever!"

Chapter 40

Apparently, enough people had gathered, because Galen said, "You're up, Nell."

"No! I'm just supposed to stand here and talk? What do you want me to say?"

"I told you."

Ellie kept expecting logic from Galen and kept kicking herself for the stupid, stupid expectation of logic from Galen.

"Listen up, everybody! Nell has something she wants to tell you."

His death grip on her arm didn't lessen, but he moved to her six o'clock. There were perhaps fifty people there, the rest of the camp still out combing through the mountain paths or being eaten by coyotes. Obviously, the leader didn't want to wait. Latecomers would not be admitted.

She did not see Angela. Perhaps, at least, this turmoil would distract her from her own agony for a while. Ellie hoped she had been sent with others to look for her and hadn't snuck back into the gym to—

Then Galen placed the end of the nail gun against the small of her back and pressed it into her spine.

Ellie froze.

A nail in her side probably wouldn't kill her. But one directly in her spinal column could, and probably would, paralyze her for life. Not an uncommon situation, but she had never realized how utterly terrifying the thought was until it literally breathed down her neck.

Her skin coated itself in ice-cold sweat. Even that felt like too much activity to be safe. She could picture the nail slicing through her vertebrae.

"Go ahead," Galen said to her.

Ellie wanted to, desperately wanted to, but she couldn't draw in the breath with which to form words. She stared at her fellow clients, the periphery of her field of vision turning black. These were people she didn't know, some gazing with distaste, some with concern, some with the anticipation of sports fans in an arena, not so secretly hoping to see the lions win. She saw Audrey, who was grinning with wild delight at Ellie's subduing. Other classmates hovered at the back, their expressions reflecting her horror. Barry watched her, stone-faced, determined to believe she had brought this on herself. Margot wore a deep frown, perplexed and worried and, Ellie thought, perhaps a titch more likely to come to her defense this time.

Don't, Ellie silently warned. *You'll only get hurt.*

Galen grew impatient. The square barrel of the nail gun bit into her lumbar vertebrae, and Ellie gave a little yelp. This forced her to breathe, and finally, she opened her mouth. "I want to apologize to you all for making you go out and look for me."

Ellie didn't know what she was saying, and didn't care. She'd pledge her soul to Satan if it kept that nail gun from firing. "I was in a bad way when I came here. I didn't even tell you half of it. My life has completely fallen apart, and I have no idea what to do about it." Lies, but who cared? "I need Galen's help, but I resented needing it at the same time."

Several of the people in the group nodded like sages, and Ellie wondered about their credulity. How could they believe her?

Because it's human, embarrassing, and messy. Most true things are, so they believe.

"I couldn't face my failure as an employee, a wife, a woman. So I took it out on Galen and fought everything put to me."

Ellie couldn't see his reaction, but the pressure of the nail gun eased a nanometer. She tried to think of what else to say that would make him happy. She *had* to say whatever made him happy.

"So I accused Galen of being, um, derivative and broke into Mrs. Coleman's house like a burglar and invented a story about a murder."

With luck, the assembly would think, *Wait. A murder*? She looked around for signs of discomfiture but didn't see many.

"But it wasn't true. Isn't true. Galen is our thought leader and—" *And what?* Her list of platitudes had grown short. "And is bringing me into the plan that will save my life. I'm a work in progress." *So if I disappear, that means there's something wrong with Galen's way of doing things. Got it?* "Again, I beg your forgiveness for my actions tonight."

No one clapped. They continued to wait, expectant. Maybe she should add more details?

Galen removed the nail gun from her back.

Her knees buckled, and she nearly fell. Relief rained down like an avalanche, so profound it forced every other sensation out of her body. She barely noticed Galen toss the nail gun to Tim and barely pondered what impact its obvious presence would have on the listeners. Would they begin, even silently, to question their leader? Would they wonder why he'd been tucked so tightly behind her with a dangerous device? Or would they wonder how she got so screwed up?

When he began, "Well, that was a pretty little speech, Nell," she didn't worry. She sucked in the first full breath she'd taken in an eternity, and cared only that her spine remained intact and she hadn't been paralyzed. He could do whatever else he wanted to her as long as he didn't do that.

Ellie would take back that unvoiced offer a minute later.

"Nell," Galen said to the crowd and not to her, "thinks she can fool us again. She thinks she can tell me what I want to hear and make me believe that she has ceased working against this project."

His voice took on a rhythm, part television preacher, part candidate on the campaign trail. He let go of her and paced in front of her and Devon. "We caught her trying to call the police, to give them her pack of lies and get this ranch shut down, to drag you all down into her pit of failure so that she wouldn't have to be alone there! And what do we call people like that?"

"Remoras," Audrey said, her voice ringing clearly in the barn. A few other people gave the same answer, but not as loudly.

"What?" Galen asked theatrically, giving the "I can't hear you" vibe to his pep talk. Ellie continued to breathe in oxygen and keep an eye on the nail gun, and let him talk. If he wanted to point fingers and drown her in abject humiliation, he could go ahead. She could handle words so long as sticks and stones stayed out of the picture.

"Remoras!" the crowd shouted.

"And what do we do with remoras?"

"Kill them," Audrey stated.

No one else had a suggestion. Ellie thought the rest of the group seemed taken aback by her bloodthirsty assumption, but she might have imagined it. Certainly no one spoke up to correct her.

Audrey, Ellie decided, was a bitch.

Yet Galen frowned. Audrey had the requisite enthusiasm but had skipped ahead on the answer sheet. "We cut them out of our lives."

Now the crowd murmured assent, and so did Ellie. Yes, fine. Kick her out. Throw her onto the paved road with nothing but the shoes on her feet and let her walk the thirty miles to town in the freezing night with the coyotes and rattle-snakes. Right now that sounded like dancing with a unicorn on a bed of rose petals.

"They must be cut out like a cancer, or else they'll devour everything and everyone around them," he went on. "They're poison, energy vampires who will suck resulters like you dry and go on to the next person. They'll never stop, because if they stop, they'll starve."

Ellie waited for him to wind down, hoping that this public humiliation would prove enough for him and fearing it wouldn't. Her breath grew shallow, the air thick and painful.

"We've stopped her from destroying your progress," Galen said, "but if we let her go, she'll just go out and destroy everyone else's."

Ah. Now he was getting to it. The mirage of her lovely, lonely trek along a dark road faded like smoke.

"It's up to us to show the world the way to success, how to put ourselves on a permanently upward path. We can't let remoras pull us back down."

"Right," Audrey said. A few others murmured accordingly, but no one pulled out a pitchfork. Yet.

Ellie waited for Galen to explain how she posed such a dire threat to the free world, but he bent down and grabbed the rope he'd brought over, and took the nail gun back from Tim. "We want to live in a world where everyone pulls their weight, right?"

Stronger murmurs.

"So you're going to show me now that you can do that. Each and every one of you is going to pull your own weight, make your own contribution to the future. Show me that you're ready to cull the remoras from society without hesitation."

Ellie could see where he was headed but not exactly how he planned to get there.

"Because you're one or the other, you know. You're a resulter or you're a remora, like Nell. You can't be a little of both. You can't be in between. One or the other, and only you can decide which it is."

Implication: *Anyone not with me is against me and will wind up just like her.*

He came nearer to Ellie, rope in one hand. "Everyone line up. Half of you on one side, half of you on the other. Here, and here. *Now,*" he added when the crowd didn't move fast enough.

They hustled.

The rope was long, longer than she had guessed. He passed an end to each side. On one, unsurprisingly, Audrey led the line. Without instructions, the rest distributed themselves along it, with plenty of slack still in Galen's hands. They had lined up on either side of her, and this left an area of egress mostly vacant, in case she felt like making a run for it. But that would be as pointless an exercise as this little tug-of-war Galen was organizing.

Galen's smiling gaze fell on her, and he came close, too close. "Now, Nell."

In one smooth motion Galen looped the rope around her neck. Nylon, at least a half-inch thick, it caught her hair and clawed at her skin and felt as heavy as chain.

A tug-of-war game, to see which side could kill her the fastest.

Chapter 41

"This is what we have to do," Galen announced, voice ringing out in clear, bright tones.

The rope scratched against Ellie's throat, and Audrey watched it hungrily, as if she couldn't wait to see it tighten. Ellie saw the young man who had spoken first in their confession circle at the very end of the line, holding the very end of the rope and staring at it in his palms as if he might cry. The rosy-cheeked woman from her class grasped it with white knuckles, and Ellie saw only teeth-gritting determination, but when her gaze connected with Ellie's, she turned away as if slapped. Barry stared with a grim, "This is on you, not me" cast to his features, his jaw set so tightly it made the small scar on the chin gleam like lightning in a dark sky.

Tim stood off to the side, working cleanup, should anyone try to make a run for it, so at least that behemoth wouldn't be in on her throttling. He had no dog in this fight. Galen could kill her, not kill her; it all made no never mind to Tim. Andre had returned and stood next to him with an identical expression.

Devon paced in an impatient arc without so much as glancing at Ellie. Clearly, her thoughts stayed more on how to salvage her takeover of the Coleman estate than on Ellie's imminent death. Ellie's mission to check up on Devon had turned into saving her from Galen, saving her from herself, and now Ellie had failed at both.

"You have to show me how committed you are to your future, and the future of people like you." Galen strolled alongside them, inspecting his troops, nodding beneficently at those with enthusiastic expressions, frowning at the ones who appeared panicky. "If you are to go out and become the thought leaders of your worlds, you have to know you have the *strength* to lead. *I* have to *know* you have the strength to lead. And part of being a leader is culling the weak and corrupt, slicing off the remoras who suck the lifeblood out of the strong."

He had reached the end of the line on one side, having made eye contact with each person, one by one. They were to know that he saw them, watched them, knew them, and that half-hearted measures would not do.

The rope made only a simple loop around Ellie's neck, not tight yet. Galen wanted to savor this process, wanted to make that tightening all the more noticeable when it occurred—and only on his command, of course. No hurry. Galen was *that* confident of his control over her and every other person in the barn. He had envisioned her punishment, and so it would happen.

But while he had everyone's attention, Ellie bent forward from the waist and ducked her head under the rope, unwrapping the loop from her neck. She didn't care about his vision.

Tim instantly moved into blocking mode, sliding between her and the doors, but Ellie didn't bother to run. Instead, she interrupted Galen in the middle of a sentence about the nature of reality and personal strength.

"Seriously?" She spoke loudly enough to be heard from

one side of the barn to the other without actually screaming. "Seriously, people? You are going to *murder* me, in cold blood, because *he* tells you to?" Now Ellie did the individual eye contact circuit, skipping Audrey, knowing she'd better do it quickly, because Galen bore down on her like a steam engine while stopping short of an undignified run. Control, always control.

"What is the *matter* with you?" she went on. "He's spouting gobbledygook about leadership mantras like some poor man's Deepak Chopra, and you're going to physically murder someone—*me*—like that's going to somehow make you *strong*? And for what? What did I do, other than point out that your fearless leader here shot a man inside that trailer you call an office and then dumped him in the river to drown?"

Galen stepped up and punched her in the mouth without further ado. The force of it knocked her on her back, her spine slamming into the rough wooden planks, barely cushioned by the sawdust and dried leaves, things already dead. Her vision clouded, and she tasted blood, but she got her feet under her and sprang back up before he could take another step toward her.

Someone shouted, "Stop!"

Angela appeared in the open barn doors. "What is—Galen, what are you doing?"

"*I'm* protecting our program here," he told her. "She's trying to destroy everything I've built."

"I can prove it," Ellie said through a swelling lip, not just to Angela but also to the crowd holding the rope, as Tim caught up with her. "I can show you Carlos Freeman's autopsy report."

Which didn't, she knew, actually prove anything of the kind, or the cops would already be there. But no one in the barn would know that.

Galen laughed. He picked up the rope, the loose middle

section, which both lines of human beings still held on to. "Why would we take the word of a thief? Tell us again how you helped yourself to the cash register."

Her "collateral," he meant. Tim dropped the nail gun into a wheelbarrow and propelled her back toward the center of the tug-of-war, where she actually enjoyed saying, "I made that up. Along with the claustrophobia and the public speaking. I invented it all, because I knew you for what you are before I even got here."

Instead of making him rash, this seemed to calm him. "Thank you for finally being honest, Nell. Thank you for admitting that you came here only to destroy this ranch, destroy me, destroy everything we've worked for here. There's nothing we can do for a pathological liar like you. Only—"

"Stop," a different voice said.

He stopped.

Margot stood on the other side of the rope line, holding out the nail gun with one hand. She pointed it directly at Galen.

This was unexpected. He had not expected a rebellion from anyone other than Ellie. But he recovered quickly. "Margot! I helped you conquer your fear of water. I set your life back on track! And this is how you repay me?"

"I was never afraid of water." This point clearly irritated her, and she enunciated each word. "I was afraid of *drowning*, and even that wasn't that big a deal, and I was never that mad at my sister."

No, but isolation from friends and family is necessary.

Her voice quavered. The nail gun didn't. "And I was too embarrassed to say so, but what you did to me was crazy. Batshit crazy. And this is crazy too."

Ellie felt Tim move from behind her, now ironically prevented from coming to his boss's aid and subduing the irrational woman—the *other* irrational woman—by the fence of people holding the rope. He hustled toward the end of the line, to scoot around it and get to Margot.

Devon stepped toward her, halted under the older woman's gaze, and decided she didn't really want to take a nail for Galen, after all. And since Galen represented her only obstacle to inheriting the Coleman estate, it might even be to her advantage if one penetrated his frontal lobe. Otherwise, she might be the next remora in the line of fire.

While Angela came forward, Devon stepped back, as if washing her hands of the whole situation.

Ellie kept up the assault, desperate to work any advantage she had. If Margot was toppled, others would follow. "We all came here for career advice and a little bit of life coaching. And what's happened? You've been convinced to abandon your families, friends, jobs, homes to camp out here and work for free. And now he wants you to become murderers too? Each of you, you're just an experiment to him—to see how far he can push you before you wake up and remember that you're rational adults."

"You can try to wound me," Galen said, "but don't you insult your classmates. They're turning themselves into supermen while you wallow in the same filthy—"

"She's right." At the end of the line, Ellie's fellow classmate dropped his tail end of the rope, and this time he did start to cry. "This is crazy. I'm not going to kill Ellen. Or Margot."

Naming them helped. It brought the idea of murder from the abstract to the real. The rosy-cheeked woman and two more people, whose names Ellie didn't even know, stepped out of the line.

Audrey, looking murderous, grabbed one of them by the forearm and tried to jerk her back into formation, but the woman easily broke her grip and said, "That's it. I'm leaving."

Tim, meanwhile, had made it around the line and headed for Margot.

Galen said, "Really, Clara? You're going to go back to your one-bedroom apartment by the docks? And that—"

Clara flinched as she returned his gaze, but did it anyway. "Yes. I am." She thought another moment and then added, "Thank you for the breathing techniques."

Galen couldn't give up, of course. If he lost a single battle, he'd lose the whole war. His voice boomed throughout the barn as he responded, "Are you forgetting what you told me about your son's real parents? And where are you going to go? Your boss fired you, and you forfeited your lease. You think your kids want anything to do with a loser like you?"

She had no answer for that but kept walking, slowly, as if the floor sucked more strongly at her feet with each step. But she stopped at the wide-open barn doors, unable to move those last few inches.

Tim closed in on Margot, and she pointed the nail gun at him. He didn't pause, perhaps assuming she'd never have the courage to pull the trigger.

Ellie could have told him otherwise.

The nail sank into his thigh, burying itself up to its wide head. Tim's eyes bulged, and he exhaled only one stunned puff as a reaction. Then he stopped, studied, considered, and limped over to a crate to sit down and decide what to do next.

In two steps Galen ducked under the rope and ripped the nail gun out of Margot's hand as she stood there, distracted by her own audacious actions. He backhanded her, knocking her down with one vicious blow, and then whirled around to aim the nail gun at Ellie. The slack at the center of the rope still existed, and she had no shield at all. His hand clenched. The clients had frozen, most still holding the rope.

The chickens outside suddenly burst into noise, as if coming to her aid. Though perhaps they'd been screeching all along, but her world had been reduced to a few square feet of rough wooden floor. She calculated distance, likely psi, trajectory. . . .

Then two men and a woman rushed Galen, and one got a nail in his bicep for his trouble. Three others piled on and succeeded in prying the nail gun out of Galen's hands. Barry stood and watched them, his hands twitching with indecision, still unable to defy his master.

Audrey jumped on the pileup, striking hard with tiny fists, until Ellie crossed the floor in three steps and pinned the woman's arms from behind. Audrey kicked at her shins, and Ellie twisted and body-slammed her into the dirty floorboards with a force that knocked the wind out of both of them and crushed Ellie's forearms. Then Ellie sat on the woman's back, reached over, and grabbed the rope meant to strangle her. One hundred pounds of muscle, Audrey did her best to buck her off, until Ellie clasped her own hands like a hammer and drove Audrey's skull into the floor. She didn't feel bad about it either. Then she used the rope to tie Audrey's wrists together.

By the time Ellie stood up, the barn's occupants had divided themselves into her rescuers on one side, having relieved Galen of the nail gun, and a small contingent of true believers on the other, who were helping their leader to his feet. Angela stood apart. So did Devon.

The master of them all snarled, shouting, "Just see how far you get in your worthless little lives without me! You came here as losers. Do you want to leave still a loser? Where do you think you're going to—"

"What the hell is going on here?" a familiar voice demanded.

Without warning, Dr. Rachael Davies stood at the entrance, flanked by two men and one woman in police uniforms. They had their hands on their gun butts, ready to grip and pull at the slightest provocation.

None was given. Galen's clients stood and blinked, arms lank at their sides, no matter which side of the now-figurative tug-of-war they were on. Tim stayed on his crate, gingerly pulling the nail out of his bleeding thigh. Devon stepped even farther back, as if hoping to melt into the wooden beams and disappear. Unfortunately for her, as Ellie had already noted, the barn had no back door.

Galen worked to keep up his glare, but with eyes turned hollow. "This is private property. You have no jurisdiction over an unincorporated . . ." His voice trailed off.

They wouldn't be there without a warrant, and he knew it. He had lost both the battle and the war. The curtain had been whisked away and could not be put back.

No one said a word.

Rachael saw Ellie, dirty, bloody, and standing over a struggling woman. "Ellie."

Everyone started talking at once. The cops spread out, assessing potential threats before moving closer, but Galen's defectors saw rescue on the horizon and went for it. The noise level shot to cacophonous.

Rachael marched over and assessed her colleague, who grinned wider than a kid on Christmas. "Are you okay? You look . . . you look—"

"I'm peachy. But we have an issue with Devon."

"So you said. Devon! Honey, come over here. Your father sent us."

And the shocked, surprised, scared offspring of Billy Diamond walked slowly over, trembling from her home-cut bangs to her worn leather flats.

Except she wasn't Devon.

She was Angela.

PART V

AFTERMATH

It was all part of a larger system of control; the longer one stayed in the Center and the deeper they rooted themselves, the more impossible it was to leave.

Jayanti Tamm, *Cartwheels in a Sari: A Memoir of Growing Up Cult*

Chapter 42

The ranch emptied out, but slowly. Some of the "students" had no place left to go. Barry was still there when Rachael and Ellie left, and he was scowling, aware that Galen had been full of hogwash but unsure where that left him and his CEO ambitions, and also completely unapologetic for his actions or lack of same. Police had interrogated Tim, Andre, and Audrey, but had had nothing to hold them on. So far as anyone knew, they had not actually harmed anyone.

A number of Ellie's classmates had reintroduced themselves as they gave her a hug, then had gone to buy tickets on the first plane out of Reno. At least three women had cried as they apologized over and over for almost participating in the deadly game of tug-of-war. Ellie tried to talk to the bloodied Jeremy, but he didn't know her and had nothing to say.

Margot made sure to tell Ellie goodbye and received a firm and heartfelt handshake, along with a fervent thank-you. Rachael waited as Ellie asked if that meant she would reconcile with her husband.

Margot said it meant only that she'd had enough of group

bathrooms. "First thing I'm going to do is lock the door and take a bath. Then I might take another one. Then I'm going to lie in my own bed in clean pajamas and order Chinese."

Before too long, Rachael returned to DC the way she'd left—on Billy's private plane. This time she had Ellie and Devon Angela Diamond in tow.

Two weeks later Rachael and Ellie walked onto the nineteen-thousand-square-foot floor of the Capital One Arena. Driving to DC's Chinatown neighborhood equaled only half the distance to Billy's country estate, and besides, he and his crew were at work setting up for a series of encore concerts before setting off across the country.

There was something thrilling and yet creepy about an empty venue as vast as a public arena. Rows and rows of seats swept upward, appearing too tiny at the farthest points to seat human beings. Sounds echoed off the concrete steps and the industrial ceiling. Most of the sounds emanated from Billy Diamond.

"There! No, there, Gus! A foot to the left. What? I know it's heavy! But I don't want it to fall off the stage!"

They had set up a stage at one end, its suspended floor extending into the seats. Huge canvas sheets fell from the ceiling to create walls to secure the backstage area. At least seven men worked with wrenches, drills, and hammers to construct the edifice. Six of them ignored Billy, who shouted something about comb filtering. Devon—aka Angela—stood at his side, the papers in her clipboard somewhat awry.

Gus shouted something about twenty-five degrees, Billy shouted that if Gus turned the speaker too far, he couldn't hear his own instrument, and Gus said that this was because Billy was going deaf in his old age. As Billy pondered a retort, Devon spied Rachael and Ellie.

"There you are! I'm so glad you came." She threw her arms around each woman.

Billy abandoned Gus and the proper placement of the stage amplifiers to greet his guests. "My angels!" He, in turn, threw his arms around each woman, greeting Rachael and proclaiming Ellie to be the woman who had saved his little girl's life. "I can't thank you enough. I can't, I can't. You get lifetime backstage passes, ladies, my jet is at your disposal, and you get front-row seats at every concert. But this, this is just from me to you."

He dug in the front pocket of his ripped jeans, and his fingers emerged with two strings of beads. They were bracelets, small, simple things of plain light-colored wood.

"This is sandalwood. Hindus believe the goddess Lakshmi lives in it, and the wood invokes the divine. It helps you focus your third eye." He looped a stretchy band around Ellie's wrist and then around Rachael's. He brought Rachael's hand to his face, as if he might kiss it, but instead he sniffed the beads. "Plus, it smells good."

"This is his *thing*," Devon—aka Angela—said. She stood close to them, her arms wrapped around her waist, beaming. Rachael noted the same bracelets, older and darkened, on both her wrist and her father's.

"I get these in China," he went on. "It's important to Buddhists too. They're not supposed to sell them in India anymore. Oh, and this."

From his other pocket he pulled out a crumpled piece of paper and handed it to Rachael. Rachael straightened it out, noted all the zeros, and her heart beat a little faster. Okay, a *lot* faster.

"They get a check?" Gus called from the stage. "When do I get a check?"

"When the job's done," Billy snapped, then confided to Rachael, "*And* backstage passes. Don't forget about that."

"Oh, I won't. Or the jet. This is a great venue." She waved her arm around the slightly intimidating space.

"Yeah. They play hockey in here, do you believe it? They flood this floor, and then something under it freezes it. Then they can let it melt and drain it off, and it's a normal floor again. Except it's white. Isn't that crazy? Does it feel cold to you? The outdoor venue was great, and the fans loved it, but half of them froze their butts off, so I wouldn't want that to happen again. How are you doing? You okay? Ellie Carr, you okay?"

Rachael's colleague had been struck momentarily dumb in the presence of someone she had heard on the radio every day of her life, but she recovered enough to say she was fine, that the experiences at Today's Enlightenment hadn't disturbed her. Rachael had her doubts about that, but this did not seem the time to air them.

Billy's manager, Newton, appeared to warn the rock star that *Rolling Stone* had entered the building. "It's Gerry again. Be nice."

"I'm always nice," Billy insisted, giving the Locard women an impish grin. Then he held his daughter's face between his hands and planted a kiss on her forehead. He walked away and disappeared in a puff of sandalwood tinged with marijuana. Old habits died hard.

Rachael turned to Newton, who glanced at the check in her hands with a pained expression. "What did you do? Discover some form of instantaneous rehab?" she asked him.

The band manager shrugged. "The concert was a hit. The comeback tour is forty shows in all, and they're all selling out. Of the two singles released from the solo album, both reached the top ten. That's what it takes. I just hope it lasts . . . for all our sakes."

He trundled out, and Devon Angela Diamond touched Ellie's arm. "I want to thank you, too, of course. You saved my life—and my sanity. But I can't get over that you thought Devon was me all that time!" She giggled, then saw the expression on Ellie's face. "It's not your fault! When I got there, Galen told me we already had a Devon, so I should go by my middle name, Angela."

"He assigned everyone a nickname," Ellie told Rachael.

Rachael got it. "A control thing."

"Totally. And I had only one picture of you, Devon, from a school dance."

"Yeah. I don't do social media, like, at all. It just leads to problems." The young woman ran one hand through her now-tailored hair. "Plus Galen 'assisted with my transformation' by chopping all my hair off with the scissors from the first-aid kit, so all my blond grew out. I thought it was exciting at the time. Daring." Her voice faded, and for a moment the only sounds in the vast space came from the stage, the clinking of wrenches against bolts and the whisper of wires snaking across the platform's rubber floor.

"How are you doing?" Ellie asked.

"Eh." Devon waved a hand, a gesture that told them nothing. "Some days I'm just glad to be alive and in my own bed. Other days, I'm so embarrassed that I want to hide in a closet for the rest of my life."

Rachael pulled on her sympathetic but firm doctor voice. "Don't be too hard on yourself. Anyone can fall victim under the right circumstances. Cults look for sensible, successful people, but ones who are at a transition point in their lives. That was you. Take advantage of the cult-deprogramming therapists your father brought in to help everyone at the ranch transition back to the real world."

"It might be a long process for some," Ellie added.

"A lot of bridges were burned," Devon agreed and then led them over to a gap where they could climb out of the rink and settle on a bench. Rachael didn't know much about hockey but thought it might be the penalty box.

She changed the subject, telling Devon, "The lieutenant from the ranch called me yesterday. He explained Devon's plot to Mrs. Coleman."

"Oh no. That must have been awful."

"It was the only way to convince her that Devon—the other Devon—is *not* Theresa. Apparently, Mrs. Coleman snapped, 'Of course not.' But her attorney will make sure she changes the will back."

"What about the real Theresa?" Ellie asked.

Rachael shook her head. "No one knows."

Devon said, "Galen said she hasn't been heard from in over thirty years and is assumed dead somewhere in Bolivia."

"Maybe she went native and lives in a cave and grows coffee."

Rachael said, "That's what Mrs. Coleman prefers to believe, according to the lieutenant."

"Speaking of him," Ellie said, "how did you talk the local police into coming?"

"I called in some favors at the FBI. Michael wanted to get on the plane with me, but they were working a violent bank robbery. He convinced the lieutenant to get a warrant, but as it turned out, he didn't need much convincing. They've had grave reservations about this ranch for a long time, ever since one or two ex-members showed up in Reno, but they had no real probable cause."

"You certainly arrived in the nick of time," Devon said. "*I'd* like to know how you talked my dad into loaning you the plane and his pilot. Of all his babies, that's his babiest."

The guys on the stage fell into another argument over the amplifier placement, but their Plexiglas box deadened the sound.

"I went to tell Billy about Carlos's possible gunshot wound and what Ellie had said about Devon—the other Devon—trying to murder Mrs. Coleman. I thought if he went out there with me, we could salvage the situation before the person who I *thought* was his daughter became a murderer. Deprogramming a cult member. . . . Well, you've seen what a shock it can be. I thought we might need his help to talk you down. But he was, um, heavily under the influence," she finished, weakly, trying to keep her opinion of Billy's parenting style out of her voice.

"Billy would never miss a show." Devon spoke without bitterness. Her father loved her, but he had his career, and that was that. "It was worth it, I guess. The concert was a complete smash despite him. Poor Newton, trying to keep a lid on him by himself. Only Isis could do that." Then she gave a little start, likely realizing what she had said.

"How?" Rachael asked. "What . . . exactly did she do to keep him under 'control'?"

"Um." The young woman shifted on the hard bench, and a struggle played across her face. Honesty or a kind lie? Honesty won out. "My dad always had a problem with alcohol. It wasn't that big of a deal. He had enough people around him that there was always someone to help me with my homework or drop me off at the airport."

"But Isis sold more than booze." Rachael made it a statement, not a question.

"Um . . . yes. He could buy that himself, no matter how much we tried to reduce the amount in the house. But when he couldn't stand up and it was time to get onstage, we'd need cocaine or meth to straighten him out. He gets nervous before a show, you see. Even after all this time."

Devon, Rachael could see, had probably been enabling her dad from a very young age, just like everyone else in his entourage. "So you knew her party-planning business was just a front?"

She lifted her gaze to Rachael's, eyes wet and brimming with sympathy. "Yes. I'm sorry."

"You have nothing to be sorry about."

Ellie said nothing, sitting like a granite statue on the other side of Devon. But the young woman didn't have the same filters—and she had a vested interest.

"Are you going to tell the police? About my dad and Isis?"

Rachael thought for a moment.

Ellie started to rise, saying that she'd let them talk in private.

"No, sit." Rachael appreciated the gesture, but it was time to be as honest with herself as she was with everyone else. "I'll have a quiet talk with the detectives who had my sister's murder case, yes, but I'll leave Billy out of it. I doubt they'll be interested in the case anyway. Nothing can be proven at this point, and there's no one left to prosecute. Isis, her bodyguard, and her killer are all dead."

"What about your mom?" Devon asked.

Rachael felt her eyes widen in surprise.

"She talked about her," Devon said. "And you. One time I wasn't very nice when she came around, but she didn't get mad. That's why I always liked her. She seemed to understand how I felt being Billy's daughter. She said she'd put you through a lot."

Rachael swallowed hard. "Thank you for telling me that. And I'll make sure my mother doesn't find out."

"Good," Devon said in relief and hastily changed the subject. "What about Devon? The *other* Devon."

Lights abruptly flooded the iceless rink, first white, then the primary colors. The staff were testing the mechanisms, sweeping the beams across the floor.

Ellie said, "Well, she's talking, giving up everything on Galen to save herself. She must figure fraud is a better charge than murder. And her fingerprints did some talking themselves. She's a twenty-four-year-old from New York, with a record for theft and dealing in stolen goods."

Devon asked, "How did she plan to get away with it when she wasn't really Mrs. Coleman's daughter?"

"She didn't need to be. The will spelled out her real, legal name, Devon Zimmerman. A journalist from the *Record-*

Courier got an interview, where Devon tried out her defense. Mrs. Coleman considered her a 'spiritual daughter.' With Theresa MIA, there would be no other heirs to contest it."

"But Galen—"

"Yes, Galen," Ellie said. "Maybe she truly wanted to convince him to marry her, like she told the reporter, but I doubt it. Her life expectancy would be in question if that went through, whereas if they were *not* married, he'd have no motive to kill her, because he'd have no legal claim to the land. Maybe she thought with the deed, she could shove him off and take over all those client payments. Maybe she just wanted to get a measure of control back after catering to him for nearly two years. Maybe she wanted to snap on a leash and yank it a little. I doubt we'll ever know."

"I hope she goes to jail for a long time too." Devon spoke with feeling.

"She might. They're charging her with accessory to the murder but may change it to accessory after the fact. Same with all the assault and fraud charges. According to her, she's just another brainwashed follower of Galen."

"But she tried to kill Mrs. Coleman!"

"For which they have only my say-so, and I destroyed the evidence."

Devon Angela watched her father walk back onto the arena floor, the *Rolling Stone* reporter in tow. They stood in the middle, facing the stage. Billy seemed to be describing the upcoming show with wide, sweeping gestures. The girl kept her gaze on that middle distance as she asked, "What's going to happen to Galen?"

"We're not sure," Ellie told her. "They plan to charge him with numerous counts of assault, fraud, and slavery. Possibly false imprisonment charges, but that would be hard to prove, since the place doesn't even have a fence. The *Record-Courier* keeps calling me for a quote and said they tracked down his real name. Gerald Lawson. He never graduated from either MIT or Harvard. He also never meditated in Tibet and couldn't find New Zealand on a map."

Devon rolled her eyes and shook her head, but Rachael felt this to be more anger at herself than at Galen. The kid had a long way to go to forgiving herself.

"Of course he'll also be charged with Carlos's death, once the autopsy report is complete," Ellie added.

"Poor Carlos," Devon said. "He was there only because of me."

"It's not—"

"No, it *was* my fault. I thought Galen's program would be a good idea—hah!—before we committed to a major and maybe a graduate program. Carlos liked it at first, but eventually . . . he could see through Galen, and I couldn't. We started arguing." She threw up her hands in self-disgust, her eyes growing moist. "I was gaga over Galen and figured Carlos was jealous. When he said he'd leave with or without me, I didn't care. I *wanted* him to go. Thought then, maybe, Galen would . . . Anyway, he had that big blowup with Galen over my bee challenge, and I didn't see him again. Galen told me he had left. I was mad, actually." A few tears overflowed and spilled onto a cheek. "I couldn't believe he didn't even say goodbye, like an adult. Now I know why."

Ellie's arm slipped around the young woman's shoulders.

"That's why I freaked out when you said Carlos's blood was in the office! I never would have thought he was *dead*."

"Devvie!" her father called, pointing her out to the reporter. "Come here a sec!"

The interruption seemed a relief to the young woman. "Duty calls," she told them with a grin, and Rachael said they'd see themselves out. Devon hugged each woman tightly, whispered yet another thank-you, and went to join her father at the center of the arena floor.

"Tell him thanks for the jet!" Ellie called after her, and Devon laughed.

Maybe, Rachael thought, the revolution Ellie had started would have ultimately saved her, even without the cavalry. Maybe the clients on her side could have physically subdued Galen and his acolytes. Maybe not, and she'd be another body floating up the Truckee River. Rachael felt a chill that had nothing to do with the unheated arena, and she and Ellie left the penalty box.

As a cult leader, Galen had barely gotten started. Cults often took a decade or two or three to morph from helpful and caring to enslaving and murderous. Galen had tried to drag his followers over a line he hadn't adequately prepared them to cross, and the newbies had balked. If, for Ellie's murder, he had gathered only sophomores and the few juniors, those he'd had more time to work on . . . well, Rachael might now be going halfsies with Billy to hire yet another investigator.

Smart cult leaders tested, tweaked, prodded, increased their control over one's life in tiny, almost imperceptible increments. Impatience had been Galen's downfall.

He had also screwed up, Rachael thought as she glanced at her colleague, by underestimating Ellie Carr.

ACKNOWLEDGMENTS

I would like to thank, as always, my wonderful family, both immediate and extended, without whose support and encouragement I would find life so much more difficult. I would also like to thank my fabulous agent, Vicky Bijur, and her assistant Claire Oleson.

And, of course, my equally fabulous editor, Michaela Hamilton, and everyone at Kensington who played a part in this book's publication.

I'd like to add a shout-out to Key Wester Albert Kelley for explaining escrow and trust accounts, and Jerri Williams and her *FBI Retired Case File Review* podcast for telling me more about detecting white collar fraud.

Author's Note

As you can probably tell, I did a great deal of research into cults for this book. *The Road to Jonestown: Jim Jones and Peoples Temple*, by Jeff Guinn, started me off. Like most of those my age, I remember discussing in school what might have motivated 918 people to drink cyanide in the middle of a jungle on the word of a preacher. If anyone in America hadn't understood what exactly a "cult" was before, they certainly did then.

A cult can be many things. At its essence, a cult is a relatively small group of people with a distinct set of behaviors and mores that are regarded as different from the mainstream. Christianity started out as a cult. The Farm, a hippie cult in Tennessee, turned out to be the most successful commune in U.S. history and is still active (with changes) today. One deprogrammer has posted how many times per year, he has to explain to someone why the U.S. Marine Corps is *not* a cult.

Scammers and fraudsters, incidentally, work much the same way, but with a specific end goal in mind. They offer quick riches or love, educate a mark in how this can be achieved with the money for a plane ticket or a "processing fee," criticize and berate any balking, and couldn't care less if workers lose their entire pension or the elderly widow sells her wedding ring to cover the sweepstakes transfer costs.

What distinguishes a *destructive* cult from a benign one according to cult deprogrammer Rick Ross, is a) an authoritarian leader, b) a leader who has a system of training or indoctrination using persuasion and influence techniques, and c) the exploitation of members for money, sex, and other forms of power. Cults can be as large as Jones's thousands or as small as one abused spouse, but the process, as I outline in my sectioning of this book, remains the same:

1. The love bombing. Despite what we like to reassure ourselves, cults do not target the stupid, the weak, the hapless. They want people who have jobs and are intelligent enough to quest for more for their lives. They do target people who are in some kind of transition—they recently broke up, lost a job, left school, are new in town. Cults seek people who are looking for a *change*, and it's helpful if recruits don't have a tight social structure at the moment. This leaves them with free time to fulfill the cult's requirements. The cult members are *so* happy you joined them and *so* confident that they can help you reach your full potential. Your new boyfriend/ girlfriend has never felt like this about anyone. You are unique and fascinating, despite what your mother or ex-spouse or boss or the industry thinks.

2. Training/indoctrination. The cult has its own language, habits, and goals, which must be learned and achieved or mastered. New members are surrounded—always— by those whose lives have been immeasurably improved by the cult's principles and its leader. The new members try hard to keep up, but continually having to ask questions makes them feel stupid, and the constant activity keeps them weary. It's better to simply comply—they'll figure it out eventually. This leaves them no time to question or, worse yet, confer with anyone from their "old" life. The new boyfriend can't bear to be without you for an evening. Your family, friends,

and boss are the ones bringing you down anyway. Ignore them. Stay in this warm circle.

3. Warm turns to hot. Remember the myth that a frog can boil to death if you heat the water slowly. The new members' loyalty is tested with ever more difficult tasks and decisions, as the leader wants to see how far they can bend their acolytes without breaking them. Will they take out a loan to give the group what they "owe"? Will they cut all ties with their parents, children, and home to live mentally and physically within the cult? Will they refrain from sex with their wife while she sleeps with David Koresh (aka Jesus, according to him)? Can they blacken their girlfriend's eye and yet convince her not to call the police?

4. In too deep. Finally, members are too immersed to leave. They have nowhere to go, as the bridges to their former support system have been thoroughly destroyed. They have no money after turning it over to the group or leader or spouse. The boyfriend never hits the kids, and they want their child to have a father, so it's not that bad. Depending upon how long they've been a member (and especially if they are born into the cult), they may have no idea how to live on the outside, how to get a job, pay a bill, go to the grocery store. But most critically, they've spent so long submitting to someone else's decisions that they no longer trust their own ability to make them.

I am by no means an expert on this topic, but you don't need to be to recognize the signs. All you need is a quiet moment to think and the confidence to trust your instincts.

Beware of anyone or anything that refuses to grant that.

Sources

I watched too many videos and documentaries and listened to too many podcasts to mention them here and, of course, I read a large stack of books. They include *Scarred: The True Story of How I Escaped NXIVM, the Cult That Bound My Life*, by Sarah Edmondson (with Kristine Gasbarre); *A Place Called Waco: A Survivor's Story*, by David Thibodeau and Leon Whiteson; *The Program: Inside the Mind of Keith Raniere and the Rise and Fall of NXIVM*, by Toni Natalie (with Chet Hardin); *Going Clear: Scientology, Hollywood, & the Prison of Belief*, by Lawrence Wright; *Cults in our Midst: The Hidden Menace in our Everyday Lives*, by Margaret Thaler Singer (with Janja Lalich); *Slavery of Faith*, by Leslie Wagner-Wilson; and *The Road to Jonestown: Jim Jones and Peoples Temple*, by Jeff Guinn.